MICHAEL JECKS

The Merchant's Partner

SIMON & SCHUSTER

London · New York · Sydney · Toronto · New Delhi

A CBS COMPANY

First published in 1995 by Headline Book Publishing

This edition published in Great Britain in 2013 by Simon & Schuster UK Ltd
A CBS COMPANY

Simon & Schuster UK Ltd
1st Floor
222 Gray's Inn Road
London

Simon & Schuster Australia, Sydney
Simon & Schuster India, New Delhi

A CIP catalogue copy for this book is available
from the British Library

ISBN: 978-1-47112-643-7
eBook ISBN: 978-1-47112-644-4

Typeset by Hewer Text UK Ltd, Edinburgh
Printed and bound in Great Britain by CPI Group (UK) Ltd, Croydon CR0 4YY

The
Merchant's Partner

Also by Michael Jecks

The Last Templar
The Merchant's Partner
A Moorland Hanging
The Crediton Killings
The Abbott's Gibbet
The Leper's Return
Squire Throwleigh's Heir
Belladonna at Belstone
The Traitor of St. Giles
The Boy Bishop's Glovemaker
The Tournament of Blood
The Sticklepath Strangler
The Devil's Acolyte
The Mad Monk of Gidleigh
The Templar's Penance
The Outlaws of Ennor
The Tolls of Death
The Chapel of Bones
The Bucher of St Peter's
A Friar's Bloodfeud
The Death Ship of Dartmouth
The Malice of Unnatural Death
Dispensation of Death
The Templar, The Queen and Her Lover
The Prophecy of Death
The King of Thieves
The Bishop Must Die
The Oath
King's Gold
City of Fiends
Templar's Acre

This book is for
Peter, Sarah,
Brill and Clive.

Thanks for your support and loyalty,
and for always having confidence.

CHAPTER ONE

It was not until much later, when winter had relaxed its grip and spring had touched the land with the fresh, yellow-green shades of renewal, that the feelings of horror and revulsion began to fade.

The knight knew full well that they were not gone entirely but merely superseded for a time by the pragmatic concerns of the villagers. The beginning of a new year forced the killings out of people's minds. Everyone was too busy for contemplation, preparing the fields and making use of the increasing daylight. But the murders had been committed late in the winter, and the long, cold evenings had given time for the storytellers to reflect and embellish. With their faces lighted by the angry red glow at the fireside, the families thrilled to hear about them time and again.

He could not grudge the people their fascination with the murders – it was only natural in such a quiet, rural shire. Devon was not the same as other parts of the kingdom, where people lived in continual anxiety. On the northern marches men feared more attacks from the Scottish raiders, while at the coast people were terrified of raids by the French pirates. Here the only concern was the possibility of a third failed harvest.

No, it was not surprising that the people looked to a story like that of the murdered witch to enliven their evenings, not surprising that every man had his own opinion of the truth behind the killings, or that some now lived in fear of her ghost in case she sought revenge on the village where she had been killed.

Thinking back now, he was not sure when it all began. It was surely not the day when Tanner called, the Wednesday morning when he first saw the body with his friend the bailiff. It was before, maybe on the Saturday, when he was out hunting and saw the women for the first time. The morning he spent falconing with the rector of Crediton.

'It's bitter, isn't it,' said Peter Clifford again.

Without looking at him, Baldwin grinned. His concentration was focused on the slender figure clutching at his gloved fist, admiring her slate-coloured back and black-barred white chest. She sat like a high-born Syrian woman, he thought. Confident, strong and elegant, not thick and heavy like a peasant, but slim and quick. Even as he gazed at her, the head under the hood turned to face him as if hearing his thoughts, the yellow, wickedly hooked beak still and controlled. It was not threatening, but she was asserting her independence, knowing she could take her freedom when she wished: she was no dog, no devoted servant – and like all falconers, he knew it.

The priest's words broke in on his meditation and, giving a wry smile, he turned back to the rector of the church at Crediton, the corners of his mouth lifting under the narrow black moustache. 'Sorry, Peter. Are you cold?' he asked mildly.

'Cold?' Peter Clifford's face appeared almost blue in the chill of the early morning as he squinted at his companion. 'How could I feel cold in this glorious weather? I may not be a knight, I may be used to sitting in a warm hall with a fire blazing at this time of year, I may be thin and older than you, I may be sorely in need of a pint of mulled beer, but that does not mean I feel the bitterness of this wind that cuts through my tunic like a battleaxe through butter.'

Baldwin laughed and looked around at the land. They had left the forests behind and now were on open, bleak moorland. The weak winter sunshine had not yet cleared the damp mists from the ground, and their horses' hooves seemed almost to be wading in the thick dew underfoot. Bracken and heather covered the hill and shimmered under the greyness.

They had left early, almost as dawn broke, to get here. Baldwin had rescued the peregrine as a young and vicious juvenile in the previous year and Peter had not yet witnessed the bird hunting, so the knight had eagerly agreed to bring her and show off her skill. For him it was a pure delight to watch the creature climb, only to float, high and silent, almost as if she was as light as a piece of wood ash.

This was ideal land for falcons, up here on the moor, away from the woods. Shorter in the wing, hawks were better at chasing their prey and were used by their astringers to hunt among trees or other cramped areas. The falconer used his long-winged birds on open land where they could rise quickly, soaring up to their pitch and staying there, touring above their targets until they stooped down like a falling arrow, rarely missing their mark.

Shrugging himself deeper under his cloak, Peter Clifford grimaced to himself as they rode along. Last night he had thought it would be pleasant to go hunting, after their meal and with plenty of Sir Baldwin's good Bordeaux wine inside him, heated by the great fire while they chatted of the latest Scottish attacks to the north. Then he had envisioned a warm day, the sky a perfect blue, the hawk swooping on to her targets . . . He glowered. Now he felt only cold: cold, damp and miserable. There was a fine sheen of silvery moisture all over his cloak and tunic, the wind cut through to his bones, and his face felt as though he was wearing a mask of ice. It was not as he had imagined.

His feelings of chilly discomfort were emphasised by the relative calmness of the man beside him. Baldwin sat as straight and alert as the bird on his fist, swaying and rocking with the slow walk of his horse. He was a strange man, the rector thought, this quiet, educated and self-possessed knight. Very unlike the normal warriors Peter Clifford met passing through Crediton. In build he was much the same, of course. Tall and strong, with the broad chest and shoulders of a fighter, Sir Baldwin Furnshill was the very image of the Norman knight, even down to the knife scar from temple to jaw that shone with a vivid heat in the cold, and he carried himself with a haughtiness to match his position. Only the black, neatly trimmed beard that covered the line of his jaw seemed incongruous in these days when men went clean-shaven.

With the hood of the knight's cloak lying on his back and the dark eyes roving constantly over the land, Peter could imagine him studying a battlefield, searching out the best points for an ambush, the line in the ground for the cavalry charge, the places to site the archers. His expression was curiously intense, as always, as if the knight had seen and done so much that his spirit could never be completely at ease.

But for all that the rector knew him to be a loyal friend and, more important, an honest representative of the law. Sometimes he looked as though he could only keep his temper at bay with difficulty while dealing with the local folk, but he still managed to hold it in check – unlike others the priest had known. Even the knight's predecessor, his brother Sir Reynald Furnshill, had been known to beat his men on occasion, though he was considered generally to be a fair man. In comparison, Baldwin appeared to be almost immune to anger.

There was a restlessness about him, though. It was there in his eyes and in the occasional sharpness of his tongue, as if every now and again the slow deliberations of his villeins became intolerably frustrating. Not like Simon Puttock, Peter thought. Simon never allowed his impatience to show. But Simon had gone to Lydford to be the castle's bailiff. At the thought, a vague memory stirred, and his brow creased. 'Baldwin? Last night . . . Did you say Simon would be here soon?'

The question made the knight turn and raise a quizzical eyebrow. 'Yes, in a couple of days – maybe three: Monday or Tuesday. He's been to Exeter, visiting the sheriff and the bishop.'

'Good. I would be grateful if you could let me know when he arrives. It's been a long time since I last saw him.'

The eyebrow lifted a little farther in sardonic amusement before Baldwin gave a short laugh. 'Peter, you asked me that last night! I said I would send a messenger to you as soon as he arrived. Do you expect me to forget so quickly?'

Smiling, the knight studied the ground ahead, searching for prey. He had not realised how drunk Peter had been the previous night. As for him, he rarely consumed much alcohol. It was too ingrained in his nature now, even if he had turned his back on the religious life of a monk. Glancing back, he saw his quiet, restless servant Edgar close behind. Peter had once said that he appeared to be so close to Baldwin that a shadow could not squeeze between them, the knight recalled, and his smile broadened at the thought. How else should a knight and his man-at-arms be? 'This should be fine. There're normally birds here. We need go no further.'

On this hill they were a little above the trees, and they could look down over the woods to the occasional plumes of smoke from the cottages. In the cool morning air they looked like strings of mist trying to rise to heaven, and Peter felt strangely calmed at the sight, as if it was proof of the need of all elements to struggle ever upwards to God. The thought helped to ease the pain in his head and the rumbling acid in his belly.

Sighing, he watched as a small fluttering flock of pigeons rose from the trees to their left, drifting off into the rising mist. The sun was quite high now, and the priest gazed up at it with concern. It looked watery in the pale sky, as if the heat which had once blazed would never return, and he offered up a quick prayer for a better harvest this year. From north and east he had heard of people being forced to resort to all sorts of extreme behaviour to survive. In parts of the kingdom all dogs and cats had disappeared, and he had heard of people eating rats. There were even rumours of cannibalism in the east.

'Please, God!' he muttered, suddenly struck with a sense of near panic. 'Let us have a good crop this year.'

'Yes,' he heard Baldwin murmur in quiet agreement. 'Let's hope it's better this year.' But his reflective mood was broken even as he spoke. From beyond the trees, where a pool lay, there was a sudden flash of feathers as a heron rose. Drawing the hood from the peregrine, Baldwin quickly loosed her and spurred his horse, crying, 'Oo-ee! Oo-ee!' to lure her on towards her prey, while Peter sat and watched and winced.

It was mid-morning when they decided to return to Furnshill for lunch. By now Peter was sure it was too late; he would never be able to warm himself again. The cold had eaten past his thick cloak, and under his two tunics and shirt, taking up permanent abode beneath his skin. Although it had been a pleasure to watch the peregrine launch herself upwards, only to stoop, plummeting like an iron crossbow bolt on to her unfortunate targets, the delight in her skill was offset by his chilled dampness.

When the knight expressed himself content with their catch and suggested they should make their way back, it came as a relief to the priest, and he agreed with enthusiasm. It was short lived: soon he gave himself up to his abject, frozen misery.

Baldwin was thoughtful too. After many years of wandering and rough living he hardly felt the cold now, but he was aware that he was becoming more used to an easy life. The muscles on his shoulders still bore witness to his days of training as a swordsman, his arms were still thick and hard, his neck corded under the leathery skin, but the definition of his belly was becoming less clear, and he found himself wondering whether he was losing his fine temper, like a blade left too long unpolished and without care.

It was no false pride that led him to feel concern at the beginning of his paunch. Under the terms of his knight's tenure at Furnshill, he must be ready to go and serve the de Courtenays, the Lords of Devon, for forty days every year. It was always possible that he could be called to go to assist his lord in the north, or on the Welsh marches – or even over to France to the king's lands there.

Riding down the slope, Baldwin gave the hawk to Edgar before they passed in among the trees. The great oaks, elms and ashes towered above them here, their branches occasionally making the three men duck in their saddles as they passed along, until they came to an open area, the common land that led up to Wefford. Here they turned right, on to the main path north that led through the village itself.

Wefford was a small cluster of houses and farms that serviced the strips to the south of Furnshill, huddled squashed together like suspicious villagers watching a stranger. Baldwin knew it to be a thriving community which contributed well to his estates, providing not only money but also men to work the fields. As with all landholders, his greatest problems were caused by the areas that had insufficient menfolk to help with the manor's estate. Money coming in to his exchequer was welcome, but if there was nobody to tend his fields, his main source of income, his land, must be ruined.

Here in Wefford, though, he had never had any problems. The villeins seemed content, placidly carrying on with their lives. Even last year, in the confusion of the disastrous harvest, the people had managed to produce plenty of food: enough not just for themselves, but to share with other hamlets on the Furnshill estates, and Baldwin felt a small stirring of pride as they came into the little village.

It was laid out on either side of the north-south road from Exeter to Tiverton, a straggling huddle of cottages and outbuildings that serviced the parallel scars of the fields. All the buildings were limewashed, stolid structures with their thatching thickly covered with moss. Up to the north lay the ford which had given the place its name, and halfway along the village, opposite the building that proudly acted as inn to the local folk, was the road west to Sandford and Crediton. Baldwin glanced at it as he passed. It led in among the woods, through the dark and gloomy trunks of the ancient trees, winding as it rose and fell over the hillocks of the softly undulating land, trying to find the easiest path for the traveller.

But the track was not well kept, he could see, and his brows jerked into a quick frown. Since he had accepted the position of Keeper of the King's Peace, he had needed to take on many new responsibilities, all going back to the Statute of Winchester. There the institutions for law and order had been reorganised and new regulations set out: how the hundred, the watch and the posse should work together; how areas should train for their own defence; and how they should protect against wandering bands of outlaws. Not only must Baldwin ensure that all men in the area were armed and trained in arms, he must keep the brushwood cleared from the public highways as well, to a distance of two hundred feet. Only three weeks ago he had told the constable, Tanner, that this track must be cleared, and Tanner had agreed to arrange it. It looked as if nothing had been done.

Sighing, he turned back to the road ahead. It was not Tanner's fault, he knew. The constable would have tried to enforce the order, but how could he persuade people to do it in the middle of winter? There would be a complete lack of interest. After all, the villagers would reckon, why bother to do all this work when it was only for the protection of the king's men, who had too easy a life already, or for merchants, who deserved to be robbed when they charged more than their goods were worth? It was not for the defence of the local people that the tracks should be cleared – for the same statute demanded that all men in the land must be trained in war and armed so that they might be able to protect themselves. No, this rule was for the safety of the wealthy, and that being so, the locals reasoned, the wealthy could clear the highways themselves. The villeins of Wefford had enough work already just keeping themselves fed.

It was while he was making a mental note to speak again to Tanner that he saw someone come on to the road from a track on the right, and he stared in surprise.

Although he had ridden through this village many times on his way to Exeter or Crediton, he had never stopped, and knew no one living here. There were too many families on his lands for him to be able to know them all, but he was sure he would have known this one. Tall, covered by a heavy, grey, fur-fringed cloak that fell to the ground and was pinned with a shining metal brooch, the figure stood quietly watching, face covered by the hood as the small group approached.

Though the body was covered by the draped cloak, Baldwin was sure that it must be a woman, and from the little he could see, a wealthy and elegant lady. Glancing quickly over at his companion, he saw that the rector was dozing, his head nodding gently with the steady jog of his horse, and when he looked back the lady had disappeared.

Frowning, he peered carefully, but there was no sign of her. Clearly she wanted to remain out of sight, but he was sure, as they rode up close, that he could feel her eyes on him. The sensation was unsettling, as if he was the quarry of an invisible hunter. It was this that made him turn, after they had passed, and glance back.

There, not far from the spot where he had seen the cloaked figure, was a short peasant woman with sharply suspicious features, gazing back at him round a tree before hurriedly jerking back as if to avoid being seen.

He turned back to the road with a grin lifting the corner of his mouth. Just a poor old woman trying to avoid the wealthy knight in case he demands food or drink, he thought. But then he felt a quick, cold shiver twitch his shoulders. Where did the other one go?

Agatha Kyteler watched the departing group with an expression so intense it was almost a glare. She waited until they had passed through the ford and carried on out of sight round the curve beyond. Drawing in her breath she let it out in a slow sigh, then muttered, berating herself for allowing her distrust to delay her. She still had much to do.

Pausing, she let her head fall back, then stretched her arms high overhead and yawned before rubbing slowly at the small of her back with her fists. After an afternoon of collecting herbs and roots she was exhausted, and her back was strained after so much bending. She relaxed and stooped to pick up her basket, patting the wiry head of her black and tan lurcher, which was seated beside her. As usual he responded eagerly and bounced up exuberantly before streaking off on the scent of a hare.

The basket was old, the wicker snapped and frayed, and she gave it a wry grimace as she hefted it. It was so much like her: ragged, worn and tired, too ancient to last much longer.

She knew that the local villagers were glad enough for her to be here most of the time, any small village was grateful for the help that an experienced midwife could offer, but they still looked at her askance. It was obvious why. They thought she was too clever. That was the risk, she knew. She was not a local, not brought up in the same way, trained in the same rules. While enjoying the results of her skills, the people around were scared of how she might have acquired them. And her accent was too strong as well. It set her apart from them and made them shun her. She was different. Of course, the fact that she lived a little outside the village in her own assart did not help matters. She gave a sudden grin: it was almost as if it made her stranger and even more awe-inspiring, guaranteeing her occult powers – in the eyes of her neighbours, at least.

She could not fully understand why. The people were genuinely scared of her, and yet she was no threat to anybody. There were rumours put about by the old hag Grisel Oatway, but they were hardly enough to make the people around go in terror of her.

In any case, she valued her solitude. Her life had been full enough. Peace was attractive in the evening of her life, and she was happy to be left alone with her thoughts; especially now she was in a new country. But she could not contain her annoyance when people tried to avoid her. They knew they needed her – they were always keen enough to take her advice or her medicines, like the poultice for Sam Cottey's bad arm, the mixture for Walter de la Forte's cow, and the potion for Jennie Miller to reduce her back pain.

'Hello Agatha.'

The voice, low and steady, soft but assured, came from her left, between her and the road, and at the sound she stiffened, her eyes searching from bough to bough, trying to see who had spoken.

A slim figure tentatively edged away from the cover of a large chestnut tree, and Agatha saw a woman, tall and slim, face covered by the fur-lined hood. 'Agatha, I need your help,' she said softly.

CHAPTER TWO

In the middle of the afternoon of the Saturday, under a leaden sky in which gulls wheeled, the wind blew up from the grey sea in a series of gusts, disturbing the branches of the trees at the shore and cutting through the clothes of the man standing on the foredeck like arrows of ice. Until the old ship was secured he must stay here, but the coldness of the middle of winter made him wish he could leave this duty to another and make his way below, to his cabin and a warm pot of wine.

It was rare for him to be sailing this early in the year. As the master of the cog *Thomas*, he tried to keep the old timbers out of the sea during the freezing cold of the winter so that the clinkered hull could be retarred and sealed, but these last few years had been so hard that any cargo of food could bring high profits, and even though the *Thomas* needed maintenance, the old ship was good for a few more trips over to France and the English ports of Gascony.

From here, the master could see most of the old town. His lip curled into a disdainful sneer, twisting the podgy face into a glower of loathing under its thatch of greying brown hair, his hazel eyes flitting over the port area with near disgust. This was not what he and *Thomas* had become used to over the years.

Usually he would try to make for the wealthier Cinque ports, or for London, where the people had money and the towns were used to entertaining sailors, but not on this trip. The Cinque ports were getting too silted, making it difficult and dangerous for a cog the size of *Thomas* to manoeuvre into the harbour, and London was far too busy at this time of year. He sighed to himself. But this was such a miserable place!

In London there was a cheery bustle, with merchants, seamen and wharfingers shouting and swearing at each other, and the occasional fight when a curse resulted in the drawing of sword or dagger. Here was very different. Four scattered villages lay to the east of the sound, and he could just make out the Benedictine abbey that owned most of the area. Apart from that the whole place looked dead. On the docks there were a couple of men splicing heavy coils of rope, but for the most part the master could well imagine that his was the first ship seen here for months – or years. It seemed as if the place was deserted after long years of desolation.

Not, he reflected, that it would have been too surprising if it *had* been left long ago by its inhabitants. The French pirates, long competitors of the Cinque ports, had for some time spread their carnage to other southern ports. Now even the smaller places like this, Plymouth, were being attacked and fired more often and, with so many tiny villages and towns on the coast, it was easy for the murderers to attack with relative impunity. After all, there was no organised navy, so the country could hardly be defended in so many places. The only answer was for each man to look to his own protection, and generally that meant helping the village or town.

Sighing again, he checked the cables to the front of the ship. When satisfied, he wandered along the side of the cog looking to the other hawsers, checking all was taut and safe. It was only when he had almost arrived at the rear castle that he found his passenger.

Startled, he stopped and cursed under his breath. It had been the same every time he had seen this man. He appeared when and where he wanted, but so noiselessly on his soft leather boots that it was as if he did not need to walk, he could simply drift to any point on the ship, quiet as flotsam on the water, suddenly arriving and making everyone jump in their surprise. He was standing by the rail and gazing towards the villages with a slight smile on his face. The master studied him, wondering who this taciturn man was and what he was doing here and feeling glad that he would soon be rid of him. Today, Saturday, he would lose him and hopefully never see him again.

It was not that he had threatened the master or his crew, but there was an aura of danger about him. Although he was cheerful enough, there was something about him that urged caution, something unsettling.

He was dressed well, with an embroidered blue surcoat over grey hose. His cloak was heavy, of thick, warm wool, and he wore light leather gloves. There was a harshness about the square face, an air of indifference in the set of the granite-like jaw, as if he cared nothing for the people around him. His thin, curved eyebrows exuded an arrogant haughtiness – like a new squire or a recently dubbed knight. It was as though he knew his own value, and that of others. He clearly felt sailors to be necessary but unimportant in comparison to himself, and although he treated the master with courtesy, there was an underlying contempt. It was there in the pale grey eyes. They looked through people, like a steel blade stabbing through paper, as if they could see a man's most secret thoughts.

If he had been older, his indifference towards others might have marked him out as a man of wealth. In one so young – for he was little more than six or seven and twenty years old – it merely served to warn. He was a man to be avoided.

He was obviously hardened in battle, from the width of his shoulders and strongly muscled arms. At his age, he was old enough to be dead on a battlefield or living as a wealthy lord: many men like him made their fortunes in their early twenties, becoming great by virtue of loyalty and prowess, or dying in the attempt. Constantly on the alert, always ready to reach for his sword, he did not look like a man who could be easily ambushed in a moment of thoughtlessness.

There was something strangely noble about him too, the master admitted grudgingly. It was in his posture, not slouching like an over-muscled, mindless fool, but rolling gently with the ship, looking for all the world like a new king proudly surveying his inheritance – or conquests.

To his discomfort, the man turned and fixed his light eyes on the master. 'When can I go ashore?' he asked softly.

Shrugging, he glanced over the last few ropes. 'We seem well enough berthed. Whenever you want. Why, are you in a hurry?' Even after the voyage he still knew little about this stranger.

'Yes,' the man said, turning to face him. 'I am in a hurry.' There was a suppressed eagerness in his voice, a slight thrill that hinted at keen excitement lying almost hidden under his calm-seeming exterior, like a harrier dog who has just seen his prey. Looking at him, the master could see that he appeared to have the controlled anticipation of a man-at-arms waiting for the order to go to battle.

'Do you have far to go?' he asked.

'No, not far. Just to the north of here, to a small manor.' His eyes turned back to their introspective study of the land. 'To a place north and east of the moors. It's called Furnshill.'

The master left him. Men such as he were disturbing, and all too often dangerous. It was hazardous enough just being responsible for a ship in these difficult times without courting additional troubles. He strode forward and began issuing instructions for unloading the ship.

As he left, John, Bourc de Beaumont, turned back to the view. He had other thoughts to absorb him. Not many memories, for they were too far in the past and his life had been full since the parting so many years before, with the continual training and service to the count, the Captal de Beaumont. All his life had been spent in serving him, his lord – and father. He did not regret it, it had been a good education for a man who would become a soldier, a man who would need to spend his time in training with weapons to be able to protect his master.

In that time he had hardly paused to regret his loss. Indeed, it was hard to think of it in those terms. All he now had were vague recollections, pictures seen as if through a milky haze, where faces and features were indistinct.

Was it wrong of him to come and see her, though? The Captal de Beaumont had felt so – had *said* so – not with anger, but with a slight sadness as he tried to explain that it could do her no good; it would not ease her last years. But the Bourc was sure it could not be wrong to see her just once, to see what she actually looked like. He was not going to punish her for what she had done: she had done the best she could, and without thinking of herself or her own safety. He was grateful for the opportunity she had given him, and had tried to take advantage of it.

At first it had been easy, of course. When he had been young it had all come so naturally, as if he had in truth been born to the Captal de Beaumont's wife and not to his mother, as if he had not been the Bourc, the bastard. He had known no better. But then, while he was still a squire training to be knight, the snide comments had started. It was not malicious, they were merely the cruel, pointed comments of young boys to a peer who was different. It meant little to them that he was the Captal's son. To them he had no mother and that was enough. He was marked with the worst scar possible for a child: that of not being the same as others.

But John, Bourc de Beaumont, had proud blood in his veins – from both the Captal and from Anne of Tyre – and he endured the comments, only occasionally defending his virtue and honour. As he grew into a tall man, fit and lean, the need to protect his name reduced in proportion to his size and the extent of his warrior training, until at last he had his spurs and became a knight.

He always knew that some day he would have to go and seek her. In the event he had remained much longer than he had originally planned. For a man trained in war who delighted in battle, there were few places better than the marches between French and English lands. Here there was honourable service, opportunities to prove himself a worthy man, and to earn coins from ransoms and protection money. But after so many years of fighting, he wanted some peace for a few months, and a chance to find out the truth while he still could.

Slamming an open hand on to the rail in a gesture of decision, he made his way to his packs, lying on the deck by the main mast. A sudden thought made him pause. She would be old now: according to the Captal de Beaumont she should be about fifty, maybe a little more, so well into old age. She might even have died. Throwing a quick glance at the coast again, he was troubled by the thought.

With an effort he calmed himself and continued to his bags. If she had died, there was nothing he could do about it, it was God's will. And his own fault for delaying the trip for so long. Collecting his things together, he walked to the plank that would deposit him once more on solid, safe, dry land, and he felt a small smile of relief twitch at his mouth. It would be good to be able to move without the constant pitching and rolling of the round-keeled ship to make him feel continually on the brink of vomiting.

Once at the shore he hefted his packs and took stock. Spying an inn, he set off for it. A drink and some food would fill the time until his horses were offloaded.

When the innkeeper of the 'Sign of the Moon' in Wefford entered his hall on the Monday, his feeling of pride was dimmed as the reek attacked his senses. It was not the ale on the floor, that acidic scent held for him the very promise of his business. The smell that assailed his nostrils was the harsh, bitter tang of vomit where young Stephen de la Forte had thrown up – again.

Even now in the early morning he felt the thrill of pride at the sight of his hall. It held the promise of comfort and pleasure, with the tables and benches laid down both sides, more at either end, and the massive hearth in the centre on its bed of chalk and soil. There were no flames now, so he set to his first task, building up the fire slowly with kindling, bending low and blowing gently but persistently until the flames, small and yellow, began to lick upwards enthusiastically and he could put smaller logs on top.

Sitting back on his haunches, he stared at it cautiously, satisfying himself that it had caught. Up above he could see the smoke drifting heavily, high among the blackened rafters. It would be some time before the room heated, he knew, but when it was, the smoke would disappear. Time now for the real work.

He began in the corner by the screens. At first he shoved the benches and chairs aside to be able to sweep underneath, but when he had got halfway, the novelty was wearing off. Realising how long he had already spent, he left the furniture where it was and merely swept around it. He was keen to finish before the first customers appeared. Arriving at the discoloured area, he could not help a grimace of disgust at the odour.

Fetching the big shovel he used in the stables, he carried the old rushes to the manure heap. It was fortunate that the pile was not far from his door, for there was a chill breeze coming from the south. A sudden shiver shook him, and he made haste to finish.

Once the floor was cleared, and all was as clean as he could get it, he found that there was only the hint of the vomit left on the air. The smoke from the fire hung in long streamers around the room like a mist over the moors on a windless day. Gradually eating its way into the atmosphere, it replaced the stench with its own healthy and wholesome bitterness. Nodding happily to himself, the innkeeper wandered outside to the store, and soon returned with fresh rushes, strewing them liberally over the floor. For some, laying new rushes was an irregular task only performed once a year, but for an inn it was the only way to keep the smells from becoming overpowering.

He had completed his task, and was standing with his hands on his hips when he heard the horses. Smiling, he reflected that new rushes worked for customers like cream with a cat. Whenever they were freshly laid the customers were sure to follow. Scanning the room one last time, he confirmed that all seemed well, then strode to the curtain that hid the passageway. At the end of the narrow corridor, he unlatched the front door and threw it open, peering out. Tall and imposing under his hooded cloak, with a bow on his back and sword by his side, was a man on a horse, leading a second by the reins.

The Bourc sprang down lightly. He had been forced to stop for the night at a little wayside inn, some miles from Oakhampton, and had set off again as early as possible in the morning. Now he was chilled to the bone, or so he felt. Puffing out his cheeks, he let his breath drift from compressed lips, then shook himself like a dog fresh from the water. 'I think I need a pint of hot ale,' he said softly.

The innkeeper nodded and smiled before turning to fetch

the drink and warm it, while the Bourc led his horses round to the stables, rubbing them down and setting out hay and water before making his way indoors. He smiled at the smell of fresh rushes, soft as the scent of hay on a summer's evening, and the promise of warmth from the burning wood at the hearth. There was a cheering tang from the beer in the pot over the flames. Sighing with pleasure, he waited silently while the innkeeper busied himself pouring the hot and spiced drink into a mug, and took it with a sigh of sheer delight. It was almost painfully lovely after the cold discomfort of the ride here. He gazed deep into the depths of the liquid before sipping, and a slow smile spread over his face.

'Am I heading the right way for Furnshill manor?'

'Yes, sir. It is only a few miles north of here.'

'Good. Good,' he said and sipped. Then, 'Tell me, do you know the people of this area well?' The innkeeper nodded. Of course he did – who else would know the local community as well as the publican, his baffled expression implied. 'Do you know where I can find a woman, an old woman called Agatha Kyteler?'

To the Bourc, it looked as though the man suddenly caught his breath, and his expression became suspicious. 'Why do you want to know about her?'

Before he could answer there was a bellow, and both men's eyes went to the door. The innkeeper sighed and rose, leaving the Bourc alone, sipping at his drink and considering the innkeeper's reaction. The man had been distrustful for some reason when her name had been mentioned, he reflected, and he offered up a quick prayer that his fear of arriving too late was not going to be realised, that she had not died.

He had turned to stare at the flames as he mused and thus did not at first notice that he was no longer alone. It was the waft of flowery scent that made him look up, and when he did he gaped in awe.

The woman who stood nearby tugging her gloves off was beautiful. She was only a little shorter than him and about the same age, with a slender body clad in a light green tunic under a grey riding cloak, and when she glanced at him, he saw that the colour of her eyes almost matched her dress. High-cheeked and with pale features, she looked frail at first sight, but as he mumbled an apology and lurched to his feet he saw that it was an illusion. Her figure was strong and supple as a whip.

'Madam, please be seated,' he said, and she turned to him. He found that she had a disconcertingly intense gaze. The way she stared, it was if she was concentrating her whole being on him, looking him full in the face with a strange stillness. After what felt like several minutes, she gave a faint smile and inclined her head, sitting on the bench he had moved for her, then unclasping the grey cloak from her throat and, with a short shrug, letting it fall. The Bourc had just sat with her when another man entered.

Glancing round, the Bourc saw a barrel-chested man in his late forties or early fifties. From his breadth and peculiar, rolling gait, the knight needed no flash of intuition to guess that he must have been a sailor. The life at sea had stamped itself on him too heavily. Although the face was not badly formed, the mass of wrinkles and scars made it ugly. There was no gaiety, no pleasure or joy in his eyes, only a cold brutality. Small eyes like those of a wild boar glared from the Bourc to the woman, and as he stepped forward, the fire seemed to strike sparks in his eyes as the flames were reflected.

'Angelina! Move over!' he said, standing behind them.

To the Bourc it looked as though she was reluctant to move. As if rebelling against the order, she waited a moment while the newcomer grumbled before shifting along the bench. Even then she moved farther than she needed, leaving a gap between herself and the man, and the Bourc was pleased to see a sneer of disgust twist her face when she looked at the man.

'Innkeeper!' the man bellowed. 'Wine! I want wine!' Only then did he turn and peer at the Gascon. 'Who are you?'

Keeping his anger under control at the rudeness, the Bourc smiled back, but his eyes were hard. 'Friend, I am a traveller on my way to see the master of Furnshill manor for my lord. I am called the Bourc de Beaumont. What is your name?'

'I'm Alan Trevellyn – merchant. Who's this master of Furnshill?'

The Bourc started and peered at him on hearing the name, then stared at the woman. She clearly felt that his gaze was in response to the man's rudeness, and softened the harshness of the question by her gentle voice. Eyes on the Bourc, she said, 'I think we have heard of him, Alan. He is named Sir Baldwin.'

The landlord arrived with a tray of wine and handed pots to the man and woman. Other people were entering now, and he was soon busy going from one group to another.

'Sir Baldwin, eh?' said Trevellyn. 'Yes, I think I remember him. He's not been there for long, has he – his brother died or something.'

'I had heard,' the woman said, 'that Sir Baldwin came here just before the abbot was murdered last year.'

'But surely you have not lived here long yourself, madam?' asked the Bourc, leaning forward and peering at her.

'She's been here long enough.' The merchant put himself between them and glared wide-eyed at the Bourc, as if daring him to continue talking.

Staring back, the Bourc allowed himself a small smile and his eyebrows rose. 'Do you object to me speaking to the lady?' he inquired softly.

'Yes, I do!' the merchant said, and suddenly his face contorted with fury. 'She's my wife! Leave her alone, or you'll have to deal with *me*! Understand?'

The Bourc could not prevent a quick glance at her in open-eyed astonishment. That such a small, frail thing of beauty should be tied to so brutish a man seemed impossible, but even as he caught her eye, he saw the beginnings of the dampness as if she was about to weep, and she looked away quickly. When he unwillingly dragged his gaze back, the merchant's lip was curled in a disdainful sneer.

'My apologies, sir, I had not realised,' the Bourc said, stiffly formal. A devil tempted him to say that he had assumed Trevellyn to be her servant he looked so poorly made, but he stopped himself. He had no wish to fight so soon after arriving here. 'Anyway, I am here to see Sir Baldwin for my master, as I said, and then I have some personal business to see to. There's a lady I must see. Do you know Agatha Kyteler?'

It was not his imagination. At the name, Mrs Trevellyn's head snapped round to stare at him and the merchant paused with his pot halfway to his mouth. Glowering at the Bourc, Trevellyn brought the mug down with slow deliberation. 'Agatha Kyteler?' he said, then spat into the fire. 'Why do you want to see that old bitch?'

He could feel himself bridling at this contemptuous treatment of the woman, but held his anger on a close rein. Sitting more upright, and resting his left hand on his sword, he said, 'If you have something to say of her, share it with me. I know her to be an honourable lady.'

'Honourable? She's a witch, that's what she is! She puts curses on people – you ask anyone around here,' Trevellyn said scornfully.

Standing, his face white and taut with anger, the Bourc stared at Trevellyn. 'Say that again. Say it again and defend yourself! I know her to be honourable – do you accuse *me* of lying?'

There was silence for a moment, as if every man in the hall was holding his breath. 'Sirs, please!' the publican called anxiously, but the three ignored him. The Gascon was still and watchful, but his rage was boiling beneath his apparent calm. Trevellyn suddenly realised how his words had affected the stranger, and now gaped with fear while his wife looked excited, but kept silent.

At last the merchant shrank back like a whipped dog. Shooting a sullen glance at the Bourc, he shrugged. 'I've said nothing that others here won't tell you, but . . . if I've offended you, I ask your pardon. Ask the innkeeper where she lives, if you want to see her. He'll know.'

And that appeared to be all that he was prepared to say.

When the Bourc drained his mug, Trevellyn hardly moved. He remained sitting, staring before him and carefully ignoring the Gascon. The Bourc looked at him contemptuously, then smiled at his wife. It pained him to see the sadness in her eyes, as if she was despairing at the misery of her life with her man, and the Bourc wondered again that such a lovely woman could have been manacled to such a brute. But there was no profit in thoughts like that, and he turned abruptly and went out to his horses.

CHAPTER THREE

'For the love of God, *will* you get down, you brute! Lionors! No! *No!* I said . . . *Lionors, NO!*'

The bellow of despairing rage carried clearly from the house and far down into the valley as the servant handed the reins to the grinning hostler, and he could hear the sound of scrabbling paws slipping on the floor and pots smashing. He sighed and shook his head in vexation. Since Sir Baldwin had returned, he had been determined to maintain the great hunting pack that his father had owned, and kept a separate kennel for the hounds. But there was one bitch who refused to leave him: Lionors.

Walking inside, he sighed again when he saw the hall. One great iron candle-holder was on its side, a bench was upset, and plates and mugs lay on the floor. In the middle of the floor stood the knight, hands on hips, red-faced and glaring, while in front of him was the dog, lying on her back, belly and legs waving submissively while her massive black jowls dangled ludicrously to display her teeth. A fearful brown eye rolled as Edgar entered.

'After food again, was she?'

'No, damn it!' Baldwin kicked the submissive dog, but not hard, and strode to a chair. Flopping down, he eyed his dog sourly. 'She was happy to see me.'

It was always the same, the knight knew. Whenever he went out and left her behind, whether it was for an hour or a day, the result was the same: on his return she would try to bring something for him. In the beginning, when he had first come home to Furnshill, he had found it an endearing trait, a sign of the mastiff's devotion. That was almost a year ago now, though. Two pairs of boots, one rug and an expensive cloak ago. 'She was trying to bring me a present.'

Edgar nodded, then bent to pick up shards of broken pottery. 'What was it this time?' Shaking his head, the knight motioned to the floor beside the table. When he glanced down, Edgar saw the short hunting spear, heavily chewed at the middle, which lay beside the table. 'She was carrying that?' he asked, genuinely surprised.

It was only a few moments later that they heard the sound of an approaching rider. Lionors heard it first, her head snapping round as she stared at the door. Wiping his hands on his shirt, Edgar went out. After a few minutes he was back, and to Baldwin's surprise, he wore a broad smile.

'Sir Baldwin, a visitor! John, Bourc de Beaumont, son of the Captal de Beaumont.'

'Of course, I knew your father well. We first met in Acre. That would be some six and twenty years ago now, of course.'

Baldwin had been surprised at the demeanour of his guest. He remembered the Captal as being a cheerful, enthusiastic man, and yet the son was withdrawn, almost depressed.

The Bourc had passed on messages from his father and some small gifts, and they were sitting before the fire, which had been stoked and now roared vigorously, lighting the room with a flickering orange glow.

'He rarely talks about those times, sir.'

'I'm not surprised. It was miserable. The end of Outremer. The end of the kingdom of Jerusalem. The finish of many brave and gallant men. Not, luckily, your father, though.'

'He told me a little about it, but never what really happened. Could you?'

Baldwin sipped at his wine as he stared into the flames, his eyes glinting. Then they narrowed – the memory was hard. 'I met your father there in the early summer, before I met Edgar. Our enemy had managed to lay siege from the land – though we still got supplies in from the sea – and were bombarding the place with catapults. I met your father early on in the siege. There were so few of us there – especially in the service of the English king – that we all knew each other. Even then he was a powerful man, or so I remember him. I was young at the time, of course. We fought together several times, and I was with him when the towers in the city wall were mined and began to crumble. We fell back together through the city as the enemy rushed in, trying to escape. It was awful.'

'He told me it was vicious work in the narrow streets.'

'Yes, because they were all connected, and there were so many men against us that even if we held them back for a minute, others could get round behind us. They kept leapfrogging us all the way back, all the way to the harbour. It was mayhem, hand-to-hand all the way. The harbour was to the south and we headed straight for it when we saw that the battle was lost. On the way we found Edgar here. He was wounded, and we helped him along with us. But when we got close enough to see the sea, we found our route was blocked. The enemy was before us, cutting us off. We had no choice: north, south and east were forbidden to us. We went west, to the Temple.'

'You were both there during the siege of the Knights of the Temple?'

'Oh, yes!' Baldwin gave a short laugh. 'Not that we were much help to them. Edgar was too ill. I myself fell on rubble on the second day and broke my ankle. Your father saved me then.' He looked over at the young knight beside him. 'We were at the main gate of the Temple when we were suddenly attacked by a strong force. They had a ram, and the bar that held the door gave way, snapping in the middle. Half of it landed near me, and that's what made me fall. A stone turned under my foot and broke the joint. Your father stood by me, holding off the enemy until I was dragged away and the gates fastened again. He managed to keep the men rallied.

'In the end, your father was hit by an arrow, and the wound soon festered in the heat. We were lucky. The Templars allowed all three of us to leave on one of the Templar ships. They took us away to Cyprus, where they tended our wounds and nursed us back to health.' Back to Cyprus, he mused. The words hardly covered the panicked rush to the ships and the feelings of relief and elation at being removed from the immediate dangers of the ruined city.

'I have been in similar positions,' said the Bourc meditatively. Drawing his dagger, he thrust it deep into the fire. When he had poured himself a fresh mug of wine, he warmed it by stirring it with the knife. 'It's hard when you're surrounded and know you cannot escape.'

'Aye. It's worse when your enemy has sworn to destroy you utterly and leave no survivors,' said Baldwin shortly. Then he glanced up and smiled. 'Anyway, that's the truth of it, for what it's worth.' He threw a shrewd glance at his guest. 'So did you come all the way here to hear that? The message and gifts hardly merit a knight as a messenger!'

'No,' said the Bourc shortly. 'No, I did not come just for that. I wanted a bed for the night as well. I will be gone early tomorrow, I came for other business, a debt which I owe from that same siege.'

'How so? You can only have been a child back then.'

'I was, yes. I was less than a year old. My mother, Anne of Tyre, had me by my father, but she could not escape from the city when it was taken. She gave me to my nurse, and this woman took me away.'

'Oh?'

'Yes, she took me from Acre and brought me home. You see this ring?' When he lifted his left hand, Baldwin saw a gold ring which held a large red stone. The Bourc stared at it for a moment, then let his arm fall and stared into the flames. 'This was given to my mother by my father. She gave it to my nurse, who gave it to my people as a token that I was my father's son. She saved my life and made sure I was safe. Now she lives near here. That's why I've come. To see her and thank her. For my life. I saw her briefly today on my way here, and will return to her tomorrow, then go home.'

'Who was she? Maybe I know her.'

'A lowly nurse? Maybe. She was named Agatha Kyteler.'

Baldwin shook his head. 'No. I don't know her. The name is unfamiliar.'

It was late in the afternoon of the next day, Tuesday, when Simon Puttock and his wife arrived. By then Baldwin was sitting in his hall. John, Bourc de Beaumont had left at noon, and the knight was beginning to wonder if the bailiff and his wife had been forced to change their plans. Looking up at the sound of horses, he walked to the door and, seeing his friends, bellowed for servants.

Though it was getting dark, the day's weak sun had not managed to clear the white spatterings of frost from the dirt and grass, and Baldwin could see that behind his guests a thin grey mist was already lying in the valley. On a clear day he could see for miles from here in front of his house, and today he could make out the moors lying under their blanket of pure white snow in the far distance, looking somehow less threatening than in the summer when they loomed dark and menacing.

Baldwin's manor house was not a modern castellated property. Built in easier times, it was thatched like a farmhouse, the only concessions to safety being in the tiny windows and its position. Standing high on the side of the hill facing south, it lay in a clearing, surrounded at a safe distance by the old woods. In front there was a shallow gully in which the rainwater drained away, and it was here that the track lay, rising gradually to the flat area before his door.

The knight watched as the small party approached. In the lead was the tall, slim figure of his friend Simon Puttock, a ruddy-faced, brown-haired man in his thirtieth year. Just behind him was his wife, Margaret, slim and elegant in her fur-lined grey cloak, hood down to show pale features glowing with the cold and exercise under thick tresses of blond hair trapped by her net. Bringing up the rear was their servant, Hugh, his dark face, Baldwin saw with a widening grin, pulled into his customary morose glower.

Spreading his arms wide, Baldwin walked forward to meet them. 'Simon, Margaret, welcome!' he shouted as they came close, his face breaking into a broad smile.

After the ride from Exeter, Margaret was frozen, her fingers feeling like icicles under her gloves, but she felt a smile tugging at her mouth on seeing his pleasure. Before her husband could drop to the ground and help her down, Baldwin was beside her, bowing low, then offering her his hand with a smile, his teeth almost startling in contrast with his black moustache. Giving him a quick nod of gratitude, she accepted his hand and dropped to the ground, then stood looking at the view while she waited for the others.

She had always loved this area, with its trees and tiny villages. The soft hills rolled gently up and down over a landscape scored with red stripes where the rich earth showed through the green carpet, smoke rising where the villeins held their smallholdings. It was so unlike the bleak, grey Devil's heathland Simon had to look after now at Lydford. Here there were happy communities still, not like on the moors.

On the moors the weather was so cold and inclement that nothing could survive but the heather and ferns. Even the trees she had seen, types she knew well from around Crediton, grew stunted and shrivelled.

Not like this lush view. Here, she felt, the land must be much as God had intended. This was how Eden must have looked: even now in the middle of winter it was green and healthy. It seemed impossible that the moors were a scant half-day's journey away.

'Come inside, both of you, out of the cold. I have food prepared. This is quite a week for entertaining!'

Baldwin led the way, chatting about his visit from Peter Clifford on the previous Friday night and the Bourc's arrival the night before, though most of what he said passed over their heads – at present they were interested only in his fire, and they hurried to the hearth.

The room was just as Margaret recalled, long and broad, with a fireplace and chimney in the north wall, and benches set around the tables. Bread and cold meats lay on platters on the table, and a pot hung from its chain over the flames, giving off a strong gamey smell. When she walked over, tugging off her gloves, and held her hands towards the flames, she saw that a thick soup was bubbling inside, and her mouth watered at the scent that slowly rose to fill the room.

As her hands gradually began to warm and struggle back to painful life, she turned to heat her back. Casting an eye over the hall, she let Simon and Baldwin's conversation float over her unheeded. They were talking about the knight's friend, the Bourc de Beaumont, and his journey to find his old nurse. She had no interest in tales of old battles, and stories of the kingdom of Jerusalem saddened her – it was depressing to think of the holy places being violated by heretics. Unfastening her cloak, she swept it off.

Baldwin stood by the table and surveyed the food, arrayed on its platters as if for inspection. Glancing down and seeing his dog, he took his knife and cut a slab of ham, tossing it to her, before turning and smiling at his guests.

To Margaret, he appeared to have changed a great deal in some ways; not at all in others. The lines on his face, the scars and weals of suffering, had almost all gone, to be replaced by a resigned submission. It was as if a sheet of linen which had been wrinkled and creased had been ironed smooth again. Where the pain had sat, now there was only calm acceptance. But still he had the quick, assured manner that she recalled from last year when she had first met him.

Simon too had noticed the signs of comfort and peace, and he was pleased, knowing that it was due to his own intervention that the knight was still free. Baldwin had admitted to having been a member of the Knights Templar when they had met the year before, and Simon was sure that his decision to keep the man's secret was the right one.

It had not been easy, especially after the murder of the Abbot of Buckland. It had been a dreadful year. There had been a band of marauding outlaws, murdering and burning from Oakhampton to Crediton, and then the abbot was taken and killed as well. For a newly appointed bailiff, the series of deaths was a problem of vast proportions, but he had managed to solve them. After hearing the knight's tale, he had been forced to search his own soul, but in the end there had been little point in arresting him, and Simon had kept his secret hidden. Now he was pleased at how the knight had justified his decision.

'Do you realise, Baldwin, how well you are considered in Exeter?' he asked as they sat.

The knight raised an eyebrow and gave him a quizzical glance, as if expecting a trap of some sort, 'Oh yes?' he said suspiciously.

'Yes, even Walter Stapledon has heard good reports of you.'

'Then I hope the good bishop keeps his reports to himself, my friend! I have no desire to be called away to clerk for the king or my lord de Courtenay. Edgar!' This last in a bellow. 'Where's the wine?'

His servant soon arrived, bringing a pot and mugs for the sweet, heated drink, serving them all and setting the pot by the fire to keep warm as he sat with them, flashing a brief smile at Margaret and Hugh, Simon noticed, but not to him. Ah well, he thought resignedly. It was only last year I had him trussed like a chicken and called him a liar.

'So how is Lydford, Simon?'

'Lydford is cold, Baldwin.'

'Cold?'

Margaret broke in. 'It's freezing! It's at one side of the gorge, and the wind howls up the valley like the Devil's hounds on the scent of a lost soul.'

'It sounds lovely the way you describe it,' said Baldwin gravely. 'I look forward to visiting you both there.'

'You'll be very welcome, whenever you want to come, but the cold's not all,' said Simon, grinning in apparent despair. 'Since I arrived I've had visits from everyone. The landholders complaining about the tinners; the tinners complaining about the landholders. God! The king allows the tinners to take any land they want – well, it's worth a fortune in taxes to the king's wardrobe – and everyone is up in arms about them, and expect *me* to do something about it! What can *I* do? All I've been able to do so far is try to keep them all apart, but now they're starting to come to blows.'

'I'm sure you'll be able to sort matters out. After all, things are never easy – you had your own troubles here last year, didn't you? Margaret, try some squirrel – or rabbit, it's fresh and young.'

'Er, no, thanks,' she said, wincing and taking a chicken leg. The knight glanced at her in surprise, while Simon continued:

'The trail bastons, you mean? Hah! Give me a group of outlaws any day; they're easier to deal with than free men and landowners, all you need do is catch them and see them hang. I can't even do that with the mob at Lydford.'

'Anyway,' said Margaret, holding up her chicken thigh and studying it as she searched for the most succulent meat. This must all be very tedious for you, Baldwin. What's been happening here? Anything exciting?'

Laughing, the knight shrugged shamefacedly and pulled a grimace of near embarrassment. Head on one side, he said, 'Not a great deal, really. Tanner hasn't cleared some of the tracks hereabouts, and my warhorse went lame some weeks ago. Apart from that . . .'

'I could learn to dislike you, you know,' said Simon with mock disgust.

Baldwin laughed, but then his eyes narrowed a little. 'What else is there, anyway, Simon? You must have heard more news from Exeter.'

Belching softly, Simon upended his mug before rising and refilling it. When he spoke, the humour had passed, to be replaced by a sober reflection. 'There's lots of news, Baldwin, but none of it's good. This must go no further, of course, but even Walter has lost all patience. He says although King

Edward was irresponsible before, now his favourite, Piers Gaveston, has been killed, he's worse!'

'In what way?' asked Baldwin frowning.

'He's playing one lord off against another, ignoring the Ordinances, allowing insults to go unpunished . . . It seems that he just wants to be left alone to play about in his boats and other frivolities. He spends his time in sailing – and playing with his common friends! There are even rumours that he was not his father's son,' said Simon quietly.

Nodding slowly, Baldwin reflected on the tales he had heard: that this second Edward was a supposititious child, a replacement inserted into the household like a cuckoo chick in a nest. Wherever there were troubles, Baldwin thought, there are people prepared to imagine the worst. 'I cannot believe that,' he said shortly. 'But it's true that the state is becoming unsettled. I have heard that tenants have revolted against their lords, even that some knights have resorted to brigandage once more. And there are more outlaws – more free companies and trail bastons – coming down from the north, displaced people who have lost their homes and villages to the Scots, who are trying to find new homes.'

'That's what Walter said. He's very worried. He feels that there has to be a compromise between the king and his barons, otherwise there must be a war, and God himself can hardly know what the outcome of that would be!'

'No, and God would not want that in a Christian country.'

'Of course not! That is why Walter has allied himself with Aymer de Valence, the Earl of Pembroke, to try to enlist support for the Ordinances.'

'Ah!' Baldwin thought for a moment. 'Yes, that would make sense. The earl could count on support from many of the barons for that. What were the Ordinances but controls to ensure good government?'

'Exactly. Walter thinks that if the king can be persuaded to agree, the troubles may be prevented from getting worse – maybe the risk of war can be averted.'

'What do you think?'

Simon glanced up and into the intense dark eyes of his friend, who sat frowning in his concentration. 'I think we'll be lucky to avoid war in some places,' he said simply. 'The Earl of Pembroke is on one side, the Earl of Lancaster on the other. Both are rich and powerful. If they fight – and they will – many men will die.'

'Yes, and many women too. In any war it's always the villeins and ordinary folk who die first and last.'

Shrugging, Simon nodded. 'It's the way of war.'

'But what of the king? You mention Pembroke and Lancaster, what about the king?'

'Does anyone worry about him? He will be with one or the other – he hasn't got enough support to make his own force without them. And would his support make any difference? After his defeat against the Scots at Bannockburn, who can trust his generalship?'

Baldwin nodded again, as if he was confirming his own thoughts and not listening to the bailiff's words. Then, as if he suddenly noticed her, he turned to Margaret. 'Sorry, this must be very boring for you.'

She stared back, her face suddenly drawn and tight. 'Boring? How can it be when you're talking about the future of the land? *Our* future?' His eyes held hers for a moment, then dropped to her belly, and she could not prevent the smile when his gaze rose to meet hers once more with a question in their black depths.

'My apologies, Margaret. I did not mean to insult you,' he said quietly. 'I tend to think that matters of chivalry and warfare are only interesting to men. I forget that they affect women too.' He sat still for a moment, his eyes seeming to gaze into the distance, Lionors beside him. The huge dog peered into his face, then rested her head on his lap, making him start, suddenly brought back to the world with a shock. 'Blasted hound!' he muttered, but affectionately, and, taking a few slabs of meat, tossed them away from the table. As the dog softly padded to her food, he rose. 'Come, let's sit by the fire.'

While the knight sat in his chair, the two servants brought the benches, and soon all were sitting and gazing into the flames, the mastiff asleep, stretched long and lean before the hearth. Edgar walked out to fetch more wine while the friends chatted desultorily, Hugh sitting and nodding under the influence of the fire and alcohol.

'What else is new, Simon?' asked the knight again, and when the bailiff shrugged, turned to Margaret with a raised eyebrow.

She laughed, shaking her head. It sometimes seemed impossible to keep anything from the knight, he had a knack of noticing even the smallest signs, although how he had spotted this she could not guess: she had only begun to real-ise herself over the last week. Now she was sure even if Simon was not – she was too late this month. 'Yes, I think I am pregnant again, but how did you . . .?'

'It's easy, Margaret. You look too well, and you seem to

dislike food that you used to love – I had the rabbits brought especially for you.'

'Well, we can hope,' Simon said. Then he leaned forward and gazed fixedly at the knight. 'But what about *you*? You were looking for a wife, but I can't see any sign of a woman's hand in this house. How is your search progressing?'

To the bailiff's delight, Baldwin gave a petulant shrug, like a child feigning disinterest. 'Well, I . . . I . . . The thing is . . . Oh damn it!'

CHAPTER FOUR

Six miles to the south the Bourc was glancing up through the woods as he rode, retreating into his cloak in the bitter cold. On either side the trees rose, stolidly impervious to the weather, but high above he could catch occasional glimpses of the stars, shining as tiny pin-pricks of light which flared and were hidden like sparks from a fire. They glittered briefly before being smothered by the ghostly clouds rushing by, clouds that made him frown with wary anxiety. They raced by as if fearful of the weather that he knew must chase hard on their heels.

Hearing hooves, he stopped and stared ahead cautiously. It was late to be travelling. Soon he saw a man riding toward him. Showing his teeth in a short grin, he nodded. The other man, dressed warm and dark for hunting, nodded back and hurried on. The Bourc smiled ruefully to himself. He was muddy from splashing through puddles, and he knew he was hardly a sight to inspire confidence in a stranger. At a sudden thought he turned, and saw that the man was staring back with frank interest. The Bourc smiled as he kicked his horse and ambled off towards Wefford.

He had travelled far enough tonight. At the first clearing that looked hopeful, he pulled off the road. Through the trees he could see a cabin, a simple affair of rough-hewn logs. Part of the roof was gone, and it was in a sorry state, but for all that it was a refuge from the worst of the wind. He led the horses inside and saw to them before starting a fire.

Chewing at some dried meat, he considered his options. His business was finished now, so there was nothing to keep him here. The sooner he could get home the better. If he continued this way, heading to the west and retracing the route he had taken from the coast, he should arrive within a couple of days, but it would surely take a lot longer than necessary. The journey west to Oakhampton and then south was quite out of his way, working its way round the perimeter of the moors. It would be more direct and quicker to cut straight south, over the moors to the sea that way.

It was still dark the next morning, Wednesday, when, over to the south of Furnshill, Samuel Cottey harnessed his old mule to the wagon and prepared for his journey, cursing in the deep blackness before dawn as his already numbed fingers struggled with the rough brass and leather fittings, pulling hard at the thick leather straps.

'Sorry, my love,' he muttered as he occasionally caught a flap of skin in the buckles, making the old animal snort and stamp. 'Not long, now. We'll soon have you done.'

All set, he stood back and surveyed his work, rubbing the bandage on his arm that covered the long gash. It was a week ago now that the branch had dropped from the tree he was felling and slashed the flesh of his arm like a sword, but, thanks to God, the old woman's poultices seemed to be working and it was healing. Sighing, he stretched and then walked back to the cottage, stamping his feet to get the feeling to return to cold toes. Inside the smoky room, he warmed himself by the fire in the clay hearth in the middle, smiling crookedly from the side of his mouth, the lips pale and thin in the square, ruddy face under the thatch of grey hair. Sarah, his daughter, smiled back into his light brown eyes as she handed his mug full of warmed beer to him and watched carefully as he drained it, smacking his lips and wiping his hand over his mouth, then burping appreciatively. Giving her a quick grin, he passed back the mug.

'That's good,' he said, then kissed her cheek briefly. 'Be back soon as I can – I'll try to be home before dark, anyway.'

When she nodded, he left, stomping quickly to the wagon and clambering aboard, whistling for his dog. After a quick wave, he snapped the reins and began to make his way from Wefford to Crediton, the dog barking excitedly behind.

As he left the light from the open doorway behind, his mind turned back to their problems. This last year had been the hardest he had known, especially since his brother had been killed by the trailbastons, down far to the south on the moors. Now the family relied on him alone to keep both farms going. His sister-in-law was right when she said that the two families could not live on either holding: both were too small to support them all, and neither could be expanded without a deal of work, hacking down the trees that fringed them. No, the only way to continue was by keeping both going.

But how to do that? There was only him, his daughter Sarah, and his brother's son Paul. There was too much work for them, now that they had to try to keep both properties working. Maybe they should do as Sarah suggested, and buy more pigs. At least they could often feed themselves, they did not need grain like cows.

The sun was lighting the eastern sky as he rattled and squeaked his way down the track into the village, head down, chin on his chest and shoulders hunched in an effort to keep the bitter cold from his vulnerable neck. Samuel had been a farmer for many years, and he was used to the cruelty of the wind and the freezing snow that attacked the land every winter, but the weather got worse with each passing year. Glancing up, he saw the sky was lighted with a vivid angry red, and sighed. The sharpness of the air, the streamers of mist from his mouth, and the red sky could only mean one thing: snow was on its way at last.

Passing the inn on his left, he glanced at it with longing, already wishing he could stop and warm himself before the great fire in the hall but, shuddering and shivering, he carried on, rubbing at his arm every now and again. Beyond was the turn he needed, and he made off to the right, towards Crediton, where his brother's farm lay, between the town itself and Sandford. He had to collect their chickens and take them into the market. Paul was still too young to be allowed to go to market on his own.

It was hard, he thought, sighing again. If only poor Judith had lived longer. But his wife had succumbed to the pestilence that followed on the tail of the rain that killed off the harvest two years ago.

The trees suddenly seemed to crowd in around him, their thick trunks looming menacingly from the thin mist that still lay heavy on the ground, almost appearing to be free of the earth, as if they could move and walk if they wished. It was this feeling that made him shiver again, peering up at the branches overhead. From somewhere deep in the trees came the screech of a bird, then some rooks called overhead, sounding strange and unnatural.

All he could hear was the clattering and squeaking of the wagon, with the occasional dull, deadened thump as the iron-shod wheels struck stones or fell into holes, and it felt impossible that any noise could be heard over the row he made, but still he caught the sounds of the waking forest, and his eyes flitted here and there nervously, as if fearing what he might see.

Then, all at once, he was out of it. The track led upwards here, to a small hill where the woods had been cleared, and he drew a deep breath of relief, blowing it out in a long feather of misted air. The feelings of dread left him, and he squirmed on the board that made his seat, telling himself he was a fool to be fearful of noises in the woods.

Here the trail was little more than a mud path, with stone walls and hedges on each side that were just below his level of vision, so that he could look over to the animals stockaded behind. Now he could see that the road opened out up in front as it passed the Greencliff barton, the old farm that had stood here for years, gradually growing as the family had cut down the trees for their sheep.

It was just before the farm, at a sudden thought, that he turned slightly, trying to look behind while keeping his body clenched like a tight fist of heat in the smothering chill. His dog had gone.

Calling out, he frowned, then hauled on the reins to stop the mule and turned, cursing. The last thing he needed was for the dog to attack one of the Greencliff sheep. There was no sign of him back on the track, so Samuel dropped from the wagon and walked back, blowing on his now-frozen hands, his face stern.

It was when he was almost level with the line of the woods that he caught a snuffling sound and then a bark from the hedge to his right, and he saw a narrow path. Shaking his head impatiently, he climbed up, catching his old russet tunic on a thorn, and swearing. At the top he could see into a field full of sheep. Beneath him was a wattle fence to keep the lambs from wandering to the hedge, but a section had fallen a little. The dog must have entered here.

Precariously balanced on the summit of the wall in the hedge, he glared round. The livestock seemed untroubled. He shouted, then heard the sudden movement as the dog started, and, seeking his master, began to return, skulking as if expecting a kick.

'No more'n you deserve,' Samuel muttered, scowling at him. 'What were you looking at, anyway?'

There was a lump, a huddled clumping, under the hedge that led to the woods some thirty yards away. He could not see what it was in the darkness, so he stepped forward carefully, his face frowning. When he had only taken a few steps, he took a quick intake of breath and groaned. It was a body. Rushing forward and touching the hand gently, he knew there was nothing he could do. It was as cold as granite.

For a moment he stood and looked down, shaking his head. Someone who did not respect the land and its dangers, no doubt, who had trusted to their own strength and found that nature in her cruelty could destroy even the strongest. Leaning down, he gently took a shoulder with his good arm and pulled, trying to see if he could recognise who it was, but the body was so cold it had frozen into its position, and it took all his strength. He gave a haul, and at last it shifted.

It was only then, when he saw the dead, unseeing eyes in the petrified face staring back at him above the wicked blue lips of the gash, that he moaned in terror. Dropping her back on her face, he stumbled back until he tripped, and then, rising quickly and glancing at her one last time, he ran head-long to his wagon.

The bailiff was on his horse and trotting fast, riding down the narrow tunnel between the trees, the leaves lighted with a bright orange glow, towards the light at the end, branches snatching at his cloak, twigs scratching at his face, and he had to slap them away with his hand until he came into the clearing, and there he found a huge fire blazing, with, in the very centre, the hottest part, the cowled figure, who slowly turned and faced him. It was the abbot who had died the year before, glaring at him with eyes of black cinder glowing red-hot at the edges, who opened a mouth like the entrance to the void, and said in a voice deep and contemptuous, 'So you thought I was unimportant? You thought my death mattered so little? You decided to let the murderer go free? Why? Why, Simon? *Simon*?'

'*Simon*! God in heaven, *will* you wake up! Simon!'

Lurching upright, his eyes wide in his shock, the bailiff sat up on his bench, staring wide-eyed until his heart began to slow its panicked beating. He blew out his cheeks, ran a hand through his hair, then held both hands to his face, shaking as the fear of the nightmare left him. He was still at Furnshill.

'I am sorry to waken you like this, Simon, but . . . Are you all right?'

The quick concern in Baldwin's voice made Simon give a wan smile. 'Yes. Yes, I was just having a dream. What is it?'

Margaret was not there. She must have gone outside. She always woke early when she was with child. Now he could only see Baldwin standing at the foot of the bench where he had made his rough bed last night, a look of wary anxiety on the knight's face.

It was not a nightmare Simon suffered from often, but he had occasionally had it over the last few months. He sighed and rubbed his eyes with the heels of his hands, trying to lose the feeling of gloom as he wiped the sleep away. 'What's the matter?'

'A murder, Bailiff.'

At the voice, Simon turned sharply and saw the constable, Tanner, standing behind him. 'What? Who?'

Stepping forward to Simon's side, the constable glanced across to Baldwin before beginning, as if seeking approval from the Keeper of the King's Peace. 'Well, Bailiff, it seems to be an old woman who lived in Wefford, down south of here. Sam Cottey – do you remember him? – he was on his way to Sandford this morning. Found the body and sent a message to me. He reckons she was murdered, says there's no way it was an accident. I thought I should come here first, see if Sir Baldwin would want to come with me.'

'I do!' said the knight with conviction. 'And so do you, don't you, Simon?'

*   *   *

The bailiff was surprised to see how seriously the knight seemed to take the matter. As far as Simon was concerned, this was surely just a local incident: probably not a murder at all, but some old woman who had met with an accident. He was happy with just his long dagger at his belt. But when he was buckling it to his waist, he caught a glimpse of the rigid set of Baldwin's face, and saw him taking his sword, pulling it out a short way and looking at it, before slipping it on over his tunic and fixing it in place.

'Anybody would think it was him who had the nightmare,' Simon thought, but then they were walking out to their horses. Taking his leave quickly of Margaret, he kissed her and swung up into his saddle, smiling at her briefly before wheeling with the others and setting off to the village.

There was a light smattering of snow as they rode, the prelude to a storm from the feel of the air, and the clouds were grey and heavy. The bailiff became aware of the knight darting quick, measuring glances upwards every now and again, studying the sky, and when he looked himself, his expression became pensive.

From the crowds it was clear that the hapless Cottey must be inside the inn. There could be no other explanation for so many people standing and waiting, all hoping to catch a glimpse of the cause of the uproar, or, ideally, a body. As soon as they became aware of the riders, they parted eagerly to let the three get to the door, and the babble began to increase with the people's excitement.

At the entrance Simon saw a short but thickset man, broad and strong with a pot-belly, glaring round from under sandy hair, trying to keep the people away by gesturing with a stout cudgel.

'Thank heaven you're here! These scum have nothing better to do than see someone else's misfortune. Tanner, get rid of them, will you?'

The constable slowly heaved his bulk from his old horse and patted her neck, looking round at the people. Tanner had the kind of build that inspired respect. Even without a weapon in his hand his poise was somehow threatening, with his stolid and compact body moving slowly as if to prevent two of the great muscles colliding under his skin. Usually the eyes in his square face held a kindly light, but not now: Simon had seen that expression before, on the day that they had caught the trailbastons. Mouth pursed, he looked over the faces with disgust and, under his gaze, there was suddenly a shuffling of feet and nervous coughing. A few turned and began strolling away. Others waited a little as if unconcerned, but soon followed.

The inn had a small screens area, a wooden corridor beyond the door to keep draughts from the hall itself, and beyond a curtain on their right they found a large square room, blocked at the other end by another wooden screen and hanging tapestry. Heavy logs were already crackling and spitting merrily on the hearth in the centre of the room. Three large benches crowded round close, so that frozen customers could get to the heat. Though the roof was high above, the room was warm and the atmosphere heavy with the cloying odours of stale beer and wine.

Simon and Baldwin tramped in together, glad to be back in the warm after their journey, and went straight to the fire. Holding their hands to the flames, they followed the innkeeper's finger, pointing at a silent figure sitting with his back to the wall on their left. His face was in the dark, but Simon could see two wide eyes staring back at him. When the flames suddenly spluttered and flared, lighting his face, the bailiff started. The farmer's eyes were wide with terror. A black and white sheep dog was seated between his legs, head resting in his lap as if trying to comfort him.

'You're Cottey?' asked Baldwin gently, and the ashen-faced farmer nodded. He looked ancient, a tired, drooping and slumped little man.

Tanner moved away, keeping to the shadows so as not to distract them, and pulling the innkeeper with him. At first it seemed to the constable that the knight and bailiff were unsure whether to question Cottey or not, he was so upset. As if to allay any fears he might have, Baldwin slowly seated himself, the bailiff following suit.

'We need to ask you some questions, Cottey. Is that all right?' asked Baldwin, keeping his voice low and soft. 'You found a body?'

Nodding, the old man stared at them, then his eyes dropped to the dog at his feet as if in fearful wonder.

'Do you know who it was?'

'Yes.' It was almost a sigh.

'Who?'

'Agatha Kyteler.'

Simon saw his friend start at the name and wondered why as Baldwin continued:

'Did you know her?'

'Yes.'

'Did you know her well?'

The farmer gave him a curious look, as if doubting his reasons for asking, before giving a curt shake of the head.

'Where's her body? Did you bring it back with you?'

'No,' Cottey said, shaking his head. 'I left her there. I . . . I thought I wouldn't be able to lift her. I asked young Greencliff to watch over her. He lives closest.'

Simon sighed. 'We were told you thought it was a murder. Why? What made you think that?'

The farmer looked up again and leaned forward, his haggard face moving into the firelight, so that his eyes glittered with a red and yellow madness of anger in the oval face. 'Her neck,' he said. 'Who can cut their own throat?'

Wincing, the Bourc felt that the crick in his neck would never go away as he rose, grunting. The fire was all but gone out, and it took time to tempt it back into life, but when it was blazing, he crouched and bleakly eyed it.

Leaving the hovel, he stood outside for a moment and looked up at the sky, sniffing the air like a seaman. Plainly the cold weather was here to stay for a while, but although the clouds above were thick and heavy, he felt that they should hold off for a day or two. There was a light sprinkling of snow on the ground, but he was fairly sure there would be no more today.

When he glanced over to the south, he could see that the blue-grey moors were almost untouched with white. Except for a few hollows, there was only the merest dusting. As he frowned and considered, a finger of light seemed to gently stroke a hillock directly in front of him, as if pointing out his path.

Nodding with a gesture of decision, he went back inside. He would collect wood first, so that he would have fire in case of bad weather, but for now it was holding. He would make his way over the moors.

CHAPTER FIVE

Refusing a jug of ale each, Baldwin and Simon led the way back to their horses. The old farmer agreed to take them to the place where he had found the old woman, and when they heard he had a wagon, they decided to take that and use it to bring the body back. The innkeeper had made sure that the mule had been fed and watered, and it was almost sprightly as it was led round to the front.

The damp chilly atmosphere outside was so sharp and bitter that it was only with a physical wrench that Simon could force himself to leave the warmth of the inn. Once out he found that snow had begun to fall, soft insubstantial flakes dropping thinly from a leaden sky making the fire seem even more appealing. The people at the front of the inn must have thought so too, because they had faded away.

Tugging on his gloves, Simon saw that there were only a few youngsters left, all of whom appeared unwilling to leave while there was a chance of seeing something interesting. He grinned at them good-naturedly as he strode to his horse and swung up, waiting for the others to mount, and while he sat there he became aware of a girl, standing a little apart and staring at him with large and serious brown eyes. She could only have been ten or eleven years of age, he thought, and gave her a quick flash of a smile. She grinned quickly, but then her eyes dropped, as if in contemplation, before she pursed her lips and turned away. It was sad, he felt, that children were introduced to death while so young, but he knew well that even here many of the children would know relatives who had starved to death in the famine. In any case, what could *he* do about it? Seeing that the other three were ready, he trotted after them towards the right-hand turn, glancing up at the sky with a frown every now and again as he wondered how bad the snow would be.

He rode along silently, watching the farmer. It was his impatience that had made the old man clam up. After he had asked his question, once Cottey had told them about the cut throat, he withdrew from them, his eyes filming over with tears as though he was in fear of something. But of what? There was something he had not told them, Simon was sure of that, and he intended to find out but, to his surprise, the farmer seemed not at all concerned by the three men, hardly even giving them a glance. His concentration was directed solely at the trees all around, eyes darting nervously from one side to the other and then upwards, as if he expected to be ambushed.

When he glanced at his friend, he saw that Baldwin was deep in thought too. The name of the old woman had surprised him, Simon knew, and he wondered briefly whether he should interrupt his friend's reflective mood. He decided

57

not to. Baldwin would explain his concerns when he was ready.

The bailiff was right. To have heard the name of the old woman so soon after hearing it from his friend's son had worried Baldwin. It was too coincidental. If he could believe the Bourc, the main reason for the man's visit was to see and thank her for saving him. There was no reason to suppose that he was involved in her death, surely.

It was only a little over a mile to the edge of the trees, and here the farmer stopped his mule and pointed wordlessly to the gap in the hedge. The knight and the bailiff were soon clambering over it and into the field.

Tanner was surprised that the old man made no effort to drop down with the others. Staring dumbly ahead, he stayed fixed to the wooden seat, reins held ready in his hands, as if daring them to ask him to join them, not even acknowledging his dog as it jumped up onto the wagon and rested its forepaws beside him to peer around. The others were out of earshot, so the constable ambled his horse alongside the older man's, and said quietly, 'What's the matter, Sam?'

When the farmer's face turned towards him, he could see the terror. 'It's *her*, Stephen. *Her*! Why did it have to be me as found her?'

Looking at him, Tanner was about to ask what he meant when Simon called him from the hedge. Nodding at the bailiff, he said, 'Wait here, Sam. You'll have to explain all this to us later.' Swinging off his horse, the constable walked to the hedge, clambered up the steep bank and followed the other two into the field.

The snow was falling more freely now, thick clumps dropping and settling gently, making the whole area seem calm and peaceful, but the constable was not fooled, he knew only too well how dangerous the apparently soft white feathers could be to the unwary. It was not this, though, that made him frown. He had known the Cottey family for many years – Samuel, his brother, their children – and knew them to be sturdy, stolid folk. He had never known any of them to display such fear, not even back in the past when they were all younger, when Sam and he had fought as men-at-arms together. Why should he be so upset at the death of an old woman?

Simon and Baldwin were a few yards away, walking towards a youth dressed in a russet tunic and woollen hose, with a thick red blanket over his shoulders, pinned like a short cloak. A heavy-looking, wooden handled knife was at his waist. Tanner recognised him immediately: Harold Greencliff.

The knight had not met him before. Greencliff was a tall, fair-haired, good-looking youth in his early twenties, broad in the shoulder with a friendly and open face browned by the wind. Wide-set blue eyes glowed with health from either side of the long, straight nose. But today they were nervous and almost shifty, not meeting the knight's gaze. From his clothes he was not poor, but neither was he wealthy. He had bright eyes, and looked quite sharp, but the knight did not judge him by that alone. He knew too many fools, who at first sight looked intelligent, to trust to his first impression.

In his hands the boy held a shepherd's crook, and his fingers moved along the stave as he watched them approach with a trepidation that Baldwin could not understand. It seemed odd that a corpse should create so much fear – first with old Sam Cottey, now with this boy. He shrugged. There must be a reason, and he was sure to hear of it before long.

'You're Greencliff?' he asked.

'Yes,' he said, peering over Baldwin's shoulder at the bailiff and constable.

'Wake up, lad!' said the knight irritably. 'You're looking after the body of this old woman for Cottey, is that right? Where is she, then?'

Silently Greencliff turned and pointed to the hedge that led at right angles to the road to keep his sheep from going into the woods beyond. There, in the darkness under the plants, they could make out a small bundle. To Simon it looked like a bundle of dirty rags lying in the space made by a fox or badger path, in the gap between two stems of the hedge itself, lying half under the plants, half in the field. He and the knight walked towards it, leaving Greencliff standing, nervously fiddling with his crook, Tanner imperturbable beside him. The two walked to the body, pausing three or four yards from it.

'Did you touch her?' Simon called back to him, frowning concentration on his face.

'No, sir, no. Soon as old Sam told me she was here, I came and stood where you saw me. I didn't want to see her.'

Glancing back, Baldwin nodded. He could see that the boy's footsteps had flattened a small area of grass, but no steps came from there, showing that the boy had been there when it began to snow and had not moved from there since. 'Did you hear anyone this morning? See anyone?'

'No, sir.'

'What about last night? Did you see or hear anything strange?'

'No, sir. Nothing.'

His face was anxious, as if he was desperate to convince, and after holding his gaze for a moment, Baldwin nodded again, then cocked an eyebrow at the bailiff and pointed with his chin. 'No tracks, Simon. We'll never be able to see if anyone came here last night. At least no one has been here since it began snowing.'

He was right. There was no mark to upset the snow that now lay almost half an inch thick on the ground, the heavily cropped grass just poking above the surface. Shrugging, Baldwin walked the last few yards to the body.

It lay partly under the hedge, face down. The lower half projected back into the field, while the head and torso were shielded under the protection of the plants and free of snow. They could see the black of the old woman's upper garments.

'Wait,' said Baldwin and stepped forward slowly to crouch, his dark eyes flitting over the ground, along either side of the body, back the way they had come, up to the hedge, then back to the inert figure itself. When he spoke, his voice was a murmur. 'The weather has been so cold there's no mark on the ground: it's too hard. Even if there were, the snow would have covered them. I don't think even a hunter could see a spoor under this.'

Simon nodded, dropping to a knee and peering back the way they had come, past Tanner and Greencliff to the hedge that bordered the road. Their own footsteps were distinct, flattened prints in the snow, but the snow had started while they were inside the inn. Now he could not even see Cottey's marks from when he had first seen the body. Glancing back at the knight, he asked, 'Could she have come from the woods? Through the hedge?'

'No. No, I don't think so,' came the pensive reply as the knight peered up. 'Look. The twigs aren't broken. No, it looks like she fell from this side. Maybe she died right here.' He chewed his lip and considered. 'Let's see her face. Simon, come on. Help me move her.'

The bailiff gave an unwilling grimace. This was the part he loathed, the first shock of seeing the corpse, of seeing the wound that killed. Sighing, he tentatively took hold of the body by the hips while Baldwin carefully moved up, taking the shoulders and rolling her over. He suddenly pulled back and exclaimed 'God!'

'What?' said Simon, nervously shooting him a glance.

Baldwin stared back, his shock slowly giving way to a quickening interest. 'I'm not surprised he was upset! He was right when he said the throat was cut – her head's almost off her shoulders!'

They carefully carried the figure a few yards away from the hedge and set it down on the snow-covered grass. Slowly shaking his head, Simon stood, hands on hips, while Baldwin knelt and studied the body carefully. The bailiff stared down at the sad little collection of cloth and flesh, thinking how pathetic it looked, this sorry little mass that had been a person – if only a villein. He was still staring when Baldwin rose.

'Whoever did this wanted to make sure. As Cottey said, she couldn't have done this to herself.'

Looking down, Simon could see what he meant. The bones were still connected, but the flesh was cut so deeply that the yellow cartilage of the windpipe could be seen as a perfect tube in the sliced meat of her throat. Wincing, the bailiff gasped and turned away, swallowing quickly. Shutting his eyes and taking deep breaths, he gradually soothed the oily feeling of sickness in his belly. He heard the low chuckle of the knight and the footsteps crunching on the dry snow, but kept his eyes shut a little longer.

'Simon, come and look at this!'

His eyes snapping open, Simon turned and strode away from the body towards the hedge where the knight crouched. At his approach, Baldwin stood, and Simon was surprised to see his puzzled frown. 'What is it?'

'Do you see anything strange here?'

The bailiff swallowed. His stomach was still turbulent after his shock, and he was in no mood to play games. He opened his mouth to give a sharp retort when he saw the pensive concentration in the knight's eyes. The words were stopped in his throat and he felt his gaze drop to the area where they had found the body.

Where she had lain, her image remained on the grass and earth. Snow bounded the lines of her legs. None had fallen under her, nor had the frost touched the ground. Apart from some twigs and flattened leaves, he could see nothing. Shrugging he looked up at the knight questioningly. 'She was obviously lying here before it snowed,' he hazarded.

'Maybe I'm ...' Baldwin broke off, then span and stomped back to the body. Reluctantly the bailiff followed.

Although he tried to avert his eyes, Simon found that they kept returning to the hideous wound, and his belly began to feel like a cauldron of stew on a fire, bubbling and thickening, making him belch. The bile rose to sting his throat, and he winced at the rough acidic taste. The corpse seemed to hold no fears for the knight, who took the head in both hands and turned it first one way, then the other, peering into the gash and at the yellowed cartilage of the severed pipes. He stared at the blue, pinched and drawn features, into the unseeing misty eyes, before rising again and frowning down, slowly walking round the body and contemplating it with his head on one side.

'I saw this woman on Saturday,' he said softly. 'I didn't know her name then. She was just some old woman on the road. I've never even spoken to her, and now I must find out who murdered her.' He stopped his musing and looked up at Simon. 'Sad, isn't it?'

'Oh . . . yes.'

The knight gave a short grin. 'That's not the point, though, Simon. Sad it may be, but there's something wrong here. Can't you see? She had her throat cut. She must have bled like a stuck pig! So where's the blood? Eh?'

For all Greencliff's nervousness, Tanner was pleased to see that he was happy enough to help carry the corpse back to the wagon while Simon and Baldwin subjected the hedge to a close scrutiny. The boy even took the blanket from his shoulders and helped the constable wrap it around the thin, frail figure, setting it beside her and rolling her into it, but while the constable took the shoulders, he could not help but notice the way that Greencliff's eyes kept going back to the gap in the hedge where Agatha Kyteler had lain.

The old constable had seen many corpses in his life, brutally wounded figures after a battle, men who had bled to death after their limbs were hacked off or who suffered slow and painful deaths from stabs to the stomach, and the sad, tortured bodies of the people that tried to cross the moors in bad weather. For him, they were the worst, their hands contorted into grasping claws as they tried to drag themselves those few extra yards to safety, their faces twisted and staring with anguish, even in death. He was understanding of people who were revolted by the sights, although he bore them with equanimity, but he was faintly surprised that Greencliff should be so calm in the face of his previous apparent fear.

It was when they reached the hedge that led to the road that he realised he was wrong. Greencliff went up the incline first, stumbling backwards. At the top he paused and Tanner caught sight of his face. The boy was not just nervous: he was terrified, and the constable was about to urge him on impatiently, 'She's dead, boy, she won't care if you drop her now!' when he saw the boy's glance flicker over to Baldwin and Simon, and the realisation hit him like a bolt from the sky: he was scared of the knight, not of the body!

From that moment, the constable kept a wary eye on him. They managed at last to heave the body down into the track, and from there it took little time to toss it unceremoniously into the back of the high wagon. Again, the constable saw that the old farmer did not move. He too seemed petrified. Even when the old woman's corpse hit the wagon and made it lurch, Cottey stayed staring resolutely ahead, shoulders hunched as if against the cold and elbows resting on his knees.

'Come on, Sam,' Tanner called. 'Let's get her back to Wefford.' Cottey whistled and clucked to the mule, but neither spoke nor turned, and the constable shook his head in a quick flare of disgust.

Baldwin and Simon were soon back. The knight mounted his horse and watched as Simon followed suit, then glanced over at Greencliff. 'We may want to see you later – when we've had a chance to find out more. You live there?' He pointed with his chin to the longhouse at the top of a small rise. When Greencliff nodded, he wheeled round, checked the others were ready, and started off back to Wefford. By the time they had entered the trees again, he found Simon had caught up with him and was riding alongside.

Smiling, the knight gave him a quick look. 'Feeling better?'

'Not really, no.' He was quiet for a moment, then said musingly, 'It's always worst just before you see them, isn't it? It's not knowing what you're going to find that makes it more revolting. Once you've actually seen the damage, it's not so bad.'

'No, I suppose not,' said Baldwin, the smile fading.

'Are you sure about the blood?'

The humour was wiped away like snow from armour. 'Yes. She cannot have died there, not with the amount of blood she must have lost. Think about it: when you slit the throat of a pig or lamb, the blood sprays, doesn't it?'

'Well, yes . . .'

'So too with humans. If she had died there, the leaves, the ground, everything would have her gore. No, she cannot have died there.'

'So where *did* she die?'

'Where?' His voice became lower and quieter, and he was musing as he continued, 'That's what we must try to find out.'

Yes, thought Simon. And why she was put there, too.

They clattered into Wefford at a little before lunch, and carried the wrapped figure into the inn, ignoring the protests of the owner, before calling for mulled wine.

Walking through into the dark interior, Simon strode over to the benches and sat, holding his hands out to the flames as if in a pagan ritual, feeling the numbness flee, only to leave stabs and prickles as sensation returned. Groaning, he stretched his legs towards the hearth and flexed his toes, grimacing in the exquisite pain.

After a moment he heard the curtain draw aside and the familiar stomp of his friend.

'God! Thank you for small gifts! That feels so good!' said the knight, baring his teeth as he stood close to the flames and sighed. 'Innkeeper! Where's my wine?'

Simon glanced at him. 'I thought you believed in moderation with your wine?'

'When it's this cold? Moderation, yes: but not to the exclusion of comfort,' he said, then roared again: 'Innkeeper!'

He entered scowling, a look of bitter dissatisfaction on his face, and walked to the other end of his hall, disappearing through the curtain. After a moment he was back, carrying a pair of jugs and mugs on a tray which he set down between them. Turning, he was about to leave when Simon called him back.

'This dead woman, Agatha Kyteler,' the bailiff mused. 'The name doesn't sound local to these parts.'

'No, sir. She was quite new hereabouts. Only came here about ten years ago.'

'You seemed surprised earlier when you heard who had died. When we were questioning Cottey.'

'I was, sir. I heard her name only recently.' The man told of the visit of the Bourc and how he had asked about the old woman. Baldwin frowned as he listened but did not say anything, and ignored Simon's questioning glance.

'What do you know about her?' asked Simon, his eyes on his friend. He felt nervous. It was clear that the knight was worried, and from what he had said of the Bourc's visit when the Puttocks had arrived, he could guess why.

'*Know* about her? I don't . . .'

'She was murdered, you know,' said Baldwin shortly, avoiding the man's eyes as he toyed with the hilt of his sword in a vaguely threatening manner. 'We want to find out who did it.'

'Yes, sir.'

'So, answer!'

Sighing, the innkeeper poured wine for them, then sat and watched morosely as they sipped the hot, spiced liquid. 'She came from far off. Some say from the Holy Land. I don't know. Took the assart down behind the Oatway place, about a mile from here, out east.'

'And?' Baldwin's eyes narrowed and Simon had the impression that he was sure the publican was holding something back. 'Come on, man. You're the innkeeper! You know everyone here, and you know all the gossip, too. What was said about her? Who knew her well? Who liked her, who hated her? What do you know about her?'

His eyes flitted nervously from the knight to the bailiff and back, then, as if afraid of what he might see in their faces, he stared at the flames. When he spoke again, it was in a low voice, not fearful, but slow and deliberate. 'She weren't wealthy, but always had enough to survive. Very clever, she was, and that upset a lot of people. She made them feel stupid. She was arrogant too. Didn't suffer fools easily. Not without letting them know what she thought of them.'

'Her friends?'

'Ask the women hereabouts. They all knew her.'

'Why?'

He looked up suddenly, a small smile playing at the corners of his mouth. 'She helped them with their babies. When there was a problem with the birth – any problem – she helped them. She was a good midwife.' He almost mused as he spoke.

'So she'll be missed?'

'Yes,' he thought, considering. 'Yes, she'll be missed by some.'

'Did anyone hate her? Could someone here want her dead?'

With a shrug, the innkeeper showed his indifference, but under the intensity of Baldwin's gaze, he spoke with a defensive air. 'Some might've. But you can't believe what people say here! "I hate him", "I'll kill him", "He deserves death", you hear it every day in here. When a man gets into his cups, his mouth runs away sometimes – it's natural. You can't believe it, it's the wine talking.'

'Who has said that about Kyteler?'

'Oh! I don't know. Many people have. They were scared of her. She seemed too clever, like I said. People get worried by women who're too clever.'

'So who *has* said that kind of thing about her?' Baldwin pressed.

'Like I say, it means nothing. There's a few have said things. Young Greencliff, he has. And old man Oatway.'

'Did they say why? Why they hated her?' asked Simon, leaning forward, his arms on his knees as he frowned.

'Why? Ha!' He gave a rich, low chuckle. 'Oatway has the place between her assart and here, and he's got chickens.

About a month ago, he saw one of his chickens was missing, and when he looked he found its feathers, all in a line on the way to Kyteler's place. He reckons it was her dog, but she swore it wasn't.'

'If it was going out that way, it could have been a fox or anything, heading back to the wild; away from the houses and back to the forest,' said Simon.

'That's what she said, too, but old Oatway wouldn't have it! He reckoned it was her dog, right enough. Anyway, he went to her and said he wanted the chicken replaced, and she refused. Since then, he's lost two more chickens, and he hates her, blames her for them.'

'Hardly enough to murder for,' said Baldwin mildly.

Simon glanced at him. 'A chicken is enough meat for a week or more for two people. After the last couple of years, I'd say it was a very good reason to kill.'

'Well,' the innkeeper squirmed in his seat, 'I'm not saying it's not, but I still don't think he could kill. Not old John Oatway.'

'No? What about Harold Greencliff?'

'Harry? No, I don't think so. He's a good lad. No, he wouldn't kill.'

'Why did he hate Kyteler?'

'I don't know. I really don't. Something happened, though. He came in here . . .'

'When?'

'Yesterday. Late afternoon, I suppose . . . Yes, it was just after dark, so it must have been about five o'clock. Anyway, he came in and took a pint of ale, and sat down over there.' He pointed at the far corner, near the screen leading to the inner rooms. 'A bit later, a friend of his came in, Stephen de la Forte, and they got talking, and I heard Harry say that she was a bitch and if she wasn't careful, someone would "see to her".'

'And?'

'Oh, they left soon after. But that's not to say he was really mad – he looked more sad to me, not really angry, just upset, so don't go thinking he went straight out to kill her. Anyway, they were back here a few hours later – before eight.'

'Who? Greencliff and de la Forte?'

'Yes. They came in again and settled down for the evening with some of their friends.'

'Where had they been?'

He shrugged. 'How should I know? To get food or something, I don't know.'

'How did they seem when they got back?'

'Oh, Stephen was noisier than usual, but I reckon they'd had drinks while they were out. It gets some people like that. Harry was quiet. He often is when he's drunk too much. He's a nice, quiet sort of a lad.'

'I see,' said Baldwin, but as he opened his mouth to say more, Tanner and Cottey came in from seeing to the body. Walking to the huddle of men at the fire, they sat and stared longingly at the jugs of wine until Baldwin gestured and the innkeeper rose with bad grace to fetch more, this time not forgetting himself.

'We put her out back in the outbuilding. She can wait there until the priest can come and see to her,' said Tanner, watching the wine being poured as he held his hands to the fire. Sighing, he continued, 'Poor old woman should be all right there. We put her up on a box. The rats should leave her alone for a day or two.'

Simon nodded, then glanced over at the innkeeper, who had returned and was staring morosely at the flames once more. 'Did she have any family?'

'What, here?' Looking up, he seemed disinterested now, as if he had exhausted his knowledge and would prefer to move on to talk of other things. 'No, not that I've seen. Sam? You seen any family with her?'

Taking a long pull at his wine, the old farmer paused before answering. Head one side, he considered. 'No. Don't think so. Mind you, you'd need to ask Oatway to know. Anyone going to see the old . . .' He hesitated. 'The old woman, they'd've had to go past Oatway's place first.'

'I think we need to see Oatway,' said Baldwin ruminatively.

CHAPTER SIX

The Bourc whistled as he jogged easily southwards, keeping the moors straight ahead. They looked beautiful, dark and soft with a vague hint of purple and blue, splashed with white in the shadowed areas where the low sun could not reach. Here, almost at the outskirts of Crediton, the moors took up the whole of the view, stretching from east to west as if trying to show him that they were the best route for him to take.

Soon he was out of the surrounding trees and winding down the lane that led into the town itself. Here he made his way to the market and bought bread and a little meat before carrying on. To his surprise, as he was leaving the market, he heard his voice called, and when he turned, he saw the merchant, Trevellyn, at the door to an inn.

'You leaving already?'

'Yes. My business is finished here. I am on my way back to the coast.'

'I see. Going to Oakhampton, then south?'

'No,' said the Bourc shortly, and explained his route. 'It should be quicker.'

'Yes,' said the merchant. There was a strange expression in his eyes as he peered at the Bourc speculatively. 'There's one easy route if you're going over the moors.' Walking a short distance with the Bourc, he pointed to where the road began, and made sure that the Gascon understood the route before returning to the inn.

Mounting his horse, the Bourc stared thoughtfully after him for a moment. The merchant's helpfulness did not ring true. It was oddly out of character after their last meeting in Wefford. But his advice sounded good.

The road led between some houses, down a short hill, and out to a flat plain. Crossing a river, he found that the road was well marked and easy to follow, and soon he was whistling cheerfully as he went.

After riding for some hours the countryside began to change. In place of the thickly wooded hills near Wefford and Furnshill, the trees were becoming more sparse and the hillsides steeper and less compromising. The road straggled lazily between the hills as if clambering up them would have been too much effort, and he found himself quickening his pace. As a soldier, he disliked enclosed places: he wanted to get to the moors and openness.

Not far from them, he found the road entered a wood which stood as if bounding the moors, far from the nearest house. There had been no other travellers for over an hour, which served to heighten his sense of solitude.

Riding into the shadows, he noticed the air felt stuffy. There was a hush, as if even the wild creatures were holding their breath expectantly. The silence was intimidating. When a blackbird crashed off a branch and squawked its way along a hedge in front of him, he stopped his horse with a frown.

It had moved too early to have been upset by him. Something else had worried it. He kicked his horse into a slow walk, and peered around with an apparent shortsighted lack of awareness. To have paused too long would have appeared suspicious, and he had no wish to avoid whoever could be ahead. But as his horse walked on, the knight was as alert as he ever had been.

Other men he had known had told him that they experienced extreme fear and a strange lassitude when they knew they were riding into a battle. He never did. To him warfare was life itself, his whole existence revolved around the fights on the marches, and without battle his life would have little meaning. No ambusher could have realised that from seeing him now.

His head moved sluggishly, as if he was dozing, and, as his horse meandered on slowly, his whole body slumped. Yet he managed to search each bush, every tree trunk, with care.

Only twenty yards into the trees he saw the first man and knew that he was about to be attacked.

The first glance merely gave him a flash of russet. If he had not already been expecting to see someone, he might have missed it, but that fleeting glimpse was enough. Considering where he would have put his own men for an ambush, he soon saw four other places where men could hide. There were too many – if he was attacked here he could be overcome too easily. With that thought in mind, he patted his horse's neck. Then, with a quick prayer, he clapped spurs to his mount and they thundered down between the trees.

Suddenly the wood was full of angry shouting. He heard the low, thrumming whistle of an arrow passing overhead, a shouted curse, cries and swearing as men realised their trap was sprung, and then he was through the woods and in the open. The moors!

Risking a look over his shoulder, he could see three men struggling with horses. One was up quickly, two others a little slower. Glancing again, the Bourc saw that the first kept ahead of the others.

In front there was no cover of any sort. A quick ambush was out of the question. He would have no chance to stop and mount an attack until he had managed to increase the distance between him and his pursuers. It would take too long to grab his bow or a lance from the packhorse. Pursing his lips, he considered as he kicked his mount again. Then, when he threw another glare back, he saw that his luck was with him. The man in front had increased his lead and was gaining while the others were falling back.

Still bent low over his horse's neck, he took the reins in his left hand and reached for his sword, checking it would pull free easily. Then he began to measure when he should turn.

It was not long. The leading man behind was a scant twenty yards away when the Bourc saw a stream ahead. Soon he felt his horse slow and pause before leaping. The Bourc just had time to drop the packhorse's leading rein before they jumped.

With his muscles coiled like huge springs, his horse bounded up and over the small stream, the packhorse following. It was then that he knew he had his opportunity. As soon as they landed, he reined in and turned, facing the man behind just he leaped over the brook.

The Bourc immediately spurred back. While the man and

his horse were still in the air, the Gascon pelted towards him, and when they landed he was only feet away. His pursuer had no chance of avoiding the swinging fist in its heavily mailed gauntlet. The blow met his chin, carrying with it the onward weight of both horses and the knight.

Seeing their friend tumble from his saddle, the other two slowed in their chase, and when they saw the Bourc draw his sword they seemed to lose enthusiasm for further battle.

'Go! Go and leave me – or accept the revenge of a knight's sword!' he shouted.

The two hesitated. Both were dark, thin-featured men, who could have been brothers, for although one was in russet and the other wore a stained blue tunic, they had the same pale skin and thick eyebrows. Their horses were cheap riding horses, not farm animals, and the men looked, although not rich, far from poverty. The Bourc's eyes narrowed as he stared at them. There was something wrong here, he felt. These men were not common footpads – or if they were, robbers in England were wealthier than in Gascony.

'Go!' he bellowed again, and the two exchanged a glance. One wheeled and started off back to the line of trees. When his companion did not move, he stopped and looked back, but before he could call, his friend had turned as well, with a last malevolent glare at the Bourc. Soon they were riding at a solid trot, back the way they had come.

Only when they had disappeared among the trees did the Bourc sheath his sword and drop from his horse. He quickly bound his prisoner's hands and feet before surveying him thoughtfully. Then, shrugging, he sat and built a fire while he waited for the man to wake.

* * *

Simon and Baldwin ate lunch at the inn, then, guided by Cottey's directions, they found their way to the dirt track that led to the Oatway holding. They rode together, with Tanner bringing up the rear, his features set in a contemplative scowl as he lurched along.

The snow had stopped again now, but was thick enough to cover most of the roadway, only the longer shoots of grass just breaking through. Nearer the trunks, the bushes and earth were untouched by the white carpet, protected by the great branches high overhead. It looked strange to Baldwin, as if they had left the winter behind in the village and now had entered a warmer area where only the road itself was cold enough to support the virgin whiteness.

While they were still out of sight of the farm, Simon began to hear a regular noise over the steady rhythm of the horses' hooves. Tap, tap, tap, then a pause, then two more. It stopped, then after a moment started again, and he cocked his head and looked over at Baldwin, who caught his glance and shrugged.

As the tapping got louder, they arrived at a fork in the trail. They chose the left-hand track, and the sound became louder as they followed it. Rounding the last bend, the forest fell back to show a large assart. In the middle stood a weary-looking cottage with stained and ancient thatch, which was allowing wispy tendrils of smoke to filter out above walls that were in need of fresh lime-wash. In front a cow stood chewing hay and watching their approach with bored disinterest, while between her legs chickens madly pecked at the earth and packed dirt of the yard. Over to the left was a strong fenced enclosure with goats, while on the right was what looked like a coppice area, with thick stems rising in clumps.

They slowly rode up and into the yard. It appeared empty, but as they looked round, Simon became aware again of the tapping. Touching his horse with his spurs, he led the way to the back of the house. Here he found a pasture area, recently cleared. Stumps still littered the rough ground, and the snow could not hide the fact that the ground was only thinly grassed. The earth showed through in red scars.

At the far end was a tall, stooping, blue-smocked man with his back to the visitors, working at a series of heavy poles set vertically in the ground. Between each were bushes.

The knight and the bailiff exchanged a glance, then slowly rode on towards him. He was plainly unaware of their approach, and as they came closer they could hear him whistling tunelessly while he worked.

In his hand was a large-bladed bill, a short, solid curved-steel tool shaped like a stubby sickle with a wooden haft, with which he was tapping branches from the bushes around the stakes to build a woven fence of living wood which would later become a hedge – thick and strong enough to keep his animals in, and forest animals out. Suddenly he whirled, the bill raised in his hand, and stood facing them, unmoving, and they halted, considering him.

He was tall, at least five inches more than Tanner, more like Simon's own height of five feet ten, but although he appeared healthy for his age, which must surely be some five and forty years, he was quite stooped. There was a slightly unnatural colour in his cheeks, as if he was on the verge of a fever. His eyes gleamed darkly from under bushy eyebrows, whose colour had faded to pale greyness like his unkempt hair. It was the eyes that Simon noticed most of all. There was an odd expression in them – not fear, but a kind of suspicion.

'There's no need to fear,' said Baldwin.

'No? Who are you? What do you want with me?'

'This is the Keeper of the King's Peace – and this is the Constable. I am the Bailiff of Lydford,' said Simon reasonably. 'Are you Oatway?'

The bill lowered a little, but the man's eyes still flitted over them in obvious doubt. 'What if I am?'

'We need to ask you some questions. Did you know there's been a murder?'

'No,' he said, and the surprise was plainly clear. His arm dropped down to his side, until the tool dangled, forgotten. 'Who?'

'Agatha Kyteler.'

'*Her!*' He hawked and spat, as if the name offended him. 'Good!'

'Did you see her yesterday?' Simon asked.

'Yesterday?' He considered. 'No. No, I don't think so . . .'

'Do you live alone?'

'No, my wife is here too.' He added more softly, with a hint of sadness, 'We have no children.'

'Did your wife see her yesterday, do you know?' Simon persisted.

Oatway glanced down at his bill, then sighed deeply and brought it down sharply on to a log. It stayed there, gripped by its own slashing cut. 'You'd better come and ask her,' he said.

When he motioned, the three men dropped from their horses and followed him back to the front of the house, tying their mounts to the rail beside his log store.

Inside they found the cottage filthy, the atmosphere rancid from animal dung. Smoke hung in the rafters waiting to drift out through the thatch from the large hearth in the centre of the floor. Entering, they had to step down. Like many older properties, to save the valuable animal dung, the floor of the house was built on a slope. As the winter proceeded, the level of the floor at the lower, byre end, would rise. When spring finally arrived, the manure could be taken out and spread over the fields and the floor level would drop once more.

Now, after some months of bad weather, the room stank, and Simon could see that the faeces were almost at the level of the door. He tried to shut his nostrils to the stench, but found it difficult. To his satisfaction, he saw that Baldwin seemed to notice the smell more than him, although Tanner appeared impervious.

Mrs Oatway was a broad, strong-looking woman of about her husband's age. She stood staring at them with a scowl of distrust as they trooped into her house, her hand gripping the large wooden spoon with which she had been stirring at the iron pot as if it was a weapon. Although her hair still had its native darkness, without the greying of her husband, her features were wrinkled with age and troubles. She looked as quick and sharp as a martin, shrewd and devious. And probably malicious too, from the look of her thin bloodless lips.

After quickly introducing themselves, Baldwin suggested that they should walk outside to talk, but she demurred. 'I've got food to prepare. We can talk in here.'

Grinning at the knight's obvious discomfort, Simon said, 'We are trying to find out whether anybody saw Agatha Kyteler yesterday. Did you?'

'Her!' A sneer curled her lip. 'I don't look for her. Why do I care for her, the old . . .'

'You disliked her after the affair with your chickens, didn't you?' said Simon flatly, feeling as he spoke that the words were superfluous, but wanting to cut off her flow of invective. It worked. She stopped and glowered at him.

'Well? What if I do?'

'Did. She's dead. We're trying to find out why. Why did you hate her so much?'

The shock was plain on her face, her mouth opening and shutting, and then she turned to her husband and stared at him. 'Is this true? Eh?'

He shrugged as Simon said, 'Answer the question, woman. Why did you hate her?'

Sighing, and after some grumbling, she told them of her suspicions about Agatha Kyteler's dog.

'Did you see her dog do it?' asked Baldwin, wincing and coughing.

'See it? No, but it was her dog, all right. We followed the feathers, didn't we?' She turned for verification to her husband, who nodded vaguely.

Simon considered. 'Did you see her yesterday?'

'I . . .' She paused, her glower deepening.

'Good. When?'

'Middle of the afternoon.'

'Why?' sighed Simon, and stared at her in silence.

'It was that dog again,' she said at last, reluctantly.

'Her dog? What did it do?'

'It attacked my chickens again. Took another one. What was I supposed to do? Wait 'til it had killed them all? I went to tell her to keep the dog tied up. I told her if I saw it on our land again, we'd kill it.'

'What did she say?'

'Her!' Her lips curled again in scorn. 'Nothing, of course! She said it wasn't her dog. Said it was in the house with her all day. Well that was a lie!'

'You saw her dog, then?'

'No, but the feathers went her way again. It must have been her dog.'

Shrugging, Simon glanced at Baldwin, who coughed. 'Very well,' he said reasonably. 'Did you see anyone else there?

Her face wrinkled with the effort of recollection. 'Yes. Yes, while I was on my way there, Sarah Cottey and Jennie Miller were talking near the house. And some other woman was in the trees – I don't know who – when I left.'

'What did she look like?' asked Baldwin.

'Look like? Oh, I don't know, Dressed well. Slim woman. Fairly tall and young, I'd say. Had a long cloak on, with fur on the hood.'

'A grey cloak?' Baldwin's face wore a frown when Simon shot a glance at him.

'Yes, it was grey, I think.'

'You saw no men?'

'No.'

After checking where Jennie Miller lived, they walked out with relief to the open air. Even the extreme cold of the gathering darkness was preferable to the stench inside. The husband followed them, standing and inhaling deeply on his doorstep as he watched them mount their horses. Baldwin whirled his horse, and was about to ride off when he seemed struck by a sudden thought.

'Oatway. Why was your wife so sure that Kyteler's dog attacked your chickens?'

He stared up at the grave knight, then quickly glanced behind to the open doorway. Moving a little away from it, to stand closer to Baldwin, he said, 'Because she thinks old Kyteler got her dog to come here.'

'What? What do you mean?'

'Kyteler never liked my wife. My wife thinks she got the dog to come and kill our chickens, one by one.'

Simon felt the hair begin to rise on his scalp as the stooping man stared up at the knight, his voice dropping as if nervous of being overheard – not by his wife, but by someone else. 'Kyteler was clever with animals. She always knew how to help hurt ones. And she could make potions for people too. She knew how to make potions, medicines and such. There's only one sort knows about that kind of thing.' His eyes held Baldwin's with a fearful conviction. 'She was a witch!'

It had not taken the Bourc long to light his little fire from one of the bundles on the packhorse, and he was soon sitting and warming himself. Munching on a hunk of bread, he watched the man until he saw a finger twitch and an eyebrow flicker, and then he stood and contemplated the supine figure for a moment before walking over and kicking it. 'Wake up! You have questions to answer!'

The man was thick-set and swarthy like a seaman. On hearing the Bourc's voice, he looked around blearily, his eyes unfocused and slowly blinking above the scuffed and bloody chin, until they caught sight of his captor and suddenly widened.

'I see you recognise me,' said the Gascon affably, squatting nearby. Pulling out his long-bladed dagger, he toyed with the hilt for a moment, then studied his prisoner with a smile. When he spoke, his voice was low and reasonable. 'Why were you trying to ambush me?'

Brown eyes narrowed and flitted around the landscape.

'I shouldn't bother, if I was you. They went. If they tried to come back, I would have seen them. They've left you here,' said the Bourc.

'They wouldn't leave me alone.' But the eyes were uncertain as they moved over the surrounding country, and the Bourc let him search for his friends for a minute without interruption. There was no need to emphasise the fact. From here the moors fell down to the stream where he had caught the man, then rose to the trees a mile or so beyond. It was clear that no rescue was to be mounted from there. The Bourc watched as the man peered round to look up the hill, and grinned humourlessly. He knew that the country was as empty for nearly as far in that direction.

Holding the dagger delicately between finger and thumb, point dangling, the Bourc glanced at him again. 'Why were you trying to ambush me? And why did your friends not shoot to kill? They had bows. I saw.'

The eyes snapped back to his face and the Bourc was surprised to see no fear there. The dark face stared at him with what looked like a vague sneer. 'Why do you think?'

'I have no idea. Why don't you tell me?' There was no answer. The man hawked and spat contemptuously. Sighing, the Bourc tried again. 'My friend, I don't know. You don't look hard done by – you aren't starving or anything. You don't seem poor: your tunic is good quality and not worn.'

Now the scornful expression grew. 'We aren't footpads!'

'Ah! So why else attack someone you have never met? You have the look of a sailor, and yet I know no sailors . . .'

Seeing a quick interest, he paused. 'So you *are* a sailor. But I know no sailors . . . No, I do not understand why you should have tried to rob me. So . . .'

'So maybe I just hate Gascons.'

'Yes, that's possible,' said the Bourc softly. With a flick he tossed the dagger up. It turned once in the air and he caught it again by the hilt. Reaching forward, he touched the point at the top of the man's breast-bone. As the eyes widened, he smiled, then dragged the blade gently downwards, so lightly he left no mark on his prisoner's skin, although it made the man squirm as it traced a mark of tickling terror down his chest. When it touched the top of his tunic, the Bourc angled it, so that it sliced through the cloth.

Speaking conversationally, he said, 'You don't look worried about dying at my hands. I suppose you aren't scared of a quick death. That's fine. But it's getting close to dark, and it will be very cold tonight. I think I might just leave you here once I have cut your tunic off. After all, maybe *I* don't like sailors.'

'You can't do that! I'm your prisoner, you must . . .'

'*I* must? I don't have to do anything. You attacked me. I can do as I wish with you – I'm a knight. And I have little time to take you anywhere, my lord expects me home in Bordeaux. No. I think that leaving you here to freeze slowly will be best.'

Now the fear was fighting to overcome the disbelief. 'You can't! What if someone finds me here and . . .'

'Finds you? Here?' The Bourc smiled at him again, his knife stilled, and he made a show of gazing round. When his eyes came back to his prisoner, he began to move the blade again. 'I think it's a little unlikely, don't you? We're not close to a road here. I doubt whether anyone would come here before morning. Of course, a wolf might come along . . .'

'*Stop!*' It was a cry of panic. 'I'll tell you why we were there . . . Stop! *Please!*'

The Bourc paused, his dagger poised under the man's heart. 'Yes?'

'We were paid to attack you. Not to kill you, just to hurt you a bit . . .'

'Who paid you? And why?' He stared. He only knew a few people here – who could have asked for him to be ambushed?

'Trevellyn – Alan Trevellyn – he lives over north of Crediton – we work for him. He paid us to follow you today, after he pointed you out to us in the inn – told us he wanted you hurt. That's all I know.'

For a minute the Bourc held the man's gaze while he considered. It was quite possible that the merchant had chosen to pay men to attack him. He had made sure of the Gascon's route by telling him which way to go. Nodding to himself, he whipped the knife down, swiftly slicing the tunic to the hem. Then he moved the blade down and cut the thongs hobbling his ankles.

'Very well. You can go now.'

'But . . .'

'What?' He mounted his horse and stared down.

'My hands! And where is my horse?' the man said, struggling to his feet and dejectedly looking down at his bare chest.

'Be grateful you have hands left. As for your horse – you lost it. You know your own way home, I believe. I should begin walking.'

He could still hear the man's hoarse shouting when he had left him far behind, but he soon put all thoughts of the robber out of his mind. His only concern was how to repay the merchant. Nothing else mattered.

CHAPTER SEVEN

Old Oatway stood and stared after the bailiff and knight as they left his holding, watching carefully as if doubting that they were truly leaving. Once out of sight of him and the house, Baldwin grimaced, glancing upwards at the sky.

'It's going to freeze tonight,' he muttered, and Simon nodded glumly, making the knight smile. Simon was not happy. Although he considered himself educated, and knew that rumours could easily accumulate around people in villages like Wefford with no reason, he felt nervous to have heard that the old woman was thought to be a witch. He shook himself. She was probably just a maligned old woman, that was all, surely. Glancing up, he saw the clouds were the colour of old pewter, angry and heavy.

'Well, Simon? Shall we go and question this Jennie Miller? Or should we go and take a look at Kyteler's house?'

'Tanner? What do you think?'

Ambling up on his horse, Tanner looked down the lane towards Agatha Kyteler's house. 'We have to see her place. We still don't know where she was killed. Maybe we'll find something there.'

It was a good quarter of a mile to the little assart where the old woman had lived, and the difference between her cottage deep in the woods and the Oatway property closer to the road was startling. Here the thatch was fresh, not more than one summer old; the lime wash brilliant and white. Even the log store appeared to have been carefully maintained, the logs stacked neatly to the left of the house under an extension of the thatch.

In front were two wattle pens in which goats and chickens roamed, and there was barking and whining at the sound of their arrival. Simon and Baldwin sat on their horses while Tanner alighted and strolled to the door, banging hard on the planks with his fist. There was no reply, so after looking at Baldwin, who gave a curt nod, he lifted the wooden latch and shoved the door open.

Immediately a thin black and brown lurcher burst out, barking excitedly and capering around the horses, jumping up every now and again in an attempt to reach the riders. Laughing, Baldwin threw a quick glance at Simon. 'The poor devil must have been in there since yesterday to be this happy to see a stranger!'

'Yes,' said the bailiff, trying to keep his horse steady. The dog unnerved her, and she was trying to keep him in sight, reversing and turning skittishly as the black and brown streak tore round below. 'Keep still, damn you!'

He was so involved he did not notice the constable come back to the door and motion to them. Grinning at his friend's discomfort, Baldwin dropped from his mount and lashed the reins to a sapling, then crouched and stroked the dog before rising, still smiling, to enter. But the smile left his face when he saw the constable's expression.

'This's where she died,' he said curtly as he stood aside to let the knight in.

That was clear as soon as Baldwin's eyes accustomed themselves to the dark inside the small cottage. It was not as well built as the other houses in the village. In place of the solid timber beams, the gaps filled with cob and dirt to give a weatherproof shell, this place was a simple wooden shed, with earth and straw plastered on the outside to stop draughts.

One window high in the northern wall gave a little light into the gloomy interior. From it he could see that there was one almost square room, with a tiny attic area which had a seven runged ladder leading up to it. Baldwin could make out the rugs and furs that made up the bed in it. Beneath, all was cluttered. In the centre sat a fireplace, around which stood two small benches. To the right was a table, covered with earthenware pots and a variety of twigs, leaves and roots. A pair of large flat granite stones sat near the fire, which must have been used for grinding in place of mortar and pestle.

All over the floor were pots and vessels containing seeds and leaves, some fresh, some dry, giving the room a soft and musty odour. Around the walls and from the beams hung clumps of other branches and drying flowers, but it was to his left that his eyes were pulled. There had been a similar table to that opposite, a simple affair built of roughly-hewn planks on top of a pair of trestles, but here it was fallen, as if pulled or yanked over into the room, away from the wall.

The collection of herbs and other plants was scattered all over the floor, and broken pots lay underneath the toppled baulks of wood.

'Wait here,' said Baldwin shortly, his eyes narrowing as he stared at the floor around the table. Walking past the constable, he moved forward slowly, gazing at the wreckage while he wondered whether there had been a fight.

Turning, he looked at the other side of the room. There, he saw, the table was standing hard against the wall. The pots around it on the floor were neatly organised on both sides, as if placed in military lines. He wandered carefully towards it and picked up a pair. One contained what looked like several twigs of yew, the other held leaves and stems from a juniper. He replaced them thoughtfully and strolled back to the fallen table.

Here, it appeared, the same pots had stood at either side, with some resting on top. There were several more smashed on the ground, and leaves and roots were scattered all over the floor. Baldwin crouched down and picked up a few. Mostly they appeared to be different herbs. He smelled thyme, basil and sage. And something else. Over the heavy musk and the thick pine, he could smell the decaying sweet-ness. As Simon came in, darkening the room as his body shut out the light from the doorway, the knight's fingers encoun-tered the slight stickiness, chilly and thick on the floor, directly in front of the table.

'Found anything?' Simon asked from the entrance. He saw the knight turn, his face sad and reflective.

'Yes. This is where she died. Her blood is all over the floor.'

Sighing, the knight slowly traced the cloying mess from one extremity to the other. It seemed to have settled in pools on the ground, as far as he could see in the darkness. Mostly it had congealed, but here and there the thickest gobs still held viscous proof of their provenance. Tanner crouched by the fire. There was no chance of resurrecting the flames of yesterday, and he resigned himself to starting a new one so that they might have light.

Soon the flames were rising languidly from a small mass of tinder, and the constable found a small foul-smelling tallow candle which he passed to Baldwin, who waited by the table, crouching.

Taking the candle, the knight peered round, grunting occasionally to himself. To Simon, standing by the door, he looked like a hog grubbing for acorns. On hearing a muttered call, the constable strode to Baldwin, then lifted the bench while the candle was held to the top and sides, then the bottom and finally the trestles. Nodding, the knight allowed Tanner to set the table down again before continuing his study. He paused for a moment and stared fixedly, then reached down and picked up something, but Simon could not see what. At last he stood and, holding the candle high, looked hard at the wall behind the table. Snuffing the candle, he walked out, passing Simon wordlessly.

Outside once more, the dog sat, head on one side as if listening to their conversation. Tanner stood silently behind them.

'So what happened?' asked Simon. 'Why would anyone kill her? It can't have been an accident.'

'No, it was no accident.' Baldwin dropped and snapped his fingers at the dog until it lurched to its feet and walked to them, head down and tail slowly sweeping from side to side.

Ruffling the fur on the dog's head, the knight continued slowly and deliberately.

'I think someone went to her and spoke to her. She was at the table when she was killed. I think she was killed as she stood there, with her back to her killer.'

The bailiff frowned as he tried to understand. 'She was standing at her table while the killer cut her throat?'

'Very likely. Blood hit the wall behind the table in a spray, so it's probable that she was facing that way when the killer struck. Blood was over the top of the table, not on the bottom, so the table was upright when the blow fell. After her throat was sliced, she fell back, and I think she pulled the table with her. No blood lay on the leg of the trestle, so I think that the table top protected it from her blood as she fell back. If she had fallen with the blow and then tried to haul herself upwards, she would have left her blood on the trestle where it faced into the room. As it is, I think she was wounded and took hold of the table, then fell back to die, taking the table with her.'

Both were quiet for a moment. It was Tanner who broke the silence. 'Why would anyone do that to an old woman like her, though? She can't have had anything to steal. Why kill her?'

Turning to him, the knight gave him a cold smile in which the bitter anger flashed. 'That's what we must find out.'

While the constable went to fetch their horses, Simon contemplated his friend. 'Baldwin, something's the matter. What is it?'

The knight stared at him for a moment. Then, holding out his hand, he showed what he had found on the floor. It was a gold ring, with a large red stone held in its flat face.

'That hardly seems the sort of ring for a poor old woman,' mused Simon, and then he noticed the knight's expression. 'Baldwin? What is it? Do you know whose ring this is?'

Baldwin stared at him dully. 'Yes,' he said softly. 'I know whose this is.'

Riding to the woods at the edge of the moors, the Bourc was frowning as he thought about the merchant. He had no desire to stay in England longer than was necessary, and could easily forget the incident, putting the attempted ambush down to outlaws. But that would be dishonourable. As a free-born Englishman, and knight, he had a chivalric duty to avenge this cowardly attack. To ignore it would leave the merchant thinking he had succeeded in scaring the Bourc, and that was not merely demeaning, it could be dangerous. If common people thought they could flout the law and attack their betters, all well-born men would be endangered.

The more he thought about it, the more he was convinced that his master would enthusiastically support him punishing the guilty man. He must go and see Trevellyn.

He was following the trail made by his horses and those of his attackers back to the copse, and slowed as he came closer. On a sudden whim, he swerved aside and rode a short way parallel to the trees, his eyes flitting over the boughs. Two men had come back this way. They could still be there.

After going east for some hundreds of yards, he abruptly cantered to the woods, crashing through the ferns and bushes at the perimeter, half expecting to feel the sting of an arrow at any moment, but he heard and saw nothing to warrant concern. When he paused, listening for any noise over the breathing of the two horses, there was nothing. He carried on.

But he kept an eye open all the way.

'Tanner? Are you all right?' Simon had watched the tall figure of the knight ride away, the small shape of the dog at his horse's heels – obviously having found another master, the dog was not willing to lose him. Now he turned, worried at the man's taciturn demeanour.

The constable was slouched on his horse as they passed the Oatway holding, chin on his breast as if asleep, but staying stiff and steady in his saddle. At Simon's question, his head snapped up, and the bailiff, to his intense annoyance, found himself being studied closely.

'What is it, Tanner?'

'I'm not sure, Bailiff.'

'Come on, you've been quiet all afternoon. What is it?'

But the constable would not say more. All he had were vague suspicions: Greencliff had been nervous; the boy was more scared of the knight than of the body. That was normal for a villein, and Greencliff lived on Furnshill's land. It was only natural for him to be fearful of his master – his master held his life and livelihood in his mailed fist. That was no reason to denounce the boy.

In his youth Tanner had been a soldier for the king, as had old Samuel Cottey. They had been men-at-arms with one of the companies protecting the Welsh marches, and had witnessed all possible human cruelties at the time, or so Tanner had thought. He had seen the murders of the villagers, the rape of the women and the slow torture of men suspected of spying or fighting against the army, and it had been there, in the smoke and fury of the Welsh battles, that they had decided to leave warfare to others. They had returned home, Tanner to take up his father's profession as a farmer until he was elected to be constable. This he found a difficult responsibility to drop, but until the previous year he had never been involved in more than the normal routine of arresting cut-purses at Crediton market.

Last year that had all changed when the trailbastons arrived and began to pillage the shire, killing and burning from Exeter to Oakhampton. That was when he rediscovered the joy of holding a sword. He had come to relearn the wicked delight in fighting, when the fighting was for a good cause. And now he had the same feeling: that something was wrong in the area. There was a killer loose. A killer who might strike again.

It was hard to believe that Greencliff could be involved. He knew the boy, had known him for over ten years, had known his father, and it seemed impossible that he could be involved in this murder. And yet he had been very nervous, and the body was very close to his house . . .

'I think I'll leave you at the inn. I want to go and see Greencliff.'

The Bourc had travelled for over three miles through the woods when he came up to the edge and gazed out at the road. There was nothing overt to cause him alarm, and he was about to kick his horse forward when a sudden caution made him stop.

In front of him the lane straggled untidily down the hill from his left, a red and muddy track cutting through the woods. He could see how it bent, falling down a steep incline to a rushing stream where a massive granite block acted as a simple bridge. At the other side the road rose steeply, soon swinging right to follow the riverbank all the way to Crediton. All seemed quiet and peaceful. There was no obvious reason for nervousness, no indication that any other person was near, but he paused and frowned warily.

Although there was probably nothing, he felt a prickling of his scalp. Partly, he was sure, it was due to the perfect siting of the bridge. If he had wanted to attack someone on the road, this would have been the place he would have chosen. The steep sides of the two hills made a fast escape almost impossible, whether forwards or back. The road narrowed at the bridge over the fast waters, funnelling the victim perfectly into a small area where it would be easy to haul a man from his horse or strike him.

Nodding to himself, he studied the trees lining the trail. They were thick, with dense bushes beneath. If someone was there, he would hardly be able to see them. But he could still feel the warning tingle of danger. Dropping from his horse, he lashed the reins to a branch and walked down the hill, along the line of the road but keeping just inside the trees. All the way he kept a wary eye on the dirt of the lane, but saw nothing alarming.

The traffic making its way from Crediton and Exeter to Moretonhampstead and beyond had chewed the path into a quagmire, and the deep ruts bore witness to the number of vehicles which had recently passed. Hoofprints scarred the red mud, leaving it cratered and pitted, looking like stew left boiling for too long.

As he walked down, pacing slowly and carefully as if hunting a deer, each step carefully measured to keep his noise to a minimum, he kept his attention on the bridge and the trees at either side. There was nothing obvious to warrant the trepidation he felt, but he had been a warrior too long to ignore his instincts. Only rarely had he known this sense of warning, but each time there had been good reason, and the feeling that this place was dangerous was not entirely due to its location. Somehow he *knew* that someone else was there.

He had covered almost half the distance when he heard a sniff and a low clearing of a throat from a few yards ahead: a man – and hidden to ambush a traveller.

Slowly, carefully, the Bourc laid his hand on his sword hilt and stepped forward softly, up to a thick oak bough with scrubby bushes at either side. Here he paused, putting out a hand to lean against the tree, listening.

'I reckon we've missed him. He's gone some other way.'

He froze at the low, muttered words. They were closer than he had realised.

'Maybe. Maybe not. Maybe he's just round that bend now, just about to come down.'

'Are you going to wait here all night just in case?'

'Trevellyn wanted him taught a lesson: not to insult an Englishman's wife.'

'But we can't wait here all night. We'll freeze.'

'We have to try to get him – do you want to lose your place on the ship?'

'It won't make much difference, will it? We never make any money on his ships now. Not since the pirates started attacking us every time we leave port.'

'Just give it 'til dusk. When it's dark we'll get back to town.'

The Bourc grinned mirthlessly, then began to make his painstaking way back to his horses. He led them slowly back up the hill for a distance before turning eastward and walking parallel to the stream. The men were too close to the bubbling water to hear his progress. He would leave them there. They would be occupied, and they could take a message back to Trevellyn, seemingly their ship's owner: although they had failed to teach their lesson, the Bourc did not seem to have tried to return to Crediton. Trevellyn would think himself safe.

The ride home for Baldwin and Simon was quiet. Neither was in the mood to talk. The knight rode along scowling fixedly ahead while Simon tried desperately to keep warm, taking the long fold of his old cloak and tossing it over his hunched shoulder as he rode in miserable, frozen silence. Every time the slow jogging of the horse would soon shake it free again. The trip seemed at least twice as long in the quickening darkness, with the wind slowly freezing the sweat on his back and the thickening mist ahead. Then, to his disgust, it began to snow again.

'God!' he muttered, and saw Baldwin shoot a quick glance at him.

'Cold, my friend?' he asked sardonically.

'Cold? What do you think?' responded Simon, throwing his cloak once more over his left shoulder.

'I have no idea!' The knight looked upwards before taking his bearings. When he continued, there was a new note of seriousness. 'We must hurry before we freeze, Simon. This snow is not going to stop.'

They were back at Furnshill before six o'clock, both pleased to see the welcoming orange glow of the sconces, candles and fire through the tapestry-covered windows. Their breath was steaming in the bitter cold, and they rode straight to the stableyard, the knight bellowing for grooms, before dismounting. Even when the men had taken the horses, he stood quietly watching as their mounts were rubbed down, and when he turned to Simon, he gave a quick grin. 'I always watch. It's a soldier's habit, I know, but old habits stay with you, and once you've lived in a war you learn that it's crucial that your horse is well fed and cared for. Hello! So you want food too, do you?'

This was to their visitor. As they had turned to walk to the manor house and the warm hall, they found the black and brown dog sitting inquiringly at the entrance to the stables, head on one side as if asking how much longer they must bear the cold.

The dog's tail began to sweep slowly from side to side, clearing a small fan in the snow, then he stood and waited for them. 'Looks like you've a new member of your household, Baldwin,' said Simon smiling. His only answer was a low grunt.

Tanner looked up sourly at the tree. His mouth twisted into a grimace of loathing as a small avalanche fell down his back and the wet trickle began its crawl towards his belt.

It was pitch black and freezing cold. The snow fell silently but inexorably. Hunching his shoulders, the constable peered ahead through slitted eyes, grunting in his misery.

After the knight and the bailiff had left, he had gone straight to the inn, drinking a couple of pints of mulled wine with the keeper. He had wanted to see if the man could add anything to his previous statement, and hoped that Greencliff might drop in, but the attempt was a failure. The landlord was happy to sell his wine, but denied knowing more than he had already told, and after morosely waiting for an hour or so, the constable decided to go and see whether he could find the youth at home. He obviously was not coming to the inn.

The track was miserable, though. Thick clumps of snow poured continually from the sky. There was nothing in his world but the cold and the snow. All creatures had fled the bitter chill and the trees at either side were invisible. In the absolute blackness there was no track, just a small patch of clear road ahead before sight was obliterated by whiteness in the dark. Now and again Tanner would see a clump of higher snow, showing where a bush lay hidden, or the branch of a tree. Other than that there was nothing.

Shuddering, he kept his muscles clenched, trying to keep himself warm. His mouth ached, and the unprotected skin on his throat and face felt tight and crisp, as if it had become brittle and would snap if touched.

He came to the house without realising he had left the woods, it was so still all round. It was impossible to see the edge of the woods, or the hedge where they had ridden that morning – all was hidden. But here at the house, he was aware that the road was rising, and suddenly there was the grey mass on his left. He gave a sigh of relief, kicking his horse into a trot to get to the front, but then a frown darkened his face. There was no welcoming glow of fire. No smell of wood smoke.

The small windows showed as rectangles of deeper black in the darkness of the walls. He would have expected to find at the least a glimmer from behind the tapestries and curtains, but there was nothing. With a feeling of anxiety, he realised that the house must be empty. Greencliff could not be there. To make sure, he dropped heavily from his old horse and thumped at the door.

After a few minutes, he tried the latch. Inside, all was silence, the fire a faint red apology in the hearth. He looked all round, then glanced behind him. The view decided him. Leading his horse inside, he took off the saddle and bridle, then groomed her before seeing to the fire.

It was when he had just managed to coax it back into life that the knock came at the door. Instantly alert, he grabbed his old sword, a heavy-bladed falchion. Drawing the single-bladed weapon, he walked quietly to the door and opened it with a jerk.

'Thank God, Harold, I . . . Who are you?'

Tanner stared grimly at his visitor, a young man with the red blush of fear colouring his face. 'I'm the Constable. Who are *you*?'

CHAPTER EIGHT

'What will you call it?' asked Simon as they entered the house, the slim figure of the dog walking ahead of them as if it had been born at Furnshill.

Throwing a quick glance at him, Baldwin said, 'I'm not so sure I'll keep it. After all . . .'

'I think you'd better tell the dog that!' said Simon. 'It's already decided to stay, from the look of it, whatever you think.'

'It's not what *I* say that matters. I was thinking of Lionors.'

'Ah! Yes, I forgot. Your wife!'

Baldwin shot him a glare of irritation, but it slowly left his features, to be replaced with a self-deprecating grin.

Lionors was apparently no difficulty. As they walked through the screens, they saw that Lionors and their companion had already met, and the two were standing and cautiously sniffing at each other in front of the fire. As they watched, the mastiff obviously decided that the newcomer was no threat, and walked away to lie before the flames, and soon the black and brown dog joined her, snuggling up against her large frame like a puppy. The mastiff lifted her head once, grumbled twice, but then flopped back down again and ignored the stranger.

'I'll think of a name,' said Baldwin with resignation.

Later, when he walked into his hall, Baldwin was amused to see Simon still standing and defensively warming his back before the fire, Hugh beside him and tossing more wood on, while Margaret stood by, an expression of tight-lipped exasperation straining her features. From her face, and from the look of embarrassed self-justification on Simon's, the knight knew his friend had been given sensible advice about not staying out too late in the dark when it snowed. In any case, Baldwin had heard the hissed fury in her voice – and the deference in her husband's – through the wall.

When he saw the quick toss of Margaret's head in his direction, the pained glance from Simon, and the straight back of the servant that seemed to imply that as far as he was concerned he would prefer to be anywhere other than with his master at the present, Baldwin smiled broadly.

'I suppose I could deny having heard your . . . er, talk?' he said, looking from Simon to Margaret, catching sight of a fleeting wince on the bailiff's face.

She raised a cynical eyebrow as she turned to face him with her hands on her hips. 'Are you going to tell me you didn't know how dangerous it can be? How bad it is to try to travel at night? You know what the lanes can be like when the snow is heavy: are you both mad?'

'I am sorry, my lady,' he said, walking to his chair in front of the fireplace. Before sitting he poured a tankard of warm wine from the jug on the hearth, then sat comfortably and sipped, his eyes fixed on her.

He looked like a bishop, sitting in his small chair as if it was a throne, she thought. Although he was not mocking her, she felt sure she could sense derision in his attitude, and drew in her breath to berate him in his turn, but before she could, he began speaking softly.

'Margaret, I'm sorry you were worried, but you must understand: there's been a murder. We could not just stop and come home as soon as it became dark. We had to see if we could discover any more.'

'Of course I know that,' she said sharply. 'But how would it profit your investigation for you both to die on a journey home?'

'Not at all, of course, but . . .'

'Exactly!' she said, cutting him off. 'Not at all! Two merchants and a monk have already died this year on the way from Tavistock. All because they carried on with their journey after dark. I will not have you two doing the same.'

'But Margaret,' Simon began, but she whirled, glaring, and he subsided.

'No more: I will hear no more!'

Baldwin grinned and inclined his head. 'Very well, lady. I will ensure that we are back in time in future.'

'Do so.' She walked to a bench and sat, arms crossed. 'And now, tell me about this woman who has died.'

The knight and Simon exchanged a glance, then, at a brief shrug from his friend, the bailiff quickly told her of their day and what they had found about the dead woman. Tentatively sitting beside her, he told of their discovery of the body, their talk with the Oatways and their visit to the empty cottage. As he spoke, the mastiff rose and walked to Baldwin, closely followed by her black and brown shadow.

'Poor woman,' Margaret mused when he finished, and Simon nodded. 'And these Oatways think she was a witch?'

'Yes,' said Baldwin. 'They seem to believe she could make her dog do as she wished. As if a dog needed any prompting to do mischief! Anyway,' he took Kyteler's dog by the head, holding it in both hands and peering into its eyes, 'how could they think this one was evil?'

'That's what they do, though,' said Hugh, and at his sudden interruption, they all glanced at him. Under their gaze he hunched his shoulders as if he wished he had not spoken, but then continued sulkily, 'Well, it is. They get animals and make them do what they want. They can call on wild animals if they want.'

Baldwin grunted, 'Nonsense!'

'It's true! And if they want, some of them can change into animals, too! There've been witches all over here since men first got here,' said Hugh, hotly defensive. 'Ever since men came here and fought the giants away there's been witches.'

'No, Hugh. There's no such thing as witches,' said the knight. 'There's only superstition and fear – sometimes jealousy. Never witchcraft.'

'Then how did this old woman get her dog to go and eat these chickens, then?' asked the servant triumphantly.

Looking up, Baldwin smiled at him, but then his face grew sombre. 'Just because some old woman has a dog, and her neighbour thinks it was that dog that attacked her chickens, does not mean it really was. I think the dog deserves the chance to defend itself. Likewise, just because somebody thinks a woman is a witch does not necessarily mean she is, and she deserves the chance to defend herself.'

'How can she? She's dead!'

'Yes. She is.' The words came quietly.

Margaret stirred. 'But, Baldwin, what if she was a witch?'

'Kyteler a witch? No, I don't think so.' His face was as gentle as his voice as he looked over at her.

'Why not?'

'Because I do not believe such people exist. I cannot.'

Simon leaned forward and peered at him. 'But surely on your travels you must have . . .'

'No. I never found any proof of a woman having been a witch. Oh, I found plenty of examples of old women accused of being evil, of being involved in magic. I have seen many of them being killed. But there was always another reason why they were accused, it was never because anyone really believed they were guilty.'

'What do you mean, "another reason"?'

'I mean, whenever there was someone accused of being a witch, it was because the accuser wanted their money, their cattle, their house – something! Always there was something that would benefit the accuser. And, often, it would only turn up later, after the poor wretch had already died in the flames. Even the priests don't usually believe they're evil, which is why they rarely get to see the Inquisition even when they have been accused. They're usually killed by the mob. No, I do not believe in witches.'

'But this old woman had all those herbs and roots,' said Simon doubtfully.

The knight shot him a quick look. 'Don't tell me *you* believe in witches?'

'Well,' the bailiff explained apologetically, 'it's not that I believe in them necessarily, or that I think Kyteler was one, it's just that there are so many stories, and . . .'

'Oh, really!' The knight suddenly stood and strode to the fire, standing by the great lintel of the chimney, and when he spoke again his face was all in shadow, his body framed by the flames behind. 'What is a witch?'

It was Margaret who answered. 'Someone who uses magic to do what she wants.'

'And what does she want?'

'Wealth. Love. Power. Sometimes to stay young. There are many things a witch can desire.'

'Kyteler had none of these. What did *she* achieve?'

Simon stirred. 'You say that, but surely witches use magic just to do evil? They don't need any benefit, they do it to please their master?'

'Their master? Who do you mean? The Devil?'

The bailiff was suddenly aware of the darkness, of the isolation of the manor as he answered, 'Yes.'

Filling his mug, Baldwin strolled back to his chair slowly. 'Possibly. I would be happier to believe in a witch who was wealthy, though, than one who was trying to please her dark master!'

'All those herbs, though . . .' Simon began hesitantly.

'Simon, really! Do you accuse all leeches of being witches? She was probably good with them and used her skills to help others. There may come a time when even *you* are glad for the help of a wise woman who can stop the pain from a broken limb . . . Or piles!'

'What do you know of her death, anyway?' asked Margaret diplomatically after a moment.

Baldwin looked up. 'Not much,' he admitted. 'She was seen in the afternoon by Mrs Oatway, but from then on we have little information.'

'No,' mused Simon. 'That's where we ought to start. We need to find out what Oatway and Greenfield were doing in the afternoon. They're the two we know who were supposed to hate her.'

'Yes,' said Baldwin, and stared at the fire. 'There is another suspect, though, Simon. I told you of my friend's son.' Glaring into the flames, he explained about the Bourc's visit to England to see the dead woman, and his ruby ring.

'Do you think he could have killed her?' Margaret asked.

Baldwin shook his head. 'He was here out of gratitude. To thank her.'

'If his story was true,' she said quietly.

The knight did not respond, but later, when he left them to go to his room, his face still wore a troubled scowl.

When Simon at last drifted off into sleep, he had the same nightmare as before, but this time the figure in the flames was not the abbot. As it turned, to his horror he recognised the face of Agatha Kyteler, her eyes sad and accusing as they held his.

The constable arrived before nine o'clock the next morning with his companion. It had not taken them long to make the journey, though the snow had slowed them.

'Sir Baldwin, I thought you should hear this man: what he can tell about Greencliff.'

The knight looked up, his jaw moving as he chewed on a crust of bread. The youth with Tanner was in his early twenties, tall, at least three inches over the constable, and with softly pale flesh. He looked fat, though his skin hung flaccid round his jowls and the hands gripping the cap were chubby. His mousy hair was cut well, and from his clothes he appeared well-to-do, with a blue tunic of wool, and woollen hose of grey. On his heavy belt he wore a small dagger.

'Who are you?'

The eyes rose and met his gaze unflinchingly. 'Stephen de la Forte.'

To Simon he appeared to be a naturally haughty man who was holding himself in with difficulty. His eyes were a surprisingly light grey colour, with glints of amber, which made them look oddly translucent, and they sat in a round face, where the definition of youthful exercise was already fading into the rounded obesity of premature middle-age. The bailiff instinctively disliked him, and rested his elbows on the table to study him the better.

'So, Stephen de la Forte, what can you tell us?'

The youth glanced quickly at the constable, a fleeting took, but Simon felt sure he could see a glimmering of devious intelligence there.

'I . . . I'm a friend of Harold Greencliff's – I've known him for years. I went to his house last night to see him, and the constable was there.'

'I went there about an hour after leaving you, sir,' interjected Tanner. 'He arrived when I'd just settled down.'

'I see. Well, then. Why were you going to see him?' asked Baldwin easily, leaning back in his chair.

'I . . .' he shot a glance over to Tanner again, suddenly nervous. 'As I said, he's a friend. I saw him on Tuesday, at the inn, and he seemed unhappy then – troubled – so I wanted to see him again and make sure he was all right.'

'How do you mean "troubled"?' said Simon frowning. The youth glanced at him with surprise and a certain distaste, as if he had thought the bailiff was a mere servant and should not try to become involved in the conversation of his betters. 'Well?'

'I don't know. He was upset by something. I took him out to the inn and stayed with him, but he didn't tell me anything about what was worrying him.'

He looked shifty, and Simon thought to himself that he appeared to be lying. Watching the boy's eyes flit away, he noted the fact for discussion with Baldwin later.

The knight was toying with a knife. Spearing a slab of meat, he studied it thoughtfully, and said, 'You were so worried after Tuesday that you want back to see him late yesterday? Why not earlier?'

'I *did* go earlier!'

'And?'

His eyes dropped. 'He wasn't there.'

'When was that?' Simon said, leaning forward.

'I don't know. Early, not long before noon.'

'I see. Tanner?'

'Yes?' The constable stepped forward.

'I assume Greencliff didn't turn up?'

'No, sir. We stayed there all night, but there was no sign of him.'

'Stephen de la Forte, can you think of any reason why your friend should have run away?'

The eyes that gazed back at him were troubled, and the youth slowly shook his head, but Simon was sure that he saw certainty there. This boy obviously thought his friend was guilty.

Baldwin took a deep breath. 'In that case, I think we'd better organise a search. It may have nothing to do with the death of Kyteler, but it certainly seems suspicious that on the day her body is found – especially so close to his house – he disappears. Very well.' He glanced at Tanner, who nodded, and then, at the knight's dismissive wave, took the youth by the arm and led him out. It was only when they were gone and the door shut behind them that Baldwin turned back to Simon and sighed in relief.

'Let's just hope they find him, eh? I think he could help us with some points about this death, especially now he's decided to run away – that looks suspicious, doesn't it. It seems like a clear sign of guilt, thank God! It *wasn't* the Captal's son.'

They spent the morning riding up over to the north on the road towards Bickleigh, the peregrine on Baldwin's arm in the hope of finding a suitable prey for their meal later, but saw nothing worth hunting. At last, when the sun had risen to its zenith, Baldwin snorted and gave a long grumbling sigh.

'This is ridiculous. I can't concentrate. Simon, Margaret, would you mind if we turned back home now?'

They exchanged a glance, then both nodded. Motioning to Edgar, Baldwin handed over the falcon, then turned his horse back home.

Up and down hills, the whole shire was smothered by the freezing blanket of white. In the distance Margaret could occasionally see the distant, grim greyness of the moors above the Dart, seeming different somehow from the rest of the countryside, gloomier and more menacing, proudly crouching on the edge of the horizon like a great cat waiting to pounce.

As they rode to the long track that wound through the ravine before the manor, Simon pointed excitedly at the path before them.

'Look at the prints! The search party must be back.'

Rounding the last bend in the trail before beginning the half-mile long section that pointed straight as a lance to the building itself, they could see the horses tied to the rail by the door, nuzzling at the ground or pawing the snow, trying to get to the grass that lay beneath.

'Edgar, see to the horses,' Baldwin called, throwing the reins to his servant before running indoors. Pausing only to help his wife down, Simon hurried after him.

The search party was waiting in the hall, sitting at Baldwin's tables and putting the knight's men to good service fetching wine and bread. Before them sat the figure they had seen the previous morning.

Simon studied him with interest. The day before he had looked nervous and scared of the bailiff and knight, but now he seemed dulled. He could have put it down to exhaustion, but Simon was sure he could see a glitter of defiance in the blue of the youth's eyes.

'Tanner?' the knight called, and the constable walked up from the bottom of the table.

'Hello, sir.'

Motioning towards the farmer on the floor, Baldwin asked, 'Where did you find him?'

Giving the boy a look of contempt, as if at his stupidity in being so predictable, the constable said, 'Down south on the way to Exeter. He walked there overnight, apparently. He says he decided to leave. He wants to go to seek his fortune in Gascony.' Shaking his head, Tanner glanced down at the boy.

Baldwin nodded. 'Greencliff?' he said. 'You know how this must make you appear to us. You're not stupid. Tell us about the day that the woman Kyteler died. What were you doing? Where did you go?'

But the youth merely stared back at him with eyes that suddenly filled with tears, and refused to answer.

After the search party had left, the constable cursing as he tried to form the ragged group of men into an escort for their prisoner, Simon stood for some minutes, gazing after them with a puzzled frown. When he turned, he saw Baldwin close by, glowering at the ground.

'I am surprised,' said the knight slowly. 'I find it difficult to believe that Greencliff is a murderer, and yet . . .'

'It's hard to see why he would keep silent if he was innocent. Especially when he must know he's the obvious man to suspect. And the body was right by his house.'

'Yes, it was. But that's what worries me. I would have expected him to leave the body in the house or dump it somewhere else. Not there, right by his own place – it's almost as if he was trying to get us to suspect him!'

'How do you mean?'

'Come on, Simon. If you were to kill someone and wanted to avoid being found out, surely you would hide the body somewhere more imaginative, somewhere away from yourself, somewhere – even if the body *was* seen – it would not be connected to you, wouldn't you?'

Simon nodded slowly, but doubtfully. 'Perhaps, Baldwin, perhaps. But equally, what if he had put Kyteler there hoping to hide her better later? He might not have expected anyone to see her there. After all, he might have thought he could get to her before anyone rose, to hide her in the trees where nobody could find her.'

Scratching at his beard, his mouth drawn up into a cynical grin, the knight nodded. 'I suppose so. But surely, if that was his plan, he would have been about his business early, before old Samuel Cottey would be up?'

'Don't forget the body was away from the road, hidden in the hedge. Maybe he thought he *was* going to be up before anyone else. In any case, why would anyone else have put the body there?'

'To implicate Greencliff, of course.'

'But wasn't it too well hidden for that?' Simon frowned. 'Away from the road, and under the hedge like that. If someone wanted to make sure that Greencliff was blamed, surely they would have made the body easier to find?'

'It was well away from the road,' Baldwin admitted.

'Yes. And yet Cottey found it . . . I wonder how . . .'

'What?'

'How did he find the body over there? He would not have been able to see it from the road. I think maybe we should go and talk to old Sam and find out exactly how he *did* find Kyteler.'

CHAPTER NINE

At the door to Cottey's old house, a ramshackle affair built half of logs, half of cob, on a small hill amid a series of small strips of pasture and crops, with a huge wood-stack before the door, they found a young woman scattering seed for the chickens that scampered at her feet.

They had ridden from Furnshill almost as soon as they had decided to see Cottey, the black and brown dog insisting on joining them. The mastiff, taking one look at the cold snow, appeared to decide that the fire inside held more delights for a lady such as herself. Now Agatha Kyteler's dog capered along in their wake, occasionally throwing himself headlong into a thick drift when the whim took him. Arriving at the door to the house, he was a great deal more white than black or brown.

The girl stopped tossing her seeds and watched as they rode forward, and then, at the sight of the dog, she put her basket down and crouched, holding her arms widespread.

The dog went into a convulsion of ecstasy, tail wagging madly, panting in apparent delight, as he danced slowly around her, allowing her to stroke and pat him.

Baldwin grinned as he swung a leg over his horse's rump. She was a reasonably attractive woman, only just out of her teens, with an agile, if sturdy, body. He could not help but notice that she appeared to be well-formed. When she glanced up at him, he saw that she had light-grey, almond-shaped eyes above a wide mouth with full and slightly pouting lips. Her hair was mousy, almost fair, and hung in a braid down her left shoulder. He drew in a breath, and let it out in a short sigh. She looked very attractive. 'Calm down, fool! She's only a villein. You're just getting desperate, that's all,' he told himself.

'Are you Sarah Cottey?' he asked, and she rose to her feet, wiping her hands on the front of her tunic. The innocent action pulled the cloth taut over her breasts, and Baldwin cleared his throat and averted his eyes.

'Yes, sir,' she answered with a smile, seeming to notice his glance and subsequent embarrassment. She wiped her hands again as if taunting him.

'Er . . . Is your father here?'

She motioned to the road behind them. 'No, he's over at my aunt's farm in Sandford. But he will be back soon, will you wait here?'

Simon exchanged a glance with Baldwin and, when he nodded, dropped from his horse, lashing the reins to a post nearby. 'Thank you. Yes, we will wait.'

She asked if they wanted to sit inside by the fire, but to Simon's surprise, Baldwin seemed happy enough to stand outside in the cold, talking by the door. Unknown to him, the knight remembered the smells from the Oatways' house.

'Do you know the dog? He seems happy enough to see you.'

'Oh, yes. It's old Agatha's, isn't it? I always used to make a fuss of him when I saw him. Isn't it sad about her, though? My poor father, he was so upset afterwards, I thought he would never calm himself.'

'Why? Was he a friend of hers?' asked Simon.

'Friend?' She looked at him with faint surprise, as if the suggestion was one she would not have expected. 'No, of course not. No, he thinks she was a witch. Even just finding her, he was scared she could come back and haunt him if he treated her wrongly.'

'Haunt him? Why should she want to?'

'Well, you know how these things are. People round here are worried if someone's a bit different. They feel anxious if someone new arrives in the village, and Agatha was different. He thinks she might come back as a ghost.'

'How? In what way was she different?'

'In what way? She came from a land far away, so she used to say, from the kingdom of Jerusalem, and had a knowledge of herbs and roots. If someone was hurt, they'd go to her, and she could often help, even if it was only by stopping their pain for a short time.'

'She was a midwife too, wasn't she?'

'Yes,' she bridled slightly, as if nervous, or perhaps shy, and her cheeks' natural ruddiness deepened. 'Yes, she was known for that. She was very clever.'

Just then they all heard the rattle and clatter of a wagon and, looking up, they soon saw the old farmer sitting on his cart. His dog leapt from the back of the wagon and walked slow and stiff towards Baldwin's adopted friend, but they knew each other and were soon engaged in a companionable chase.

Samuel Cottey appeared unsurprised at the presence of his visitors, and he nodded at them both before springing lightly from the seat and beginning to see to the mule. While Simon and Baldwin waited, Sarah disappeared inside and soon came out again with a mug of warmed ale for her father. Taking it, he smiled at her, his face creasing into familiar wrinkles before tilting it and drinking deeply.

'So . . . What do you want, sirs?' he asked equably as he finished and wandered over to the men at his door.

'We had a few questions to ask about how you found the woman yesterday,' said Baldwin by way of explanation. As he spoke, the farmer's daughter appeared again by the door, holding two pint mugs of ale for them. Smiling thankfully, Simon took both from her and passed one to Baldwin, but she hardly noticed his gratitude. She was staring at the knight as he spoke to her father, and looked pale, as if she was worried about something.

'First, can you tell us exactly how you found her? You can't have seen the body from the road.'

'No, I didn't,' said the farmer. His eyes were downcast, but then they rose to the knight's face, and Baldwin saw the defiance in them, as if the old man knew that he should not be scared of the dead woman, but was still not afraid to admit his fear. He quickly explained how his dog had wandered and found her body. 'Daft bugger never was a sheep worrier. No, but he had found the old witch . . .'

'She wasn't a witch!' The hot defence came swiftly from the girl, surprising Baldwin.

'No, I don't think she was,' he said gently, but then turned back to the farmer. 'Then?'

'I . . .' His eyes became reflective as he thought. 'I pulled her up a bit – she was so cold she couldn't be alive – so I lifted her a little to see who it was. I couldn't see from the way she was lying there, so I had to lift her by the shoulder. Well, when I saw who it was, I had to drop her, it was such a shock.'

'Yes, yes. What then? You saw who it was, you saw how she'd died, what did you do then?'

'I buggered off! She *was* a witch.' He glared at his daughter. 'Everyone knows that. So I left her there and went up to the Greencliff place.'

'Greencliff was there?'

'Oh, yes. He was there all right.'

'How do you mean?'

'He was just out to see his sheep, he said. He was just getting ready to go.'

'So he was dressed and ready? What time would that have been, do you think?'

'What time?' The farmer stared at him, then gazed at the view for a moment. Talking slowly and pensively, he said, 'It was still dark, but I think the light was just starting . . . I don't know, really . . . I think it was around dawn, just before, not after . . .'

'But he was dressed and ready to go out?' Simon said, and the farmer turned to him and peered at his face.

'Yes, he was about to go out. He already had his cloak on, that bright red one. Why? Why does it matter?'

'The innkeeper said that he had made some comment about the woman on the day she died, something about her doing something. Greencliff said that if Kyteler wasn't careful, someone would do something to her. We think he might have killed her.'

'That's mad!' Sarah's sudden interruption made them all turn in astonishment. 'Harry wouldn't do anything like that. He's a good man, kind and gentle. He wouldn't kill like that – especially not an old woman.'

'Be quiet, girl!' The old farmer's voice was harsh and thick, his face stiff in his anger at being interrupted.

'No, wait!' Baldwin's order made Sam Cottey fall back, as if the quick fury had exhausted him. 'Now, Sarah,' he said more quietly, 'why do you think that?'

Glancing briefly at her father, she paused, but then decided that, having come so far, she should continue. 'Because I know him. He's not cruel, he couldn't kill someone like that.'

'The innkeeper seemed sure.'

'He's wrong. Harold wouldn't kill an old woman like that, cutting her throat. He's too gentle.'

Baldwin's eyes held hers for a moment, and then her gaze fell, and Simon was sure he could see the embarrassment there in the way that her face suddenly reddened.

'Perhaps,' said the knight softly. Looking back at the farmer, he said, 'Cottey, what would you say about that? Would you expect Greencliff to be able to kill an old woman in that way?'

'Not an old woman, no.' Then his voice became bitter again. 'But a witch? *I* should think he could have killed her and been glad! He might think it was a service – a Godly act – to kill the old bitch!'

*   *   *

Leading their horses from the house, Baldwin stopped for a moment and scratched at his head with a speculative grimace. 'What do you think?'

Simon paused. 'I don't know,' he admitted. 'I think she's as convinced it couldn't be Greencliff as her father is that Kyteler was a witch. Maybe . . .' He was cut off by running feet crunching on the soft snow.

'Sirs, sirs! Wait a minute!' It was Sarah again, rushing along the track with her skirts held high in her hands, giving Baldwin a glimpse of her legs.

'Yes?' he said.

She stopped in front of them, her face bright from her exertion, panting a little, then somewhat breathlessly leaned forward. 'It can't have been Harold.'

'Why?'

'He never thought Kyteler was a witch. He was sure she was clever, and she knew about plants, but he never thought she was evil or made magic. Anyway, he was a kind, gentle lad . . .' Her voice faltered as she caught sight of the knight's raised eyebrow. Baldwin smiled and said:

'So he didn't believe Kyteler sent her dog to the Oatways chickens?'

'That!' She dismissed the idea with a curt movement of her hand, as if slapping away the suggestion. 'How could anyone believe that! It was a fox or a weasel did that, not a dog. If her dog wanted to eat chickens, he would have eaten her own, not gone all the way to the Oatway holding to eat theirs.'

'Hmm.' Simon could see that Baldwin's eyes were looking over her shoulder, and when he followed the knight's gaze, he saw that the dog was lying in front of the door to the house, head between his forepaws and watching the huddle of humans, while the chickens strolled and pecked around him.

'But why then would Greencliff have said that about her? Why should he be so annoyed with her?' Baldwin asked after a moment.

'I don't know.'

'Did he have many friends?'

'Not really, sir. Some of the other lads in the village. I suppose mainly he was friends with Stephen de la Forte.'

'I see.' He appeared to think for a moment. 'All right, thank you for your help, anyway.' He mounted his horse, then glanced back at the dog, and his voice held a hopeful note as he said, 'Her dog seems happy enough here . . . I don't suppose you'd like to . . .?'

She smiled, but shook her head. 'No, I don't think father would like to have the old woman's dog here. He'd always be afraid that she might be watching over him, ready to protect him or attack the man that strikes him. No, you'd better take him back with you.'

Baldwin sighed. 'I suppose you're right,' he said with resignation, and whistled.

Back at the road, Simon looked over at him. 'Well?'

Baldwin shrugged. 'It seems clear that the boy was ready to leave the house as Cottey got there, but that could mean anything! Maybe he was on his way to look after his sheep, like he said, or maybe he was going to move the body, to bury it or hide it . . . I don't know.'

'What if he *was* going there to move the body? The girl seems sure that he could not have killed the old woman.'

'Yes . . . It was strange, that. She was very defensive . . .'

Simon gave a short laugh. 'Not that strange! She's young, so's he. He's good looking, so's she. I don't think you need look further for a reason than that.'

'Possibly.' Baldwin mused for a moment. 'Let's see this friend of his – what was his name? Oh, yes, de la Forte. Let's see what else he can tell us.'

Quickening their pace, they rode off to the inn to ask for directions. It seemed that the de la Forte house was on the way to Exeter, some three miles outside Wefford, so they turned their horses to the south and were soon there.

As they approached the property, Simon could not help letting a small whistle of approval pass his lips. 'The de la Fortes seem well enough off,' he said.

Baldwin nodded. The house was a large and rambling place, quite long, with a number of stables and outbuildings. In size it was bigger than his own manor, with the roof probably higher. The whitewash was fresh and clean, making the house almost seem to rise from the snowy ground in front as if it was made of the same material. Above, a thick mass of thatch was visible only from the chimney rising high overhead: around it the snow had melted, showing the greying straw beneath.

The roadway passed close to the front of the house, which itself lay in a shallow dip, while between the building and the trail was a stream, cutting a neat and precise line through the snow. As they followed the track to the house, they slowed, moving at a walk through the ford at the little stream's shallowest point before trotting up to the door.

Here the house had two stubby arms projecting forwards like horns from a cow's head, and the door was in a yard formed between. There was a hitching rail, to which they tied their mounts before Simon knocked loudly at the door, while Baldwin tied up the dog with some twine he found dangling from the rail. He did not want his new dog to fight with the de la Fortes'. They did not have long to wait.

An elderly servant, a thin, gaunt man with an expression of intense trepidation, opened the door and peered out at them. Trying his most winning smile, Simon nodded to him. 'Is Stephen de la Forte here?'

'I . . .' As he began to speak, there was a bellow from behind, and the servant spun round, quickly explaining to someone inside. 'No, sir. No, I don't know who it is. He's asking for Master Stephen, sir.'

'Out of the way!' came the voice, and the servant disappeared, his face replaced with that of an older man.

Simon felt he must be middle-aged from the thick and grizzled hair. Stout, not fat but thick in body, he stood a little shorter than the bailiff, but was almost half as wide again at the shoulder. He had a vast barrel chest, with arms that would have looked well as tree trunks, they were so massive.

His face was a maze of creases, some of them so deep that they appeared to be separate flaps of skin roughly butted together and sewn, and among them Simon could see the lighter marks, thickened with age, of old wounds from knives or swords. In the midst was a mouth, itself a colourless gash. A thick and broken nose sat between two bright and intelligent eyes, blue-grey like his son's, which stared unblinking at Simon.

'Well? Who are you and what do you want with my son?' he said, his voice harsh with distrust.

'You are de la Forte? Father to Stephen?' Simon heard the knight ask softly from behind.

'Yes. Who are you?'

Baldwin slowly paced forward until he was beside the bailiff and stared back unblinking. 'I am Sir Baldwin de Furnshill,' he said, announcing his title with careless pride. 'I am Keeper of the King's Peace here, and my business is with your son, not with you. You will bring him here to me. Now.'

Initially, Simon felt sure that de la Forte was going to explode like a child's firework. His face appeared to become suffused with blood until the veins stood out at his temples and neck. His eyes seemed to want to start from their sockets, as if they could themselves leap out and attack the knight. But as quickly as his rage appeared, it passed. After a moment's thought, he stood aside, albeit with bad grace, to let his visitors enter.

'My apologies, sir. I did not realise who you were. Please, come inside and seat yourselves by my fire while I fetch him out for you.'

'Thank you,' said Baldwin graciously as he swept inside.

This was no rude hovel. The screens gave into a broad and airy hall, with a huge fireplace built into one long side. Richly coloured tapestries hung from the walls, with narrow-looking gaps where sconces lay to brighten the interior. Two large candle-holders in wrought-iron stood before the fire, shedding pools of light. A massive table built from thick oak timbers stood at the opposite end of the room, while a bench from it had been dragged to the heat, leaving the earth bare in two great sweeps where the rushes had been dragged apart by the bench legs. A chair and small writing table stood near the hearth, and a man, dressed like a monk in a habit, stood nearby.

'My clerk,' said their host dismissively before walking to a chair and sitting, shouting at his servant to 'Fetch him out!'

'You have a very pleasant house,' said Simon tentatively, watching the clerk clearing his papers and hurrying from the room.

'Yes. It took many years to build, but now it is as we want it. I only hope,' his face became sour, 'we can make enough profit to keep it.'

'To keep it? Why, what's the difficulty?'

'The Genoese, they're the problem!' he said, a sneer curling his lip. 'The whore-sons want my money.'

The knight turned and watched impassively as the man carried on. 'I have been a successful merchant for many years, with my partner, Alan Trevellyn, and now these *Italians*—' He spat the word. '—want us to pay them back the loans we have with them. It's madness! They know we can't. They just want to bankrupt us, that's all.'

'Why would they want to do that?' asked Simon reasonably.

The grey eyes fixed on him. 'Why? So that their own people can take over the trade from us, of course!'

'My friend has had little experience of trade. Perhaps you could explain for him,' said Baldwin suavely, and Simon threw him a look of sour distaste. To his knowledge, his grasp of trade was as good as any man's.

'Alan Trevellyn and I hire ships and use them to bring wine over here from Gascony. We've been doing it for years. Going the other way we take what we can, wool mainly. When the ships arrive, they sell the cargo and use the money to buy the wine to bring back. We've been very successful over the years, but for the last two we've been unlucky. The pirates have caught our last two ships, and wiped out the profits from the previous ten. The profit is too low now, with the high costs since the harvests. So now the Italians want back the money they loaned us some time ago. What it means is, they want everything. It could mean losing our houses . . . Everything!'

They sat for some minutes in silence, and just as Simon opened his mouth to inquire about the consequences should he refuse to pay, they heard the sound of approaching feet, and through the curtain to the screens came the boy they had seen earlier, with a thin, mousy-looking woman who had enough similarity with Stephen to look like his mother. She stood just inside the doorway, darting little glances at each of the men, while her son strode in, boldly enough to Simon's eye, although his face held a curious expression. It was almost petulant annoyance, as if he were close to anger that the knight and bailiff should dare to invade his father's household.

He moved directly to a chair and sat, his pale features turned to the knight. 'Well?' he asked, impatiently.

Baldwin sat quietly contemplating him. Then he sighed. 'Your friend will not talk to us. It's as if he wanted to be convicted. I am not happy that he did it, though, and I want to be sure that I have the right man. So tell me, why do you think Greencliff ran away last night?'

'Last night? I've no idea,' said Stephen, leaning back and crossing his legs. He appeared to have a slight smile on his face, which Baldwin felt looked a little like a sneer.

'You said to us that you went there because he was upset. In what way was he upset?'

The boy haughtily raised his hands as if in exasperation. 'Oh, I don't know! Upset! Depressed! He just seemed to think that there was nothing to keep him here. He wanted to go: leave and travel. He's often said he'd like to go to Gascony.'

Frowning, Baldwin peered at him doubtfully. 'So although he could give no reason for his misery, you felt he was so upset that you tried to go and see him twice in one day?'

'Yes,' said Stephen, and uncrossed his legs.

'How long have you known him?'

'How . . .? Oh, almost all my life.'

'You are of the same age?'

'Yes. We are both twenty.'

'I suppose you must have talked about everything.'

'Yes.'

'So why was he upset, then? He must have told you.'

To Simon it looked like a gesture such as a theatrical player might use. The boy half turned to his father, opening his mouth, then faced the knight again with a thoughtful frown on his face.

'It is difficult for me to tell you this . . . I do not know if I should, for he told me in confidence, and I swore to keep it silent for him.'

'What?'

'A woman.'

Baldwin sat back, his eyes still fixed on the boy, and Simon found himself immediately thinking: Sarah Cottey! It must be *her.*

'Who?' he heard Baldwin rasp.

'I cannot say.'

'This is nonsense!' said Baldwin, standing abruptly. 'You expect me to believe that he knew you since childhood, that you talked about everything, that you were close friends, and yet something like this, something so important, he kept from you?'

'No, sir. You don't understand.' The voice was low now, almost sad. 'She is well-born, not a villein. And married.'

'Ah!' The knight faced him again.

'Yes. Of course I know who she is, but I swore to keep her name secret when he told me. You must understand, I cannot break my vow.'

'No. No, of course not,' said the knight hastily.

'But there's one thing I can tell you.'

'Yes?'

'He couldn't have killed the witch.'

'How can you be so sure?'

'He was with me all afternoon on Monday, and all evening.'

'So?'

'I heard from the innkeeper that old Kyteler was seen by Oatway in the early afternoon, so she was killed later in the afternoon or in the evening. I was with Harry all that time. It can't have been him.'

CHAPTER TEN

The father stood at the door and watched as the two walked to their horses, untied the dog and mounted, turning and slowly making their way back down the path, through the ford, and on to the road back to Wefford.

There was a bitter wind blowing that felt as though it was licking at Simon's skin with a tongue of pointed ice. His cloak, tunic and shirt were of no use in defence.

'The weather doesn't improve, does it?' he remarked after some minutes of silence.

'Hmm? Oh! No, no it doesn't.' Baldwin was jogging along with his mind completely absorbed.

Sighing, Simon said, 'What part of his speech did you find confusing?'

'Only the one part that matters. Who is she?'

'This lover of Greencliff's?'

'Yes. Who could she be?'

'Unless Greencliff himself decides to tell us, I doubt whether we'll ever find out.'

'No. Unless, of course, the boy de la Forte could be persuaded. I wonder . . .?'

'What?'

'Was he lying, do you think?'

'Ah!'

Baldwin glanced across at him. 'Well?'

'Well what?'

'Aren't you going to tell me not to jump to conclusions? Tell me I'm being fanciful?'

'Would you listen to me if I did?'

The knight considered. 'No.'

'Good!' said Simon and chuckled. Then, with a small frown, he said, 'What did you think of the boy de la Forte?'

'Think of him?' Baldwin shot him a glance. 'I don't know. I don't trust him. I think he is telling the truth about the woman, though.'

'That Greencliff was having an affair with one?'

'Yes.'

'I thought so too,' said Simon, nodding. 'So what do we do now?'

'I suppose we must release him. There can be no doubt that after Stephen de la Forte's evidence the boy could not have been close to the woman when she was killed.'

'No, unless de la Forte was lying. I felt he was this morning, and again just now. It wasn't just a case of holding things back. I got the definite impression he was deliberately lying.'

'Yes. I thought so too.' Baldwin glanced up at the clouds overhead. 'There's at least another hour and a half to dark.

Do you think Margaret would begrudge us a warming drink on our way home?'

If it had not been for the innocent expression on his face, Simon might have thought he had no ulterior motive. As it was, the bailiff knew well that the knight had a reason to want to visit the inn and his grin broadened as they increased their pace to a canter.

The innkeeper was sitting at a trestle in his hall when they arrived, both flushed from the sudden warmth after their ride. He was not alone.

This late in the afternoon, the inn was filled with people after their day's work. Farmers and labourers, local villeins and others lounged on the benches or stood near the fire. Round and portly, slight and thin, no matter what the drinker's figure, all became silent at the sight of the knight and his friend. The black and brown dog followed, slinking quietly as if he realised the impact of their entry.

'I think we've been noticed,' said Baldwin quietly, almost laughing.

Simon could not find their situation amusing. His eyes were darting over the men in the room, trying to find a friendly face. There was none.

'Sirs! Please, come in and sit,' said the innkeeper, evidently trying to put them and the others present at their ease. Walking to them, he quickly led the way to a table in a dark corner, at the back wall, near the curtain to the screen, and pulled over a pair of chairs.

'Wine,' said Baldwin shortly, and the landlord nodded as he walked away. Pulling off his gloves, the knight looked around the room, and as he met the eyes of others there, they looked away. Gradually they began talking again under the firm gaze of the knight. The dog curled up under the table.

'Here, gentlemen, your wine. Warmed and spiced.' The innkeeper set the tray down and poured them each a large measure.

'Good,' said Baldwin, smacking his lips as he drew the mug from his mouth. 'Ah, yes. Very good, innkeeper. Will you join us? Will you take a drink?'

The expression of harassed nervousness disappeared. 'Yes, sir, I'd like one. Here, let me . . .' He waved to a woman at the far end of the bar, a short and stout woman of a few years less than the landlord himself, whom Simon took to be his wife, and soon another tankard arrived.

'It seems to be a busy inn you have here, keeper,' said Baldwin appreciatively.

'Yes, sir,' said the publican, smiling as he looked around his empire. 'Yes, we have some good customers here.'

'Are they all locals?'

'Yes, all of them. We don't have many travellers at this time of year, not with the snow. That trade begins again later, in the springtime.'

'I see.'

Simon leaned forward and set his pot down, resting his arms on the table, while Baldwin leaned back and gazed at the man sitting with them. The bailiff stared thoughtfully at his hot wine, then said, 'We've been to see the de la Forte family. Do you know much about them?'

The innkeeper took a long pull of his drink and glanced from one to the other. 'Not very much, no.'

'So you do not know about their business?'

He shrugged. 'Merchants. They import wine. Well . . .'

'What?'

'Oh, I was going to say, they used to, that's all. I think they've suffered more than most over the last few years. I used to buy my own stocks from them.' He waved an airy hand vaguely towards the far side of the room, where he kept his barrels. 'But then, when they began to lose their ships, I had to go elsewhere. Now I buy it from . . .'

'So you know the father, then?'

'Old Walter? Yes,' he chuckled. 'He still comes here every now and again, but not too regularly.'

'What is he like?'

'How do you mean, what's he like?'

Before Simon could answer, Baldwin leaned forward conspiratorially, beckoning the landlord closer and peering round as if to make sure no one could overhear their talk. 'You see, my friend,' he said quietly, 'Walter has suggested, in a way, that perhaps I might like to invest in some of his ideas.'

'Oh yes?' The landlord's eyes were large moons, bewitched by the confidence.

'Yes.' Baldwin peered over his shoulder, then beckoned again, settling farther forward on his elbows. 'But . . . You will understand I'm a little suspicious, eh? I hardly know the man. What can you tell me of him?'

'Ah well.' He settled, convinced of his audience by the knight's firm and steady gaze, and Simon could not help a small smile at the similarity between the innkeeper and a bird preening itself. He suddenly realized that this man spent the whole of his life having to listen to other people, and he was rarely asked to give his own opinion or express his feelings. He was enjoying the experience.

'I think he's a steady sort of businessman, in truth. He's been a merchant now for many years, and knows all the ways of the sea, and of Bordeaux in Gascony. Yes, if you want someone who knows his trade, he is good. He learned it while aboard ship as a boy, and soon managed to make enough to start to hire his own.'

Frowning, Baldwin said, 'But surely he would have had to make a fortune to be able to charter his own ships? How could a man who began as a crewman make that much?'

'Well, sir, I've heard tell . . .' His eyes darted nervously towards Simon and back, then his voice dropped. 'I've heard tell that he was in Acre. I think he helped bring people out of the city when the Saracens took it, and he could charge as much as he wanted for that.'

'Ah!'

In the dark, Simon found it difficult to read the knight's expression, but he was sure that he caught an angry glint. He recalled the knight's stories of how Acre had fallen, of how the seamen of all nations had appeared, like carrion crows to a corpse, demanding gold and jewels for taking people away to safety. After centuries of life in the Holy Land, families were ruined over a few short days, while the mariners became fabulously wealthy.

'I think it was after that he managed to earn enough to hire his first ships. And build his house. But recently it seems he has suffered from the French pirates. I think he has lost several boats, and cargoes. That's probably why he wants a new partner.'

'Yes, because he already does business with . . . Er . . . He told us his partner's name. Who was it?' The knight snapped his fingers as if frustratedly trying to remember.

'Alan Trevellyn, over towards Crediton. Yes, they have both been badly hurt by the troubles. You know, there have even been rumours that Trevellyn has somehow been responsible for the failures. I've heard that he was in debt to the French and told them when his ships were leaving, so he could pay back his debts with his partner's half of the shipment as well as his own.' He sat back, his head nodding knowingly.

'Where would you have heard that from?'

Winking confidentially, the innkeeper said, 'Walter de la Forte's son, sir. Stephen.'

'So you think I should be careful, then?'

'Oh, yes, sir. Yes, very careful.' His eyes flickered to the hilt of the sword at the knight's waist. 'It's said he was quite a warrior in his youth, you know. That he was in many sea battles, not just at Acre, and that's how he got all those scars. Yes, I hear he's a bad enemy to have.'

'Thank you, my friend, I am very grateful to you. You have given me a great deal to consider.'

'Sir, I'm sure it's an honour to help,' said the innkeeper, recognising the dismissal and rising slowly to clear the table. When he had finished and left them, Simon glanced over at the knight.

'If he was in so many battles, that explains his scars.'

Baldwin nodded. 'Yes,' he mused. 'But there seems to be little to connect him to Agatha Kyteler apart from both of them being in Acre when the city fell – and that was over twenty years ago.'

'Well surely that itself is enough of a coincidence.'

'By the same token you might as well suspect *me*, Simon,' said the knight drily. 'No, I don't see it. But who did kill the old woman?'

'Sorry, Peter,' Simon managed at last. 'No, you're right. We didn't expect you to have any better idea than we ourselves.'

Standing, Baldwin yawned and stretched. 'Since we all agree that it was not Greencliff, I should get to the gaol!' Sighing, he glanced at the priest and explained about the evidence from Stephen de la Forte. 'So you see,' he finished, 'we are here to release him. It's not fair to keep the boy imprisoned for no reason, and now Stephen de la Forte says he was with Greencliff all afternoon and evening, there's little reason to keep him locked up. No, Simon. You might as well wait. I shan't be long.'

'Bring him back here. I'll not see him go without being fed – not in this weather,' said Peter.

The town gaol stood at the entrance to the market beside the toll-booth, a small square block used mainly for those traders found to have given short measures of grain or bread, and only occasionally for holding vagabonds found in the town. Strolling along the street and trying to avoid the slush, it took the knight only a few minutes to cover the short distance, and soon he was at the entrance, wrinkling his nose at the smell from the market, which had not yet been cleaned from the last market day, and consequently was bathed in an all-encompassing stench of animal and human ordure. He glanced at the area, wincing, and then rapped his knuckles on the heavy door.

Tanner had apparently been sleeping, for when he opened the door, his hair was tousled and his eyes bleared. At the sight of the knight, he seemed to wake rapidly, and hauled the stiff door wide on its hinges.

'Good morning, sir.'

Stepping into the murky gloom of the gaol, the knight sniffed with distaste. The men who were usually held here tainted the very atmosphere with the pervasive, metallic scent of fear. Convicts knew what would happen to them once they were judged in court. There were not many sentences available for a judge, and justice usually followed swiftly after pronouncement of sentence, most often involving a brief meeting with the executioner. There was good reason to be fearful of the result of the legal process.

He shrugged. After all, that was the whole idea of justice.

'So, Tanner. How is the prisoner today?'

'Greencliff, sir? He seems well enough in body, but I wish he'd say something.'

'Why? Has he stayed silent?'

'Yes, sir. Since the hour we brought him here.'

Baldwin sighed. 'Take me to him.'

The cell was an unpleasant, square chamber dug under the floor of the main room. To get to it, Tanner had to lead the knight through the curtain at the back. Here, in the wooden floor, was a trap door with a simple latch secured by a thick wooden peg. Lifting this, the knight could peer into the dank and murky interior. 'Greencliff?' he called doubtfully.

There was a sudden stir in the far corner, then a small splash as the boy stepped into a puddle, before his face suddenly appeared under the trap, and Baldwin could not help shaking his head and sighing. The boy who so recently had been a strong, tall and proud youth was a pale shadow of himself. His features were gaunt and strained, the skin appearing yellow in the half-light, his eyes vivid and unhealthy, his cheeks sunken and wan. His whole appearance was that of a man close to death, of someone who had fallen victim to an unwholesome disease.

'Tanner, get him out of there.'

Fetching a ladder, the constable wandered back to the hole in the ground and slipped it down. 'Come on, lad. The knight wants you up here,' he called, offering his hand.

Leading the way to the front room, Baldwin stood with his arms akimbo and looked at the boy, shaking his head. Greencliff held his gaze. There was fear there. The knight could see it deep in the boy's eyes, but he still appeared defiant. 'Do you have anything else you want to say to me about the old woman's death?'

'The witch, you mean.'

The knight peered at him. The boy's voice sounded as though he was caught between emotions. It was as if anger and impatience were struggling for dominance, but Baldwin was sure he could see contempt, and self-disgust as well. 'Did you think she was a witch?'

'Me?' The question seemed to surprise him.

'Yes. What did you think of her?'

'I didn't *think* anything of her. I *know* what she was. *Evil!* She deserved to die!'

'Why?'

The boy held his gaze firmly and squared his shoulders with resolution, but kept silent. After a few moments Baldwin sighed.

'Very well. If you do not wish to answer, I cannot force you.' Greencliff glanced across at the imperturbable Tanner, and looked as though he was sneering. Turning, he was about to return to his cell when Baldwin stopped him. 'No. Your friend has told us the truth.'

'What?' Greencliff spun round and stared at the knight. Strangely, Baldwin thought he was now scared. 'Who?'

'Yes, we know you were with Stephen de la Forte all afternoon. He's told us.'

Later, he knew that what worried him most was the fleeting glimpse of absolute surprise as the boy said, 'Stephen?'

CHAPTER ELEVEN

They left the youth with Peter, consuming a large bowl of stew with minced meat, the priest happily organising more bread and ale as his guest ate.

Simon rode quietly with his chin on his chest. The three were silent, as though they were all contemplating the murder. At last, he said, 'Baldwin, we must go back to Wefford and ask other people what they saw.'

'Yes, you're right. We've spent two days thinking that Greencliff had to have been involved. Now we must get back to trying to find out who really was,' said Baldwin and sighed.

'Calm yourself, Baldwin.'

The knight threw him a puzzled glance. 'Eh?'

'Just because it wasn't Greencliff, that doesn't mean it was your friend's son.'

'No, but it's suspicious, isn't it? That he was here, trying to find out about her just the day before she . . .'

'Look at it this way – nobody saw him there, did they? Let's see whether someone else *was* there.'

'Yes,' he said, but not convinced.

'So, where do we start?'

The knight stared ahead, towards the town itself, as if there was a clue in the scenery. 'Jennie Miller, I suppose. Oatway said she was there with Sarah Cottey. Let's see her. She might know something that can help us.'

The mill was a large sturdy building to the east of Wefford, and they found their way to it by the simple method of riding through the woods until they came to the stream, then following it north. It stood in a small, sheltered valley. Looking at it, Simon thought it looked like a safe and warm property, with thick walls and a pleasing drift of smoke rising from the tall chimney. At the eastern end lay the stream from which it gained its power, quiet and sluggish now, but wild and fast when the countryside was less frozen. They had to cross the leat to get to the buildings, and were able to use a small wooden bridge that had been thrown over to help the farmers bring their grain.

Baldwin nodded approvingly as he gazed at the mill and the stream. Mills were jealously guarded by their parishes, and although the knight had only been here once before, and then only briefly, he was proud of this one. It had been built by his brother only five years before, and he was glad to see that the walls were maintained well, their limewash shining in the light.

But then, as they approached, they heard a high scream, and they spun in the saddles to look for the source. It seemed to be a young girl's voice.

At first there was nothing, then the cry came again, shrill and urgent, from the woods to their left, on the other side of the water. Baldwin felt at once for his sword and drew it, scanning the trees with a frown while Simon fumbled for his knife and spurred his horse alongside. They exchanged a glance, then both prepared to leap the stream.

'Ignore them, they always make a lot of noise.'

Turning, Baldwin saw a smiling, chubby woman in her early twenties standing in the doorway. He motioned toward the noise uncomprehendingly. 'But . . . Who?'

Her smile broadening, she put a finger and thumb to her mouth and gave a piercing whistle. Immediately the sounds stopped, and were replaced by giggling and laughter, quickly approaching. After a few minutes four children appeared, two boys and two girls, the oldest being perhaps ten or eleven years old.

The knight's eyebrows rose in sardonic amusement as he carefully stowed his sword away. Simon frowned as he watched the oldest of the two girls walk sedately to her mother. It was the girl from outside the inn, the one he had seen when they had brought the witch's body back from the field. His eyes rose to take in the mother as Baldwin asked: 'You are Jennie Miller?'

Her grin broadening, she nodded as her brood accumulated around her, their eyes fixed on the strangers. 'Yes. It was the children playing. I'm sorry if they troubled you.'

Clearing his throat, Simon glanced at his friend as he shoved his dagger back in its sheath. 'It's no trouble. We . . . er . . . thought someone was being attacked. That was all.'

The knight dropped from his horse and glanced up at Simon, then over at Hugh, who sat glowering with a face like thunder. When he turned to the woman, Baldwin was laughing. 'No, it's no trouble, apart from having a fit of the vapours!' He strode forward. 'I am Baldwin Furnshill. Can we speak to you?'

At her nod, Simon leapt down, threw his reins to Hugh and told him to wait with the horses. She led them inside, sending the children away to play.

The cottage was sparsely furnished, but welcoming and homely. There was a large table, benches, and chairs at one end, and at the other was a huge chimney and hearth, now filled with logs and roaring. Motioning towards the flames, Jennie Miller said, 'My husband isn't here right now, he's woodcutting. If you want him, you're welcome to wait by the fire . . .' Her voice trailed off inquiringly.

Taking a seat at the fire, Baldwin sat and smiled. 'No, it was you we wished to see.'

'Me?' Her eyes seemed huge, but not from fear, only amusement. This was no mindless peasant, Baldwin thought to himself, this was a quick-witted and intelligent woman. She was also clearly not afraid.

'It's about the death of Agatha Kyteler,' said Simon as he too dragged a chair to the fire, then sat contemplatively staring at her. 'Did you know her?'

She laughed as she sat. 'Everyone knew old Agatha! She was always helpful to people who needed her sort of aid.'

'What sort of aid?'

'Anything,' she shrugged. 'A salve for a burn or wound, a potion to clear the bowels, a medicine to stop pain – she could give help to almost anyone. She was very clever.'

The bailiff peered at her. 'You know what the people say about her? That she was a . . .'

'A witch?' She laughed. 'Oh, yes, some said so. Why? Do *you* believe that?'

From his side Simon heard a low chuckle. He subsided back into his seat and left the knight to the questioning, faintly offended by his friend's amusement. It was not surprising that he should believe, after all. He was not credulous, but everyone knew that the Devil was all round, trying to win over the forces of good and subvert them. Shrugging, he watched the woman as Baldwin began to question her.

'You didn't think she was a witch?'

'No,' she said dismissively. 'That was only a rumour. Old Grisel wanted to blame her bad luck on someone else. Bad luck happens. When we lose a sack of corn to weevils we don't say someone put a curse on us. It just happens. When something steals chickens, there's no reason to assume that it must be because of a witch. It was probably a fox!'

'But you said she was good with herbs and making medicines. Is that why people were prepared to think it was her, do you think?'

'Yes, I think so. She was very skilled, she knew all about different plants. That doesn't mean she was a witch, though, and after all, everyone was happy to take advantage of her knowledge when they needed her.'

Baldwin nodded thoughtfully, and Simon was sure he was thinking of Sam Cottey, the man who denounced the old woman as a witch but still used her poultice when he hurt his arm.

'When we spoke to Grisel Oatway, she said that she saw you there, at Kyteler's house, on the day she died. Tuesday. Why were you there?'

'Tuesday? Yes, I was there. I went to speak to her about my pains. Last time I was with child she helped with the sickness and cramps. I wanted to see her about some more herbs, like the ones she gave me before.' Seeing the knight's raised eyebrows, she giggled. 'Yes, I'm carrying a baby again.'

'Oh . . . Fine, well . . .' To Simon's amusement, he saw that it was the knight's turn to be embarrassed. 'I see. You *did* see her?'

'Oh, yes. Yes, I was there early in the afternoon.'

'Do you know when?'

'Not really. About two hours after noon, maybe.'

'How was she?'

'She was fine. A bit tired, I think. She used to spend so much time out collecting plants, and I think it was getting to be a bit too much, really.'

Simon cleared his throat and leaned forward. 'You seem to be one of the very few people who knew her, like Sarah Cottey, but no one seems very sad that she's been killed.'

'Why should we be sad? The poor old woman never tried to make friends here.'

A picture came into mind of the Kyteler cottage, fresh painted, with a new roof. 'The house was well-looked-after. She was surely too old to paint and thatch – who did that for her?'

Jennie Miller smiled knowingly. 'She wasn't stupid,' she said, and her voice seemed to imply that she was not certain that the same could be said for Simon. 'Whenever someone went to her, they had to pay in some way. She was not anxious for money, she had little need for it. No, she asked for things that were useful. If someone needed her help, they had to help her.'

'How long were you with her on the day she died?' asked Baldwin.

'How long? About an hour. Maybe a little more. I don't know. Sarah might be able to help, she was there just as I left.'

'Do you know why she was there?'

'I think you should ask *her* that, don't you?'

Baldwin studied her with a small frown, but slowly began to nod his head. 'Perhaps we should,' he agreed. 'Grisel Oatway said you and Sarah were still there when she arrived?'

'Yes. I waited until Sarah had finished. She's an old friend, and I wanted to speak to her. We started to walk up the lane towards the village . . .'

'How long was she with Agatha? When roughly did you leave?'

'Oh . . . She was there maybe a half-hour. Anyway, that's when Grisel came rushing down towards the cottage. She was mad! Another of her chickens had been taken.'

'She was mad? Mad enough to . . .?'

'If you're going to ask me whether she was mad enough to kill, I'm not saying yes or no,' Jennie Miller said tartly. 'How could I say? She was furious, certainly, she could hardly talk without spitting. When she got to the cottage we could hear her voice clearly, shrieking at poor old Agatha while we walked back.'

'You didn't go to help?'

'Help who? Would *you* have gone to separate two strong old women like them? I'd think even a knight could be nervous of doing that!'

'Yes,' Baldwin said, with a sudden smile. 'You may well be right.'

'When you left, did you see anyone else on your way home?' asked Simon.

'Anyone else?' she paused, then spoke more quietly. 'I thought I did, but Sarah didn't.'

Leaning forward, both men kept silent as they waited.

'Back towards the road, I could swear that I saw a woman slipping off the track and into the trees as we came close.'

'Who?' Simon felt as though they were getting closer to the details now, nearer to an understanding of what had happened.

'I don't know,' she said, glancing at him with a sympathetic smile, seeing his near despair. 'It was dark there under the trees like I say. It was a woman, I think, but she was wearing dark clothes. Both cloak and tunic.'

'And Sarah didn't see her?' he persisted.

'Ask her, but I don't think she did. She would have said. *I* didn't mention it because I wasn't sure myself.'

'Do you know of anyone who hated her enough to want to kill her?' Baldwin asked.

She screwed her face into a cynical wince. 'It's hardly the sort of thing people are going to talk about in the lane, is it? No, I've never heard anyone talk about murdering her.'

'Not Grisel Oatway, for example?'

'No.'

He sighed and gazed into the fire for a moment. Looking up, he caught a thoughtful glance from her.

'There *is* something else.'

'No,' she said, but she looked troubled.

'It is very important, Jennie,' the knight persisted, seeing her waver. 'Whoever did this could kill again. He's like a mad wolf: once it's tasted the blood of a man, we have to kill it because it's not scared of people any more. It kills once, then it knows it *can* kill. Whoever killed Agatha Kyteler can do it again, because he *knows* he can do it.'

It was then, when his friend sat back, looking like a kindly father persuading his daughter to obey for her own good, that Simon saw her expression change. She stared at Baldwin with a curious resolve, as if the decision was as difficult as agreeing to take a lover, but once her choice was made, she was committed.

'Very well. But I cannot believe it was him.'

'Who?'

'Harold Greencliff. When we came to the edge of the trees, where the lane meets the road, I saw him.'

'With Stephen de la Forte?'

'Not that I saw. I didn't see Stephen, only Harold. I thought he was alone.'

'What was he doing?'

'Nothing. Just standing there with a horse.'

'His own horse?'

She gave a quick laugh. 'Harold have a horse? No, he does not need a horse. Anyway, it wasn't a man's horse. It was a nice little mare, brown with a white flash on her head and a small white mark on her left foreleg like a short stocking. He was standing and holding her just off the road, almost in the trees. He looked like he was trying not to be seen.'

'If it was Greencliff, did Sarah Cottey see him?'

She smiled sadly, but shook her head. 'No. Sarah would have commented. She couldn't have seen him.'

'Why?'

'Sarah and Harry grew up together. They were as close as brother and sister. I think she still expects him to . . .'

Baldwin gently prompted her. 'Expects him to what?'

Sighing, she stared at the flames. 'To ask her to marry him. She's always loved him. But he doesn't love her.'

'Who is he in love with?'

'I don't know, but find the owner of the little mare and I think you'll find out.'

Outside once more, they found Hugh lurking sulkily, still holding the three horses by their reins. He was about to make a comment when he caught sight of the two men's expressions and decided quickly not to. The look on his master's face told him that this was not a good time to mention the weather. Handing their reins to them, he watched sullenly while they mounted their horses, then climbed on to his own and, shivering slightly, trotted off after them.

There was no conversation as they went. His master and the knight were sunk deep in thought, and Hugh found himself wondering what had been said in the mill. Both seemed morose, glowering at the trail ahead as they retraced their tracks to the road. He shrugged, putting their mood out of his mind. His priority was a warm meal and drink. Drink mainly: a pint of mulled wine or ale. It was so cold out here, with the wind whistling and howling between the branches of the trees like lost souls.

At the onslaught of a fresh, bitter blast that cut through his flesh to the bones beneath, he turned his head aside and groaned with the sheer pain of it.

'Are you all right, Hugh?'

Looking up he saw Simon swivelling in his saddle to peer back. Seeing the question in his master's eyes, he tried to answer through his chattering teeth, but all he managed was a grimace. It was with relief that he heard Simon say, 'Baldwin, we'll have to stop to let Hugh warm up. I think he's frozen colder than the mill leat.'

'If you're sure,' said Baldwin giving Hugh a sour look. 'But what with him not liking horses and needing to sit in comfort with a fire, I honestly cannot see why you don't simply pension him and have done!'

'He's not that bad!' Simon laughed as they continued. Hugh carried on in silence, but kept his ears open. 'And he was outside all the time we were indoors by the fire.'

There was a pause for several minutes, and then Hugh heard Baldwin mutter, 'So what do you think, Simon?'

'About Greencliff? It looks suspicious, doesn't it? He was there, after the women seem to have left the witch alive, we know he was nearby.'

'Yes,' Baldwin mused. 'But why? Why was he there? And whose horse was it? Why would Greencliff *want* to kill Agatha Kyteler?'

'Are you going to arrest him again?'

'I don't think so. Let's see if we can find out more first. Maybe it was just sheer coincidence he was there. I don't want to arrest the boy every other day! And what about the horse, and this other woman? Maybe she can help us.'

'Maybe. But who is she? How can we find out *who* she is?'

By the time they clattered into Wefford, Hugh felt as if he was frozen to his saddle. His hands seemed to have taken on a will of their own and refused to obey him as he tried to force them to open and release the reins. When Baldwin sprang lightly from his horse, at first he stood impatiently

157

and watched with his face set into an irascible grimace. Then, slowly realising that Hugh was having difficulty, he stepped forward, peering at the servant with concern. Seeing the miserable set of Hugh's face, he quickly moved up and helped the dejected man from his horse, assisting him to the door of the inn while Simon handed the horses to the hostler.

Coming into the hall, he saw the innkeeper bustling, moving men from the fire and making space for Baldwin and the frozen servant. Simon could see that the knight had a look of perplexed concern, while Hugh merely wore his usual glower. But there was no mistaking the pain on his face as the heat began to thaw him, the warmth sinking into his flesh like stabs from needle-sharp darts of pure agony.

Sitting near his servant, the bailiff contemplated him. 'How are you feeling?'

'I'll live. I've been worse,' Hugh grunted.

The innkeeper returned with jugs of heated wine, setting them beside the fire to keep hot, and nodded to Hugh while pouring a mugful. To Simon he looked like a leech trying out a new quack remedy, watching intently while the servant took a gulp, then leaning forward to top up the mug before standing and walking off to see to another customer.

Baldwin took another mug, then sat with his head down, staring at the hearth, sipping every now and again at his drink like a merchant testing a new batch of wine. When Simon glanced over at him, he was surprised to see that the knight had stiffened, his eyes gazing into the distance.

'What is it?'

'I was just thinking . . .' He broke off as the innkeeper came back and stood near Hugh, watching him carefully as if to see whether his medicine would work or not. 'Ah. I was about to call for you. Tell me, has Greencliff been ill recently?'

'Harry? No.' His eyes flitted to Hugh, clearly comparing the strong and healthy farmer with this weak-seeming servant. 'He's been fine.'

'Oh. And his friend? Stephen de la Forte? Has *he* been unwell?'

The man's face was baffled as he shook his head.

'Trying to find out if Greencliff or de la Forte might have needed to go to Kyteler for something?' asked Simon with amusement as the innkeeper hurried off to serve another customer.

'It was worth a try!' said the knight. He shrugged. 'But it's no help again. Greencliff was there the day Kyteler died. He was in the lane after Oatway saw the old woman. Some other woman might have been there too, after Oatway. Apparently Greencliff was very annoyed with the old woman that afternoon, so he may have seen her, though we don't know why. He may have had a chance to get to her.'

'But de la Forte said . . .'

'That they were together all afternoon? That's true.'

'He would, wouldn't he?' said Hugh glumly.

Simon glanced at him. 'What do you mean?'

'They're close friends, aren't they? Maybe this de la Forte knows Greencliff has done it and wants to protect him. So he told you he was with Greencliff all afternoon when he wasn't.'

Baldwin grunted assent. 'It *would* make sense.'

'I don't know,' said Simon thoughtfully.

'The only other people who had a real reason to kill Kyteler were the Oatways,' Hugh continued doggedly.

'But if Kyteler was still alive after she'd been there . . .' Baldwin began, and was interrupted by Simon.

'Was she? We don't know that. Grisel Oatway could have killed her. We don't know for sure that any other person saw the witch alive afterwards. If they did, we haven't spoken to them!'

'Witch!' muttered the knight with a brief display of disgust, then took another sip at his drink. 'All right, so we cannot be certain that Oatway did *not* kill her. Likewise we cannot be sure that Greencliff didn't. There appears to be another person involved somehow as well, this strange woman in a grey cloak. Oatway saw her, so did Jennie Miller. Sarah Cottey didn't mention her, though. Who could she be?'

'There is the other side, don't forget.' Simon gulped wine, then leaned back and sighed contentedly as he felt it heat a simmering trail in his body. 'Why was she carried away from her house up to Greencliff's field?'

'Maybe Grisel Oatway admitted to her husband that she had killed their neighbour and he carried the body away to hide the fact that they'd done it?' said Baldwin.

Hugh looked up. 'That's daft,' he said flatly. Baldwin was so surprised at the contemptuous comment he could not respond, but simply stared at the servant, who suddenly seemed to realise what he had said. Flushing an embarrassed red, he quickly carried on, 'What I mean is, sir, that they're not young, the Oatways. If they were going to hide the body, why would they take it so far away? They'd dump it nearer, somewhere they knew, somewhere they knew other people wouldn't go.'

'He's right,' said Simon frowning. 'If they had done it, they would hardly carry it so far. And, if they *were* trying to keep it all hidden, they wouldn't have left the Kyteler house with blood everywhere, would they?'

The knight mused. 'That's an interesting thought. But the only conclusion must be that it's even more likely that it was Greencliff. The body was close to his house – maybe he was intending to go and hide it somewhere *he* knew, but Cottey interrupted his plans? It's possible.'

'Yes. The only reason for thinking he must be innocent was the fact that Stephen de la Forte gave him an alibi, but from what Jennie Miller said, that wasn't true,' Simon said. 'Which means he must have been lying to protect his friend.'

CHAPTER TWELVE

In the middle of the afternoon they left Wefford and began to make their way back to the manor house at Furnshill. They had to take the journey slowly, for Hugh's sake, but now even Baldwin did not grudge the servant his speed. It was too clear that the man was in pain.

They were home again by three, and when they arrived, Simon insisted that Hugh stay before the fire for the rest of the day, an order with which the man appeared to be well satisfied. It was the small grin of gratitude that showed the bailiff just how poorly his servant was feeling. Usually he would have expected a grimace and complaint even for such a welcome command.

Leaving him staring at the flames with a blanket over his shoulders, Simon took Margaret outside to where Baldwin stood contemplating his view. Turning, the knight pointed to the house with his chin. 'How is he?'

Margaret shrugged. 'He seems all right, but he'll need to stay indoors for a while. He got very cold.'

'It was my fault,' said Simon. 'I should have waited while he got his clothes, but I thought he was making excuses to avoid coming with us to Crediton.'

'It's easy to forget how cold it is in winter,' his wife agreed. 'But make sure in future that he's got his cloak and jacket if you're taking him with you.'

He nodded grim-faced, feeling the implied rebuke. She was right. The winter here, so close to Dartmoor, was always brutal, as he knew well. To change the subject, he said, 'Did Hugh tell you what we have learned today?'

From the look on his face she knew he felt the blame for Hugh's illness. That was only right, she thought. If they had not been quick once they realised how badly chilled Hugh was, the man could have died. Although he was the son of a moors farmer, and had himself spent much of his youth out in all weather looking after the farm's flock of sheep, he was not indestructible. The weather here was so cold as to stop a man's mind. It was foolish not to take the correct precautions when there was time. Now, though, there was no reason to make her husband feel any worse. As she gave a brief nod and listened to him explain about the conversation with Jennie Miller, she studied his features with frowning concentration.

'So you have three real suspects, then,' she said at last.

'Grisel Oatway, Greencliff and his woman, you mean?' said Simon.

'No, Oatway sounds as though she only really bore the old woman a grudge,' she said, frowning. 'If she wanted Kyteler dead, she sounds shrewd enough to have persuaded the villagers that her neighbour was a witch, and let them do her work for her; let the mob lynch her. She doesn't sound

163

like she's a killer herself.' She shot a sharp glance at Baldwin.

The knight sighed and looked out over the hills as if seeking inspiration. 'I know. There's only the one other suspect. But I find it hard to believe that my friend's son could have been involved. He was too grateful to this woman to want to kill her.'

'Maybe you're right, but you'll need to speak to him.'

'He's probably back in Gascony by now. He has not been seen since Tuesday. For now, I think it's the woman who is the problem. How can we find out who she is?'

'Oh, really!' her scathing tone made both men turn and stare. When she saw their puzzled expressions, she said, 'The woman lives somewhere near. There can't be many for you to consider.'

'But we have no idea where she might have come from, Margaret,' said Baldwin, peering at her with a small frown. 'It could be from miles away!'

With a small laugh, she shook her head in mock disgust. 'You think so? I doubt it! She must be close by – it's surely unlikely that Greencliff would have taken a lover who lived far away. How often could he meet her if she lived far off?'

'So? How many women do you think live . . .'

'Simon, that's not the point. De la Forte said she was well-born, didn't he? And how well she was dressed! How many *wealthy* women are there round here? That's the point!'

To her relief, she saw the understanding dawn. Baldwin looked as though he had doubts, but Simon grabbed her, tugging her to him, and embraced her, hugging her tight.

'I married a philosopher,' he said, gazing into her eyes and smiling.

Baldwin turned back to the hills. It was good to see his friends happy, but ... He grinned as he accepted his jealousy.

Noticing the way he averted his gaze, Simon pulled away from his wife. He knew how much his friend wanted a wife and a son, and was sympathetic. It was impossible for him to understand how a man could live alone. But he could not stop himself patting his wife's belly affectionately, hoping again that this child would be strong and healthy, that the birth would not be difficult. He wanted a son badly, but more than that he wanted his wife to be safe and well. A passing thought struck him. Did this woman of Greencliff's have children? Then another idea leapt into his mind: was she pregnant? Had she gone to the midwife to get medicines for a birth, like Jennie Miller?

He frowned as he stared at the moors in the far distance. Who could this woman be? Was she the last person to see Agatha Kyteler before her murderer – if she herself was not the killer? Who was this mystery lover of Harold Greencliff?

But the hills gave him no inspiration.

The next morning, Jennie Miller winced, tugging her old woollen shawl tighter around her shoulders as she rattled her way towards Crediton on their little wagon. It was still freezing here on the road through the woods, even with the sun up. The ground crackled under the steel-shod wheels as ice on puddles and streams fractured under their weight.

Usually it was Thomas, her husband, who would ride into town. He would make his way in, calling cheerfully to his friends and customers, before delivering their sacks or collecting the items he needed. But this winter was hard and he must fetch more wood while it was possible in case the snow stayed.

When they had bought the wagon, it had seemed to be a good idea. Then they had only been in the mill for two or three years. The steady flow of grain from the manor had been enough to keep them busy and provided them with a good income, even after paying the taxes to the manor. That was in Sir Reynald de Furnshill's day, of course, before his death and the arrival of Sir Baldwin. Their trade had been so good with the new mill that they had been able to bring in corn from other parts and make a good profit. That was why they had decided to purchase the wagon. It meant they could buy corn from farms far distant and sell their flour in Crediton to the bakers.

Now, though, after two years of appalling harvests, the wagon seemed less of a good idea. They could hardly afford to keep and feed the old horse, and with the prices demanded in the town for the simplest goods, Jennie felt that they were better off staying in Wefford. At least in the village most things could be bartered.

She passed the new house, where the de la Forte family lived, with little more than a cursory glower. She felt it was unfair that some were able to buy whatever they wanted when so many of her friends were starving or freezing to death for want of fuel. At the thought of death she shivered, thinking again of poor old Agatha.

The old woman was sometimes difficult to deal with, Jennie knew that. But even so, there was a strain of decency in her that was missing in others. Old Agatha was always prepared to come and see anyone in pain, always happy to help. She may not have been as subservient as some would have wished, but that was no great problem to Jennie. She was not overly humble either, except to the priest in Crediton, Peter Clifford. He was a *holy* man; he deserved respect.

Agatha Kyteler's death was very sad, she reflected. It was all round that the old woman's throat had been cut. The innkeeper had charged people a fee to look, and many had taken the opportunity, giving gory details later to the others waiting eagerly outside, and that made her feel sad, as if the old woman had been molested. Jennie was happy enough to go and watch the executions when she had a chance, but that was different. That was seeing other people who did not matter. It was quite an exciting time, usually with a small, thriving market to supply food and drink to the crowds waiting for the first hanging, waiting to see the criminals being lined up, having the ropes set around their necks until they were hauled upwards, spinning slowly, twitching and jerking in their struggle for life, while the hemp tightened and stopped the breath in their throats.

If the felon was particularly strong and muscled – she had seen it a few times – one of the executioners would have to grab the swinging body, then leap up and embrace it, using his extra weight to jerk the victim down hard and fast to snap the spine. But they only did that if the felon was still alive after fifteen minutes or so, not before. After all, they had to make sure that the crowds were satisfied with their viewing first, even if there were a lot more criminals waiting for their turn. Otherwise there could be arguments over the gambling, with accusations that the executioners had intentionally killed the victim before the allotted time, that they had been bribed, and they could all do without the problems that kind of altercation produced.

At the outskirts of the town, she took a wineskin and sipped at the freezing liquid. Then, taken by a sudden urge, she halted the wagon and dropped to the ground. Crunching through the thick layer of snow, she walked to a bush at the edge of a field strip, lifted her tunic and skirts and squatted, giving a sigh of relief. It must be the jogging of the wagon that always had this effect, she thought.

Then, over the sound of her little stream as it died to a slow trickle, she heard a merry, tinkling laugh, and the steady clopping of hooves. Lifting herself, she peered over the shrub toward the road, where she saw two riders. One, she saw, was a middle-aged man, thickset with a heavy belly, and a face like a mastiff's, all wrinkled and creased, with two small and cruel eyes. The other was a younger woman, tall, slim and dark, with long braided tresses lying over her shoulders as black as ravens' wings, framing a face as beautiful as the Madonna's. Her hood was back, but the fringe of rabbit fur showed light against the darker grey of the cloak. She glanced at the miller's wife, then through her as if she was no more important or interesting than the shrub she squatted behind. The man ignored her completely.

As Jennie stood and let her skirts fall, her hands automatically smoothing her tunic over the top, her eyes remained fixed on them.

Simon and Baldwin arrived at the de la Forte house in the middle of the morning. Both felt the cold today, as if Hugh's misery of the previous afternoon had reminded them both how chill the weather was. It had not snowed again overnight, but this morning the clouds were thick above, looking as soft as goose-down in the heavens, and promised more snow to come.

Today they were prepared. Edgar rode with them, and each carried a sack of provisions and a wineskin. The bailiff had felt the bitterness in the air early when they left, and glancing at Baldwin, he could see that the knight was feeling the cold as well. His chest was rigid, his shoulders hunched and his mouth pursed, looking as resolutely slammed shut as an iron door. Gentle though the breeze was, it made up for its lack of speed by shearing through any protection, seeming to aim straight for the vitals.

Arriving at the house, he thought it looked very peaceful and quiet, with the smoke rising and gently swaying before dispersing in a straggling feather that trailed languidly northwards. Here, between Wefford and Crediton, even the noises from the strip fields would be hidden by the thick woods all around on a clear summer's day. Now there was nothing. Not even the lowing of the oxen in their byres could be heard. The only sounds were of their hooves crunching and the occasional tinkling of their horse's harnesses, like soft bells in the pale sunlight.

With the glory of the view, with the gently rolling hills looking smothered by the tree-tops that stretched off, over to the horizon, and with the air chill and fresh in his lungs, Simon felt good: strong and healthy, alert and sharp. The ride had honed his senses, and he waited for the door to open with a keen excitement. He wanted answers from young Stephen de la Forte.

The thin, pinched face of the manservant at the door was an anticlimax, as if his temper needed immediate expression and any delay was merely frustrating. The feeling made him curt with the man, and when the old figure retreated, cowed, into the screens, he was ashamed of himself. There was no need to vent his spleen on this man.

Baldwin noticed his sharpness and smiled to himself as he followed the bailiff into the main hall. Here they were left alone for a moment while the servant disappeared through to the solar. The knight walked to the table, pulled out the bench, and sat, his eyes on his friend.

The bailiff was strolling round the room casually, his hands clasped behind his back, the very picture of suave relaxation. But Baldwin could see the suppressed excitement in the way that his head kept snapping towards the door at the faintest sound. He was clearly on edge.

They had been waiting for several minutes when they heard the clumping of feet in the solar, and shortly afterwards the door opened to show Walter de la Forte. He paused, glaring from one to the other, then gave what looked like a sneer and walked to the table where Baldwin sat watching him with calm and detached interest.

To the knight it looked as if the merchant was taunting them, as though he felt they were both so insignificant as to hardly merit any respect, and Baldwin was intrigued. It was strange that a man of lowly birth should feel superior to a bailiff and a keeper of the king's peace.

It seemed to Baldwin that Simon was as interested in the man's attitude as he was, and began to question him with a soft, almost gentle voice.

'After our last meeting, we have released Harold Greencliff.'

Watching closely, Baldwin saw the man's sudden doubt. Walter de la Forte glanced across at the knight before staring back at Simon. 'Released him?'

'Yes. Your son made it clear that they were together all day, so of course Harold could not have been involved, could he?'

'Oh. No, I suppose not.'

'Yes, but if Harold Greencliff *didn't* kill Agatha Kyteler, who did? We can find no one who can suggest any good reason so we wondered if it could be someone from her past. We've heard that you were involved in the escape from Acre with your partner.'

'So what? Anyway, who told you?'

'Did you know that Agatha Kyteler came from Acre? That she came over with a boy and saved his life?'

At first Walter de la Forte looked merely astonished, but when he spoke, his voice was as forceful as before. He asked truculently, 'What's that supposed to mean? What is this? Are you accusing *me* of something? Is that it? You feel you have the right to come to my house and accuse *me* of murdering some old woman just because we were in the same place ages ago?'

'We have the right to go anywhere and ask anyone about the matter. I work for the de Courtenay family, and my friend works for the king. We have the right to question even *you*!'

Something snapped in him. The merchant half rose from his chair, his feet sliding back under him as if he was about to leap up and attack Simon, but even as he moved, Baldwin coughed and twitched his sword hilt with studied carelessness, making the steel stub at the end of the scabbard scrape over the floor with a harsh, metallic ringing. When Walter de la Forte shot him a glance, there was an expression of faint inquiry on the knight's face, as if he was merely waiting for the man's response. But Walter de la Forte saw that Baldwin's hand remained on the grip of his sword, and the meaning was clear.

Clearing his throat, he glanced from the knight to the bailiff with a slight nervousness. Then, slowly, he appeared to accept his position, stretching his legs out once more with what looked to Baldwin to be a physical effort, as if it was hard for him to surrender in this way. When he spoke, although he had made an effort to compose himself, Baldwin could hear the anger thickening his voice.

'What do you want to know?'

Simon walked to a chair by the fire and sat, leaning forward on his elbows. Staring at the ground at first, he said, 'It's a coincidence, that's all. You are an important man in this area, do you know of anyone who could have had a motive to kill her?'

Shrugging, the merchant shook his head and folded his arms. 'No.'

'In that case, are you aware of anyone who had a particular grudge against her from Acre? We have heard that you made a lot of money from taking people out during the siege.'

The eyes were suddenly narrow and shrewd. 'If that's what you've heard, it's not true!'

'Really?' said Baldwin dubiously, and saw the merchant's eyes flit to him. 'You must understand, though, that all we have to go on is what other people tell us. All we know is what they have said about you. If you want to put your own side to us, you should do so now. Otherwise we'll have to assume . . .'

'Yes, yes, yes, you've made your point!' He reflected a moment, then gave a quick shrug, as if mocking himself for unwarranted fears. 'I don't see why not. I have nothing to hide.' Pausing, he stared into the fire, and looked as though he was collecting his thoughts into a coherent story. When he started, his voice was low and thoughtful, almost as if he had forgotten their presence.

'Alan Trevellyn and I were in that hell-hole, Acre, during the last days of the siege – before it fell. We were shipmates on a French galley, both young and fit. We were ideal for the life. God! When we were young, a man had to stand on his own! Not like nowadays.' His brows pulled into a short glower of fury, but then they cleared again and his voice became reflective once more, while his eyes moved from Simon to Baldwin. The bailiff was sure that there was a shiftiness in them, and watched him carefully as he spoke.

'When we left, it was without the ship's master. He had taken some of our men to help with the fighting near one of the city gates, and while he was gone a group of English knights with Otto de Grandison came up. They were all that were left of the English soldiers sent by the king. De Grandison took a ship, and some of his men took over ours. If we hadn't agreed to go with them, they said they would kill us. We had to agree. De Grandison slipped his lines almost immediately, but the men on our ship insisted that we must wait, and while we did they brought on men and their wives, taking all their money in exchange for organising their escape. Gold, diamonds, rich jewels, spices: the knights took it all. But only those with a lot of money could come aboard. Others had to stay behind. If they had nothing, they had no escape. It was that easy.'

Baldwin frowned. He recalled de Grandison, a strong Swiss, tall and proud. It sounded odd that he could have allowed his men to take advantage of the siege in such a way. He peered at the merchant, who now scowled back with a glower of sulky self-justification. 'It wasn't our fault,' he protested. 'If we'd argued, what could we have done? We couldn't have fought the knights – they'd have killed us. Anyway, when the ship was full, the knights told us to make off, and we rowed out to sea.

'All was well. We got back to Cyprus and there the knights paid us off. We took the ship. They had no need for it. Alan and I shared our profits, and with them we thought we'd make our fortune. With the ship we could afford to trade, and we did for some time, all over the coasts around Outremer and back to France. After a few years, we had earned enough to be able to settle down, but we chose to carry on. We bought another ship – a cog – and sold the galley to the Genoese. With the new ship we could carry more cargo, and we took to trading between Gascony and England. We were successful, and that was where we made a good amount of money. But then things began to go downhill.

'We began to suffer from the prices,' he continued, frowning moodily at his boots. 'When the French king took over Aquitaine, at first we made good money from King Edward, taking men and provisions to his lands, and bought more ships. But as things began to get worse, it was hard for us to get our pay, and it was soon obvious that we'd have to get some money some other way. So we began raiding French shipping in the channel. We did well. We kept our eyes open for any kind of profit, and never turned our noses up at anything. Well, that was how Alan met his wife, Angelina. We took over a ship that was sailing from Sluys to Calais, and found we had a better prize than we had at first realised.

The owner of the ship was wealthy, very wealthy. Alan caught him, and his was the prize. At first we thought the money and cargo was all that was there, but Alan realised the man himself must be valuable, and he struck a bargain, taking his daughter and half the cargo.'

He stared unseeing past Simon's shoulder. 'But that was the high-spot of our careers. Since then, things have gone from bad to worse. Two years ago we had a bad time when we just couldn't seem to do anything right. We even had a ship taken by the French: lost the whole cargo. That hurt us. And since then, we've had our ship attacked twice and damaged, and lost I don't know how much money. So you see it's wrong to think we made all our money from Acre.'

'How did you lose so much? Just bad luck?' asked Baldwin mildly.

The eyes flashed towards the knight. 'Luck? I suppose so. We made some unlucky decisions, telling the ship's master to take this course or that, and then finding a French pirate waiting, but I think most of our problems stem from misfortune of one sort or another.'

'So you don't believe in witches?'

'That's rubbish,' he said scornfully. 'I know that's what they say, but it's not true!'

'That Agatha Kyteler was a witch, you mean?' asked Baldwin.

'Yes. She had nothing to do with us. It was just bad luck.'

'But people thought you were being cursed by her?'

'Some did.'

'Why should they think that?' mused Simon, then, catching a sullen glower from the merchant, his eyes suddenly widened. 'She left Acre on *your* ship, didn't she!'

175

'She might – how can I tell? It was years ago!'

'Was it your partner who thought she might have cursed you?'

'He . . . He can be a little superstitious.'

Baldwin stirred, his spurs tinkling. 'She never spoke to you about her escape from Acre?'

'This has nothing to do with her death. I'll not answer stupid questions.'

'Very well,' said the knight. 'But tell me, your partner is Trevellyn, isn't he? You told us that when we last met.'

'Yes. The business is ours.'

'You have no other partners, but you are in debt to the Italians?'

'Yes.' He gave a sad grin which seemed to offer a glimpse of personal fears. 'As I told you before, the business is sailing towards rocky shores. The Italians want their money back.'

Just then they heard feet in the screens and, looking up, saw the son standing before them. Baldwin was surprised at the change in Stephen. Whereas before he had been relatively cock-sure, now he looked chastened and almost shy. Not nervous, Baldwin thought to himself, but certainly not arrogant – or as arrogant as before, anyway, he admitted to himself with a small grin.

It was only when he approached and his face was lighted by the sconces and fluttering candle flames that the knight saw the reason. One side of the youth's face was a livid bruise with painful-looking yellow and purple edging. Above it, his left eye was marked too, and as Baldwin raised an eyebrow in surprise, he felt sure that the wound must have been inflicted by the boy's father. What, the knight wondered, had Stephen done to justify a beating?

Looking at the father, he found himself thinking that it could have been anything. The brutish face glared at him, defiant and cruel, as if daring him to make any comment about how his household was organised.

Stephen walked across the room, glancing at Simon but ignoring the silent Edgar, to a low-backed chair. Whereas before he had haughtily held Baldwin's gaze, today his eyes were cast down like a shy maiden's. He did not seem to know where to put his hands, either. They rested at first in his lap, then on his knees. Soon he resolutely placed them on the chair's arms and sat still.

Baldwin smiled faintly. 'When we saw you on Thursday, you said that Harold Greencliff had taken a lover. You said she was a married woman.' There was a slight movement of his head, but other than that Baldwin saw no sign that he had heard. 'It is difficult for you, I know, but it is possible that she might know something about the death of Agatha Kyteler. We must find out who she is.'

Slowly Stephen's eyes rose to meet the knight's. 'Like I said, you'd better ask Harry. I cannot betray a confidence. I swore . . .'

'Very well. I cannot force you. There is something else, though.' He paused, head tilted as he considered the youth. 'Why did you lie about being with him all that day, the day that Kyteler died?'

'I . . . I didn't lie! How can you suggest that? I . . .'

'We know that you lied. What I now want to know is the truth. When did you meet him and what did you do together?'

His mouth opened, but then snapped shut as if he thought the better of further blustering. He glanced away for a moment, and when he looked back, Baldwin could see some of his previous pride rising again. 'We were together almost all of the time. I met him at the "Sign of the Moon" in the afternoon, and we spent most of the rest of the day together. If you want to check, ask the innkeeper, he'll . . .'

'We *have* asked him,' Baldwin said flatly. 'He said you met him there at around five, late in the afternoon, and left shortly after, getting back at eight or so. Is that right?'

'I suppose so. I don't know . . .'

'Because we have someone who saw him in the road with a horse at about four, maybe just after. That means he could have gone to the house, killed the old woman, and still met you at the inn.'

'But . . . He's not a murderer!' The words came softly, almost hesitantly, and Baldwin was sure he was thinking hard about his friend, wondering whether he could have been wrong about him. How hard, the knight thought, to have to doubt an old friend.

'Have you seen him since he was released?'

The question, shot out so fast, took the youth by surprise, and his head nodded before he could stop himself.

'Did he say why he decided to leave the area?'

Stephen hesitated. His eyes held a sudden fear, a hunted look that made Baldwin realise how young he still was. The knight was about to prompt him gently when his father slammed his fist on the bench beside him in rage. 'Answer!'

The boy's eyes shot to his father, and his mouth framed the word 'Yes.' It was so soft that Baldwin could hardly hear it, but at the sound he breathed easier.

'Tell us why, Stephen.'

'It was his woman. She rejected him. He felt that there was nothing here for him anymore. He just decided to go. He was trying to get to a ship, so that he could sail for Normandy or Gascony, but he hardly got anywhere when he was caught. That was all – he *swore* to me that he had nothing to do with her death! You don't really think he killed her, do you?'

Baldwin gazed at him with sympathy. There was little doubt now. Whatever else was unknown, they would be able to find out by questioning the youth again. He had little doubt of that. But in the meantime, this friend, who had been so loyal, was bound to be hurt. At the least Greencliff had lied to him, to his best friend, who had kept his secrets even when questioned by the Justice.

Sighing, he stood and motioned to Simon.

'Let's go and see Greencliff,' he said.

They had only just crossed the threshold when the messenger arrived, a young lad, flushed and panting from an enthusiastic chase that had taken him all the way to Furnshill and back.

'Sir! Sir!' Riding up to them, he was close to falling from his saddle as he reined in his horse before them.

It took little time for him to tell them, gasping out the message from Peter Clifford, his eyes darting from one to another of the silent men before him. When the boy had finished, Simon and Baldwin stared at him, then at each other. Snatching their reins from the waiting hostlers, they leapt up and, setting spurs to their mounts, set off to Crediton.

CHAPTER THIRTEEN

At the yard before Peter Clifford's house, they turned in and
dismounted quickly, their messenger taking their reins and
leading the mounts to the stable area. The door was opened
by Peter himself, who gave them a short nod and stood back
to let them all enter. His face was serious. He did not smile
at the sight of his friends, but silently led the way through to
his hall.

Inside, sitting like a queen on her throne, Simon saw
Jennie Miller near the fire. She looked up quickly as they
came in, but although she registered a brief pleasure – or was
it relief – at the sight of them, she was reserved. Looking at
Peter, Simon felt sure that his reaction to her news was the
cause of her seriousness.

'I understand you've already had a conversation with
Jennie,' the priest said. 'She arrived here just over two hours
ago and . . . Well I shall let her tell her own story.' He walked
to a seat in the shadows near the screens and sat. Glancing

quickly at her, Simon saw her eyes studying the knight with a kind of suppressed excitement now that Peter was out of sight. As Baldwin sat in front of her she leaned forward to stare at him, as if he and she were alone in the room; friends meeting to gossip about old acquaintances.

'I've seen her!'

'Yes? Where? Tell us exactly what happened.'

'I was on my way into town, but I had to stop for a piss just outside. Well, I just finished when I heard these horses coming. There was this pair. She was the one, though. She was wearing the same things I saw on her out in front of Agatha's place: long grey riding cloak with fur round the edge, with a blue tunic and skirts underneath, and it was the same horse. A nice little mare. Pretty little thing she was.'

'Are you quite sure? You couldn't have made a mistake? It wasn't just a similar horse?' interrupted Simon dubiously. She threw him a withering look.

'It's not only knights can see the difference between a tired old hackney and a good young mare,' she said, then added tartly, 'and my eyes are perfectly good enough to tell colours from a couple of yards away.'

Baldwin coughed discreetly, bringing her attention back to him. 'That's good. Can you describe the man?'

'Oh, yes. He's short in build, not your height, sir. Very dark face, with scars and wrinkles all over. His mount was a palfrey, a grey with dappled sides. Both horses had good leather fittings with brass.'

'Good!' Baldwin stood. 'We should be able to find a couple like them easily enough.'

'Yes, sir. I can take you there if you're worried you'll lose them.'

He spun around to stare at her. 'You know where they are?'

'Of course I do!' she said, seeming amused at his surprise. 'I know everyone round here. I'm the miller's wife.'

Simon grinned at Baldwin's dumbfounded expression, and asked: 'Could you just tell us who these two people are, please, Jennie?'

'Oh, sorry, I forgot. Mr and Mrs Trevellyn. They're from over to the west, at South Helions.'

'Trevellyn?' Baldwin glanced at Simon, who shrugged. 'Now that *is* interesting!'

'Do you need anything else from this woman?' Peter's voice sounded strained, Simon thought, and as the priest stepped forward into the pool of light from a large candle-holder, the bailiff saw that his friend's face was taut and pale, and his face registered distaste when his glance fell on her.

Stirring, Baldwin shook his head quickly. 'No. Thank you, Jennie. You've been very helpful.'

She stood. 'Suppose I'd better get on with buying what we need, then, and get on home.' She smoothed her tunic and grinned at the knight before walking out enthusiastically. This was an important day for her. There was the excitement that her story would have for the people in the 'Moon' later, as the only person who saw the woman in the trees and who also saw Greencliff with her horse. *That* should start some heads shaking, she thought with satisfaction. And then there was the interest there had been over the apparent break up between Greencliff and Sarah Cottey. Was that because of Mrs Trevellyn? She paused at the door, caught by the idea as she pensively straightened her shawl. Now *that* was a thought!

Inside, Baldwin and Simon stood and prepared to take their own leave when the priest caught them both by the arms. 'Wait, I want a word with you two.'

Baldwin was surprised by the urgency in his voice. 'What is it, Peter?'

'What on earth have you two been saying about Greencliff? Or Mrs Trevellyn?'

'What?' Simon was confused, but he ran through the sequence of events that so far made up their search for the killer of the witch, leading to the discovery of the identity of the woman who was involved. 'What is troubling you? All we're trying to do is find Agatha Kyteler's murderer. What's wrong?'

'It was what she said. That woman will make sure that this is all over the parish within hours. And what will happen then? Everyone will assume that Mrs Trevellyn was responsible, whether or not she was. Just as they will all think Agatha Kyteler was a witch.'

'You don't think she was?'

'Agatha?' He was so amazed by the idea that his eyes opened wide at the very thought. 'Good God! No, why on earth should I? She was a very pleasant woman, always ready to assist the people of the parish who hurt themselves. No, I'm sure she was no witch.'

Baldwin grinned sidelong at the bailiff. 'You see, Simon thinks there may be something in it because of all her roots and herbs.'

'*Simon*!'

'I'm sorry, and I'll pray for her if that will help, but so many others think she was, I . . .'

'Agatha Kyteler was a good and kindly woman. Ignore

the rumours. But you see how gossip can spread? What if news of this gets back to Alan Trevellyn?'

'Ah!' Baldwin seemed to understand this, although Simon was left looking from one to the other with growing exasperation.

'Why? Who is this man? Why should this be a problem?'

'Don't you know Alan Trevellyn?' Peter asked. 'I thought you would be sure to ... well, he is a powerful man, a merchant...'

'Partner to Walter de la Forte,' murmured Baldwin softly.

'Precisely. They bring wine from Gascony. Anyway, he is known for his boldness.'

Baldwin turned to Simon. 'What the good priest is trying to say is that this man Trevellyn is a hard man, known to be cruel to his servants, and who takes the law into his own hands on occasion. I had not thought before, while we were speaking to de la Forte, but now I remember Trevellyn. He almost beat an hostler to death late last year. How will he react, I think Peter is wondering, to us asking if his wife is having an affair with a local farmer?'

Peter nodded dejectedly.

'But surely,' Simon said frowning, 'all we're doing is asking her about what she was doing at Agatha Kyteler's house.'

Peter and the knight exchanged a glance, then the priest scratched his head while he threw a speculative frown at the bailiff. 'I don't think that will help much. You see they have no children after several years of marriage. At the same time as starting rumours about the faithfulness and honour of his wife, you are asking her why she went to see the midwife – I don't *quite* see how that's going to help.'

'Ah!'

It was not until they were riding on the road to Wefford from the Tiverton road that Simon threw a speculative glance ahead and suggested that they leave questioning the woman until the morning.

'Why?' asked Baldwin, swivelling in his saddle to peer at him.

'At least we'd have a better chance of thinking what we need to ask her that way. If we can frame the questions carefully, we may not need to ask her about things like . . .'

'Like whether she's been faithless to her husband, you mean?' Baldwin sighed. 'I don't know. Maybe it *would* be better. But what if by the time we get there Trevellyn has already heard about the rumours? You know how fast news gets around in these parts.'

'Surely they will not have heard first thing in the morning.'

Baldwin gave him a sour look. 'Don't bet on the fact!' he said. 'I once smiled at a serving girl at an inn on the Exeter road. Next day a rumour began that I had used her that night.'

Simon grinned. 'And?'

'No, I had not!' he declared hotly, giving the bailiff a black scowl. At the sight of the bailiff's sceptical smile, he shrugged shamefacedly, then became pensive. 'You see how it is, though? I did nothing, but the rumours still started. And there was nothing I could do to stop them – it ended up with a projected date for my bastard's birth!' He subsided, glowering gloomily ahead. A quick smile lightened his features, and he turned conspiratorially to his friend. 'But the worst of it was, I would have liked to!'

He paused, scowling and shrugging himself deeper into his cloak, before continuing in a quieter, more pensive tone, 'And that's why I find these rumours about an affair between Greencliff and Mrs Trevellyn hard to believe. A wealthy merchant's wife and a villein? It hardly seems likely. Gossip is always so easily started, but stopping it is like halting a war horse in full gallop – very difficult until it has run its course.'

Looking up at the sky, Simon said, 'It's getting close to dark. Let's get back and sleep on it. We can get the answers we need in the morning, and if we speak to her well rested, we'll be more likely to be able to be careful and save her from embarrassment.'

'Very well.' Baldwin nodded. 'But let's go home past her house. At least you can see the place. It's not far.'

This part of the land was not an area Simon knew well, being too far to the east of his old home. He had always spent more time to the west or the north, in the country where he had grown up, and thus it was a surprise to see the great manor house of the Trevellyns at South Hellions.

Baldwin's house at Furnshill could easily be mistaken for a farm, with its cosiness and simplicity, while the place built by Walter de la Forte was imposing, showing the wealth of its owner. By comparison Trevellyn's was a castle. It stood in its own clearing, a massive property of grey and ochre, with granite walls topped by castellations, showing that the owner had money and influence: all kings for many years had been trying to reduce the number of fortified houses to stop the internecine warfare that still continued between lords when they had squabbles. A man who could build a place like this was wealthy and important, and the house spoke of his power.

The windows at the base were small, but those higher had been enlarged to allow more sunlight and were mullioned. The door was a small, blackened timber slab set in a tower formed of a projecting section of wall, with an overhang above in which Simon knew there would be trap doors so that defenders could drop rocks or burning oil on any attacker. Overall it gave a feeling of threatening solidity, as if it was glowering down at the humans riding past.

The land all round was set to pasture, and there were a number of sheep grazing, scraping with their hooves at the snow to get to the grass beneath. A small stream led from the house to the lane, so the bailiff correctly assumed that it had its own fresh water from a spring.

'I think I prefer your house, Baldwin,' said Simon meditatively as they rode on.

'Maybe.' The knight was surveying the ground around as if assessing the best point for an assault. 'But if we have a new war between barons in England, and this shire is attacked, I think I'd soon get to prefer this to my own!'

The lane curved round in a great sweep after the house, avoiding the hillock it was set upon, and then began the long and steady climb up the hill west of Wefford. It took some time for them to wander up it, both deep in their thoughts, with Edgar silent, as usual, behind. At the top they could see the lane winding through the trees ahead, dark in their leafless splendour against the snow that had fallen through their branches to the ground beneath.

There, only a half mile away, stood a solitary farmhouse, and Simon regarded it with a jealous scowl. It stood so calm and quiet, a single building with a small barn nearby. The smoke drifting from the thatch promised a warm welcome.

As his eyes roved over the surrounding country, he could see that a light mist was rising from the cleared areas, making them appear grey and somehow insubstantial, as if he was looking through fogged glass. The sun was setting slowly behind them now.

It was only then he realised that the farmhouse ahead must be Greencliff's. Pointing to it, he said, 'Baldwin. We could save ourselves some time and see Greencliff now, before we see Mrs Trevellyn. Get his side of the story before going to her.'

'Do you think he'd tell us more than he already has?' Baldwin mused, staring at the house. He seemed to be talking to himself as he continued, 'I suppose we could try. He doesn't know how much we've learned or guessed. The trouble is, will we learn more from her? Should we wait until we've spoken to her before we see him again?'

'You're probably right,' Simon said, staring at the peaceful house again. 'There's a chance we may learn something from Mrs Trevellyn that could help us question Greencliff. Yes, let's leave it for now. We'll see him when we've been to the Trevellyn castle.'

Once inside Baldwin's manor again, they were welcomed by the smell of a pair of roasting fowls, spitted on iron skewers by the fire. Hugh sat nearby, stretching occasionally to turn them.

Laughing, Simon saw that his servant appeared to have made a complete recovery. He looked as though he must have spent the whole day in front of the fire. At Baldwin's mild inquiry, Hugh nodded towards the screens, and soon Margaret appeared holding two jugs which she set on a table before greeting her husband.

Glancing at Hugh, Simon said, 'Has he been making you run around all day?' with mock seriousness.

She registered surprise. 'Shouldn't I have looked after him? Don't be stupid! Of course not. I've done little today, and so has he. I wasn't going to send him out when his master nearly killed him yesterday, was I? No, but at least he's cured now.'

'Good,' said Baldwin, sitting by the fire and pulling his boots off. 'That's better! Good, so he can come with us tomorrow, then.'

Hugh's face was immediately frowningly suspicious. 'Why? What are we doing tomorrow?'

Sitting, Simon grabbed his wife around the waist and hauled her on to his lap. 'We're going to go and see the mystery woman who was there when Kyteler died. The woman who, according to gossip, has a fancy for strong young farmers,' he said, and kissed her.

Baldwin smiled at the sight of the bailiff and his struggling wife, then turned to face the fire. Yes, he thought. We'll surely find out more tomorrow.

The dark was crowding in as the Bourc settled again, squatting as he gazed at the Trevellyn house. He smiled to himself as men hurried past nearby. None could see him, hidden as he was behind the thick fringe of bracken and bramble. Two men were talking as they lopped branches from a fallen tree only a few feet away. They had been there almost from the time that he had arrived, late in the morning, and were still unaware of him.

Since he had seen the ambush, he had carefully considered what to do. The first night he had been able to find a room in an inn in a hamlet to the south of Crediton – keeping to the woods had meant taking a great deal longer on his journey than he had expected, and he had been surprised at how far to the east he had been forced to travel before finding a bridge.

The next day, Thursday, he had risen early and crossed the stream at a small wooden bridge built by the villagers. Taking his time, he had made his way back to Wefford by quiet trails and paths, avoiding any large villages or towns. This way it had taken him until dark to get to the little hut where he had stayed before, and he had been glad to merely light a fire and tumble down to sleep.

It was the Friday when he began to plan his revenge while he spent his morning fetching wood for his fire. He knew where the man lived, so it should be easy enough to waylay him.

Any wealthy man was predictable in his habits, as the Bourc knew. Rising with the sun, he would take a light meal with his servants before dealing with whatever business his clerk wanted to bring to his attention, maybe handing out punishments to wrongdoers. The main meal would follow, and then it would be out with the dogs or hawks to see what game could be found, and back home with the carcasses.

It followed that the Bourc must try to catch him while alone to have any chance of success. There would be no likelihood of taking Trevellyn while he was out hunting – he would have too many men with him.

Late in the morning he had ridden off to the Trevellyn house. Finding a high point in front where few seemed to wander, he saw to his delight that the master of the house did not hunt. He saw the men leaving with the dogs, and stared at the group, but Trevellyn was not there. Shortly afterwards he heard a bellowing, and saw a stable-lad being beaten. The hoarse shouting and pitiful crying came to his ears, making him set his jaw with distaste. It sounded as if the boy had taken too long in bringing the master's horse when it had been called for.

And now it was Saturday and he was no closer to seeing how to catch the man on his own. Whenever he had thought he had an opportunity, he had been thwarted by the proximity of others. Even now, sitting as he was high on the land behind the house, where the day before Trevellyn had wandered alone and aimlessly for the earlier part of the afternoon, he could see the workers all around, hewing wood or taking it back to the house under the watchful eyes of Trevellyn's seneschal. The master was there too, close to the house where the Bourc could not reach him.

The smile was still fixed on his face even as he decided he must leave and go back to the hut for the night before he died of cold. He placed his hands on his thighs to begin to rise, but then stilled himself as he heard the hated voice thundering at the two men before him.

'Why have you not finished? Hurry with that wood, you lazy sons-of-whores! Why should you eat when you can't even fetch the logs we need to cook on?'

There was more in the same vein, but the Bourc was surprised to see that the two men did not answer but redoubled their efforts to cut the branches away from the bough. Their faces set and troubled, they hacked and chopped with a curious silence that was at odds with their frenetic actions.

Usually men would answer back if their master shouted at them, or so the Bourc had believed from what he had seen of the lower orders in this country, but these two hardly spoke. They looked terrified of the man blustering below.

'I can't finish, I'm too tired,' he heard one say.

'Hisht! Save your breath! We have to, or he'll take the skin off your back. You know what he's like.'

'I can't. I've got to rest, or I'll die here.'

'Such talk! Just get on and . . .' He was cut off by an enraged bellow.

'What are you doing?' The Bourc saw with surprise that the merchant had suddenly come round from the edge of the trees and now stood, hands on hips, glowering at the men. 'Well? Why have you slowed? Maybe this will give you some energy!'

As he spoke, his hand reached back over his head, and the Bourc saw he held a short whip. It made a hideous whistling noise, as full of venom as a snake. Then the younger of the woodsmen cried out as it cracked. A fold of the tunic above his elbow opened and flapped, and a red flood began to stain his arm. Whimpering, the boy hefted his hatchet high over-head, but even as the axe fell, the whip slashed across his back.

The older man stoicly chopped at the branches, but he was not safe. Two strokes caught him, one around his waist, one on the chest which made him stumble and forced the breath to sob in his throat.

'Pick up the branches you've already cut and carry them to the house!'

'The wagon, sir, it's not back yet, and . . .' The boy's voice faltered. His objection earned him another crack from the whip.

'Do as I order, unless you want to feel this again!'

From his vantage point the Bourc watched as the two men, one snivelling, the other silent with a kind of taut agony, collected armfuls and walked back to the house.

'And hurry. You have to finish this tonight!' the merchant shouted at their retreating backs. Then he turned and looked at their work with a sneer. 'Fools!' he muttered contemptuously. He kicked at a branch, walking farther along the trunk towards the trees, and the Bourc smiled to himself.

Giving a polite cough as the merchant passed by, he was pleased to see sudden fear in the man's face as he turned and saw the Gascon for the first time. 'Mr Trevellyn, I am so pleased to see you again. I think we have some things to talk about.'

He saw the whip rise and leap back, and then it was whistling towards him.

CHAPTER FOURTEEN

The innkeeper at the 'Sign of the Moon' was very busy that night. It seemed that everybody from the village had come to his hall to drink. There was little else to do on a cold and snow-bound night, and while it was a delight to have the room filled with people wanting his ale, it still created havoc. He only hoped that his stocks of beer would survive until the next brew was ready.

'Yes, yes,' he muttered when a new hand stuck in the air or a fresh voice called to him. If it carried on like this until the spring, he would have to get someone to help. As it was, he and his wife were running witlessly like headless chickens, out to the buttery where they refilled their jugs with ale or wine, then to the hall again, where they struggled to fill the mugs and pots before they were all emptied. It was like trying to limewash a city wall, he thought. Just when you think you've finished, as you get back to the beginning, you find it's already old and worn and you have to start again.

One group he watched with a particularly sour eye. He took no delight in gossip, even if it was a stock currency here in the 'Moon'. He especially disliked malicious rumours that could hurt or offend, and the Miller family had an effective monopoly of them today.

Seeing a man lift his tankard in a silent plea, the innkeeper wove his way through the groups of people. As he stood pouring, he could hear the Millers.

'But how do they know it was Mrs Trevellyn as was carryin' on with young Harry?' he heard one man ask.

Jennie leaned forward, her face serious. 'Who else could it've been?' she said. 'It was her who went to Greencliff and tempted him. And then they went to Agatha. You know what *that* means. And then they went back, after killing her.'

'So you sayin' as it was both of them did it? They both killed Agatha?'

The innkeeper walked away sighing. It was bad hearing such talk, ruining people's characters to fill a boring evening. There was one thing for certain: it was bound to get someone into trouble. He glanced back at the little huddle, his eyes looking for empty pots, but always they were drawn back to the group. Was it worth telling them to shut up? No, they would carry on. Throw them all out? They would just hold court outside, and he would lose business at the same time. He shrugged. May as well let them continue, he thought, and went out to refill the jug again.

There was another man who was not amused by the talk. Stephen de la Forte sat near the screens, his back to the room, his face twisted as if his ale was vinegar.

His mug was empty. Turning, he tried to catch the eye of the innkeeper, but instead found himself being fixed by the gaze of the Miller girl, the oldest one, who stood and subjected him to a close scrutiny before tugging at her mother's tunic.

Jennie saw the white-faced youth staring and her voice failed. Following the direction of her gaze, the group saw Stephen, and their chattering died, as if the sluice that fed their conversation had been shut, and suddenly all talking in the hall stopped.

Now Stephen found himself the focus of all attention. He stood and walked to the table where the Millers sat, the woman staring at him with large bold eyes. 'You ought to be ashamed of yourselves,' he said deliberately. 'You're all saying it was those two, when there's nothing to prove it, apart from *her*,' he pointed to Jennie, 'saying he was in the road that day. There's nothing else says they had anything to do with it. Nothing.'

'Come on, Stephen,' came a voice. 'Nothing wrong with wondering. That's all we're doing, just wondering who might have done it.'

He spun to face the talker, an older man with round, jowled face and grizzled hair. 'Nothing wrong? You've all set your mind to it that they're guilty, haven't you? Eh?' He looked around the table, staring into their eyes, until he met those of Jennie Miller. Only then did his lip curl into a sneer. Shaking his head with contempt, he spun on his heel and left, yanking so hard at the curtain as he left that he nearly pulled it from its fixings.

The wind had built again, and was whipping the snow into mad, whirling smoke before him, obliterating the view and making it hard to see the ground under his horse's feet. It was with a curse of sheer fury that the Bourc dropped from the saddle, wincing as the movement pulled the fresh scabs on his back, and led his horses on, trying to keep his head to the south. This was worse than anything he had experienced before.

Here, this far into the moors, it was hard to maintain any course. All sense of direction had left him, and now he found it almost impossible to guess which direction was south. But he was tenacious and determined. He had never before failed to find his way, even when high in the mountains, and he was confident that he would win through, even if occasionally he would curse the thought of the easy lanes and roadways to the north which he had forsaken in favour of this bitter route.

At first he had managed to make good time. He had collected more wood, storing it as faggots on the packhorse. The sky had been clear over to the south where the moors lay. Only to the north did clouds darken the sky. But that had changed as soon as he rode on to the rolling hills. Immediately the wind had begun to gust and blow, bringing the salty taint of the sea at first, but by late morning it was full of bitter coldness.

A flurry of snow blew at him, and he tugged his cowl over his face. Here, high on the moors, the wind could change direction and dart around at will like a well-trained knife-fighter. It was impossible to find his way.

He turned and stared back the way he had come. Now he could not even see his own trail. As soon as his feet lifted, his prints were filled. Cursing again, he hauled his horse's head round and began to search for any protection: a wall, even a tree, anything that could give some relief from the elements.

* * *

Leaning on the front of his saddle, Simon stared down the hill towards the square, grey house and sighed. 'I'm still not sure I'm ready for this,' he admitted.

Baldwin blew out his cheeks and peered ahead. 'No, neither am I,' he said.

They had set off just before light, this time with Edgar again. Their packs filled, their wineskins sloshing merrily in case they became stranded, they had ridden through thick drifts to get here.

At points the drifts were so bad that they were forced to leave the lane and move into the woods at either side where the snow did not drift. Using sheep and deer trails, they had managed to continue, occasionally returning to the lane for short periods before moving aside to circumnavigate drifts. Whenever they left the shelter of the trees, they saw that the fine powder had taken possession of the land outside.

Finally they had been forced to leave the tracks completely. Where the lane opened out below Greencliff's house, the snow had completely blocked their path. They had chosen a diversion to the north, taking a path Baldwin vaguely recalled, which led them up the side of one hill under the cover of the woods until they had passed over a mile beyond the field where they had found Kyteler's body. At last, when they left the trees behind, they found themselves on a smooth and rounded hillside, and it seemed that here the snow could not drift. It had been blown away before the strong overnight winds.

At the top of the hill overlooking the house, they could see that the master and his wife must be inside. Smoke rose calmly from the chimneys. There were some tracks leaving the property by the road, but they only went a short distance, up as far as the first drift, before returning to the house.

While Baldwin stared, he could see no signs of movement. Sighing, he watched his breath dissipate on the freezing air, then glanced at Simon. 'At least there should be something hot to drink down there.'

'Yes, thanks to God! I'm so cold my hair will snap off at the scalp if I touch it,' said the bailiff through teeth firmly clenched to prevent their chattering. 'God! Come on, let's get to sit before a fire again before we die!'

At the bottom of the hill they had to ride well to their right to find a passage through another thick drift that lay deep and impassable. Once round it, they were in among the trees again and here the snow was thin. But then they could not see any route through the snow on the farther side, and after some minutes of trying, Simon heard Baldwin muttering and Edgar cursing.

In the end it was Simon who lost both temper and patience together, and with his jaw fixed, his head down, he forced a path for them, whipping his horse on. The snow was over his heavily built rounsey's chest, but the horse was strong, and barged on, whinnying slightly, taking short bounds in an effort to leap the freezing obstacle.

Once through, Simon rode for the house at a loping speed, half canter, half trot, without even glancing behind to see if the others were following. Indeed, he was not sure that they were until he drew up to the little tower that housed the main door and heard the chuckling of his friend. Even Edgar seemed amused, but when the bailiff's glowering countenance shot towards him, the servant appeared to be busily concentrating on the parcel tied behind him on the saddle.

Even so, Simon was sure he caught a brief, dry chortle as he turned away.

After hammering on the door, Simon turned and glared at the white landscape. To his disgust, it began to snow again, a thin and fine drizzle of minute, dry particles, soft as pure wood ash. It was like watching a rain of flour.

'We had better be quick,' said Baldwin as he approached, his eyes cast upward at the leaden sky. 'If this gets worse, and it looks as if it might, we could get stuck here for days.'

Simon grunted, but just then he heard the latch being pulled, and they turned to see a young servant girl. 'Ah, good. We're here to see your master, is he . . .?' He paused as the girl started, a fist rising to her mouth as she stared at him from terrified eyes. 'What is it, girl?'

'The master, sir. He's disappeared. We don't know where he is!'

She led the way inside. The stone-flagged screens beyond the door were long, reaching all the way to the other side of the house where another door gave out to the stable area and outbuildings. To their left were three doors, and when Simon peered in, he could see that the first led to the buttery. The others must lead to the pantry and kitchen. On the right were the two doors to the hall itself.

Entering, Simon was awed by the magnificence of the great room. It was vast for a family home, nearly as big as the hall in Tiverton castle, with a high ceiling above and stone pillars supporting it, very like the church at Crediton. Benches and tables lined the walls, leaving a central aisle to the dais. Simon could not help but study the rich-looking tapestries on the walls and the immense fireplace. It roared with massive logs that in his own house would have had to have been shortened and split. Glancing round, he saw that behind him the screens had a rail at the top, and to one side there was a staircase for musicians, so that the master and his lady could hear singing and playing while they sat to eat.

Clearly, this was a house where the old traditions still held sway. On the dais at the far end, the master's table stood, with platters and mugs spread over its surface. The family still ate in the hall with their servants and friends, then, not like so many masters and the ladies who went to eat alone in their solar behind the dais.

But as he and Baldwin marched across the floor, Edgar striding respectfully behind, it was not the hall itself that commanded their attention, but the solitary figure sitting alone on the chair just before the dais. The slim figure of a young woman dressed in blue.

This was the first time that Baldwin had met the lady, and he considered her at first with a calm and studied indifference, noting her dress and deportment. She could only be in her early twenties. Her hair was deepest black, shining blue as the light caught it, and was hung over each shoulder in braids as thick as her wrists. The heavy tunic looked as though it must be woollen, and had four decorative gilt clasps at the breast. But it was not her clothing that caught his eye, it was *her*. She was almost painfully beautiful.

The face was an oval with high and elegant cheekbones, above which her green eyes slanted slightly down to her nose. The eyebrows were matching bows of black. Her nose was thin and straight and under the delicate nostrils was a voluptuous mouth whose lips pouted invitingly. Slim and elegant, confident and proud, she sat with her hands upon the arms of the chair and appeared to be subjecting them to a close scrutiny.

She rose languorously as they walked towards her, as if weary from lack of sleep, then turned to her servant, who hesitantly explained who they were. Baldwin watched her carefully as the maid spoke, but apart from a swift glance from her splendid green eyes, he could not see any particular reaction to the news that the Keeper of the King's Peace had arrived. Was it his imagination, or were the eyes a little red-rimmed?

'Gentlemen, you are welcome. Please be seated at the fire and accept our hospitality.' Her voice was soft and low, and the gentle motion with her hand towards the flame was so graceful and ingenuous that he found himself turn to the hearth as if all will had left him. And he rather liked the sensation.

Walking slowly, he followed Simon to a trestle by the fire, and stood waiting for her to join them. Closer to her now, he could see that she had a smooth skin, tinted a warm dusky colour. As she sat he could not help but float his eyes over her figure, from the slender neck to the swelling of her breasts under her tunic, and on down to the narrowness of her waist and widening of her hips. He brought his eyes back to her face as quickly as he could, but he could see in her measuring gaze that she had noticed his inspection, although not apparently with displeasure. Her mouth twitched, as if she was close to smiling at him. But then her face turned inquiringly to Simon.

He began hesitantly, staring at his lap. 'Madam, I am sorry to have arrived like this, it must be difficult for you. Your maid said that your husband is missing.'

'Yes,' she said, and sighed. 'He left the house late last night, and when we awoke this morning, he was gone.'

'His horse . . .?'

'In the stables. That is what is so surprising . . .' Her voice trailed off as she frowned at the fire.

Baldwin said, 'Has he ever disappeared like this before?'

'No. Never in the five years I have been married to him, never has he done this before.'

'Has anything happened recently to make him go?'

She hesitated a little, then flashed him a quick look, which he could not fathom. 'No.'

Simon coughed and sighed. 'It may be lucky that he *has* gone for now,' he said, shooting a nervous glance at Baldwin as if looking for confirmation that this was the right time to broach the subject. The knight gave a slight shrug of indifference. 'Madam, we came here to speak to *you*, not your husband.'

'Me?' Her surprise appeared genuine. 'But why?'

'Madam . . .' He broke off again, looking to Baldwin for support. 'This is very difficult . . .'

Baldwin smiled at her as he leaned forward, his eyes intense. 'Mrs Trevellyn. I am sorry to have to ask this, but we are investigating the murder of Agatha Kyteler.' He was sure that she started at the name. 'And we must know what you were doing at her house on the day she died.'

'At her house?' She seemed to be considering whether to deny having been there, so to prevent her lying, Baldwin quickly interrupted.

'Yes, madam. You were seen at the lane going towards the old woman's house, you were seen trying to hide. You are a little too distinctive to be able to hide from the people of the village.' She inclined her head to this, as if accepting it as a compliment and, to Baldwin's annoyance, he was not sure that he had not intended it to be. 'Your horse was seen there too. With Harold Greencliff.'

'Ah! It seems that you know I was there anyway.'

'Yes, madam. But we don't yet know *why*. That is what we would like you to tell us now. '

She held his gaze, and there was defiance there. 'I was there to buy a potion. I had felt ill for some days. I saw her on Saturday to ask for this potion, and she told me to return when she had been able to collect the right elements to make it. That was Tuesday.'

'Why did you hide?' asked Simon, his face frowning.

'Hide?'

'Yes. When people came along the lane, you hid in the trees. Why?'

It was as if she was fascinated by Baldwin. As she spoke she kept her magnificent green eyes on him, answering Simon's quick interruptions with scarcely a sidelong glance. 'What would you have done? There are any number of gossips in the village. I did not want people to know I was going there. After all, she was supposed to be a witch. I wanted not to be associated with her. She was useful, but I wanted to see her privately, not with the whole village watching.'

Simon looked at Baldwin and shrugged, and the knight grinned as he accepted the bailiff's defeat. He studied the beautiful face before him. Was she capable of murder? Even as he wondered, he saw her eyes seem to fill with liquid sadness, and she had to blink to clear them. But when she spoke her voice was strong and even. 'It is no crime to keep such things private?'

Shrugging again, Baldwin sat back as she continued. 'So, yes I hid, but only so that the village's gossips would not see me. When they had passed, I went on to the house. I saw the old woman and took the potion, then I left . . .'

'My pardon, madam,' said Baldwin. 'But were you alone with her the whole time?'

'Yes.'

'And no one saw you enter the house?'

'No,' she said, her brows wrinkled with the effort of recollection. 'No, I do not think so, though . . .'

'Yes?'

'I did have a feeling I was being watched – it felt like there was a man in the trees . . . But I saw no one.'

'Please continue.'

'As I say, I took the potion and left. I walked back to the horse and came home.'

'What time did you arrive home?'

'What time?' she appeared surprised by the question. 'I do not know. After dark. Maybe half an hour after five?'

'And you were with Agatha Kyteler at about what hour?'

She shrugged indifferently. 'Maybe four o'clock. I do not know.'

Frowning, Simon asked, 'And you only collected the potion? So you could only have been there minutes . . .?'

'No,' she said equably, 'I was there long enough to take the mixture – you know, to drink it. Then I left.'

'Was there anyone there when you *did* leave?' said Baldwin.

'I . . .' She hesitated.

'Yes?'

'I did not see anything, but I thought someone *was* there. It was just a feeling, you know? But I *did* think there was someone there in the trees still. I don't know why. And Agatha seemed keen to be rid of me.'

'And that was all?'

'I think so, yes.'

'And then you went straight back to your horse?'

She looked at him. 'Yes.'

'And Greencliff was there?'

'Yes. I had seen him earlier and asked him to mind my mare while I went to see Kyteler.'

Simon interrupted. 'But you said you didn't want the villagers to know you were there: that was why you hid in the trees on the way to her. Why didn't you mind him?'

Looking at him, her mouth opened but no sound came for a moment. Then she turned back to Baldwin as if in silent appeal. 'I know the boy. He is gossiped about as much as I am. He agreed to look after my horse. That is all.'

The knight nodded slowly. It would make sense, he thought. To his mind it was a great deal more likely than a high-born woman such as this having an adulterous affair with a lowly farmer.

'What about Grisel Oatway?' asked Simon. He felt he had an advantage somehow and he was determined to press it.

This time she did not even look at him. 'I did not see her.' The tone of her voice carried finality.

Baldwin leaned forward again, and he was about to speak when the door in the screens flew open and a manservant ran in excitedly. 'Mistress! Mistress! Come quickly! Oh, please come quickly!'

They all sprang to their feet and stared at the man as he halted before her, his boots and the bottom of his tunic and hose covered in dripping snow. 'What is it?' she demanded, apparently angry at the interruption.

'Mistress – it's the master – he's dead!'

Simon gaped at him, and when he looked at Baldwin, he could see that the knight was as shocked as he, but then, as the bailiff glanced at the man's widow, he stopped, his heart clutched in an icy grip. In her eyes there was no sadness. Glittering in the depths of the emerald pools was a cruel, vicious joy.

CHAPTER FIFTEEN

It was not there for long, and it was speedily covered by an expression of, if not grief, at least a degree of respectable regret. 'Where?' she asked simply, and the man led them outside, Edgar silently bringing up the rear.

Walking quickly, the servant kept up a constant stream of apologies and pleas for pardon until she cut him off with a curt gesture, and he fell silent. Out through the door to the stable he took them, across the snow-covered yard, already trampled and flattened into a red-brown slush, to an open picket gate in the wall that gave on to the pasturage behind. Here they could easily make out footprints, leading straight to the woods. It was a place where the trees looked to Simon as though they were being cleared for a new assart, or perhaps merely to increase the lands available for the hall. Up at the treeline was another servant, moving from one foot to another in obvious agitation and wringing his hands. They made their way to him without a word.

At first the ground fell away, giving the house a solitary prominence. A small stream lay at the bottom, curling lazily round the house. The snow had not covered this rippling water. It lay with small sheer cliffs at either bank like a miniature gorge, almost, Simon thought to himself, like a tiny replica of Lydford itself.

The servant took them to a bridge built of sturdy planks, wide enough for a wagon, then they were climbing the bank to the figure waiting at the trees. He was a middle-aged man, with a face flushed from the cold. His square, stolid features showed his terror. It was as if he feared even to talk, his muscles moving as if with the ague, mouth twitching, brows wrinkling, eyelids flickering. He pointed wordlessly, then remembered his place and would have fallen to his knees if the knight had not sharply ordered him to take them to his master. With a hesitant glance at his mistress, and seeing her nod, he turned and stumbled in among the trees. It was not far.

The assart was a small semicircular clearing, with stumps cut off a few feet above the ground, and Simon realised it was a coppice. The trees were being cut to allow for regrowth. When the new long-stemmed shoots grew, they could be harvested for fencing, staves or just for burning on the fire.

At the far end, to which the servant now led them, there was a spur cut into the forest like a thin, invasive finger of land thrusting the trees apart. Inside was a recently felled oak, lying on its side waiting to be cut into planks or logs. The man led them up to it, and there, just beside the bough, was a rolled-up form. Baldwin stepped up, a hand held out to stop the others, and then crouched by the figure.

On hearing a small gasp, Simon said, 'Wait here!' to the others, and went forward to join him. 'Oh, God!'

All around he could see the snow was dappled and clotted with frozen black gobbets of blood.

He stood motionless, his eyes on the ground for fully a minute. Then, though waking, he took a deep breath and let it out in one long jet. Breathing slowly, he peered around the small glade. Baldwin was beside him, his eyes on the figure. Beyond was the thickest concentration of blood, as if it had jetted forward under great pressure, thick gouts lying nearby and thinner droplets farther away.

Studying it, he could see that it was almost as if the stream had all been impelled in one direction. It had not all sprayed in a circle, but started to his left, in a thinnish drizzle, then fanned round to the great thick line ahead. When he looked down he could see that the body pointed in this direction too.

Alan Trevellyn lay partially covered with snow. He was down on his knees, his torso and arms outstretched as if praying, his head on the ground between. Only one side of his body was cleared, the other was still as white as the ground. Simon paused and peered down, then crouched, hands on his knees, and stared.

Standing, he pointed at the agitated servant. 'You! Did you find him here?'

'Yes, sir. I was here to collect wood for the log store when I stumbled on something. I thought it was a log . . . Or a stump . . . I had no idea it was the master . . . When I kicked at it, all the snow fell away, and I saw it was . . . Was . . .' He seemed to run out of energy.

'Did you clear away the snow with your hands?'

'No, sir. I kicked, and the snow fell away, and . . .'

Simon interrupted harshly. 'I know all that. Did anyone

else come here to see the body after you found it? Did anyone touch the body?'

'No, sir. I stayed here with the master until you got here just now, sir. I didn't leave, sir.'

Nodding, the bailiff turned back to the frowning knight.

'What is it, Simon?'

'Look!' He pointed. 'There's snow over the body. But the blood's on top of the snow.'

'Which doesn't make much sense,' Baldwin agreed.

'No. He would hardly bury himself in the snow after dying, would he? No, someone else piled the snow around him after he was dead. And there,' he indicated the rows of lines on top of the mound that covered the dead man's side, 'are the finger-marks to prove it.'

'Let's see what actually killed him.'

Simon grunted assent, and they carefully began to clear away the snow from around the corpse.

'Do you want one of the men to help you?' asked Mrs Trevellyn.

Looking up, Simon glanced at the two men before returning his gaze to her husband. 'No,' he said. 'I think we can do this. Could you send one to fetch a wagon, though, to bring the body back to the house?'

'Yes, of course. I'll be inside if you want me.' She shivered and wrapped her arms around herself. 'It's too cold for me up here.'

Simon nodded, and watched as she began to make her way back to the house, followed by her two servants, who straggled along like confused dogs expecting to be beaten. Turning back, he caught Baldwin's eye. The knight was watching her too.

*   *   *

211

To Simon's surprise, it did not take them long to clear the snow from Alan Trevellyn's corpse. After only a short time they had wiped it from his back and sides, and now they had a small moat around him. His stance was clear to see now, with the arms reaching up as if in supplication.

'More than likely he just fell down like that,' was Baldwin's own curtly expressed view when the bailiff pointed this out to him. 'Come on! Let's roll him over.'

Both taking a shoulder, they pulled hard. At first he seemed to have frozen to the earth itself. Simon felt it was as if the ground knew that he would be buried soon and had no wish to give up what it knew to be its own. But then it reluctantly gave up the struggle with a sudden loosening of its grip, and Simon nearly fell back as Trevellyn's body moved, then toppled over on his side.

Simon stared at the bulging eyes, the blackened tongue, the black and red mess around the mouth where the blood had spurted and frozen or dried, at the deep wound beneath where the murderer's knife had sliced through the yellowed cartilage of the windpipe before severing the arteries, and found himself swallowing hard to keep the bitter bile at bay.

'Interesting,' said Baldwin, rocking back to squat on his heels after studying the wounds. 'Just like Kyteler.'

The bailiff's voice was thick as he said. 'Yes. Just like the witch.'

The knight took a close look at the face, and Simon could see a series of scrapes where blood had been drawn. It looked as if he had been hit with a heavy weapon of some sort.

'Mace, or maybe a cudgel,' he heard the knight mutter to himself. Apart from that there was little they could learn from the body.

It was not long before the men arrived to carry it back to the house, and Simon relinquished it with pleasure. As he watched the men collect it up, rolling it in a blanket and staggering with it to the cart, he stood well back, away from the gaze of those sightless, dead fish-eyes.

Even last year's killings had not been quite as bad as this. At least then it had been a series of murders caused by a group of trailbastons, wandering outlaws with no other means to earn a living. Nobody was safe from the increasing prices that made food so expensive, that made lords have to reconsider how many retainers they could afford and threw out those they felt to be a burden. It was not surprising that some resorted to violence to gain what they needed. Especially since now, by law, all men had to own weapons for their defence, and by law must practise using those weapons for the better defence of their communities and themselves. No, it was not surprising that some decided that when their world refused to give them an honest way to earn a living they should resort to violence.

That was different, an almost comprehensible reason for a life of brigandage. But now? Two deaths like this? These were made more horrible, in some strange way, by the fact that they were unique. Perhaps if there were other bodies they would not seem so shocking. Maybe it was their stark, lonely individuality that made them so hideous.

As the wagon began the slow progress back, bumping and rattling over the lumpy ground, he paused a moment. It was just the same as the witch, he thought again. And it was only then that he felt the prickle on the back of his head as the hairs began to rise erect, and he felt as if he was suddenly smothered in an ice-cold sweat.

'What is it, Simon?' he heard his friend ask as he stopped in his tracks.

'I was just thinking. How was his body? Kneeling, sort of like he was praying – or maybe begging on his knees? Could he have been pleading for his life?'

When they returned, it was obvious to Angelina Trevellyn that they were deep in thought. They walked in without talking, stepping to a bench and sitting, their servant standing behind them. As soon as they were seated, she clapped her hands, and was pleased to see how quickly the manservant came in to serve them. He gave them mugs and poured mulled wine for them, then left the jug by the fire to warm.

'Can you tell me how he died?' she asked at last.

'Madam, he was slashed. His neck.' Baldwin was silent for a moment, peering into his mug, then looked up. 'Do you have any idea who could have done this?'

Looking up, Simon was sure he could see a look quickly veiled – fear? Uncertainty? As soon as it appeared it was gone, and her face seemed to melt into repose as she reflected. 'No, I cannot think of anyone who could do such a thing. Alan always had a temper, but to do this someone would have had to have hated him, surely?'

'Has he argued with anyone recently?'

She looked at him with a serious expression. 'Sir, if you know anything about my husband, you will know that he was always strong and resolute. He was brave and never feared any man. He never hid his feelings.'

'Is it true that he nearly beat a servant to death recently?'

'Oh, I do not know about that. It is true he would beat the men if they were slow or stupid, but so many of them are!

You know what servants are like! They are like dogs, and must be trained. He had to beat them to keep them alert. That is not a reason to kill him.'

'Did he know the witch?' Simon burst out, and she turned her face to him with sudden fear.

'The . . . The witch?' she said at last with an attempt at surprise. Under Simon's gaze, she appeared uncertain. Licking her lips with a nervous gesture, she half-shrugged, then turned once more to Baldwin.

'The bailiff wondered if there could be something . . . You see, your husband died from the same kind of wound as Agatha Kyteler.'

She stared at him, and Simon felt instinctively that this was no play-acting. Her shock had every appearance of honesty. 'What do you mean, the same?' she said at last.

The knight shrugged. 'Exactly the same. It was just how she died, with a single cut across the throat.'

'I . . . I need to think. Gentlemen, I am sorry, but this is very hard. Would you mind leaving me now? I must . . . Please go!' There was no refusing that last desperate plea. Leaving their wine, Simon and Baldwin stood, bowed, and walked out.

They found their horses in the yard and were soon mounted. At the gate, Baldwin turned back to glance at Simon. 'Where to now, do you think?'

'There's only one thing I want to know right now, and that is, where was Harold Greencliff last night?' said Simon shortly. When he looked up, he thought the knight was still looking back at him, but then he realised his friend was peering over his shoulder. When he glanced round, he saw that Angelina Trevellyn was standing in her doorway, watching them leave. He sighed as he turned forward again and saw Baldwin's face. It held a small, far-off smile.

As the light faded, the land was covered in a uniform dull greyness as if there was no distinction between heaven and earth. The snow took on a sombre shade that seemed reflected by the sky. There was no shadow to help him, and the Bourc tripped and stumbled as he carried on, leading the horses by the reins.

At least the wind had died now, and the ground glimmered palely under the soft cloak. On all sides were gently undulating hills, and here and there he could see a craggy outcrop of stone at the highest points.

He dared not ride in case he took his horses on to dangerous ground. Better by far that he should lead them, testing his steps all the way. But soon he must stop, find a place to rest and recover from the toil of the day. Stopping, he wearily drew a hand over his brow and gazed around. His eyes flitted over a number of hillsides before they rested on one.

It stood a mile away – maybe two – a hill with what looked like a scattering of rocks on the summit, as if a house had been left to collapse there. A tall spike pointed to the sky like the jagged reminder of a corner, while there appeared to be the tumbled remains of other walls, and even the hint of an enclosure.

Sighing, he let his head drop for a moment, then dragged at the reins in his hand. He must get there before the exhaustion overtook him.

The snow had not dissipated in the least. As they trotted down the hillside towards the lane, it became clear to Simon that they would have as slow a struggle as they had endured earlier.

At first it looked like their worst fears were unwarranted. The lane that wound round before the house appeared relatively clear, and even as they rode farther up on to the top of the hill, it was still reasonably easy going. It was only when they began to descend once more that they found that the drifts had accumulated, and all at once they were bogged in snow which at times was over their feet as they sat on their horses. At one point Edgar showed his horsemanship, keeping his seat as his mount reared, whinnying in fear and disgust at the depth of the powder and trying to avoid the deepest drifts, and the servant was forced to tug the reins and pull the head round, to turn away from the obstacle. Standing and gentling the great creature, he glanced over at Baldwin.

'I think I'll have to walk this one.'

He dropped from his saddle and, strolling ahead, spoke calmly to the horse as he led it forward, keeping a firm and steady pressure on the reins. Once it stopped and tried to refuse to carry on, shivering like a stunned rabbit, but then it accepted Edgar's soft words of encouragement and continued.

That was the worst of it. Now the land opened up and the snow was less thick. There was hardly enough to rise more than a couple of inches above their horses' hooves, and they all felt more confident, breaking into a steady, loping trot.

The house was soon visible. Simon could see it, a welcoming slab of grey in the whiteness all round, and he breathed a sigh of relief. He was about to make a comment, turning to look at Baldwin, when he saw a troubled frown on the knight's face. He appeared to be staring at the ground near their feet.

'Baldwin? What's the matter?'

'Look!' When Simon followed the direction of the pointing finger, he saw them. They were unmistakable, and his mind swiftly returned to the hunched figure of the dead merchant. The blood had been laid over the top of the snow, as if a geyser had spouted it up, and over the body the snow had been piled up into a makeshift hide-out. There had been little fresh powder over the body or the bloodstains. Trevellyn had died after the snowstorm had stopped.

And here were the clear marks, slightly marred by drifting, rounded and worn by the strong winds but still recognisable, of a pair of feet and the hoofprints of a horse, leading the way they were going. Back to the door of Harold Greencliff's farm. Exchanging a look, the two men trotted on.

There was no doubt, the marks clearly led straight to the trodden mess in the ground before the door, the tracks of a horse and a man. Shaking his head, Baldwin tossed his reins to Edgar and sprang down. Simon followed, unconsciously testing the dagger at his waist, making sure that the blade would come free if needed. Noticing his movement, Baldwin smiled suddenly, and Simon saw that he had been doing the same with his sword. Leaving Edgar on his horse, they strode to the door, and Baldwin pounded heavily on the timbers with a gloved fist.

'Harold Greencliff! I want to speak with you. Come out!'

There was no answer. He thumped the door again, calling, but there was still no reply, and Simon suddenly found himself struck with a feeling of nervousness. He felt an extreme trepidation for what they might find inside. Involuntarily he stepped backwards.

'What is it?' snapped Baldwin, angry at being left outside. 'God!' The sky was again starting to fill with tiny feathers of purest down, light specks of glistening beauty. But these minute granules were composed of pure coldness, and they could kill. Baldwin swore, then slammed his fist a last time on the door. '*Greencliff!*'

But there was no response. Glancing at Simon, he shrugged, then reached for the handle.

Inside it was almost as cold as out. Calling to Edgar to bring the horses in, Baldwin crossed the threshold and strode immediately for the hearth. Crouching, he studied the ash for a moment, then tugged off his glove and held his hand over it, swearing again. 'Damn! We'll need to light a fresh one!'

Simon busied himself gathering tinder and straw, then set to work relighting the fire. As he blew gently but firmly at the glowing sparks, carefully adding straw and twigs as the flames started to creep upwards, he was aware of Baldwin noisily clumping around the room, peering into dark corners and searching under blankets and boards. Meanwhile, Edgar unperturbably saw to the horses, removing their saddles and bringing their packs to the fire. Tossing them down, he gave Simon a quick grin before returning to the mounts.

The fire starting to shed a little light, he carefully piled smaller pieces of wood on top, then balanced logs above, and soon the house was beginning to fill with the homely smoke, catching in their throats, making them cough and rub at their eyes to clear away unshed tears. But as the fire caught hold the smoke rose to sit heavily in thick swathes in the rafters, and the air below cleared.

'He's not here, that's for certain,' Baldwin grumbled, crouching nearby.

'The footmarks seem to show that he was here last night,' said Simon calmly as he watched the flames. 'Maybe he's out to look after his sheep.'

Baldwin jerked his chin to point at the fire. 'And left his fire to go out? In this weather? Come along, Simon. Nobody would let his fire die at this time of year. It could mean death.'

'Well . . .' Simon nodded slowly. 'If he's gone, where has he gone to? We can't follow now, not with the snow coming again, that would be too dangerous.'

'No, but I can take a look and see which direction he's going in,' said the knight and stood. He walked outside, shutting the door behind him.

Already the weather had changed, and the small flakes were replaced by large petals falling at what looked like a ludicrously slow speed.

Peering, he narrowed his eyes as he tried to make out any marks in the snow. It was hard to see, the light was too diffuse behind the clouds, and with the failing light as day slipped towards night, he found that bending and looking for some differentiation in the contours was no help. All was uniformly white. There was not the relief of greys or blacks to mar the perfect apparent flatness. It was only when he stood again and stared farther away, wondering in which direction the youth would have gone, that he thought he could make out a depression left in the snow, like a shallow leat pointing arrow-straight to a mine. It led down the lane towards the trees, towards Wefford.

The wind began to build, whisking madly dancing flakes before his eyes, occasionally knocking them into his face. This was impossible, he thought. There was no way they could find out where the boy had gone in this: it was too heavy. He turned back to the door with a mixture of despondency and anger at being foiled.

*　　　*　　　*

The cry started as a low rumble on the Bourc's right. He might easily have missed it, but his ears were too well attuned to sounds of danger, even after the punishment the wind had inflicted during the day, and he immediately stopped in his tracks and stared back the way he had come.

He could feel the shivering of the horses as the call began again. First low, then rising quickly to a loud howl before mournfully sliding down to a dismal wail of hunger: wolves!

Putting out his hand, he stroked his mount gently. There was no sign of them yet. They must be some distance away. He threw a quick glance at the hill ahead. The shelter it offered was a clear half-mile farther on. He gauged the remaining ground he must cover, then set his jaw and pulled at the reins, setting his face to the hill. It held the only possible cover here in this darkening land.

The howls came again, but their tone had changed. They must have found his trail, for he thought he could hear a note of fierce joy. The cries were no longer full of anguish and longing; now they were a paean of exultation. Desperation was replaced by harsh, cruel delight, as if the creatures could already taste the thick, hot blood in his veins.

When he peered at the hill again, he knew he could not survive on foot. Throwing an anxious glance behind, he could see the dog-like animals running towards him. It would be dangerous to ride, God only knew how many hazards lay just under the surface of the snow, waiting to break his horse's legs, but to walk was suicide.

Clambering on to the horse, he whirled, checking the distance once more. They were only a few hundred feet away, seven of them running at a steady lope with their eyes fixed on him. The sight of their implacable approach sent a

221

shiver of expectant fear down his back. He knew what would happen if they were to catch him. Turning, he spurred his horse into a gallop.

The two horses ran madly with their terror. There was no need to urge them on, both knew their danger. The calls of the wolves had seen to that. All he need do was hold on, clinging for dear life as his mount bolted, ears flat back, head low, pelting forwards. The Bourc let him have his head, occasionally twitching the reins a little to keep the great horse heading in the direction that would lead them, he hoped, to safety.

'Thanks be to God!'

The heartfelt prayer of gratitude sprang to his lips automatically as they stumbled into the ring, and he fell from the saddle just as the second of his horses galloped in.

Grabbing the packhorse's leading rein, he managed to haul the horse round, and then he could tug the bow free. Calling softly to the petrified animal, trying to calm him, the Bourc grabbed the arrows from the top of his pack. Only when he had them in his hand did he set the point of the bow on the ground and pull down sharply to string it. Then, arrow ready and nocked, he moved forwards to the perimeter, a string of great stones that encircled his small encampment.

The howling had not stopped. Ahead the Bourc could see them approaching, not now with the mad enthusiasm of the hunting pack, but with the wary caution of dogs who have seen the boar to his lair and now watch carefully to see how to pull him down without danger.

Teeth showing in the dark, the Bourc waited while they approached, bow held firmly in hands that now felt clammy with anticipation.

CHAPTER SIXTEEN

Every now and again Simon or Edgar would stir from the fireside and peer out, but each time the view was the same: clouds of tiny swirling and pirouetting motes sweeping by in the breeze, a pageant in white and grey. The knight sat and stared morosely at the fire.

It was still early when they decided they must remain for the night. The snow was here to stay for some hours and they all recognised the need to keep warm. Once the horses were fed and watered, they opened the packs that Margaret had forced them to bring and sipped at the cool wineskins, then huddled in their blankets around the fire and began to talk desultorily until sleep took their them.

Simon found himself nodding soon after sitting, and his voice dropped, his words coming slower and slower, until Baldwin and Edgar were aware of a rhythmical droning as he started snoring.

'Noise like that could waken the dead,' said Edgar, but not unkindly.

Baldwin nodded. It was many months since he and his servant had slept away from their new home. In the past, when they had travelled more, they had always tended to avoid other people on the road. Someone always snored, and they preferred their own sleep undisturbed.

'At least the snow's not too heavy,' he said. 'We should be able to get on tomorrow.'

'Yes. And then we'll need to hunt for Greencliff.'

Nodding, the knight sighed. 'So long as the snow stays like this, we should be able to follow him.'

'Yes, God forbid that it could get any worse – we could get snowed in here for ages. No one even knows we're here.'

'Oh, I shouldn't worry.' He peered at the bailiff's body and threw a quick smile at Edgar with a quizzically raised eyebrow. 'There's a good amount of meat on *him*! We'll survive!'

His servant smiled, relaxing back and laughing silently. He was the only man Baldwin had ever met who did so, opening his mouth and letting the breath gasp out in that curious, inaudible exhalation. Baldwin had seen him laugh that way before battles, showing his teeth in a purely natural delight, taking pleasure while he might, even if were to die shortly thereafter.

'So if we're snowed in for a while we can eat him?' Edgar said after a moment. 'Ah, that would be good. There're some good joints on him! Mind, he'll be heavy to haul to the fire. How would you cook him? On a spit?'

Leaning back, the knight squinted at the recumbent figure. 'I don't know,' he said musingly. 'He looks a bit heavy. Is there a spit strong enough in this place?'

Rolling on to an elbow, Edgar stared at him too, grinning. 'I don't know. No, you're right, we'd need to paunch and joint him first. Maybe we could hang the rest of him in the open air outside? At least that way he'd keep well.'

'Maybe, but he might be too tough. Perhaps we should boil him into a stew?'

That's possible. Yes, with carrots and a thick slice of fresh bread.'

There was a grunt from the bailiff, then they heard his voice. Although muffled by his blanket, the disgruntled tone was unmistakable. 'When you have both finished discussing my merits as food on the hoof, perhaps you would like to go to sleep so that we can all be fresh in the morning.'

Laughing, Baldwin rolled himself up in his blanket, and was soon breathing long and deep, but now Simon found sleep evaded him. He kept seeing, as if in close juxtaposition, the two gaping wounds, one which had killed the old woman, the other which had killed the merchant. And then he saw the face of Harold Greencliff next to Angelina Trevellyn.

The first attack was easy to fight off. As the Bourc watched, the pack circled, some slinking from side to side in the expanse of clear ground before the wall, others sitting and peering back, like soldiers at a siege checking on the defences. But then he noticed one in particular, and concentrated on it.

It was a tall dog wolf, from the look of it, lean, taut and strong, with thick grey hair and eyes that stared fixedly at the Gascon. As the others in the pack walked up and down, this one slowly and deliberately inched forwards like a cat, staring unblinkingly. Then, as if at his command, they hurled themselves forward.

The leader died first. John drew the string back, sighted the cruel barbs of the arrow head between the eyes of the grizzled dog, and let the arrow fly. He snatched another arrow and fixed it to the bow, drawing again. But there was no need. The wolf died instantly. The arrow sank deep into his brain, and the animal somersaulted on to his back, then lay, shuddering in his death throes. Immediately the others pulled back, withdrawing dismayed to the gloom where he could not fire with certainty. The death of their leader made them pause, as if they suddenly appreciated their prey was not defenceless. They kept just out of clear sight, silently circling his camp, a series of grey wraiths in the gloom.

The Bourc knew wolves, and now he had found a defensible area, he knew he could hold them off. Satisfied that he was safe for a moment from another attack, he investigated his camp.

He was out of the vicious wind at last. The tall walls of stone offered a barrier against the worst of the weather – the ground beneath was free even of snow. Here he tethered the horses.

Nearby, beyond the line of stone, some bushes stood, twisted and stunted as if blasted by magic into weird shapes. He took his knife and hacked at them, wrenching branches off and tossing them into a pile. While there was firewood handy he would conserve the faggots on the packhorse. Nearer the horses he found a small hollow and set himself to lighting a fire, looking around as the flames began to curl upwards.

By their light he saw that he was in a natural bowl on the top of a low hill. Its perimeter was bounded by a low wall to the south, but northwards it had collapsed. Behind, what he had thought was a derelict building was a rocky outcrop, three or four great slabs, one on top of the other, with a narrow, low gap like a door between the two lower ones. Peering through, he saw that there was a cavern inside. A place to sleep, safe from wind and snow.

It was while he was peering inside that the second attack began. From the corner of his eye he glimpsed a shape leaping noiselessly on to the wall. Even as the Bourc grabbed his bow and notched an arrow to the string, drawing it back and letting the shaft fly, he heard the screams of terror from the horses, and, spinning round, he saw the packhorse rearing in terror as another wolf jumped, jaws snapping, trying to reach the horse's throat.

Lurching to his feet, the Bourc tried to aim, but the wolf was too close to the horses, and he dared not risk the shot. Cursing, he ran forward shouting, and as he did, the wolf's teeth scraped a ragged tear in the horse's neck. Shrieking, the horse rose once more, but now the smell of blood appeared to enrage the Bourc's mount and made him lose his fear. Lifting his bulk up onto his hind legs as the wolf passed before him, he suddenly dropped, both hooves falling, legs stiff, the whole of his weight behind them. With a petrified screech, the wolf was crushed to the ground, forepaws scrabbling in the dirt, eyes wide in agony, as the horse rose again and again, only to bring his whole weight down on the wolf's back, not stopping until the hideous cries had ceased.

Before running to his horse's side, the Bourc stared around his camp carefully, arrow still set on the bowstring, every sense straining. There was nothing: no noise to disturb him. He slowly rose, walking along the line of the great rocks until he came to the horses. Squatting, he put aside the bow, and drew his dagger to make sure the wolf was dead. It was unnecessary. A quick look at the ruined body was enough to show that.

The horse was still shivering, eyes rolling in horror, and the Bourc stroked it for a moment. A few yards away was the packhorse, and he stared at it anxiously. He could see the blood dripping steadily from the long gash, but he gave a sigh of relief as the fire spluttered and flared. The wound was not deep enough to kill the animal. Walking to it, he made sure, then patted the horse and spoke softly to him.

It was while he was there that he heard the panting. Turning slowly, his heart beating frantically, he saw the sharp features of the wolf crouched low, eyes fixed on him as it stalked forward. He glanced at his bow, lying useless only yards away. It was close, so close, but already nearer the approaching wolf than him: he would never be able to reach it. He showed his teeth in a snarl – though whether in fear or rage, he was not himself sure – and grasped his long-bladed dagger.

When Simon awoke, it was to a sense of mild surprise, wondering where he was. At least over the night he had not suffered from the dream again. It was as if it only wanted to seek him out while he was idle, not now, while he was searching for the witch's killer. While he was employed on that task the nightmare would leave him alone, although its memory would stay with him as a spur to his commitment to the hunt.

It took them little time to saddle their horses, roll up their blankets and prepare to leave. The snow appeared not to have been so strongly blown by the wind this time, and lay evenly rather than drifting, so the three men felt that the journey to Wefford should not be too difficult. From the front of the house, they could look over to the east where the woods began and see where the lane made its way in among the trees, the hedges at either side standing out as two long ramparts. The trail itself looked like a ditch between them, like some sort of fortification, from the way that the land rose on their left to form the small hill.

As they mounted and turned their horses' heads to the sun in the east, which seemed to hang larger and redder than usual in the pale blue sky, they had to squint from the already painful glare off the snow. Baldwin rode alongside the trail he had seen the evening before. In the bright sunlight the tracks still stood out, and they led the men along the lane a short way. But then the marks were obliterated under a fall of snow from the branches of the trees overhead. Taking their time, they set a slow pace, between a trot and a walk, as they went under the trees, casting about for a continuation of the tracks, but they saw nothing.

'We'll have to get Tanner, of course,' said Baldwin after a few minutes.

Looking across at him, Simon sighed as he turned back to the road ahead. 'Yes. And raise a search party; see if we can hunt him quickly.'

Another manhunt, the knight mused sadly. He enjoyed the chase for an animal. After all, that was only right, to hunt and kill for food and sport was natural. But tracking a man was different, demeaning for the man and his hunters as well.

229

It would be different, the knight knew, if he felt that there had been any justifiable reason for the murders, but there did not seem to be. He frowned and bit his lip in his annoyance at one thought: if he had kept this boy Greencliff in gaol, or put him back when they had heard from Stephen de la Forte that the two of them had *not* been together all the time when Agatha Kyteler had died, maybe Alan Trevellyn would not have died. That meant that a little of the guilt for the murder, he felt, now lay with him for making the wrong decision at the time. As his eyes rose to the road ahead, they held a frown as he swore to himself that he would catch the criminal and avenge Trevellyn's death.

Jogging along quietly beside him, Simon was not so convinced of Harold Greencliff's guilt. Why? That was the question that plagued him: *why*? Why kill the merchant? Or the witch, for that matter. The boy had made comments about her at the inn that night, but nobody could explain why he hated her. And there seemed no reason why he should kill Trevellyn either.

Then his eyes took on a more pensive look and his head sank on his shoulders. Mrs Trevellyn was very beautiful, he admitted to himself. Was it possible that she *was* the mysterious lover? That Jennie Miller was right? Could the boy have killed her husband to win her? But if he had, why run away afterwards? It made no sense!

The admission of what she had done at the witch's cottage had launched Harold Greencliff into a nightmare that would not stop. All he had ever wanted was to be able to live out his life like his father before him, a farmer. To be able to earn his living honestly. He knew he would never be rich, but that did not matter when none of his friends and neighbours were. Money and cattle were pleasant to dream of, but he felt it was more important to be satisfied and content, to work hard and earn a place in heaven, like the priests promised.

But since the death of Agatha Kyteler last Tuesday, there had been no peace for him. Maybe if he had managed to run away then, he would have left all this behind. If he had got to Gascony, perhaps then he might have been able to forget the whole affair, but it was too late now. He was marked by his guilt.

At first, when he got back home from the Trevellyns' hall, he had sat down as if in a dream, his mind empty. It felt impossible to move, and he stayed there on his bench, sitting and occasionally shivering in the lonely cold of his house, not even bothering to stoke his little fire so deep was his misery. But soon the despair returned, and the disgust, and he stood and walked around his room, sobbing. Ever since that *witch* had ruined everything, his life had been wrecked. It was all her fault: she had deserved her end.

It was like a dream, the way that he had made his decision and started taking up his meagre essentials, stuffing them into his old satchel. He had picked up his ballock knife, the long dagger with the single sharp edge, from where it had fallen on the floor. He might need it, and it was good in a fight, with the two large round lobes at the base of the solid wooden grip to protect the hand.

For food, he took some fruit and dried and salted ham, which he dropped into the bag, followed by a loaf of bread as an afterthought. Then the satchel was full. He pulled a thick woollen tunic over his head, draped his blanket over his shoulders, took his staff, and left. He would never return. The shame would be too painful.

At first he had wandered in the darkness without any firm direction in mind, aimlessly following where his feet led him, and he had found himself heading south. Soon he was in among the woods. Usually he would stride through there, knowing each trunk and fallen bough like the furniture in his hall, but in the bitter cold and his despair he had meandered witlessly.

Now he knew it was a wonder that he had managed to survive and had not succumbed to the freezing temperatures. He had been lucky. The woods appeared to go on for ever, leading him up gentle hills and down the other sides, through lighter snow which the winds had not been able to pile into deep drifts, heading away from his home and his past life.

Only when he had begun to smell woodsmoke did he realise he had almost arrived at Crediton, and he stopped. Almost without consciously making a choice, he had found himself starting to walk again, following the line of trees to circumnavigate the town, always keeping to the shelter of the thick boughs. When he had passed by the town, he had discovered a strange lightening of his spirit, as if he had truly left his old life behind. He had only rarely been this far from home before.

All that day he had continued, ignoring calls from other travellers, concentrating solely on the steady trudge of his feet, careless of his direction, neither knowing nor caring where he was heading, until he had realised that the snow was falling again.

It forced him to waken from his mindless, daydreaming tramping, and he stopped dead, staring around with no idea where he was. He had arrived at a flat area, an open space fringed by trees, and now, as the first few flakes began to fall, he could see that there appeared to be no houses nearby.

Here he was quite high up, his view unimpaired, and to the left he could see over the top of some trees to a hilltop some miles away which wore a circle of trees at its summit like a crown. Before him he could see along a small cleft in the land, which appeared to forge ahead like a track, with both sides hidden under a light scattering of trees. Narrowing his eyes against the thin mist of snow, he had set his face to the valley and determinedly carried on.

But it had been no good. The snow had begun to take hold, the air becoming colder, and each fresh gust of wind felt as if it blew a little harder than the last, making the snow swoop and dive like millions of tiny, white swallows.

The random movement of the white dust held an almost hypnotic fascination, and he found himself beginning to stumble more often as he fell under the spell of the all-encompassing whiteness that now appeared to form an impermeable barrier around him. It was as if the dance of the snow motes before his eyes was an invitation to sit and sleep. He had the impression that they were soothing, calming, as if asking him to rest.

And then he had fallen.

Possibly it was a gnarled tree root hidden from sight, maybe a fallen branch, but suddenly he had discovered he was not walking any more. He had tripped, and was now lying headlong, his face resting against what had felt like a warm soft pillow of the smoothest down. Rolling, he could not help a sigh of relief. He stretched and groaned in happiness. At last he could relax: he had come far enough. Now he could sleep.

It was not until much later that he could be grateful for the interruption. At first it had seemed to be a growling, then a moaning as of pain, low and persistent. Just at the edge of his hearing, it had penetrated his thoughts and dreams like a saw cutting through bark. He had mumbled to himself and rolled, trying to sleep and lose the insistent noise, but it had continued, and as his mind grew angry at the interruption, the anger started to make him waken. It was sufficient.

The snow had strengthened, and as he lurched unwillingly back to consciousness, he realised that he was smothered in a film of light powder. Recognising his danger, he stood quickly, his heart beating madly, while his breath sobbed in his throat, and he gazed around wildly, a feral creature recognising the sound of a hunter. The snow had cocooned him, swaddling him under its gentle grip of death. If he had not heard that noise, he would soon surely have died, sleeping under the soothing influence of the murderous cold.

But what had made the noise? As he turned here and there looking for the source, a slow realisation had come to him: it was the noise of cattle, and it came from nearby.

As soon as he had recognised the sounds, he had started off towards them. There, hidden behind a line of oaks, was an old barn. The walls were red-brown cob, not limewashed, and if he had not heard the animals inside, he would not have seen the place. After carefully looking to see that there were no people nearby, he had entered. Inside there was a store of hay, and he fashioned a rough cot from it, sitting and preparing to wait for the snow to stop.

The sudden lack of movement freed his mind from the shackles of exercise and he had found his thoughts returning to *her*. To his pain at leaving her behind. He had wept tears for her last evening as he had sat alone and miserable at his house, he could now remember. Hot, scalding tears that seared his soul. He had loved her. Inevitably, his thoughts turned to her again. To know that he could never see her again, never feel the smooth softness of her body, never hold the thick, blue-black tresses of her braids in his hands like silken ropes, never kiss her again, hold her, feel the warmth of her breasts and the flat sweep of her belly, was maddening. He had once thought that he had loved Sarah, but this was much more: this was almost a religious loss. It felt as if, after the horror of her face in the dark only two nights before, a part of him had died. When she saw him there, and spoke with such loathing, a spark of his soul had weakened and finally faded to dullness. There was nothing there any longer.

He sighed at the memory. Now, in the morning, he could accept that he could never see her again. Picking up his satchel, he swung it on to his back and made his way to the entrance, carefully peering out. There was no one there, so he walked out. He could break his fast later. For now the main thing was to get away, as far away as possible from this area. Could he get on a ship? Would it be possible to find one to take him away?

Pausing, he considered. There were docks at Exeter, he knew, but last time Tanner had found him there. It was further, but would they expect him to head down to the south? To Dartmouth or Plymouth? Weighing the satchel in his hand, he debated the two options. He would need more food on the way if he was going that far. It was a great deal further, but if he could make it, they would never think of searching for him there, would they?

Making his choice, he set his shoulders and set his face to the south. He must go to the coast, then on to Gascony and to freedom.

The village looked like a slumbering animal, as if the area had chosen hibernation in preference to the freezing misery of the winter weather, and Baldwin gazed around sourly as they rode along the street.

'God! Why aren't these people up and working yet?'

'It *is* very early, Baldwin. And I have no doubt that some are up. They will be out tending to their sheep and cattle,' said Simon calmly. 'Especially after the snow last night.'

Baldwin grunted, and maintained a disapproving silence for the rest of their journey. It was not far. They stopped outside the inn, and at a curt nod of Baldwin's head, Edgar dropped from his horse and walked leisurely to the door. Watching, Simon saw him casually glance up at the sky, trying to assess the time. The bailiff nodded to himself. It was very early to waken the innkeeper. But then he realised his error.

After looking up to reassure himself as to the earliness of the hour, the servant grinned back at him quickly, then beat on the door in a shockingly loud tattoo before retreating a few yards.

It was a sensible precaution, from the bellow of rage that issued from inside. Simon heard rapid steps, the sound of bolts being drawn, and then the door was yanked open and the unshaven and furious features of the publican appeared, mouth wide to roar at whoever had woken him. At the sight of the knight with his servant and friend, his mouth snapped shut as if on a spring.

'Sir Baldwin,' he managed at last, with a snarl that appeared to be his best approximation to a smile. 'How can I serve you?'

The knight grunted. 'You can fetch hot drinks for three, prepare cooked eggs and bread for our breakfast, and start to organise a search party. Then you can send word to my house that we are all well, find Tanner, and tell him to come here immediately. Prepare provisions for three days for three men.'

'I . . . Er . . .'

'And you can do it all now. We must hunt a man.'

CHAPTER SEVENTEEN

It seemed to the bailiff that no sooner had they sat to watch the innkeeper's wife cooking their eggs on her old cast-iron griddle over the embers of last night's fire than the men from the village began to arrive. Farmers and peasants walked in, strolling casually as if the matter was nothing to do with them, or cautiously and reluctantly sidling through the curtain as though expecting to be arrested themselves. Each was told by Edgar to go and arm himself and return as quickly as possible, with food for at least three days.

It was not until Tanner arrived, covered in snow almost up to his knees and dripping, that Baldwin looked up and began to take an interest. The old constable walked straight to him. There was no need, he knew, for subservience with this knight. Glancing up as his bulk approached, Baldwin gave him a slow grin and waved a hand to the fire. 'Have you eaten? Would you like to have some eggs?'

Glancing carelessly at the griddle, Tanner shook his head. 'What's the matter, sir? The innkeeper's boy told me to come here straight away. Said we had to hunt a man.'

'That's right. Greencliff has run away again.'

'Harry's gone? Oh, the daft bugger!' He shook his head as if in tired annoyance, then said, 'But so what? If he wasn't there for the death of the witch, because he was with de la . . .'

'It's not that easy. He was not with de la Forte,' the bailiff broke in, and explained about the change in Stephen de la Forte's evidence. When he spoke of the murder of Trevellyn, there was a sudden hush in the room, as the men all around realised why they were being asked to chase Greencliff. When Simon had finished, he found he was immediately bombarded by questions from all sides, and after a moment Baldwin stood with a hand raised for silence.

'*Quiet!*' he thundered, and gradually the noise died down. 'That's better. Now, Harold Greencliff was not at his house last night. The fire was cold, so it's likely that he left the night before. Otherwise it would at least have been warm when we got there. So, where has he gone?'

The room was quiet as the men thought, then one said, 'He could've gone to Exeter, to the docks again. That's where he went after the witch was killed.'

Baldwin nodded. It was certainly possible. 'He could, but was there anywhere else he might go? Did he have any family or friends he could have gone to stay with? Anybody outside the area with whom he could rest?'

All round the room heads slowly shook.

'In that case, we have no choice: we must try to search for him on all of the roads.' Baldwin sighed. The only result of this would be long hours in the saddle. To think that he had felt sympathy for the lad when he had been in gaol! He sat, glowering.

Simon stirred thoughtfully. 'We saw the footprints in front of the house,' he said. 'Were they going to it or leading from it?'

'What do you mean?'

'We thought he was going home *from* Trevellyn's house, but we could have been wrong. He might have gone to Trevellyn's house, killed him, then carried on towards the west on the road. Or he could have done the murder, then headed home and carried on from there. We can't be sure which.'

'Yes,' Baldwin agreed. 'So those are the directions we should concentrate on. Beyond Trevellyn's place, and back this way.'

'He can't have come this way,' said a stocky man in a tough jerkin of leather and skins.

'Why not?' asked Simon, frowning.

'I'm a hunter. Mark Rush. I was up at the lane all last night between his house and here – there's been a wolf or something attacking sheep in the pens over that way – and I was sheltered there all night. When it snowed, I went into my hut, but when it was clear enough I was out again. He never passed me.'

'Are you sure?' said Baldwin dubiously. He found that the man's eyes moved and fixed on him, curiously light and unfeeling as he spoke.

'Oh, yes. I'm sure. Nothing living passed me that night I wasn't aware of. Harry did not pass.'

Simon eyed him thoughtfully, then nodded. 'In that case we should look in the woods to the north and south of the lane, especially near his house.' He thanked the woman, who passed him a platter with two eggs and a hunk of roughly torn bread. 'I suggest we have three parties: one to ride to the west and look for signs, one to search for tracks in the woods north, the last to look in the southern woods. Whoever finds anything should return here with a message to be left with the innkeeper.'

They talked a little longer about the details, but agreed to this simple plan. Baldwin and Edgar would take the western road, Simon the southern woods, and Tanner the northern. Splitting the men into three groups of four, Baldwin and Simon quickly finished their breakfast, went out to their horses, and mounted.

Simon was pleased to have been able to enlist the light-eyed hunter for his search. The man looked capable and confident. Although quiet and soft-spoken, he moved with an alertness and graceful ease which spoke of his skill and strength. He was older than Simon, probably nearer Baldwin's age of forty and odd, although whether he was older or younger than the knight was a different matter. The bailiff could not guess.

As they rode along to the lane leading to the Greencliff farm, Simon studied him. He wore a heavy-looking short sword by his side. There was a bow at his back and arrows in a quiver tied to the saddle over his blanket in front of him, where he could reach them quickly. Before the three groups divided, Baldwin, Simon and Tanner had held a quick conference to confirm the main plan. Whoever was to find what could be Greencliff's trail was immediately to send a messenger back to Wefford so that he could guide others there. If

Simon's or Tanner's teams found no sign of the youth, they were to carry on and join Baldwin's, for it was in his direction that there were going to be the highest number of roads to search, and thus he had the greatest need of men.

With the details agreed, they had separated and made their way to the areas allocated to them for searching.

Baldwin knew, as he urged his horse into an easy lope, that his would almost certainly prove to be a wild goose chase, and reviewed the road ahead. This lane led to Greencliff Barton itself, then on up the hill to the Trevellyn house, and past it to the crossroads on the Tiverton road. Where would they go from there? Into Crediton itself? Or north-east to Tiverton? Or should they carry on west? Where would the boy have gone?

In among the trees, Simon had an easier time. At the beginning of the line of trees he had called the hunter aside. 'Mark Rush, I've heard of you, even if we haven't met before.'

His eyes were a very pale grey, as if the rain and snow he lived in had washed the colour from them. Set in the leathery, square face, it made him look as if the eyes were a reflection of his soul, which had been so worn with his outdoor life that it was weary now of continuing. But when the eyes fixed on the bailiff, he could see the glittering intelligence that lay behind.

'Yes, Bailiff?' His tone expressed polite interest, bordering on indifference.

'I have no idea where this boy has gone, or how to seek him. You do, you're a hunter. You're in charge: you can read his spoor if we find it, I won't be able to.'

The hunter nodded, then glanced ahead at the waiting men. 'In that case, sir, we'll come out of the woods again.'

'Why?'

'It's hard going here. We'll go another half mile down the road, then go into the trees there. If he went into the trees to lose someone following him and made a big curve, we could end up following it all the way back on ourselves. If we go in further down, we can see if he left the woods south of the village or whether he went on at all. If he didn't leave them, we know he's waiting for Tanner or the knight to find him.'

'So if we enter further on, we stand a better chance of finding him if he's there.'

He nodded. Then, apparently taking Simon's shrug to be acknowledgement of the transfer of authority, the hunter called the other two men to them and led the way down the road to the south, with Simon taking second position behind him.

When Mark Rush stopped, it was some way past the last of the houses in the village. Here Simon knew that the woods were bordered by a grassed verge before the road, but now the grass was hidden by the layer of snow. The hunter appeared to be measuring, gazing back the way they had come for a moment, then, seemingly satisfied, he took his horse to the verge and on into the trees.

Following, Simon was again taken with the sudden hush, the stillness that existed inside. It was as if the troop had entered an inn as strangers, causing a void where there had been noise. Here it was as though the trees were intelligent beings who were suddenly aware of the invaders, and who were stunned into uncomprehending dumbness. He almost wanted to apologise to the towering boughs that loomed overhead for their noisy presence.

Smothering the feeling, he carried on, over the thin bracken and ferns that lay under the snow at the edge and into the woods. He was faintly surprised how thin the snow was even after only quite a short ride. Above the trees were leafless, and he could see through the apparently lifeless branches to the sky above, but still the ground had little more than a thin crust of snow, a mere few inches.

On the floor he could see that several animals had passed by, their prints firm and clear on the white carpet: birds, animals running purposefully in a line – twice he saw the marks of deer, with the distinctive twin crescents of their hooves. All stood out distinctly on the thin surface, and when Simon saw the attentive gaze of the hunter, seeming to notice and catalogue them all in his mind, the bailiff relaxed. There was obviously no point in trying to see the tracks before Mark Rush. The man was clearly more than capable. Sighing, Simon lapsed into a private reverie.

What was Margaret doing? Probably ordering Hugh to help her with her work! He must surely be fully recovered by now, and Margaret was good at getting him to work, using the right amount of acid and sweetness in her voice to persuade him. He smiled fondly. She always did know how to get her men to do what she wanted.

That was the kind of woman Baldwin needed, he felt sure. One who could not just excite the senses, but one who would always keep him on his toes, one who could keep his interest going. Above all, one who was intelligent. Simon was sure that the knight would need a woman who could discuss matters with him, not a pretty ornament.

The thought led him down a new and different track. What about Mrs Trevellyn? She certainly seemed to have attracted

Baldwin. Simon's lips twitched in remembered humour at the way the knight had turned in his seat to gaze back at the house as they left the day before. Yes, he had been interested!

And there was no denying her beauty, the bailiff reflected. Of course, he was more than happy with his own wife, but refuting the beauty of another would be stupid and, in the light of his own devotion to Margaret, pointless. He could cheerfully confirm that he was happier with the warm and summery fair looks of his wife than he could be with the cool and wintry attraction of the brunette from France, with her calculating, green eyes, cold and deep as the sea. They were nothing like the merry, bright blue cornflower of his wife's. But still, he could appreciate her slender and willowy figure, with the long legs and tiny waist. And her flat belly, below the rich, ripe splendour of her breast, promising warmth and comfort. Yes, there was much to admire there. But was she intelligent enough for his friend?

Then suddenly the smile froze on his face as his thoughts carried on to the inevitable question: if she was clever enough, if she was capable, and if she had taken Greencliff as her lover, could she have persuaded him to kill her husband for her?

Deep in his musings, Simon nearly rode into the stationary horse of the hunter in front. Looking up, he was surprised to see that the man wore an amused grin. Thinking his humour was at his absent-mindedness, the bailiff was about to snap a quick retort when he saw that Mark Rush was pointing down at the ground.

'There he goes!'

Staring down in complete surprise – for he had not truly expected this troop to find anything – Simon saw the footprints. As the other two riders approached, he and Rush dropped down and studied them, crouching by the side of the spoor.

The hunter reached out with a tentative hand to softly trace the nearest print, then Simon saw his eyes narrow as he glanced back to their right, the direction where the man should have come from. Seemingly satisfied, he turned and gazed the opposite way, then ruminatively down at the prints once more.

'Well?' asked Simon.

Mark Rush sniffed hard, then snorted, hawked and spat. 'This is too easy. He's not trying to hide.' His brow wrinkled. 'I wonder why not.'

Shrugging, Simon gave a gesture of indifference. 'What does it matter? We'll find out when we've caught him.'

'Yes,' said the hunter, then grunted as he rose, a knee clicking as he moved. 'Right, well I suppose we'd better get on after him. These prints're from yesterday from the look of them, they're worn. See that?' He pointed at a small round hole beside the trail. Glancing at it, Simon saw it repeated beside the footprints. 'That's a walking stick. See how it hits the ground in time with his left foot, although he holds it in his right hand? He's carrying a stick, so we'd better be careful. Don't want him braining us.'

They mounted, then sent one of the men back to the inn. Before he left, Simon looked up at the sky. 'How long have we been in the woods, do you think, Rush?'

Squinting at the sky, the hunter seemed to consider. 'Maybe two, maybe three hours?'

'I think so too. You!' This to the waiting messenger. 'Get to the inn as quickly as you can, but then go on to Sir

Baldwin – understand? Tell him too, and ask if he can send a couple more men, just in case we do have to fight to catch him.'

'No need to worry about that, sir,' said Mark Rush, indicating his bow with a jerk of his thumb.

'I'd prefer to take him alive, Rush. We'll avoid any unnecessary violence.'

'Yes. I'll avoid unnecessary violence, but I'll use any that *is* necessary,' he said meaningfully.

The three rode on in file now. There was no real need for a hunter to follow this trail. If the man had wanted to leave an invitation his path could not have been more easy to detect. It straggled on, winding unnecessarily round shrubs and saplings, sometimes seeming to halt, both feet placed together, and then starting out afresh. Once or twice Simon felt sure that the man must have stumbled or tripped. At one point there was a definite mark where he had fallen, and the outline of his body remained, his hands making deep prints in the snow, looking strangely sad, as if they were all that remained of him.

Simon shivered. It was curious, but he felt a kind of sympathy with this man, for no reason he could fathom. Perhaps it was merely empathy for the hunted creature? He had felt that once before, when, as a boy, he had watched a deer at bay, the hounds snapping at it, the animal's eyes rolling in his terror, knowing that he was about to die. Then, when the huntsmen had egged on the dogs, and the deer had fallen, legs flailing uselessly, beneath the pack, Simon had felt the same sadness. It was not for the hunt itself, but for the inevitability of the end. For that buck it had been death at the teeth of the hounds. For Harold Greencliff it would be the slow strangling as he was hauled up the gibbet by the rope around his neck.

With a shrug, he concentrated on the trail again. Had the boy given any compassion to the witch? Or to the man he murdered? The bailiff doubted it.

It was getting close to dark when the man at the back of the troop called out, and Baldwin had been getting short-tempered long before that.

Their ride had been slow and painstaking, searching care-fully along the lane, with Edgar on one side and the knight on the other, both looking for tracks that could have been left by the farmer, but they found nothing. Baldwin had even insisted on going into the sheep's pasture to see whether they could find a trail there leading into the woods, but the sheep had trampled the whole area and scraped at the surface to get at the grass underneath so effectively that there was nothing that the two men could find.

Carrying on, they had slowly worked their way along the lane, up to the Trevellyn house and beyond, and Baldwin had managed to throw it only the most cursory of glances, preventing himself from staring and searching for the extraordinary beauty of Angelina Trevellyn. It was not purely his willpower that stopped him. It was the raised eyebrow and sardonic smile on Edgar's face when he happened to catch the servant's eye.

As he turned back to the road ahead, he wore an expres-sion of vague perplexity. The look from Edgar showed more clearly than any words just how obvious his interest in the woman was. Baldwin was no fool. If it was that obvious to Edgar, it would surely be as clear to others who knew him.

His problem was, he did not know what his feelings were. Was it just sympathy for a woman recently widowed? He slumped in his saddle as he tried to analyse his emotions. Although there was a sense of lust, that was hardly enough to explain his desire to see her again. It was quite a poignant sensation, one that he had never experienced before. Was it normal to feel like this after such a brief introduction? Who could he speak to about it? Edgar?

They had almost arrived at the end of the road, and Baldwin was debating which direction to take, when the call came. Stopping his troop, they waited, and soon saw the figure of Simon's messenger.

After hearing the message, Baldwin looked at the two men in his squad. 'You two go back. Find Tanner and tell him he can call off his hunt, then go back with this man and join the bailiff and the hunter.'

There was a little grumbling, but they finally agreed, and Edgar and the knight sat on their horses and watched as the three disappeared round the curve in the road. Then Baldwin sighed and flicked his reins, setting off at a slow walk, his servant behind.

'Well?'

Edgar grinned at the gruff word, and at the implied question. 'Sir?'

'What do you think?' Baldwin had stopped his horse and now sat frowning at Edgar with his brow wrinkled in perplexity. 'Of Mrs Trevellyn, I mean?'

'Mrs Trevellyn? A very beautiful lady. And very marriageable, I would think, with the money she must have. Her dowry would be high, I imagine.' He maintained a wooden and blank expression.

'Yes, but should I . . .? Well, for a woman whose husband's just been killed? She's hardly begun her mourning. Should I . . .?'

'I'm sure if you catch her husband's murderer she'll be very pleased. And grateful, sir.'

As Baldwin wheeled his horse and set off, his face purposeful once more, he could not contain his glee. That the capture of Alan Trevellyn's killer would delight her had not occurred to him, and now he could tell her that they had found the trail. He squared his shoulders. He must go to her at once to tell her.

Not having to search continually for tracks made their return along the road a great deal faster, although the snow was thick enough to ensure that they must exercise caution. They could not risk going so fast that their horses might slip on ice or on a hardened rut of frozen mud.

At the turn-off to the house, they slowed and ascended the hill at a walk. It was strange, Baldwin thought, that from here, outside, there was no sign of the sadness that inevitably follows the death of the master. Smoke still issued cheerily from chimneys, there were sounds of shouting and woodcutting from behind the property, and if he did not know of the death, he would have thought that nothing had happened here.

When they had dismounted and tied up their horses, Baldwin thumped on the door. It was soon opened by the same young maid who they had seen on the day before, but now, the knight noticed, she had undergone a transformation. Whereas before she had appeared timid and fearful, now she seemed gay as she opened the door, smiling as she recognised the men waiting, and he found himself grinning in return.

She led them through to the hall again, where the fire blazed in enthusiastic welcome. Striding in, the knight and his man stood warming themselves by the fire while the maid left to go into the solar at the back of the dais. After a few moments, she returned, indicating that they should follow her, and they soon found themselves in a warm and comfortable family room with another roaring fire. Sitting on a bench nearby was Mrs Trevellyn, sewing quietly at a tapestry, and she glanced up questioningly as the two men entered.

At the sight of her cool green eyes, Baldwin felt the blood begin to thunder in his veins. She looked so soft and vulnerable, so warm and defenceless, he wanted to gather her up in his arms and gentle her. The feeling was so strong that he stood for a moment and stared, taking in her slim and languid dark beauty. It was impossible to suspect her of being involved in the murder of the old woman, let alone the killing of her own husband. He felt quite certain of that now. But when her eyes met his, he was sure that he could see a quick impatience, and at the sight he dropped into a chair, waving Edgar out to the hall. Her maid followed, so they were soon left alone.

With a sigh she set her needlework aside and subjected him to a pensive, detailed study. 'So, Sir Baldwin. You wanted to see me?' Her voice was low and calm.

'Yes.' Now he was here, he realised that raising the death of her husband was going to be difficult. Mentioning Alan Trevellyn must recall to her the pain of seeing his twisted body out on the hill among the trees. Taking a deep breath, he said, 'Mrs Trevellyn, I know it must be very hard for you, but we have been fortunate in our search for your husband's killer.'

An eyebrow rose, and he was sure he could see a sceptical smile form. 'Really? And how is this?'

'After the death of Agatha Kyteler, we found some evidence that a local man might have been involved, and when we went to see him, he had disappeared. Harold Greencliff. We went to see him yesterday, but he has gone again. Run away. But we have found his trail, and . . .'

Her eyes had widened, as if in great surprise, and a hand raised to her throat. 'Harold?' Her voice quavered, suddenly weak.

'It looks like he ran away almost immediately after the killing of your husband, lady. We have sent a search party after him. The men are following his tracks in the woods. My friend the bailiff is there, and he should soon bring the boy back to be tried for the murder. Lady? Are you all right?'

She had dropped her face into her hands, as if about to weep, and the knight leaned forward a little, his hand held out tentatively, longing to touch her and try to calm her, but he let his hand fall. He dared not.

After a minute or two, she cleared her throat and looked into the flames.

'Lady? Can I fetch you anything?'

Looking at her, he was struck by the fresh sadness in her eyes, and his heart went out to her for feeling sympathy for the young farmer, even if it was misplaced. But then her eyes returned to his, and he could plainly see the fear in their emerald depths. It was that which made him stiffen with a sudden cold doubt. This was not just womanly compassion for a hunted villein. She was scared for herself.

CHAPTER EIGHTEEN

'Damn this snow!'

They had managed to follow the tracks all around the perimeter of Crediton, Mark Rush staying in among the trees, stumbling over the bracken and thin, straggling shrubs at the very edge so that he could follow the footprints while the others rode on happily in the clear area that bounded the town, listening with amusement to his muttered curses. Every time he passed too close to a tree and jogged its branches, more snow fell on him, causing another outburst.

It was not until they had passed round the town and were at the south that the trail began to turn away from the others. Rush was no fool, and he knew that if he was the fugitive he would try to confuse any pursuers. He might double back when it was not expected, or find a stream where he could travel without his prints being seen and where no hound could detect a scent, although it would be dangerous and painful to do that now with the waters frozen. What else could he do? Leave tracks and then make a trap?

These were the thoughts that kept forcing their way into his mind as he followed the prints slowly making their way south. 'Bailiff?'

At the call, Simon left his horse with the last man and wandered into the trees. 'Yes?'

Pointing, the hunter glowered at the ground. 'He's going south now. It's late. We can try to carry on after him if you want, but I reckon we'd be better off finding somewhere to lie up for the night and get on after him in the morning.'

Simon nodded. Already the sky was darkening, and it would soon be difficult to see the prints. They had seen a farm not long before, in a new assart to the east, so they made their way to it, and were soon sitting before a fire, eating their cured meats and drinking wine. The farmer had been concerned to have three well-armed men appear at first, and had nervously fingered his dagger, until Simon explained who they were, and then he had agreed with alacrity to allow them to use his hall. As he said, if there was a killer on the loose, he would be safer with them in his house.

The house possessed a large hall, with the animals segregated by a fence, and there was plenty of space even when the constable arrived with two men. He had sent the other members of his party to their homes when he had received the message about the spoor. There seemed little point in having so many men to chase one.

They had arrived within an hour of Simon's group finishing their meal, complaining bitterly at having to track not only the outlaw but also Simon's troop to the farmhouse, and sat in front of the fire until the snow melted and steam began

to rise from their clothes. The farmer bustled around enthusiastically, giving them pots of ale and cider from his buttery
and providing extra blankets for those who needed them. In
one corner was a table with a bench at either side, and here
the constable, the hunter and the bailiff sat.

Tanner chewed meditatively at a loaf as he eyed the other
two. 'So you're sure we're on the right trail?'

Mark Rush and Simon exchanged a quick glance. Then
the hunter nodded. 'Yes, I'm sure. We picked up the tracks
leading away from the lane by his house, like he was avoiding the roads. When it came to Crediton, like you saw, he
avoided the town and kept going.'

'It doesn't make much sense, though,' the constable mused.

'What doesn't?' asked Simon.

'Well, he's heading south like he's thought it all out and
decided to run away, but I didn't see any sign of a fire. Did
you?'

'No,' he admitted.

'So I suppose he must be trying to cover as much ground
as possible before resting. We've come at least twelve miles
or so already. He could have gone another seven or eight
before he needed to stop.'

'Yes,' the hunter agreed. 'He's all right. He can go at his
own pace. We have to make sure we can follow his tracks, so
we can only work with the sun.'

Nodding, Tanner glanced at the bailiff. 'Where do you
think he'll be going?'

'I've no idea. I can only assume he's heading for the coast,
but he's taking a great risk.'

'Yes. He's heading for the moors. If he keeps going, he'll
end up as feed for the crows.'

255

Mark Rush glanced up from his pot. 'Won't take long. Way he's going, he'll be dead before he gets to the moors themselves if he's not careful.'

'Why do you say that?' asked Simon.

'The way he's going. His walking's all stumbling and tripping, like he's drunk. I think he'll be lucky if he makes it to the moors. I don't know, but I think tomorrow we may find his body.'

Greencliff was not dead, though he was frozen to the bone. He was sitting in a small depression in the ground, a tiny natural shelter, with a little fire cheerfully throwing small shadows. But it was not enough to warm him. There was an absence of tinder, and he had been forced to make do with some green branches snapped from a tree which cast little heat. Now he sat shivering, gloomily considering a dismal future, huddled under his blanket.

There was no doubt in his mind. If he did not find somewhere warm where he could rest and eat hot food, he would freeze. His teeth chattered like a sour reminder of his predicament. There must be somewhere here for him to beg a warm place to sit. And a bowl of soup.

Here he was just inside the edge of a forest, although he was not sure where. At either side of the depression the trees marched away into the distance, while in front, to the south, the land was bare and barren: Dartmoor. He had never been this far south before – there had never been reason to come here – and the view of the rolling hills ahead was awesome. There was no definition to them. One hillock merged into another, the series of flattened peaks seeming almost to be one great, flat plain. But when he strained his eyes, he could see variations in the greyness. There was a long patch of darker ground sweeping across from his left, leading on to the horizon, there was a series of whiter areas on the hill tops where the moon lighted them. And between them he could just make out the shading that showed where valleys lay.

Sighing, he rubbed at his eyes with fingers that were swiftly losing all feeling. He was tired out, completely exhausted, as if his very soul was drained. It had taken the last tiny sparks of defiance to light the fire, because all he really wanted to do was lie down and sleep. It would be so good to shut his eyes and drift off for a time, to let the drowsiness steal over him and give him some peace, some real peace, such as he had not known since he put the witch's body in the hedge. If only he had immediately buried her. Why had he gone indoors to sleep and not hidden her away at once?

Just then he noticed a small star and, for some reason, his eyes were drawn to it. There was something wrong with it. Frowning and wincing, he stared, trying to focus, to see what was different about it. There were several other stars above it. They all seemed about the same size, so it was not that. What was it? There was certainly something strange about it. It looked like it was flickering, as if maybe a cloud was passing in front of it – but there were no clouds, or he would see them in the moonlight. He felt a quick, stabbing fear rise in his breast: fear of ghosts, of the demons of the moors that he had heard about. His breath caught in his throat as he thought of the stories about ghouls wandering, trying to capture men to take to hell. If Agatha had a pact with the devil, like they said at Wefford, then she would be capable of sending one for him.

Then the panic fell, as quickly as the blanket from his shoulders as he suddenly lurched to his feet, his face white in the dark as he stared, his breath catching in his throat.

It was a fire!

There was no choice to make. If he stayed still, even with his little fire, he would die. That much was obvious. The cold was too severe, the shelter too exposed and his clothes too damp from his sweat and from the occasional clumps of snow landing on him and melting. With a last, longing stare at the weak flames he recognised that they offered no safety and no chance of survival. The fire would be sure to go out if he slept. The twigs and branches he had managed to collect were too damp to stay lighted and would need constant attention. No, he had no choice.

Leaving the fire to die, he hefted his pack and stick and began to make his way towards the flickering light ahead. He could not tell how far away it was, but it looked as though it was something over a mile. It appeared to be quite high on a hill, which was why he had mistaken it at first for a star.

There was little wind, only a slight breeze, and he made good headway at first. The snow was not deep, and the ground beneath felt solid and fairly flat with few stones or holes. But then, after only a few hundred yards, it became more difficult.

It started when he tripped and fell headlong. Gasping with horror, he rose, his face and head smothered in the white, clinging powder. That was not the worst: under the surface apparently there was a stream, and his legs were soaked with freezing water. He must keep moving, to try to keep warm; to stay alive.

With a new resolution, he set off again at a faster pace, his forehead wrinkled with the concentration of his effort, straining with determination. He would not die – he must not!

The ground now was worse. It was broken, with granite stones liberally sprinkled under the white covering, which now itself became a serious obstacle, not only hampering his movements but hiding the stones beneath. He could hardly move more than a few yards without stumbling, and he was so tired he would inevitably fall.

At one point he felt that he would never reach the fire. After yet another tumble, as he lay sobbing in frustration, he lifted his head to find that the rising land before him hid the flames, as if its promise of warmth and rest had been snatched away as he approached.

Gasping with the effort, he slowly rose to his feet and began to carry on, the breath shuddering in his throat in a continual, weeping groan, his face turned towards the fire. All his energy was gone. His boots kept striking rocks, and his toes were bruised, creating a blunted, numbed ache of pain that managed to seep over even the dulled senses of his frost-bitten feet. His stick grew heavier with each step, and the energy used to lift it and place it down, lift it and place it down, sapped his failing resources, but he kept hold of it as if it was a talisman offering some support and strength of its own.

He breasted the hill and could see the fire again more clearly. Standing still for a moment, he savoured the sight as he caught his breath. It lay under an overhanging rock, at the entrance, apparently, of a cave, and the cheerful flames beckoned to him, promising peace. His breath caught in his throat, and he was not sure whether to laugh or sob. Letting his breath out in a great sighing gasp, he started off again, down the slight incline to the bottom, then up the other side to the fire, to safety and warmth.

It was when he was almost at the upward slope that he heard the howling. The voices of wolves calling to each other – and realised that *he* was their quarry.

'I think you'd better get up here a little faster,' came a contemplative voice from above. 'They sound a bit hungry!'

The rest of the way was a mad scramble up the hillside. He dropped his staff, his satchel fell from his shoulder, pulling his blanket with it, and it may have been this that saved him.

As he reached the top of the slope he slipped and fell, slithering face-first into a depression ringed by rocks. Behind him he heard a sudden snarling and snapping, and when he managed to rise, staring with terror, he saw four wolves tearing and ripping at his package and attacking his blanket. They had attacked his belongings rather than following and attacking him immediately.

Suddenly his legs gave way and he fell to his knees in petrified horror at the thought that the animals could have been on *him*, their teeth at his throat, their hot breath in his nostrils as they tore at him, savaging him like the bag they had just ripped apart. He gave a small cry, and was faintly surprised by how high and childish it sounded. Then he saw them turn.

'Ah, they'll be coming here now.' The Bourc spoke calmly. After years of hunting wolves in Gascony, he knew how to defend himself, and now he watched carefully – he was prepared for them. Before him was a handful of arrows, their points in the ground, standing like a makeshift fence. When he gave Greencliff a quick, appraising glance, the farmer saw his dark eyes glittering in the shadow under his hood as the firelight caught them.

The Bourc gave him a nod, then pointed to the fire with his chin. 'You get back. Warm yourself. Don't think you'll be any help right now.' He turned back to the scene below, pulling an arrow from the ground and nocking it on his bowstring, his hands moving with the assurance of long practice.

Greencliff felt his head move in slow acceptance, and he began to walk, stumbling in his tiredness and chill. His limbs felt leaden, his head heavy, and he moved as if in a dream, his feet moving automatically like ponderous weights in a great machine. But as he got to the fire he heard a roar, and spinning round, saw a huge animal streak forward. The bowman seemed to stand still, the wolf running straight for him, and then there was a thrumming sound and the wolf fell, an arrow in his head.

Even as he seated a fresh arrow on the bow and drew it back, two more of the evil-looking animals appeared, but they were undecided, slinking from side to side at the edge of the camp like cavalry trying to see a weakness in a line of foot-soldiers, while the Bourc's arrow-tip followed them.

With a snarl as if to boost flagging spirits, both streaked forward, and the Bourc hesitated a moment, as if unsure which to attack. Then, quickly drawing the bowstring again, he let his arrow fly at the leading animal, but perhaps in his haste, perhaps because of the darkness, his shot missed its mark.

To Greencliff's horror, the wolves rushed on, and one of them launched itself at his saviour's throat. To his astonishment, he saw the man fall back, one arm held up to protect his neck, and the wolf caught his arm in its mouth, his leap carrying the man backwards. But almost as soon as the man had dropped, he rolled, then sprang back to his feet. The farmer's shocked eyes shot to the figure of the wolf, which lay shuddering as it died, and when he looked back at the Bourc, he saw the short sword in his hands, now flashing and glinting as it dripped red in the firelight.

The last wolf had followed almost on the heels of the first, but had held back when it had sprung, and now hesitated, circling the man warily. Its eyes flitted from the Bourc to Greencliff with uncertainty, and while it paused the Bourc dropped his sword, snatched up his bow, nocked an arrow to the string and fired in one smooth action. This time he made sure of his target. The wolf dropped as if felled by a pike.

When he had stood for a minute or two, the Bourc slowly lowered his bow and sighed. Holding a fresh arrow in place, he cautiously walked to each of the figures, kicked them briefly, then strode to the perimeter of the camp and peered into the darkness. Seemingly the view satisfied him, and he sauntered back to the bodies with a low but cheerful whistle. Dropping the bow, he collected his sword and went from one body to the next, slitting the animals' throats.

Looking up, he gave a quick grin. 'Always best to make sure with these evil buggers!' he said contentedly. The last thing Greencliff saw as he slowly toppled sideways was his grin slowly fading in perplexed surprise. The farmer's exhaustion had won at last.

Simon and the troop were mounted and ready early the next morning just after light. He felt stiff and had a kink in his back from sleeping on a bench, but it was, as he knew, a great deal better than how he would have felt if they had tried to sleep out in the open.

They were soon back at the trail and Mark Rush began his careful perusal of the prints once more. He was convinced that today they would find a corpse at the end of the trail. It was easy to see why.

The steps were almost like a pair of long lines with deeper indentations where the boots had dropped. Between the footprints were scraping drag marks where the man had been too tired to lift his feet. Simon had no doubt that Mark Rush was right. The boy had little chance of surviving.

When they had been riding for an hour, they came across the flat area where the boy had lain. After this the steps changed direction, seeming to stagger and falter into the trees, and they found the byre. Dropping from their horses, Tanner and Mark Rush slowly drew their swords and walked in, half expecting to find Greencliff's body. While they searched, Simon glanced around at the snow nearby, then gave a cry.

'There're more prints!'

Mark Rush came out, his face expressionless, and followed the bailiff's pointing finger. To Simon he seemed to doubt what he saw. He stood staring down, his head shaking in disbelief, then he sighed and walked back, putting his sword away as he walked. 'He lived to rest, then. He must have made it to the moors.'

The weather was not so cold this morning, and a dampness had set in. The trees overhead occasionally dropped great clods of ice and snow, occasionally hitting one of the men. Riding along, the men were all warm enough. Even at a slow trotting pace, the exercise kept them glowing with an internal warmth, and Simon was grateful for the slight breeze.

They found that the tracks kept them going almost straight south-west, so Simon knew that they were going towards the moors. It would not be long before they were out of the trees and on the moors themselves. There they would be certain to find the boy.

Margaret had passed an uncomfortable night, and she rose late to find that Baldwin had already left the house. She spent an idle morning wondering what Simon was doing and where he was. She had not been overly concerned when they had not arrived on the first evening, and she was quite sure that he would be safe, but still felt an occasional twinge of concern.

She picked up her tapestry and managed almost half an hour of work before she tossed it aside impatiently, startling the old woman's dog. 'Sorry, it's not your fault,' she said apologetically, holding out her hand and snapping her fingers, but the dog stared at her with unblinking accusation before meaningfully standing, stretching, then lying down once more near the fire, this time with his back to her. She grinned at the obvious rejection, then rose and walked out to the front of the house.

Here she found Edgar supervising other servants splitting logs for the fires. He looked up and gave her a welcoming smile as she emerged into the sunlight, blinking at the sudden glare.

'Morning, Edgar,' she said, peering at the horizon with a hand shielding her eyes.

'Hello, my lady.'

'Has Baldwin gone far?'

He shot her a quick glance, then she was sure she caught a glimpse of a grin as he turned back to the men at the logs. 'I'm sure he won't be too long, madam.'

This was puzzling. She had never seen any sign of the humour from the normally taciturn servant, and she suddenly wanted to know where the knight had gone. 'Walk with me a while, Edgar. I'm very bored.'

Looking up, he considered, but then he nodded and, after issuing instructions to the men, walked to her. 'Where do you want to go?'

'Oh, just down the lane.'

They set off in companionable silence, but once they were out of earshot, she gave him a quick look. 'So where has he gone?'

His expression was wooden. 'Just into Wefford, I think.'

'Why? And why was he in such an odd mood last night when you returned?'

'Odd mood, madam?' He turned guileless eyes on her.

'You know he was. He would hardly talk to me. Every time he opened his mouth he got embarrassed. I thought he must have done something foolish.'

He smiled and she suddenly stopped in amazement as a flash of intuition suddenly blazed and she caught her breath. The knight's embarrassment, his apparent shyness, his servant's amusement, all pointed to one thing in her mind.

'It's not a woman! He hasn't found a woman!'

'Madam, I didn't tell you that!' said the servant earnestly, but still with the smile transforming his features.

'But *who*?' She gasped with delight – and a little surprise.

'Ah,' he turned to the view with a slight frown. 'Mrs Trevellyn.'

'So you think he's gone to see her?' she asked doubtfully, and he spun to face her with horror on his face.

'No, madam, no. He wouldn't do that. Not when she's only just lost her husband. No. I think he's gone out to decide whether he ought to even think about a wife.'

The servant was right. Baldwin was riding slowly, his peregrine on his wrist, but his mind several miles away.

'After all,' he thought, 'there are conventions. The poor woman has just lost her husband. She might not want to even think about another man until her mourning period is over.'

He sighed. That was not the point, and he knew it. She was so desirable, especially now when she appeared so vulnerable. Her expression on hearing of the manhunt had made him want to hold her and comfort her, she had looked so scared. Clearly she feared for herself while her husband's killer was free, in case he might return.

For her to have heard the cruel gossip about her and a local farmer must have been painfully wounding, and to have then lost her husband seemed a vicious turn of fate. But if nothing else, Baldwin was at least now sure that she was innocent of adultery. A wanton could surely never have shown such emotion. And if the malicious rumours were untrue, she would make a wonderful wife for a knight.

It was so attractive the way that she licked her lips after sipping at a drink. So provocative, somehow.

'This is ridiculous!' he muttered viciously and glared balefully at the bird on his wrist. 'Why should I even think that she'd . . . It's not as if I have huge wealth or titles . . .'

He broke off as his mind mischieviously brought a picture of her to him. Of her sitting at the fireplace in the warm and comfortable solar, the long black hair falling down her back, her eyes so green and bright, staring him full in the face with her red lips parted a little, as if she was close to panting, and he smiled fondly again.

CHAPTER NINETEEN

'So, you're awake now, are you?'

'Ah.' No words could convey the same anguish and pain as the simple, soft and quiet groan that broke from Harold Greencliff's lips as he tried to sit up. Moaning gently, he rolled on to his side and peered through slitted eyes at the man who stood looking down at him with grave concern. When he opened his mouth, it felt as if there was a week of dried saliva encrusted around his lips, and he winced as his skin cracked.

'Keep quiet, friend. Sit back. You can't go anywhere.'

As his eyes began to focus, Greencliff stared at him. He was dressed in thick and warm-looking woollen clothes, his tunic woven of heavy cloth and his cloak lined with fur. He must be a wealthy man.

His face was arresting. Swarthy and weather-beaten, square and wrinkled, it seemed as rugged as the rocks around them. Two gleaming black eyes gazed back at the farmer with interest under a thick mop of deep brown hair. Although there were lines of laughter at the eyes, now they contained only concern, and Greencliff realised what a sorry figure he must appear. Then, as the memories returned, he felt a sob rack his body in a quick shudder of self-pity.

'Calm yourself. Drink this.'

The liquid was almost scalding hot, but he thought he had never tasted anything so wonderful. It was a warmed wine fit for the king himself, Greencliff thought. Though he sipped carefully, it still seared the flesh around his mouth and burned a trail down his throat, seeming to form a solid, scalding lump in his stomach. Meanwhile his host crouched and watched.

After a few moments, Greencliff took stock of his surroundings. He was in a cave of some sort. Outside, through a small doorway, he could see the fire, whose heat wafted in with the smell of burning wood. He was lying on a straw palliasse with his blanket over him, and his new friend had clearly let him sleep on his own bed because a roll and blanket on the floor showed where he had slept.

'Do you feel well enough to eat?' At the question, the farmer felt his stomach wake to turbulent life as if it had been hibernating until then, and a low rumbling started to shake his weakened frame. The man gave a short laugh. 'Good. I'll have some stew ready in a little while. I have bread too, so don't worry about losing your own food.'

An hour later he felt well enough to rise from the mattress and walk outside to where the man crouched by the fire, meditatively breaking twigs and branches to feed the flames. He looked up as Greencliff came out, bent double to save himself from hitting his head at the low entrance.

'How're you feeling now?' the Bourc asked.

Wincing, Greencliff sat warily on a rock near the fire. 'A lot better. I'm very grateful, if you hadn't helped me, I'd be dead.'

'One day, I might need help, and I hope that I will be protected as I protected you.'

'Who are you?'

'I'm called John, the Bourc de Beaumont.'

'You are not from here?' It was an innocent question, and the farmer was surprised by the laugh it brought.

'No! No, I come from far away, from Gascony. I would not live *here* from choice!'

Greencliff nodded, morosely staring at the moors all round, 'I can understand that!' he said. 'So, why are you here?'

Grimacing, the Bourc explained about his decision to cross the moors. 'The wolves chased me here, and I was attacked by one – night before last, that was. I killed it, but I got little sleep, so I chose to stay here for another day. Anyway, I thought it was easier to defend myself here. If they catch you on horseback, they'll chase you 'til your horse drops.'

'Why were they trying to attack you? Are they just evil?' asked the farmer, shivering at the memory of the slavering mouths tearing at his belongings.

'No, not really. It is just the way they are. They saw me – and you – as a meal, that's all. There is not enough food for them right now. They thought we'd be easy enough to catch.' He almost shuddered at the memory. The way that the beast had leaped at him had terrified him. In his mind's eye he could still see the jaws opening and smell the foul breath. In that moment he had been sure he was about to die.

The fear had almost caused his death. It slowed his reactions, so that the huge creature had almost succeeded in tearing his neck with its wickedly curved fangs, just missing and slashing his shoulder. The pain had woken him to his danger, and turning quickly, he had stabbed deep, again and again, in a fit of mad panic.

Afterwards he had built the fire and waited, nursing his shoulder, but they had chosen not to attack again. The next day they were still there, and he had kept an eye on them as he sat and kept warm.

He glanced up shrewdly. 'So why are you here? Who or what are you running from?'

'Me?' His start of surprise seemed to strike the Gascon as comical.

'Yes: you! Nobody who knows this place would come here to the moors in the snow unless they had a good reason. Especially at night. It's a good way to make sure of death, but nothing else. Who are you running from?'

'I . . .' He paused. There was no reason to doubt his grim-faced saviour, but the truth was, he had no wish to admit to his guilt. Opening his mouth to speak, he found the breath catching in his throat again, and he had to keep silent. The sob was too close. He gave a small cough, an involuntary spasm that could have been from misery or joy, and covered his face in his hands.

'You've been through pain, I can see that,' said the Bourc matter-of-factly, finishing his wine. With his eyes on his guest, his mind ran through the items he had found from the satchel. A little food the wolves had left, a flint and a knife. A long-bladed ballock knife: a single-edged blade with two globular lumps where the wooden grip met it, held in a leather sheath. When he had found it, he had been going to return it, but then he had wondered. If this boy was an outlaw, if he was escaping from justice of some sort, it might be better to keep his knife back for now. 'Of course,' he thought, 'if he wants to tell me what made him leave, I can give it back. But not yet. Not quite yet.'

It wasn't just the distrust of a man for a stranger in these difficult times. It was also the thick clots he had found on the blade, the dried brown mess of blood.

'Wait here!' Mark Rush ordered as he dropped from his horse. He wandered slowly and carefully round the little dip in the ground, following the line of staggering foot-prints. 'Yes, he was here. He walked up here, tripped and fell. There's the mark where he lay. Looks like he got up and then began to make a fire. Not much of one, though.' Kneeling, he sniffed contemplatively at the blackened twigs. 'Not enough to keep him warm for more than a minute. He sat here.'

Rising, he stood and stared at the ground for a minute, hands on hips as he considered. Glancing up at the bailiff's face, he shrugged. 'Didn't wait long, from the look of it. Seems like he made his fire, sat by it for a bit – not for long – and went on.'

'Fine. Let's get on after him, then.'

Tanner ambled forward. 'One minute, bailiff. Mark? How was he when he left here?'

The hunter pulled his mouth into a down-curving crescent of dubious pessimism. 'Put it like this: I wouldn't gamble on his chances. I'd rather put my money on a legless, wingless cock in a fighting ring.'

Nodding, Tanner glanced back at the men behind, then at the bailiff. 'Sir, we may as well send the others back. The three of us are enough to catch him, even if he's well. The way things are, all we'll need is a horse to bring his body home.' When Simon nodded, Tanner turned to the men, telling them to return, the bailiff instructing one to ensure that a message went to the inn, to be passed on to Simon's wife, to say that they were well. Not that it mattered much, as Tanner knew. There was little hope that they could find the boy alive now. They should be able to return home before long.

As they set off again, leaving at last the line of trees and beginning to make their way on to the moors, he found himself reflecting sadly on the last Greencliff. Tanner had known him since he was a boy.

Good-looking since he was a child, he had always been able to win apples from the women in the village while young. As he had grown, he had kept his innocent charm, and then he had taken other gifts – or so it was rumoured. Why, even Sarah Cottey was supposed to have carried on with him recently, and she was only the last in a long series. The boy was lucky to have lived so long without getting a thrashing from an enraged father or brother!

Murder was a long way from enjoying a woman's embrace, though, he mused. Just because a man was popular with the local girls did not make him a killer. It was different, as the constable knew, with soldiers. He had witnessed enough rapings and people having their lives taken quickly or slowly to know the difference between the brutal and the gentle taking of a woman. Harold had only ever been kind with his women, which was why none had ever denounced him to their families. All still liked him. Even Sarah Cottey – she was infatuated with him.

But love was possessive, and perhaps that was why the boy had found the courage to kill, stabbing Trevellyn in a jealous fit so that he could have the woman he wanted. If so, that did not answer why the youth should have killed the witch, though. The reason behind *that* was still a mystery. Tanner dawdled behind the others as the thoughts drifted through his mind, making him scowl darkly as he stared with unseeing eyes at the ground.

At a sudden gasp from the hunter in front, he kicked his horse and rode forward to where Simon and Mark Rush stood pensively gazing down at a mess of confused prints.

'Looks like he walked to here, then fell,' said the hunter. He peered up the shallow slope to a small group of tors huddled together as if for warmth on the top of the hill. 'Wolves were about, but he managed to get up there.'

'Let's see if he's still there, then,' said the bailiff, and they began to make their way up the slight incline.

Tanner stayed at the back again at first, but then he shrugged and put the thoughts from his mind. If he was alive, they would be sure to find out as soon as they caught him. There was no point in speculating.

'Morning, gentlemen.'

The call made them all stop and cautiously glare at the rocks before them. Then Simon tentatively rode forward a couple of yards, 'Is that *you*, Greencliff?'

'No.' There was a dry chuckle. Then there was a movement above them, and they saw what had appeared to be a boulder detach itself from the tor and spring lightly to the ground before them.

For a moment they contemplated him in silence, then Simon rode forward a pace or two. The man held himself alert and had the look of a fighting man, but did not look as though he was dangerous. Merely wary at the sight of three strangers out here in the wild.

Glancing to his side, Simon saw that Rush had come up alongside.

'I know this man,' the hunter muttered, 'I saw him trotting away from Wefford the day the witch was killed.'

Simon nodded, then looked back to the Gascon. 'Good morning, friend. I am a bailiff. We are hunting an outlaw, a man who is running from justice. His feet led us here – have you seen him?' He gave a brief description.

'He is not here now,' said the Bourc.

'What do you mean? Have you seen him?' Simon asked eagerly.

The Bourc put his head to one side thoughtfully as he peered up at the bailiff. 'I have, but he did not seem to be an outlaw. I gave him a place to sleep last night. He was here with me, but he left some time ago. Come to my camp, I will show you the path he took and you can warm yourselves by my fire for a while,' he said quietly, and, turning, led the way to the ring of old stones that stood at the summit, just under the tor.

To Simon it looked like an enclosure. It was about fifteen paces across and roughly circular, lined with boulders of the local grey granite, with here and there a patch of orange or brown lichen peeping out from under a thatch of snow. At one side was a pile of the Gascon's tools and belongings, with, beside them, his pony and a small packhorse. To the right, beyond a fire of fresh kindling, was a low gap in the rocks of the tor. Near the fire were the carcasses of two wolves, freshly skinned, the flesh clean and glistening with silver where the membranes held the muscles. The pelts were stretched on wooden frames nearby. Simon walked to them and kicked one corpse thoughtfully while their host strode to the fire and crouched contemplatively in front of it.

'So he was here. Where did he go?' he asked.

Looking up, he saw the Bourc grin. 'Oh, yes. He was here.' With a jerk of his chin, he pointed towards the middle of the moors. 'He left about an hour ago, just as you all appeared through the trees. Made an excuse and ran for it. He won't have gone far.'

'Right!' Mark Rush tugged his horse's reins, pulling it over to the far side of the enclosure, Tanner following, while Simon stood and looked out in the direction John had shown. There, clear against the white background, were the footsteps. Now they were more purposeful, each step defined as an individual print without the dragging lines where the feet seemed too heavy to lift above the crust of snow. As he looked, he became aware of the man at his side.

'What are you after him for?'

'Murder. He's killed two people.'

'Really?' The note of sadness made Simon turn to him with an eyebrow raised. 'I'm sorry, Bailiff. It just seems so unlikely, he is a pleasant enough lad.'

'It seems he's killed a man and a woman. Both over the last week.'

There was a brief pause, then the black eyes met Simon's in a frown. 'How did he kill them?'

'He cut their throats.'

The Bourc sighed, then told him of the blood-stained ballock dagger. When he had finished, the bailiff stared after the men on their horses, now riding slowly away after the fugitive. 'That more or less proves it, doesn't it?' he said musingly.

These were the steps of a rested man. His prints showed deep at the toe, light at the heel, and Tanner saw that the boy had been running. He sighed. It was sad to think of the youth, only just an adult, bolting in fear of his life, trying to escape his death.

Because that was what the outcome would be if he was found guilty of the murders, and the boy must know that. There was only one penalty to avenge the murder of a man or woman: hanging.

There was a small gasp of excitement at his side, and when he looked over, Mark Rush's eyes were fixed on the horizon. Following his gaze, Tanner saw a tiny figure in the distance, a slender, stick-like shape, seeming to pelt across the snow.

'Come on!' cried the hunter, and both whipped their mounts.

Tanner stuck rigidly to the footprints. It was possible that the boy had thought of taking any pursuers over rough or broken ground to try to throw them off. If he had led them towards a mire, they could get stuck. The constable kept his eyes down, but saw no sign of any obstacles. Jolting and lurching, they rode up one slope, then down the other side. Now they could see him, some distance off, making for a copse in a valley. 'Bugger!' he thought. 'Must stop him before that, it'll take hours to find him if he reaches it.' But he need not have feared.

As they pelted forward, he saw the shape take a tumble, tripping and falling, rolling, to lie for a moment as if winded. Then he got up again, and set off once more, but this time he was slower, and looked as though he was limping. His speed was gone, and the two men chasing felt confident enough to slow to an easy canter, taking the pursuit more carefully to protect their horses.

They rode up in front, swinging round in a curve, to come to a halt facing him, sitting on their horses between him and the protection of the trees. As he sat and watched the wretched figure of the man staggering towards them, Tanner felt the sadness again. It looked as if he had been ruined. His hair was matted and slicked down over his head, damp from falling in the snow. His tunic and jacket were covered in white as well, making him look like a weird monster of the winter. But his eyes were full of his grief. Even from a distance Tanner could see that.

'We hunted *that*?' He heard the hunter say in wonder, as if he too was feeling compassion for a destroyed life. The constable nodded and let out his breath in a long drifting feather on the frozen air.

A few yards from them, Greencliff stopped and stood surveying them with a frowning face that seemed close to breaking into tears. When they both kicked their horses forward, he took a half-pace back, then twitched the front of his tunic aside, and pulled his dagger out. 'Leave me alone!'

'Come on, Harold. You can't stab *me*.' Tanner felt that the words sounded ridiculous even as he said them.

'I can't go back. I *won't*! There's nothing for me. Just let me go. Please . . .' His eyes filled with tears. 'Just let me go.'

'You know we can't do that, Harold. We have to take you back.'

'Why? Sir Baldwin doesn't need me . . .'

'Bugger Sir Baldwin,' said Mark Rush from Tanner's side. 'We can't let you go after you murdered Alan Trevellyn. What's it to be? Alive or dead?' As he spoke he pulled his bow over his head and checked the string.

'Alan Trevellyn?' Tanner was sure that he saw absolute horror in the boy's eyes. 'Dead?'

The bow was ready. Mark Rush took his time over selecting an arrow, then tugged one free and fitted it. 'I suppose you wanted to just scare him? That's why you cut his throat, like you did with the old witch too. Never mind. You can apologise to them both when you get to hell.'

Tanner watched as the boy gaped, but then, as if with a sudden resolution, he pulled his dagger's sheath free and put the blade away, tossing it towards the men. 'You can put up your bow. I surrender to you. Yes, I killed them both.' The words were said calmly, but with what looked to Tanner like a kind of tired but firm defiance. He stood patiently while the constable swung from his horse and strolled over to the prisoner, tied his hands with a thong, then picked up his dagger and pointed back the way they had come.

'Come on, Harold. Let's get back.'

Simon watched the slow approach of the three men, two on horseback, one staggering slightly on foot, with a feeling of relief. At least there was no one else hurt. Greencliff had not managed to stab one of the men when they captured him.

He heard the crunch of snow as the Bourc strolled over to stand beside him. At the sound of a sigh, Simon turned with surprise. It seemed out of place for the man. From what he had seen of the stranger, he had appeared to be strong and self-sufficient, not the sort to express sympathy for a murderer and outlaw.

Catching the bailiff's eye, the Bourc shrugged, ashamed. 'I know. He's a killer. But he's a likeable sort of lad. I wouldn't have thought he was capable of murder. He seems too quiet. And he seems more sad than cruel.'

'But you said you found blood on his dagger!'

'So I did. So I did. Could it have been in defence?'

Simon paused and considered. 'Defence? No, I don't think so. Both murders were from behind, both of them had their throats cut. I don't think they could have been killed except by a man who wanted to murder them. I can't see it was defence. In any case, what defence would he need from an old woman?'

'Old woman?'

'Yes, he killed an old woman in Wefford.'

Simon became aware of a sudden tenseness as the man leaned forward and said, 'What was this woman's name, Bailiff?'

'Her name?' The three men were almost with them now, the lone walker struggling in the deeper snow that lay beneath the hillside, moving slowly and swinging his arms as if trying to maintain his balance. 'She was called Agatha Kyteler.'

There was a sudden intake of breath from the man, and Simon turned to see that his eyes were filled with horror as he stared at the figure labouring towards them. 'Agatha? You killed Agatha Kyteler?'

The bailiff gasped. 'Of course! You must be the Bourc de Beaumont!'

'Yes, I am, but how . . .?'

'I am friend to Sir Baldwin. He mentioned you had been staying with him. He would like to see you again, I am sure. Would you ride back with us?'

The Bourc stared past the bailiff towards the centre of the moors, and when he glanced back, he smiled ruefully. 'My friend, I think it would be a very good idea for me to return with you, and when I next leave for the coast, I think I shall take the roadways like others do, and avoid my own short cuts! Ah! Here they are.'

Turning back, Simon saw the men entering the ring of stones.

Now he could see the youth close to again, Simon felt that he was unwell. He had the feverish red and apparently sweating face of a convalescent. Was it that or was it just his guilt? Was it illness from his nights out in the cold or a deeper sickness at the knowledge of what he had done, of what his price must be now he was captured? His hands looked blue, as though the blood was cut off, and the bailiff made a note to get the thong tying him loosened.

His eyes were bright and steady, not ashamed or worried. They almost looked relaxed, as if he had tested himself and found himself to be stronger than he had expected. Although he appeared dirty and unkempt, he still stood tall – a bit like Baldwin, Simon thought. Proud and arrogant in his confidence.

The boy stood staring at him for a moment, then peered over his shoulder. Throwing a quick glance behind him, Simon saw that the Bourc was crouching by the fire and feeding it with fresh branches. The bailiff saw that the boy was struggling to control a shiver, and wordlessly led the way to the heat, Greencliff squatting and holding his bound hands to the flames with a small grunt of pain. After a moment Simon pulled his dagger free and, reaching over, sliced through the thong. The boy gave him a nod of gratitude before returning his gaze to the fire.

Tanner hobbled his horse before walking to the three by the fire. He stood and watched his prisoner for a moment, then pulled the ballock knife from his belt and tossed it to the ground beside the bailiff.

Looking up, Simon saw his serious – sad? – gaze and picked it up. Pulling the blade from the sheath, he saw the stains and picked at them with his fingernail. There was no way to tell for certain, but it looked a dirty brown, like dried blood.

'Whose blood is this, Harold?' he asked.

The light eyes glanced at him, then down at the knife for a moment with apparent disinterest before he shrugged and faced the flames. 'Trevellyn's, probably.'

'He admitted the murders,' said Tanner, and dropped down beside the bailiff.

'Why did you do it, Harold? Why kill them?' Simon said, frowning at the gasp from the Bourc.

The boy did not even bother to turn to face them. 'I wanted to get away. I wanted money. They refused to give me any.'

'But you must have known that Agatha Kyteler had nothing! I suppose Alan Trevellyn was wealthy, but she had nothing! Why kill her?'

But they could get nothing more from him. He ignored their questions, sitting silently, his face set, with his hands to the fire, and his shoulders hunched as if they could act as a barrier to their questions.

CHAPTER TWENTY

It was nearly dark when Jennie Miller walked into the inn and sat at a bench near the door with her pot of cider. It was too early for most of the people to have arrived, but there were already some men standing and talking in hushed voices. She knew why. Her husband had been told earlier that some of the men had returned from the hunt. They had found where Harold Greencliff was. He would be brought back soon.

In a small village like Wefford, this was news of the first order. Unused to the excitements normal in more populous or busier places, where the number of travellers passing through led to their own difficulties, Wefford had experienced its first taste of real crime in decades, and found that it had a sour flavour.

But where there were problems, there were also compensations, and this affair was no different. After all, nobody would miss old Agatha too much. She had scared too many people after the rumours put about by that old hag Oatway. Her death had caused more interest than anything she had done while living.

When the curtain opened to show a slightly nervous, scowling and dark-haired man, she looked up with interest. The face was familiar, but she could not remember where she had seen him. Thin featured, with weather-beaten skin and thick dark hair that straggled at the sides. Appearing shy, he hung back at the screens as if nervous of crossing the floor. Not tall, he looked quite thickset, but quick and lithe, a bit like her husband's horse. Where had she seen him before? Surely he had been *on* a horse? It was then that she recognised him – it was the bailiff's servant . . . What was his name? The one who had waited outside with the horses when the knight and bailiff arrived to ask her about the day that Agatha died.

Shifting quickly on her bench, she smiled at him, and saw a minimal relaxing of his glower. Patting the bench seat beside her, she beckoned to him, then waved at the innkeeper.

'What would you like to drink?' she asked innocently, and he asked for a strong ale, sitting ungraciously beside her.

'Aren't you the man that came to see me with Sir Baldwin Furnshill and the bailiff the other day?' she said when his beer had arrived and he had taken a deep draught.

He nodded, wiping his mouth with the back of his hand, and now his face had lost some of its black dejection. The flavour of the beer restored some, if not all, of his equanimity.

Hugh was annoyed. So far today he had been told to help two serving women (either old enough to be his mother) with moving barrels in the buttery, then Margaret had asked him to help an hostler in the stables area, and finally, he had been instructed by a haughty man-servant that Hugh had been assigned to *him* to help with the mews, the sheds behind the stables where the falcons were left to mew, or moult.

When he had gone to Margaret to demand some sympathy, she had been short with him. Of course he understood that she was upset at the continuing absence of her husband, but that was no reason to take things out on him. On seeing him, she had made it very clear that he was expected to help wherever he was needed while they stayed under Baldwin's roof, and that meant doing whatever the servants felt was useful. After being peremptorily ordered to go out and help with the mews, he had obeyed, but had then made sure that he could not be seen afterwards, and had quickly saddled his horse to come into the village for an evening of peace before he could be asked to do anything else.

Now, as he sat and glared moodily at his pot, he was struck with a sense of the unfairness of it all. After all, he was the servant of a bailiff. He should not have to mess about helping hostlers – the knight should have enough men to look after his horses and those of his guests!

Looking at him, Jennie could see that he was feeling gloomy, and quickly ordered him another pot of ale. After all, if the bailiff's man knew nothing, especially when he had been living with the knight, the Keeper of the King's Peace, then no one could know anything.

'I hear they're bringing back young Greencliff,' she said tentatively, as if musing. 'Shame that. He's such a nice lad, too.'

'Yes. They should be back later, or first thing tomorrow.'

'Your master? He's with them?'

'He's *leading* them,' said Hugh tetchily, then resumed his gloomy stare at his pot. 'They all seem to think Greencliff must be dead, though. He was out in all that snow, so it's unlikely he'll survive.'

'Oh.' She was quiet for a minute, then said, 'What about *her*? That French wife of Trevellyn?'

Hugh stared at her uncomprehendingly, wondering what she was talking about. 'Eh? What, the widow? What about her?'

'Didn't you know? She was having an affair with Greencliff. That's why he was with her horse when she went to see the witch. He was helping his lover, looking after the horse of the woman he was having an affair with. I think *she* killed old Agatha while he held her horse!'

When the little group rode into town the following morning, Simon was pleased to see Baldwin, Edgar and Hugh standing outside the inn opposite the gaol. Saying, 'You see to him, Tanner,' he dismounted and led his horse to the group of men standing on the patch of brushed earth, which showed red where the snow had been swept away.

'So, Bailiff. You were successful,' the knight said smiling, nodding towards the man being led into the little gaol, then, with surprise, he said, 'John! I thought you left for Gascony days ago.'

He was about to question them about the hunt and where they had met, when he noticed the pinched look on Simon's face and called out for the innkeeper. Soon, mulled wine was brought, the steam rising steadily from the liquid, and the smell from the sweetened mixture with its strong spices made the bailiff's mouth water. Taking a mug gratefully, he cupped it in his hands and blew on the surface to cool it a little, then took a sip of the scalding drink as the Bourc accepted another pot from the innkeeper.

'And, surprisingly enough, he's alive, too!' Simon said, voicing the knight's thoughts as he stared after the figures entering the gaol. 'Yes, and it feels like I nearly died of the cold myself on the way.'

Mark Rush soon joined them, and they walked indoors out of the cold.

After his initial pleasure at seeing the men returning, Simon saw that Baldwin had sunk into a pensive reverie. The Keeper of the Peace was wondering whether he would shortly see the boy, his villein, hanged in the market square for the murders. It was surely not pleasant, Simon thought, to have to see the last remaining member of an old family on the estate coming to this kind of ignominious end. Far better that the boy had died on the moors or in the woods. To an extent, perhaps, it would have been better for all concerned if Greencliff had put up a defence and had died with an arrow in his head. At least that way there would have been an end to the matter. Now there would have to be a trial, with the lad perhaps attempting to defend himself – though how he could try to was beyond Simon's imagination. The evidence all pointed to him.

As the knight called for more drinks, an eyebrow delicately rising at the speed with which the men finished off their first pots, Simon leaned forward on his elbows and jerked his head towards the Gascon. 'Your friend knows a little more about the day Trevellyn died, and the day Agatha Kyteler was killed.'

'Really?' said Baldwin, glancing across the Bourc, who looked up inquiringly. 'John? Simon says you can help us with the death of your old nurse and the merchant. Is that right?'

Before the Gascon could answer, Simon fixed him with a gleaming eye. 'Be very careful how you respond, John. Your father's friend thought you might be the killer.'

The Bourc stared at him, then at the sheepish knight. 'You thought *I* did it?'

Shifting uneasily, Baldwin grimaced. 'It did seem odd that you were with the old woman when . . .'

Laughing, Simon enjoyed the sight of his friend's embarrassment. 'Don't worry, Baldwin. Anyway, he has an alibi, even if we didn't already have Greencliff. Rush saw the Bourc on the road at dusk that day, far south of Wefford.'

'So what do you know of these killings, John?' the knight asked.

'I saw them both before they died.'

'Both?'

'Yes. When I left you on Tuesday morning, I went to see Agatha, as I said. I told you about the escape from Acre, but not the last detail. Agatha told me that herself. My mother wanted to save me, so she went to the boats to ask for a passage. You know more about it than I do, of course, but apparently it was mayhem. Boats everywhere, and all of the sailors demanding huge fees to save people. My mother carried me along the harbour, pleading for passage, but no one would help. Then she thought she had found one. Trevellyn's ship.

'The master was happy to take her, he said. Pleased to, he said. But then he named his fee. Not money, not her jewels, just her. He wanted *her*!' He sipped his drink sullenly, but then grinned lopsidedly. 'My mother apparently refused his kind offer, and asked that he accept a more sensible fee, but he insisted, and she came away empty-handed. Anne of Tyre, my mother, was of an important family, and I suppose she could not comprehend how low things had sunk by then. Anyway, she gave me to my nurse, and pleaded with her to take me to my father's house. That was Agatha.

'To shorten the story, she managed to get on board, and refused to leave. She had all that remained of my mother's wealth, and that was the cost of her passage. You have seen the man Trevellyn's house? I would guess many of the stones of his walls were purchased by my mother's jewels. A sobering thought, eh?'

'What became of your mother?' asked Simon.

'She died, I hope,' said the Bourc shortly, and Baldwin gave the bailiff a quick glare to stop him asking more. Time enough later, the knight thought, to explain about the horrors of capture by the besiegers of Acre, about the multiple rapes, the slow and painful murders – or, worse, the lifetime of slavery, owned by a fat merchant or prince. Far better, as the Bourc said, for the poor woman to have died quickly. Perhaps she was in the Temple when it collapsed, mercifully crushing all those who could not escape together with the remainder of their protectors, the last of the Templar Knights in the Holy Land. They were all buried together, in the one massive tomb.

'And you said that the ring you wore was the token of your position?' asked Baldwin.

'The ruby? Oh, yes. My father gave it to my mother, she gave it to Agatha, and she used it to prove who I was when she finally got me to my father.'

'You are not wearing it . . .'

'No, I gave it to her when I saw her on Tuesday.'

'You gave it to her?'

The surprise in the knight's voice made the Bourc glance up at him. 'Yes. She was not wealthy, and I thought it could be useful to her. I gave it to her as a token that my family would always remember her protection of me. Now . . . Well, now I wonder whether that is why she died.'

'What do you mean?'

'Perhaps Greencliff saw the ring and killed her for it. She might have died because of the present I gave her.'

Baldwin untied his purse and withdrew the ring, setting it on the table before the Bourc, whose eyes grew large and round as he stared at it.

'But . . . How did you find it?'

'It was not stolen. Greencliff did not see it – or did not care about it. We found it in her house after her death.'

The Gascon gingerly picked it up and studied it for a moment. 'That is a relief, I suppose,' he said at last and passed it back to Baldwin. 'At least I know I was not responsible for her murder.'

'I'm sure you were not,' said Baldwin. 'But the ring is yours. Take it!'

'No. Let it be buried with her. She has little else. At least that way her act toward me will always be with her.' Baldwin nodded and replaced it in his purse.

'Why were you here to see her?' asked Simon frowning thoughtfully. 'Was it just to give her the ring?'

'I have no reason to hide it. For many years I have sworn to find the woman who saved me, to thank her and to find out more about my mother. But where do you begin to search? She had left my father's court when I was weaned, many years ago. Where she had gone seemed a mystery to all, but then a letter arrived.'

'A letter?'

'Yes. It said that Agatha Kyteler was here. As soon as I heard, I set off to find her. It did not take so very long.' He settled back in his seat as if that explained everything.

Now Baldwin leaned forward. 'This letter,' he said. 'Who was it from?'

'We weren't supposed to know,' the Bourc said smiling, then shrugged. 'It was not signed, but it came from England, that much we found from the messenger.'

'And the messenger came from . . .?'

'He came from a town just outside Bordeaux, from a wealthy family. I asked them. They said it had come to them in a letter from their daughter, with a note asking them to send it on to me.'

The knight mused, wrapping his right arm around his chest and resting his chin in the palm of his left so that it covered his mouth. Shooting a quick glance at the Bourc, who sat imperturbably sipping at his pot, he said, 'There's more, isn't there? Why did you disappear? And why did you go down to the moors?'

The Bourc explained that he had thought it would be faster, and then paused. With a short laugh of pleasure, he set his pot down. Looking up, he stared at the knight, resting both hands on the bench at either side of him. 'There is no reason not to tell you now, sir. Not now that the boy confessed to the murders. I admit it! When I stayed with you that night I was thinking about killing Trevellyn!'

'What?' said Simon, sitting suddenly upright and spilling his drink in surprise. 'In God's name, *why*?'

'Simon, have you not heard a thing the man has been saying?' said Baldwin curtly. Then, to the Bourc, 'So, you would have killed the man who had caused you to be separated from your mother. What stopped you?'

'Agatha was not at all how I had imagined. She was bitter and cruel, all she wanted was what she called revenge. But when I came to think about it, there seemed little point. Would the man be able to remember my mother? She was probably nothing more to him than just another refugee. And he did not touch her. She decided not to pay the price he demanded, but he did not actually do *anything* to her!' Under the stern gaze of the knight, he gave a quick shamefaced grin. 'I don't know, sir, whether you have been in a position where you have had control of refugees. I have. I know that it is easy to take advantage when you have power like that, power to give or take away life.'

Baldwin nodded. 'So the choice did not seem so easy once you realised what Agatha wanted you to do for her?'

'Not, it was not at all easy. But one thing was odd.'

'What?'

'She never wanted the message to be sent to me. It came from a friend of hers, and was not Agatha's idea.'

'You are sure of that?'

'Oh, yes. I asked Agatha. She was surprised to see me on the Monday when I explained who I was. She had not expected to see me again.'

'And she told you all this on that Monday?'

'Yes, sir. Some of it she told me later, on Tuesday, when I went to say farewell. I thought I should return home and leave the merchant. I had done what I wished. I had given her the ring and found out more of my mother. But when she asked me to kill this man Trevellyn, on the Monday, I had to have time to think about it. She said it would be revenge for what he had done to my mother. I thought, and made my decision: I could not.'

'And you left her well on the Tuesday? You saw no one else there?'

'No, there was nobody there that I saw.'

'What about when you left? Which way did you go? Along her lane?'

'No, I left in among the trees. Agatha told me that she was often having people go to see her, and I might scare them away! She asked me to stay hidden, and I did as she asked.'

'On your way back from seeing her? Did you see anyone?'

'Ah, yes. Coming back I saw a woman.' He smiled. 'It was Mrs Trevellyn, Agatha told me that! She thought it was quite funny. The woman went to see her often, she said, and she found it amusing. Alan Trevellyn wanted children, but his wife did not.'

Simon heard his friend draw in his breath. 'But I thought . . . Was it Mrs Trevellyn who sent you the letter saying where Agatha was living?'

'Yes. I suppose she had heard of me from the old lady and thought I could ease her last years.'

'So, you say Agatha wanted you to revenge your mother?' said Baldwin.

'Yes. But I couldn't. Oh, I had seen the man, and I disliked him, but that's no reason to kill, and as for my mother . . . I am a soldier. I have seen what happens when a city is captured, and I have taken part. How can I condemn or kill a man because he took advantage of his position, when I have done so myself? No, I decided that I should leave him.'

'And then you left?'

'Yes. She asked me to go.'

'It's interesting that the man she wanted you to kill died only days later,' said Baldwin pensively, and the Bourc nodded and shrugged.

'I have nothing to hide. It is more strange than you realise.' He explained about his meeting with Trevellyn at the inn, the ambush, and his subsequent visit to the merchant's house. 'He tried to whip me, and I wasn't expecting that, but I think he was used to whipping men who would do his bidding: his servants, maybe even sailors. He worked in the east, perhaps he ran a galley for a time . . . I do not know. Anyway, the blow caught me on my back as I ducked, and that made me very angry.'

His eyes misted as he remembered the lash sweeping back ready for another strike, and as he told them, he saw it all in his mind's eye: the way that the pain had lanced across his back like a slash from a razor, the way that he had sprung forward before the merchant could attack again. He had not even drawn his sword, the rage and pain were too intense. As the handle of the whip came forward again, the Bourc had swiped a gauntletted fist and caught him on the cheek and temple, felling him like a sapling under the axe.

By the time the merchant came to again, the Bourc had calmed, but Trevellyn did not know that. All he could see was the heavy blade of his sword at his throat. That was when the Gascon told him who he was and saw the terror spring into the small, black eyes.

'He honestly seemed to think I was a ghost,' he said. 'He was horrorstruck at seeing me.' He gave a short laugh. 'I don't know what he thought was worse: that I had reappeared from his distant past, or the fact that I had bested his men!'

'Did you do anything else to him?' asked Baldwin.

The Bourc glanced at him and grinned. 'What? Cut his throat, you mean? No, my friend, I'm afraid I did not! I left him there when I heard some of his men coming back, then made my way back to Wefford. Next morning I started south. I was happy that Trevellyn would not try anything new.' He went on to describe his journey south and the attacks from the wolfpack.

When he had finished, Simon leaned back in his chair and gazed at his friend. 'Well? It fits with what we know, doesn't it?'

'Yes,' said Baldwin pensively. 'And now Greencliff has confessed, that is an end to the affair, isn't it?'

CHAPTER TWENTY-ONE

Once they had passed through from Crediton and were
making their way along the winding road north to Tiverton,
Simon tried to break the depressed silence. 'Did you know
he still had the knife with him?'

'Eh?' Baldwin's face registered bafflement.

'I said: the knife – he still had it with him. It even had the
blood on it.'

'Oh, you mean Greencliff. No, I didn't know that.' he
returned to his gloomy perusal of the trees ahead.

'Baldwin?' Simon attempted. '*Baldwin*!'

'What is it?' The knight turned to him irritably.

'What the hell's the matter?'

At the exasperation in his voice, the knight smiled
apologetically. He looked as though he was about to deny
any concern, but then, after a quick glance around, seeing
that Edgar and Hugh were some distance behind and that
Mark Rush was a little way in front of them, he dropped

his voice conspiratorially and leaned over towards the bailiff.

'This is very difficult, old friend. I think I might have . . . No, that's not right . . . I feel that there could be a . . . Well *now*, since . . .' He suddenly broke off, and Simon almost laughed aloud at the sight. Here was a brave and resolute modern knight, completely lost for words. His eyes met Simon's and the bailiff saw near panic in them.

'And what does *she* say?'

'I haven't . . . How did you know?'

This time Simon did laugh. 'Baldwin, did you really think you had kept it secret? God in heaven! The very first time you saw her it was like watching a cock with a hen. It was obvious what you were thinking . . .'

'Please, Simon, save my blushes,' the knight murmured.

'So you have not yet said anything to her?'

'How can I, after the death of her husband?'

'Baldwin, at the very least you must get to know her better. Otherwise she may not even think of you. If you don't let her know you are interested, how can she tell you are?'

'*You* did!'

'That's different. I *know* you.'

He digested this in silence for a moment. 'But what should I do? I can't just go to her house and say, "Hello, Mrs Trevellyn, would you like to be my wife now your husband's been murdered?" can I?'

The bailiff sighed. 'Look,' he said, 'you need to find ways of getting to know her. Ways to get her alone so that you can both talk. Maybe take her hawking, or just out for rides sometimes.'

'Is that how you won Margaret?' the knight said, his eyes clouded with anxiety and doubt.

'No, I simply asked her father.'

'Well, shouldn't I . . .'

'No, Baldwin. I was winning a young girl. You're trying to get a woman, one who knows her own mind, possesses her own household, has her own land and wealth. You have to win *her*, not her relatives.'

'Oh. I see.'

'Then why do you look so worried?'

'I'd rather be riding into a battle than trying to take on this role, old friend. That's why!'

Simon laughed, but then his face grew serious for a moment as he gazed ahead with a pensive expression, chewing his lip. 'We're not far. Come on, we'll drop in on her now.'

'No, Simon, I think . . .'

'Come on, Baldwin. To battle!' the bailiff laughed, and to the knight's abject misery, he turned to the servants and called, 'Hugh! Edgar! We're going to the Trevellyn house first, before going back to Furnshill.'

The bailiff was still grinning as they clattered up the hill to the Trevellyn manor, and his good humour did not fade as he banged on the door with his fist. It was only later, after they had entered, that the doubts began to assail him, but the thought had its inception with the opening of the front door, the rest was merely the gestation period.

When the door swung open, Simon found himself confronted by a pretty maidservant, a slim young woman of maybe twenty, with pert breasts and a cheeky smile. Her face was prettily framed by curling brown hair, and her lips parted in a smile as she saw him. Acknowledging her, Simon led his

friend through to the hall, where both waited for the lady of
the house to enter. Their servants waited with the horses in
the stables, feeding them.

Upon the arrival of Angelina Trevellyn, Simon glanced at
Baldwin expecting to see him step forward, but seeing his
friend transfixed, he instead took a half-pace back. The
knight appeared to be tongue-tied, standing as if in a dream
as she approached, and Simon was pleased to see the way
that the woman's face changed on seeing Baldwin. It was as
if her features were lighted by a subtle glow, and her step
quickened as though she was keen to be close to the knight.

Looking at her, Simon felt a warm delight. It was not only
her obvious pleasure at seeing Baldwin, it was also partly the
sight of a woman in the perfection of her youth. There was
no hardness to her. Her face, her body, all were composed of
soft curves. Under the rich-looking blue tunic, her body
moved with the grace and elegance of a well-bred Arab
horse, all controlled energy carefully harnessed. Her hair
was pulled back and today she was bare-headed, emphasis-
ing her wide brow, unmarked by lines, above narrow
eyebrows. It was the eyes that immediately caught the interest, though.

To Simon they looked like twin chips of emerald, glinting
in the firelight, not with cold arrogance, but with a warm and
calm joy. Self-confident, self-possessed, she radiated a
distinct and deliberate sexuality, and even Simon found it
difficult to take his eyes from her.

While she chatted inconsequentially, she kept her eyes on
the knight, hardly seeming to acknowledge the bailiff, and
led them to chairs before the fire. Then she ordered wine,
and it was then, when the maidservant returned with a jug

and three pots, that Simon's eyes quickly hardened. It was then that the idea took root.

Suddenly the whole room felt full of danger and risk, the warmth of their welcome hollow and empty. The bailiff's eyes glazed for an instant as he reviewed every moment since he and the knight had entered the place, and then focused back on his friend. He was talking to her and stammering as he invited her to join him in a day's hawking. The bailiff watched the maid as she walked to the door, having filled their pots. Picking up his own, he rose.

'Excuse me, madam, but I find it a little warm. I'll just go out for some air,' he said, though the others hardly noticed him. Leaving the room by the screens, he saw the girl walking into the buttery, and quickly strode after her.

In the little room, filled with pots, jars and barrels, he found the maid drawing a pot of beer for herself. As he entered, she turned quickly, then, seeing who it was, she gave him a quick smile, shooting a glance to the door behind him.

'I wanted to speak to you. What is your name?'

Her eyes dropped demurely. 'Mary, sir.'

'You seem a very happy girl, Mary.'

'Thank you, sir. This is a happy household.'

'It is now, isn't it?'

'Now, sir?'

'When I first came here, you were very different, you know.'

Her fingers began to play with a cord dangling from the neckline of her tunic. 'I don't understand, sir.'

'Oh, I think you do, Mary. I think you do.' He sat on a barrel. 'Did he beat you often? I suppose that was not all he did, either, was it?'

'Beat me?' Her eyes seemed to grow large in her face as she stared at him, but not with confusion. There was complete understanding there.

'When I first saw you, you were a nervous, shy thing, scared and fretful. Not now, not since he died. Not since he stopped hitting you, is that it? And what about his wife? Did he beat her too? She wasn't sad to see him dead either, was she?'

'No, I wasn't.'

He spun around. There in the doorway was Angelina Trevellyn.

'You can go, Mary.' When the girl had scampered past, relieved to be free, the lady turned back to the bailiff. 'Well? Do you wish to interrogate me here, or shall we go back to the hall?' She picked up a jug, filled it with wine, and motioned with her hand towards the door.

Entering the room, the bailiff found Baldwin standing before the fire, his back to it, and staring at the door hopefully. Seeing Simon, his face fell a little, but then he grinned. At the sight of Mrs Trevellyn behind, his face cleared and he smiled again.

'Please sit down, Baldwin,' she said, and pointed Simon to another chair before filling their pots with wine. 'I have some things to tell you; things you may not like.'

The knight's eyes moved over her, then flashed to Simon, black with suspicion. She carried on softly, sitting and resting her hands in her lap with an almost deliberate attempt at composure.

'Your friend is most astute, Baldwin. He has noticed the change in my house since your first visit. It is not surprising, really, but I should have admitted it to you before. It was not fair to let you think . . .' She paused for a moment, as if in sadness. Taking a deep breath, she carried on.

'Anyway, he is right to think that we are all much happier now. My husband, Baldwin, was a monster! He was a brute. He took me when I was young, and forced me to marry him. He trained the servants well, and beat them often when they displeased him, but he treated me the same! He thrashed me as if I was one of his hostlers! When he wished to, he ignored me and took the maids to his bed – and they dared not refuse him, just as I dared not complain.'

Baldwin stared at her in silence, but Simon was sure that there was pain in his eyes.

'So, my friend,' she continued, 'when you found his body, I think none of us here were sad. Oh, no! How could we be?'

Leaning forward, the bailiff gazed at her intently, but she kept her eyes downcast, refusing to meet his. 'Mrs Trevellyn, why did you stay with him? You could have left him and gone home again.'

She looked up at that, with an unmistakable look of sadness. 'Could I? How? My home is in Gascony, a little to the south of Bordeaux, so yes, I am English, the same as any other Gascon. And my father was always loyal to the English king, so I should be able to get home. But when your husband owns ships and knows all the people in the ports, how can you gain a passage? And even if there was someone to take me, how could I pay? My *husband*,' it sounded as if she wanted to spit at the word, 'kept control of all our money. He even refused me permission to keep my jewels. Oh, no. There was no way I could leave!'

'Why did you agree to marry him in the first place?'

'I did not.' Her voice dropped and her head fell to her breast, as if slumping with exhaustion. 'How could I marry a man like him? No! He captured my parents and me when we were travelling from Normandy to our home. He took all our cargo, *everything*, and then bargained with my father. He would have me, and let my father keep half of his goods. I was bartered like a slave! But that is how hostages are treated: whether the daughter of a merchant or the king of a province, all are treated the same.'

Nodding, Simon contemplated her. It was common enough for a man to be held until his ransom had been paid, and if her father saw a way of retrieving half of his cargo, paying the rest as a dowry, he might well consider it a good arrangement. 'I understand, madam. Could you tell me what happened on the night your husband disappeared as well, please?'

'Simon, you don't think she had anything to do with the killing of her own husband!'

Looking at his friend, the bailiff was saddened to see the anguish in his eyes. He gave Baldwin a grave shake of his head, and then faced the woman once more. 'Madam?'

Her eyes rose to meet his again, and she spoke simply, expecting to be believed. 'I was outside and walking. It appears that my husband came running inside. He had decided he wanted to speak with me, and he asked all the servants where I had gone. When they said they didn't know, he beat two of them, including little Mary, my maid. Then he stormed out. I came back inside an hour or so later, and spent the evening in trying to calm the servants. When he didn't appear, I thought little of it. He often went out to visit the inns of the area. Usually drinking made him violent towards me, but when he went to an inn he was often too drunk, when he finally got home, to be able to hurt me.'

'And the next morning?'

'I awoke as usual. He was not with me, but that was not unusual. I was surprised, though, when I found he was not asleep in the hall. When he was incapable of making his way to the solar, I usually found him there, spread out on a table or a bench. Still, it was no real surprise, not when I saw how much snow had fallen over the night. I would have sent out a man to ask at the village, but the drifts were too deep. I was surprised when you managed to get here.'

'Tell me, madam. When Agatha Kyteler died, why were you there that day? You are not with child, and you have not had any children, is that right?'

'Yes. We . . . We were not lucky with children.'

'So why were you seeing the midwife?'

Her face rose in a faintly haughty manner. 'I cannot tell you that. I did not kill her. Or my husband!'

Simon held her gaze for a moment, his face serious. 'Very well,' he said at last. 'I will not force you. But I would like to know this. Did you see anyone that night? The night that your husband disappeared. Was there anyone here?'

She seemed to become even more pale as she stared at him, her eyes wide and seeming to hold a secret fear as her lips mouthed the word 'No.'

It was then that Baldwin stood decisively and bowed to her. 'Madam, I think we should leave you in peace now. I am sorry that we have caused you distress. Simon, come on. We must leave.'

The bailiff rose and walked to the door behind the impassive knight. At the screens he turned, partly to take his leave of the woman, perhaps also to apologise, but when he caught sight of her face, he turned and left.

Her features were contorted with loathing, and it was concentrated and focused on him.

They had ridden almost to the door of Greencliff's house before Baldwin turned to face the bailiff. 'Simon you can't believe that she was involved. How could you think . . .? After all, Greencliff's confessed . . . And she's far too beautiful to be a murderess. God! Why did you have to be so hard on the poor woman?'

'Baldwin, be still! Calm down.' Simon stared at his friend and the knight could see his misery. Baldwin was torn between his strong attraction to the woman and his friendship to the bailiff, but although his loyalty to Simon was intense, he was so moved by Angelina Trevellyn that he felt a sense of near disgust for Simon after the interrogation he had just witnessed. Even so, the signs of misery on his friend's face compelled him to be silent and wait for the explanation.

'Look, we *know* she was there. She was with the witch on the day the poor woman was murdered, after the Bourc had left. She won't say why. We *know* she hated her husband – she hardly hides the fact, does she? Even her servants were not with her when her husband disappeared, from the sound of things.'

'Simon, for the love of God! You can't believe this! How could a woman like her kill? It's not possible – it's mad!'

'Listen to me, old friend. You know as well as I do that there have been warlike women before, women who could kill, or wage war. You know this. Why should Mrs Trevellyn be different?'

'But Simon . . .'

'You recall how her husband's body was? Lying as if outstretched? You remember I said it was as if he was pleading? Couldn't she have got Greencliff to cut his throat while he was begging *her* not to kill him?'

'But Simon! You cannot believe that, surely! A woman like her . . .' Through his horror, Baldwin, realised that his friend was pleading with him, his face set, his eyes intense.

'Baldwin, I don't know, I don't know! That's the point! I have to make sure she's innocent of the murders.'

'But *you* said that Greencliff admitted to them.'

'Yes, and he had a knife with blood on it, but even so, he might have had help . . . Or he might have helped another. I don't know. All I do know is that she *is* involved somehow. I don't know how or why, but I'm sure she knows what happened. Baldwin, I must know what she has done. So must you!'

Margaret was worried by the sight of the two men. She had expected Simon's return to be a joyful occasion, not miserable like this. The two men were hardly talking.

They entered the hall together, but almost immediately Baldwin muttered about wanting to change out of his clothes, damp as they were from his journey, and left them alone. Simon stood and watched him go, then sighed and dropped on to a bench.

'Simon, what has happened?'

Briefly he explained, telling her about their visit to Mrs Trevellyn, and his conclusions. Margaret listened with misery. She could not comprehend the feelings of the knight, who at last appeared to have found his ideal woman, only to have his best friend suggest that she could have been involved in a murder – maybe two.

When the door opened, both looked up. Seeing it was Hugh, she turned back to her husband. 'But you only have some suspicions against her, nothing concrete, nothing that should make Baldwin doubt her. Why not leave him to make his own choice. If she is as beautiful as you say, then . . .'

'But that's the point!' he exclaimed despairingly. 'If I'm right, she might have been involved not just in one murder, but two! And one of the dead was her own husband. If she killed her own husband, would she not be a danger to Baldwin?'

To Hugh it looked as if his master was ravaged by doubts. It seemed as if he was pulled in different directions, by his friendship to the knight and the wish to see him happy, and by his confusion over the woman's role in the death of her husband. Clearing his throat, he interrupted. 'Sir?'

'What?'

'I don't know if it's important, sir,' the servant said, and quickly explained what Jennie Miller had said about Harold Greencliff and Mrs Trevellyn.

It was one of the few times he had ever been able to shock his master, and Hugh rather enjoyed it.

'You mean Jennie Miller thinks that Mrs Trevellyn herself killed old Agatha?'

Their evening was quiet. With Baldwin's reserved and withdrawn manner, there was little conversation. Simon and Margaret sat opposite Hugh and Edgar at the great table. Baldwin was at his place at the head, but he was unwilling to talk, and soon after he had finished his meal, he announced that he was ready to go to bed.

Before he could rise from his seat, Margaret went to him and poured him more wine, then stood beside him. 'No, you need to talk with Simon,' she said, and motioned to Hugh to clear the table. Sighing he got up and began to collect the plates. After a glare from Margaret, Edgar stood too, and began to help. Soon they were taking out the dishes, and when they had both disappeared, Margaret turned to her husband.

'Right, Simon. Tell Baldwin what we heard today from Hugh.'

He gazed at her in surprise, and then looked apologetically at Baldwin, who stared back impassively as he was told of the rumours in Wefford about Mrs Trevellyn and Harold Greencliff. Then, with a sigh, he picked up his pot and sipped at his wine.

'All right, but there's no proof that she has been unfaithful to her husband, no proof of an affair, and certainly nothing to suggest that she killed Agatha or her husband. It's pure gossip, as you say.'

Margaret sat down again, looking from one to the other. 'Baldwin,' she said, 'did you think her evidence was strange?'

'Strange?' he glanced at her in surprise. 'How do you mean?'

'From what Simon told me, Mrs Trevellyn will not say what she was doing at the old woman's house. And there really isn't anyone else who seems to have had a reason to want to kill her husband. Doesn't it seem strange?'

'Well . . .' He shrugged, dubious.

'And yet this boy has admitted to it. I don't see why he would do that unless he was involved, but I think you should question him and see what he has to say.'

'There's no point trying to do that,' Simon interrupted. 'I tried to get him to speak about it yesterday and all the way back today, but I got nothing from him. He just didn't seem to want to talk about it at all.'

'What?' Baldwin frowned at this. 'Not at all?'

'No. He refused to talk about it. He wouldn't talk about Agatha Kyteler's death or Alan Trevellyn's. As soon as I mentioned either he went as silent as a corpse and said nothing until we spoke of something else.'

'But he *did* confess to killing them?'

'Oh, yes. In fact, when we asked him, he kept reminding us that his knife had their blood on it. And it did – well, it had *some* blood on it, anyway.'

'That *does* seem odd.'

'What does?' asked Margaret.

The knight glanced at her. 'The fact that he confessed without giving any reason why. Usually people boast of the reason why they murdered someone if they admit to it. "He robbed me", or "he threatened me", they say, and use that as justification for the killing. If they don't confess, and it's more common that they don't, they deny all knowledge of the crime. At least, that's *my* experience.'

'So you think that because he said he *did* do it, it looks odd?' she said slowly.

'Yes. Nobody wants to surrender themselves to a punishment or death for no reason. It would be mad, stupid – or . . .' He suddenly broke off, and his eyes turned to the fire with a frown that spoke of a level of intentness Simon had not seen before. It was as if he was consumed with a total concentration which absorbed him completely. A low gasp escaped from his lips, almost a moan of pain.

'What is it? Are you all right?' asked Simon, and was surprised to be silenced by a curt wave of the knight's hand.

There *was* a reason, Baldwin thought to himself distractedly. If a man was committed, or if he was devoted in his life, tied to a cause, he could subject himself even to death. Who could know that better than he, he who had seen his comrades sent to torture and to death by the flames. They were all dedicated because they all believed in their cause: in the honour and purity of the military Order, in the Poor Fellow-Soldiers of Christ and the Temple of Solomon: the Knights Templar. They had refused to agree to the confessions put to them by the Inquisition, they had suffered and died, not for a lie, but because they believed: in themselves and their masters and their God. And now Harold Greencliff was behaving in the same way, as if he too had a cause. A *love*, greater even than his own love for life.

Simon's eyes flitted from his wife to the knight in his bewilderment. What Baldwin was thinking was totally hidden from him. What had he been saying? Something about not surrendering to something not done? That was it, he had been saying that anyone would be mad to admit to something that they had not done. The bailiff's eyes narrowed: was that what he was thinking? That Angelina Trevellyn had killed her husband and would be mad to admit it? That she would never confess, that someone who *did* confess to a crime must be a fool or mad? And she was neither?

He felt his eyes drawn to the fire. But why kill old Agatha Kyteler, he wondered. Then a quick frown pulled his brows down and he gave an angry sigh as he felt the frustration rise: why, for God's sake, *why* was he thinking about *her* still? She was irrelevant; unimportant – just a sad little old woman. Why did her murder keep impinging on his brain? As he glared at the flames, he found that with no effort he could again conjure up a picture of her from his dreams, dressed in her hooded cloak, her eyes glittering with bright red fire, her expressions intense – and yet not threatening.

It was not a terrifying face. Instead it was sad, as if she was trying to help him, nudging and prompting him towards her murderer.

This was foolish. Thrusting the thought aside, he considered. The only thing that mattered was finding the killer of Agatha Kyteler and Alan Trevellyn. And right now he was not sure that they had the right man in the gaol. Glancing up he saw Baldwin's face set into a pensive scowl.

Right, the bailiff thought, so who wanted the witch dead? Even Harold Greencliff did not appear to have a motive. And who could have wanted to kill Alan Trevellyn? To find that out the bailiff would need to know more about him. Could one of his servants have wanted to see him dead? It sounded very much as if they all suffered under him. Who knew the man well?

He gave a start, making the brown and black dog stare at him in sudden reproach for waking him before dropping his head down again. He said, 'I know what we have to do. Tomorrow we need to see Jennie and Sarah again and check a couple of points – I think I'm getting close to the truth at last!'

CHAPTER TWENTY-TWO

After leaving their horses with the hostlers at the back of the inn, they entered and took a table near the front of the room. Baldwin haughtily summoned the innkeeper with a curt wave of his hand, while the bailiff stared round the room. After hearing what Hugh had to say about his conversation with Jennie Miller, he was interested in seeing her again, and putting some other questions to her.

But today the inn was quiet. Although it was lunchtime, there were few people there, and Simon reflected that the people from the village would still have many tasks to perform. Even with the fields under snow, there would still be animals to look after, tools damaged over the year to be repaired, and some jobs, no doubt, to be done in their houses.

There was no sign of Jennie Miller. Over by the fire there was a little group of four men, one of whom Simon recognised as Samuel Cottey, but that was all. Perhaps it would become more busy as men finished their lunches and went to the inn for a quick drink before getting on with their afternoon duties.

Wiping his hands on a thick rag, the innkeeper strolled to them. 'Sirs. What can I offer you?' he said.

Simon raised an eyebrow towards Baldwin, who shrugged. 'Two pints of ale, and food.'

'We have cold meats, sir. Is that all right?'

Nodding, Simon turned to his friend as the publican left to fetch their order. 'Well, Baldwin? Come on, what do we do next?'

The knight glanced up at him, and gave him a wan smile before returning his gaze to the matted rushes on the floor. 'I don't know, old friend,' he admitted. 'Everything we have heard would seem to support your doubts about Mrs Trevellyn. But Greencliff had the knife, and the prints led to his door after Alan Trevellyn's death. Then there's Agatha Kyteler's death. He was there, we know that.'

'So was *she*, though!'

'I know, I know. She confessed to that. But I wonder . . .'

'What?'

'I was just thinking: why did she want to see the old woman? Agatha Kyteler was supposed to be a midwife, but Angelina Trevellyn says she has never had a child.'

Just then their food arrived, and they set to with gusto. Breakfast felt like it was a long time ago. Speaking between mouthfuls, Baldwin's eyes narrowed as he peered at Simon. 'If Harold Greencliff was having an affair with Angelina Trevellyn, isn't it likely that he was trying to kill her husband so that he could take her for himself? It would make more sense than thinking that she was involved.'

'I'm not so sure, Baldwin. I don't know her that well, but if she really hated her husband that much, especially after the way that he apparently abused and mistreated her, I think she could easily become angry enough to kill. And don't forget, she *is* a Gascon. She's French.'

'*French*?' The knight stared at him open-mouthed. 'What on earth's that got to do with anything?'

'You know,' Simon's eyes were suddenly hooded and he glanced around quickly. 'They do tend to get overexcited, the French.'

'God in heaven! Simon, you and I must talk soon. You believe in witches, you trust to all the old superstitions, and now you think all the French are mad as well!' The humour had returned to the knight's eyes, Simon saw with a degree of bitterness.

'No, not all French. It's just that . . .' Simon shrugged. He knew he would not win this argument, so he changed the subject. 'You know, I think I'm beginning to understand dimly what actually happened.'

'There's still a lot we need to find out.'

'We need to talk to the people of Wefford again and find out what they haven't told us.'

'How? We've already spoken to most of them. How can we find out more?'

'Well, first I think we ought to go back and see Sarah Cottey – especially,' he nodded towards the group in front of them, 'especially while her father's in here. Then we must see Jennie Miller. She knows more than she's told us, she seems to know all the gossip in the village, if Hugh's right. And I want to speak to Harold Greencliff again. I don't know how to get him to talk to us, but he *must* know more.'

'That's a lot of work. It'll take time to get into Crediton to go to the town gaol.'

'Have him brought up to the manor, then. The innkeeper can get a man to fetch him and Tanner. It'll save us a journey, and probably do them both some good to be able to stay in a warm place, compared to that cell.'

Having decided on their course of action, they finished their drinks and made their way to the Cottey holding, but when they arrived, there was no sign of life. Simon hammered on the door, and rode round to the back, but there was no sign of anyone, apart from the thin streamers of smoke drifting idly on the wind from the roof. After looking all over the plot, they decided to go on to Jennie Miller's instead.

Here they were more lucky. As soon as they came through the trees into the clearing, the sound of voices, shrill and laughing, met them. Coming to the small bridge, they could see the Miller children running and playing tag over at the line of the trees, their mother sitting on a stool and watching as she plucked the feathers from a chicken, laughing every now and again and calling to them to urge them to greater efforts.

At the sound of the horses, she spun round, and Simon was vaguely sad to see the happiness die from her features as she recognised her visitors. The cries from the children faded too, as if the slight breeze was taking away their pleasure and enjoyment with its gusts. The bailiff urged his horse on with a rueful grin. Such was power, he thought. To bring joy, but also to destroy it. Sighing, he brought his horse to the door, to where Jennie Miller had now risen, the fowl forgotten beside her, wiping her hands on her apron to rid herself of the tiny feathers clinging to the blood on her skin.

It was the knight who greeted her, sitting and watching her gravely from his horse. 'Jennie, we have come to speak to you again about the death of Agatha Kyteler. Can we come in?'

At her shrug of apparent indifference, they dropped from their horses and followed her inside. Sitting at the same place, she watched them take their seats and sat back, waiting for them to begin with a slightly nervous mien, as if she was anxious of what they wished to know from her.

'Jennie, we wanted to find out from you anything that could help with these two murders,' Baldwin began, and her eyes swiftly sought his face.

'What do you mean? You already have the killer, don't you?'

Simon gently interrupted. 'You mean Harold Greencliff?'

'Yes,' she nodded. 'You have him held in gaol, don't you?'

'Yes, but do *you* think he could have killed them'

'No!' The answer was categoric.

Baldwin stared at her. 'But why? Who else had a chance?'

At this her gaze dropped and she stared at the floor in silence. Simon tried again.

'Jennie, you must tell us anything you know. After all, you wouldn't want Harold to be sent to trial and executed if he had nothing to do with it, would you?'

She shook her head, but no words came.

'Jennie, it's obvious you have some idea about this. Why? Who do you think it was?'

She started to speak in a low and halting voice. All the time her eyes remained downcast, and her features anxious. 'I knew after I'd spoken to your man at the inn . . . I would have been better to hold my tongue . . . It was the drink got to me . . . But it's true, I'm sure of that.'

'What . . .' Baldwin started, but Simon cut him off with a short movement of his hand.

'Carry on, Jennie.'

She gave a sigh, a massive effort that looked as though it rose from the very soles of her boots, then looked at Simon and held his eyes. 'When I came out of the woods, I was sure who it was I'd seen. I was certain it was Angelina Trevellyn. At the lane, I saw Harold Greencliff. And I know Sarah Cottey saw them too. She's a good girl, is Sarah. But she has not been able to admit to herself what sort of a boy Harold is.'

'What sort of a boy do *you* think he is?' asked Baldwin. She ignored him, her eyes staying fixed on the intent bailiff before her.

'You see, Harold and Sarah, they've grown up together, been with each other for years, and they've always been very fond of each other. But now Sarah wants to marry and settle, she thinks Harold does too, and he doesn't. He never has, really. He's always been a boy for enjoying himself, and no girl ever could say no to him, he was always such a good-looking lad . . .' As if in answer to an unspoken question in Simon's eyes, she suddenly reddened and half-turned away in apparent embarrassment, but then faced him once more with an air of defiance, as if she knew her words might shock, but was now careless of effect.

To Simon it looked as though she was almost proud, and he realised with a quick insight how she must feel, working every day to bring up her family, toiling as she tried to help her husband keep the mill profitable so that there would be bread on the table for them. Would it be a surprise if a few kind words from a "good-looking lad" like Greencliff could remind her of a time when she was free of worry and had the opportunity to enjoy the comfort of another man? 'And?' he asked softly.

'There are many he has known in the area. Sarah was one. But over the last few months, he has been seeing another woman, one who was not from Wefford. She was married, so he said . . .'

'What? Harold Greencliff *told* you this?' Baldwin cried, leaning forward suddenly.

'Harold?' There was a faint sneer on her face at this. 'Oh, no. Harold didn't tell me. No, but there's been a few he did tell. Like Stephen de la Forte. *He* told me.'

'What exactly did he say?' asked Simon gently.

She frowned in concentration. 'When was it? Oh, yes.' Her brow cleared a little and she glanced up at Simon quickly, looking as if she wanted to confirm that he was concentrating. 'It was at the inn. Maybe . . . Maybe a month or so ago. He was laughing and joking about his friend, that is, Harold. Harold wasn't there at the time, and Stephen said that he was out with his new lover. He said that her husband was a fool to be cuckolded like that by Harold, but he said there's no fool like an old one. Stephen said he wished his friend good luck, and drank a toast to him. Well, as you can imagine, we all wanted to know. We asked him who it was, and at first he refused to answer, but later, when there was only a few of us left, he swore us all to silence, and then told us.'

'He actually said who it was?' asked Simon.

'Well, he hinted. But it was impossible to miss who he was talking about. He said it was a woman he knew, someone married to a man close to him, someone wealthy, living close to the village. It could only be Mrs Trevellyn.'

'Do you think it was *her*, then?'

She looked up with a fire of bitterness glinting angrily in her eyes. 'Who else? She hated her husband, everyone here knew that. And it's not surprising either, the way he treated her and his servants. I'm sure she loathed him enough to kill him or to have someone else do it for her. I'm sure it wasn't Harold.'

'You said,' Baldwin said pensively, 'that you saw them at the woods. Did Sarah?'

'Oh yes. She must have done. And she knew what the rumours were about Mrs Trevellyn and Harold, too. So when we saw her in the trees on the way to the witch's house, and then him at the roadway, she went quiet. She put the two together. Why else would they be there like that?'

Now it was Simon's turn to frown. 'I don't understand, do you mean that she was ill and . . .'

Jennie Miller gave a sudden harsh laugh. 'Ill? It's no illness to be with child, Bailiff!'

He stared at her open-mouthed. 'You . . . You mean the woman was pregnant? That she . . . She was to have Harold Greencliff's child? They went to the midwife to get her help with the delivery?' he stammered, but it was Baldwin who answered, with a tired kind of sigh to his voice.

'No, Simon, not like that, anyway. I should have realised. It's obvious, now I think about it. A midwife can be useful to a woman to help in bringing a child into the world, but she can also sometimes be of help in stopping a child, too. That was why there was yew in Kyteler's cottage. Yew can be used to make a mixture that will make a pregnant woman lose her child. It forces a miscarriage.'

When he looked at Jennie, she nodded. 'Yes. I think that's why Angelina Trevellyn was at the witch's house: to lose the child she and Harold had produced.

They were both quiet as they rode away from the mill towards the road, and they had travelled some way before Simon dared to interrupt the knight's thoughts. When he looked over at Baldwin, he could see that the knight was deeply troubled. The evidence of Jennie Miller had thrown the whole matter into a different light.

'Well, Baldwin?' he asked as they turned into the Cotteys' lane. 'What do *you* think?'

Looking up, the knight's face registered a bleak sadness. He felt that the evidence was so overwhelming now that there was certainly good cause to doubt that the boy had confessed honestly. But what teased at his mind was why the boy should have admitted to a crime he had no responsibility for. And whether Angelina Trevellyn could have killed her own husband. It still seemed impossible somehow that such a beautiful woman could be capable of such a deed.

But then his mind went back to the chronicles he had seen and read while he had been in Cyprus and other countries while he was still a member of the Order of the Temple. There were many examples there of women prepared to take up weapons, from women who killed and threatened to take control of lands they wanted, to others who were more subtle and devious in their approach. Alice of Antioch was one, Constance another. Both had tried to take over lands and rule them alone. It was possible that Angelina was struck from the same mould.

'I have no idea, Simon,' he said heavily. 'All I know is that it seems that there is some reason to doubt whether the boy Greencliff was truly responsible for the murders. And we need to hear from the lady herself why it was that she went to Agatha Kyteler's house. I don't know.'

They had almost arrived at the cottage now, and Simon nodded thoughtfully as they made their way to the door, through the flocks of chickens that scrabbled at the dirt for any food missed by their sisters. Dismounting, he lashed his reins to a tree and banged once more on the front door. This time there was only a short pause before it was opened to show Sarah Cottey, whose eyebrows rose at the sight of her guests.

'Sarah,' Simon said, 'we have come to ask you about the day you went to the witch's house again, and about Harold Greencliff.' To his horror, she immediately burst into tears.

Baldwin was still on his horse, but swung down and walked over to join them with a grimace of sympathy twisting his mouth. Throwing a disdainful sneer at Simon, who stood staring at him with frank amazement at the response to his words, the knight barged past, took the girl by the shoulder and gently led her indoors.

'Come on, Sarah. Don't worry, we know most of it already.' He helped her to a bench at the table and sat before her, holding her eyes with his, and she began to calm, sniffling. Eventually, rubbing at her nose and drawing in gulps of air, she glanced up at Simon, then began to weep again.

'Come now, child,' Baldwin said. 'We must know what really happened. Otherwise, you know what will happen, don't you? Harold must die. He has admitted both killings. He has confessed to them both. *You* can't believe he killed them. Tell us the truth.'

Looking up, she found herself gazing into the knight's dark eyes. Under that solid stare she found herself relaxing, as if she was becoming entranced by their deep brown depths. 'He can't have meant it. None of it.'

'Meant what, Sarah?' the knight asked softly.

'What he promised me,' she said, her eyes filling again with tears, one huge drop forming in her right eye and slowly descending like a feather dropping in a clear air. 'He promised me he would marry me as soon as he could.'

'When did he promise, Sarah?'

'Months ago. He said he loved me, that he wanted to live with me for ever. But he was lying. I heard about him and that French cow, and how they were carrying on . . .'

'Where did you hear that?'

'At the inn. They were all talking about it up there. But when I asked him about it, he said it was untrue! He said it was all lies, that he'd never seen her, there was nothing in it. He said he still wanted *me*!'

Baldwin looked at her steadily as the tears fell in a constant drizzle, but he could almost feel her pain and it was only with an effort that he stopped himself from touching her to try to offer some comfort. 'What happened to make you doubt him? Why did you think he was untrue to you?'

'Because he was *there*! He was at the road to that woman's house. I didn't realise at the time, I couldn't really see . . .'

'Did you see the woman in the trees? Did you see Mrs Trevellyn?' Baldwin interrupted quickly, and saw with relief that he had brought her back to her story again.

'*Her*? Oh, yes, I saw *her*! She was there in the trees, hiding a little back from the lane, dressed so clean and expensive, like a lady, she was. But she was still there for the same reason . . .' She broke off suddenly, and her eyes glanced away.

'I think we know why she was there, Sarah,' said Baldwin.'You had gone there for the same reason before, hadn't you?'

Her head came up once more and she looked him full in the face with a kind of pride as she said, 'Yes.'

'Why did you think she was there at the time? Is that what you thought immediately, or did you think she was there for some other reason at first?'

'I . . .' Her eyes lost their focus with the effort of recollection. 'I didn't think *anything* at the time. I think it was just like seeing anyone. No, it was later, when I came to the lane and saw her horse there that I knew.'

'What do you mean? Why?'

'I never saw Harold, he had dropped back into the trees, but he must have been there holding the horse.'

'Why do you say that? Surely it could have been anyone there holding her horse – she might have brought an hostler to do that. Why do you think it was Harold?'

There was withering scorn in her eyes as she sneered at him. 'Why? Because *I* may not have seen Harry at the time, but when I spoke to Jennie later, she admitted she saw him there, before he ducked back into the trees. He hid when he saw me. I'm not surprised he wanted to stay hidden from me.'

Leaning back, Baldwin gazed at her with doubt. 'So Harry Greencliff was definitely there – but as far as you could see, he was alone? You saw no one with him?'

'That's right. She must have been in the trees on the way to see Agatha by then. There was only one reason for him to be there – he was there to give her comfort after she had been to see Agatha. And then she killed the poor old woman.'

'*What*?' It was almost explosive the way in which the word forced itself from his lips.

'Well, of course she did. Just like she killed her husband. And with both killings, she tried to blame other people!'

'But why?'

'Why?' Again he could see the disdain in her eyes. 'Because when the witch knew she was pregnant, Mrs Trevellyn had to kill her so that her secret was kept. Then she killed her husband too.'

'Wait!' Baldwin held up a hand and sighed. This was becoming impossible, the suggestions and allegations were flying around too quickly for him to be able to think them through. 'Why would Mrs Trevellyn have killed the old woman? Surely she could rely on her to keep the thing quiet?'

'Oh, I don't think so. How could she trust the poor old dear to keep her mouth shut? It's one thing for me, an unimportant woman, unmarried, I knew *I* could trust her. But her? Angelina Trevellyn? She had lots to lose.' Her head tilted and she looked as if she was giving the matter judicious consideration. 'I imagine she never thought of killing her husband, but then she realised how easy it was after killing old Agatha, and then I suppose the next time her husband tried to threaten her, it seemed like the best thing to do.'

Baldwin threw a glance of desperation at his friend, and Simon leaned forward. 'Sarah, when you knew Harold, did he always carry a dagger?'

'Yes, of course!'

'What was it like?'

'Just an ordinary ballock dagger. A thin blade with one sharp side. The handle was wooden, I think, and the sheath made of thick leather.'

'And he always kept it with him?'

'Yes. Of course he did.'

'So it comes to this, then,' said Simon at last as they rode back to Furnshill Manor in the creeping darkness of the twilight. 'We know that Mrs Trevellyn was there. We think she was obtaining the same kind of medicine as Sarah, and she had some sort of reason to keep the witch quiet.'

'But why did the boy run off? And why would he admit to the crime?'

'Baldwin! If you were young and in love, wouldn't *you* protect the woman of your dreams, even if you *did* think she could be a murderer?'

Drawing up his horse, the knight stared at him. 'What do you mean? That *he* thought *she* had done it?'

'Yes!' Simon stopped his mount and turned to face Baldwin. 'If you were him, and you had gone with her to see the witch, waiting for her with her horse, only to hear later that the witch had died around then, you'd wonder, wouldn't you?'

'Yes, I'd wonder, but I wouldn't run away immediately, though. Why did he do that?'

'I don't know, but I think the second time, after Alan Trevellyn had been killed, I think that was because he found out that the man had died. Maybe he came across the body in the snow? Or perhaps she told him she had done it and that revolted him so much that he decided to leave. The fact that he admitted to doing it seems to show that he was trying to protect her. After all, if he had not run away, if he had not confessed, it would not have been long before you and I began to wonder about her, would it? We would have to begin to think that she must have been involved, surely, after hearing about the way her husband used to beat her, and the way that she and the servants suffered.'

'But the knife? It was covered in blood!'

'Ah! There's a simple reason for that, I'm sure.'

'And why confess to doing it himself? That was madness!' said Baldwin incredulously.

'Why confess? That's the easy part. Because he loves her! It may be misplaced, but he wanted to protect her because he still loves her!'

Chapter TWENTY-Three

Entering the hall, they found an unkempt-looking Greencliff tied to the beam of the middle of the floor, watched by an attentive Tanner who was reflectively drinking from a large pot of warmed ale and sitting by the fire. As the two men walked in, the constable stood quickly, conscious of his position compared with the two officers. Setting his drink aside, he greeted them.

'Hello, Tanner,' said Baldwin, acknowledging the constable's nod before turning to the huddled form of Harold Greencliff. Striding across the floor, he carefully seated himself in his favourite chair and fixed a narrow-eyed glower on the unfortunate man. Seeing the frown of concentration on his face, Simon grinned to himself as he crossed over to a bench nearby. He had seen that expression on the knight's face before. It looked as if Baldwin was wearing a magisterial attitude of distaste, but the bailiff was sure that it was no more than a front to hide his bafflement.

But as he sat, he caught a glimpse of something deeper. There was pain in his friend's eyes, a pain that struck at the knight's very soul, and Simon realised what was so affecting him. The knight was a man of honour, who would want only to see that the law should be upheld. He would not want to convict the wrong person and he would not want to let the guilty go free. But that may well mean that he must find this farmer innocent, and if so, there was only one conclusion: Angelina Trevellyn must be guilty. The Bourc had confirmed she was there.

'Harold Greencliff, do you know why we had you brought here?' the knight began, and the shape by the beam stirred.

To Simon it looked as if the youth was beyond fear. His pale face stared back at the knight, but without any apparent care. He seemed disinterested, unfeeling, as if whatever happened to him was irrelevant now. Nothing could shake him more than the events of the last few days. It was as if he had already decided that his life was forfeit, and that there was no point in even hoping for any reprieve. Seeing the look in the knight's eyes, he appeared to recover a little, though, and struggled to get up, rising from a sprawl to kneel beside the post as if he was drunk and embracing a support. He nodded.

'You have admitted to killing Agatha Kyteler and Alan Trevellyn. Do you still affirm your guilt?'

'Yes.' It was said with a note of contempt, as if the knight should not have harboured any doubts.

'When did you kill Agatha Kyteler? Was it after Angelina Trevellyn went to . . .'

'Leave Angelina out of this . . .' The pain of his expression and the suffering in his voice were all too obvious, and

Simon nodded to himself. That barb touched a nerve, he thought.

'Leave her out of it?' Baldwin's voice was deceptively soft at first, but then it hardened as he leaned forwards and continued more harshly. 'How can we leave her out of it when she must bear part of the responsibility? If you killed them both, you killed them *for* her. You murdered the old woman so that your secret should be safe and you murdered Trevellyn so that his wife could be free of him, didn't you?'

The boy stared at him, mouth gaping in shock as he slowly shook his head from side to side.

'We know why Mrs Trevellyn went to see Agatha Kyteler. We know that she went to get rid of the child she did not want.'

'No.' It came as a low moan, but Baldwin continued doggedly.

'She went there to keep her pregnancy secret, to hide it from her husband.'

'No!'

'And then your knife was used to kill Alan Trevellyn as well, I suppose because he found out about the secret. We know you were there with her at the time. We followed your trail back. Your knife was still covered in blood when Simon here arrested you.'

The knight paused. The look on the boy's face had become contemplative, and now a faint smile tugged at his lips. He nodded slowly. 'Yes,' he said. 'That's what happened. I had to kill the witch after she realised that Mrs Trevellyn was pregnant, and I had to kill Trevellyn when he heard about our visit to the witch.'

'How?'

Greencliff stopped and stared at the knight at the simple question. 'How? What do you mean?'

'How did Alan Trevellyn hear about the visit to the old woman? Who told him? I doubt whether *you* did, after all!'

'I . . .'

'And why did you need to kill Agatha Kyteler?'

'To keep her quiet!'

'But she always kept quiet before, didn't she?'

'Oh, I don't know, I . . .'

'But you *did* know, didn't you? You knew that Sarah Cottey had been to see her, didn't you? And you knew that no stories had spread afterwards.'

'No, that's not true . . .'

'No? Do you mean you didn't know that Sarah had been to see old Agatha?'

'I . . . No, I didn't know, I . . .'

'You knew.' The flat statement cut him off, and he sat with a red face as the knight continued. 'You knew full well that the old woman never spoke of the women who visited her, just as she never spoke of the men who went to see her. She always held her tongue, unlike others. No, you would not have killed her for that. And Alan Trevellyn? Why would you have killed him? So that you could have his wife?' The youth opened his mouth as if to agree, but the knight made a terse gesture with his hand to cut him off. 'That's nonsense. Why kill the man and then leave? Why kill him to win his wife and then leave her behind? You broke yourself off from your life and your woman at the same time. Are you really that stupid?'

Now the boy was staring blankly at the knight. Looking at him, Simon was reminded of a hare gazing at a harrier. He was left with the impression that he and Tanner need not be present.

'So why, then? Why did I do it? Tell me that.'

It was almost as if that simple demand for factual reasoning was enough. Harold Greencliff seemed to relax, nearly slumping back against the post, with an almost contented, a smug, expression on his face.

But his face changed as soon as the knight rested his chin on his hand and gazed at him, saying, 'Very well. I shall tell you what happened. I shall tell you *why*, but not as you mean. I don't think you killed anyone.

'When Agatha Kyteler died, you were standing by Angelina's horse. She left you and went to the old woman's house. You waited there and when she returned, you both went home. You didn't go to the house and kill. You couldn't have! When you went to the Trevellyn house, you didn't see Alan Trevellyn. You went to see your lover, and she took you to the places where her husband could not be. She was not stupid enough to take you somewhere he could see you together.'

'Then how did my dagger get his blood on it?'

Baldwin waved a contemptuous hand. 'There are many ways for a shepherd to get blood on his blade! What did you do that morning? Kill a ewe? A lamb? I'll bet was something other than Trevellyn's blood on the knife!'

Simon pursed his lips. It did not seem likely. No, it was more probable that it *was* Trevellyn's blood. If a shepherd killed a sheep – if any man used his knife – he would clean it before putting it away again.

'No! It was me! I did it! I killed them both, I . . .'

But if that was the case, Simon frowned, if that was so, then why was the blade still dirty? Everyone always cleaned their blades, didn't they?

Could it be because someone wanted it to stay bloody? Harold must surely have cleaned it if he had used it, but if another had used it to murder, would they have left it filthy to prove Harold's guilt? Was it to put the blame on him?

Now the knight leaned back as if exhausted, his features seeming somehow older, his face suddenly grey and ancient as though the fatigue made his flesh sag like an old man's. 'No,' he said softly. 'You aren't a killer. A man, certainly, but not a murderer. You couldn't have killed the old woman and Trevellyn later, not even for the love of a woman like Angelina. But you could lie for her. You could lie and say that you *did* kill for her. You could do that and make us believe you. So that *she* was safe. So that she went free.'

'*No!*'

'Because all along, all the time, you knew who had really done it, didn't you? All along you knew that only one person *could* have done it. Only that dear woman, only dear, sweet Angelina could have had the chance to kill both the old woman and her own husband. Nobody else had the chance. Did they?'

And it was then, as the knight asked the question, that Simon suddenly realised. 'Oh, my good God in heaven!' broke from his lips in a soft cry that was almost a prayer as the truth dawned and he saw what had truly happened.

As if he was looking at a sequence of pictures that built up a large tapestry, he saw in their turn the house of the old woman Kyteler, her body, the form of Alan Trevellyn under the snow, the tracks in the snow leading from the Trevellyn house back to the Greencliff house, and the footprints that he had followed down south towards the moors. Snatches of the comments he had heard with Baldwin struck him and now they seemed to build a tight framework around the killer, with threads as strong as hempen rope around a neck.

He leaned forward and gazed at the boy with an intensity that Harold Greencliff could almost feel. He turned to face the bailiff slowly and nervously.

'Harold, I think I can prove that the killer was not who you thought it was. If I can show it most certainly was not Mrs Trevellyn who killed either of these two people, would you tell us the truth?'

There was a cynical question in the lifting of the boy's eyebrow as he stared at the bailiff, but then, as Simon suddenly gave a wolfish smile, he thought he could discern a slight puckering of Greencliff's brow as if in confusion.

'What are you talking about?' asked Baldwin. They had both gone outside and were standing at his front door where the youth in the hall could not hear them.

'We can clear up two suspects in one session. Send a boy to ask Mrs Trevellyn to get over here for an early lunch tomorrow. Make sure there is no mention of us having Greencliff here. I think we should keep that quiet for now. Then we'll need to go out for a ride, I think.'

'Simon, you can be exceedingly unpleasant on occasion, especially when you are smug. Tell me what is going on!'

But the bailiff refused. He ignored entreaties and threats alike, and merely smiled to himself as Baldwin tried to prise the truth from him. 'You have heard and seen the same as me, Baldwin. I think I may have seen something you haven't, that's all. I won't tell you what until I've had a chance to see whether I'm right or not,' he said and changed the subject.

By the time Margaret came out to see what they were doing, they had stopped talking, and Simon was gazing out over the scenery towards the moors with apparent calm contemplation, while behind him the knight was meditatively kicking at the ground with a face like thunder.

'Are you two all right?' she asked anxiously. She had never seen them like this before. When they glanced at her, she could see that they were both deep in thought, though her husband's thoughts appeared more pleasing to him than Baldwin's. Simon gave her a quick grin, while the knight appeared preoccupied and apparently hardly noticed her.

'What is it?' she asked, not sure whether to laugh or show sympathy, they both looked so absorbed.

In the end it was Simon who answered. Speaking slowly, as if still considering his words carefully, he said, 'I think I may have discovered who could *not* have killed either of the two victims. I *think* we are almost in a position to arrest the real murderer!'

'And . . .?'

'And I'll tell you both tomorrow when I'm sure!'

The next morning was clear and calm. The sky was filled with enormous clouds that floated past slowly and majestically like massive ships under a light but steady breeze, and the sun occasionally burst out from between them to give a wintry glow to the land.

It only served to heighten Simon's expectancy as he walked slowly at the front of the house, trailing aimlessly along the track that led back to the road, then turning off to wander on the snow that still lay over the grass at the side. Every now and again his eyes floated to the lane itself, as if they were being pulled there against his will, as he searched for any sign of approaching horses, and Angelina Trevellyn. Baldwin had been like a boar with a spear in his side all night. Tetchy and fractious, he had snarled even at his servant when Edgar apparently failed, in the knight's opinion, to meet his usually high standards of service. It had little effect on Edgar, who simply smiled, and even threw a knowing glance at Simon, to his faint surprise. It looked as if the man was acknowledging the bailiff's presence, and giving Simon his approval. When the bailiff gave him a slight nod, the servant's mouth twitched, as if he was trying to show a degree of sympathy for the guests in the strained atmosphere.

Smiling again at the memory of Baldwin's petulant expression when he had refused again to answer the knight's questions, he slowly ambled over to a tree trunk that lay not far from the woods. Wiping away the excess snow, he sat down.

He was still there when Margaret came out, followed by Agatha Kyteler's dog, who jumped up at the bailiff with every indication of delight, then, after managing twice to slobber on his face and making him turn away in disgust, began to walk around with his body bent like a strung bow, wagging his tail and panting.

Margaret watched the dog's antics with a small smile. The previous evening had been miserable. She hated dissension, and her husband and their friend had both been so edgy: though for very different reasons, that much was obvious.

It was curious that Simon wanted to keep the matter to himself. That was not like him, especially if he knew, as he must, that the affair was causing Baldwin real discomfort. And the fact that it was distressing the knight was plain to see. Usually Simon would leap at a chance to calm a friend, but with these murders he seemed almost to be taking a perverse pleasure in keeping Baldwin in suspense, and the ploy, if it was a ploy, was working. Strolling thoughtfully, she went to her husband's side and sat on the trunk with him, and he glanced up at her as he patted the now quickly calming dog.

'Hello, my love,' he said, smiling at her. She did not return his welcome, but sat quietly with her hands in her lap. 'What is it? Are you all right?'

'Yes, Simon. I'm fine, but I'm worried about you.'

'Me? Why?'

She looked up into his smiling grey eyes, searching them for a sign as she spoke. 'What you're doing is so cruel. Can't you see what it's doing to Baldwin? The poor man's in a torment. He has no idea what you're thinking of doing today or why! You're making him mad – *why*?'

'I'm sorry, Margaret, I didn't mean to worry you. It's nothing that you need fear,' he said, but then his eyes drifted to the view again. 'It's just that I'm not sure myself how it's going to go today. I'm fairly certain that Harold Greencliff is innocent, and I think we'll show that today, but the trouble is, what will the result be for Angelina Trevellyn? I think maybe she *did* have something to do with it, and if so, it's quite likely that today I'll have to hurt Baldwin's feelings. And I don't want to.'

'What makes you think young Greencliff didn't do it?' she asked matter-of-factly after a moment.

Glancing at her, he smiled. It was typical of his wife to get straight to the main issue without being sidetracked. He considered, but before he could speak there came the tinny jingling of harnesses from the lane before the house. 'Come inside, and you'll hear all about it any moment now,' he said and, rising, gave her his hand. Looking briefly down to the road, he confirmed it was Angelina Trevellyn before he turned and led the way to the house.

Baldwin appeared at the door as they approached, peering past them to the people on horseback. Watching him, Simon saw the concentration, the intensity of his stare. He felt his belly churn at the thought that the woman might be involved. Oh, God, he prayed, please let it be someone else. I couldn't face Baldwin if I made it clear it was her!

CHAPTER TWENTY-FOUR

When Angelina Trevellyn and her manservant arrived at the house, they were met by the stern-featured Edgar, who took her horse and pointed her to the front door. She curtly passed him the reins and entered. In the screens, she found herself glancing up and around, assessing the property. It was clearly not as good as her own place, neither as new nor as spacious, but it was warm and appeared to be comfortable. She could see rooms off to her left, but before she could investigate, a taciturn, dark-faced glowering man came out from the furthest and indicated the door near her that led into the hall itself.

She haughtily looked him up and down briefly, and when her gaze returned to his eyes she was angered to see that he stared back. If he had been one of her own servants, he would have been whipped, then thrown out of her house for his presumption. At least Alan had always treated the men correctly, she reflected, even if he was wrong to beat her and

her maid. After staring at him for a moment, she conde-
scended to enter, but she had only gone a few paces when
she felt her legs begin to falter.

To Margaret it looked as if the poor woman was close to
fainting. At first she entered as if she owned the place – and
if she was as aware of Baldwin's infatuation with her as
everyone else was, Margaret thought, she had good reason
for arrogance. But her steps began to stumble at the sight that
met her gaze. The brown and black dog seemed to understand this too, and walked to her with his tail wagging as if
trying to sooth her, but she recoiled from him, and he withdrew, offended, to sit beside the figure of Harold Greencliff.

Looking at her husband, Margaret suddenly realised how
well he had arranged the benches and tables. Simon had
insisted on pulling the table to the far end of the hall so that
Mrs Trevellyn must walk across the length of the floor to get
to a chair. Ranged opposite at the table were Baldwin, then
Simon and Tanner. Margaret was at one end, and at the other
sat Harold Greencliff. Thus, as she entered, the woman saw
the knight at first, directly in front of her, then as her gaze
ranged over the other people, it met the unflinching stares of
the bailiff and constable. Only after meeting their eyes could
she glance over at the last actor in the sad little drama:
Greencliff.

Whereas the representatives of the law were sitting grimly
pensive, the youth had at first looked enthusiastic. He
appeared to want to leap up and greet her, but realised that it
would not be right. Seeing how her gaze flitted over him, and
seeing the contempt in her eyes, his face fell. When she
looked back at Baldwin, the boy almost fell back as if
suddenly nerveless.

They had exercised no torture, no cruelty against him, but the seriousness of his position was clearly apparent in the dejected way that his body slumped, an elbow resting on the table top, his head hanging as he stared at the floor. Now he understood he had lost her too. He looked up and all she could now see in his eyes was a pathetic, total and abject misery before his eyes fell, full of shame.

The look had not gone unnoticed by the others. Simon cleared his throat authoritatively and motioned to a chair set before the table. 'Please be seated, madam.'

She strolled to the chair, then stood beside it while she tugged off her gloves with a contemplative air. Sitting, she raised an eyebrow and stared at Baldwin. 'So, sir? I thought I was asked to come here as a friend, to join you in a meal. Why am I subjected to an inquiry? I assume that this *is* an inquiry?'

The knight opened his mouth to speak, and she thrilled to see his expression of hunted apology. He clearly had not had much desire to see her here like this, then. Glancing at the others, her gaze fixed on the bailiff, and she knew she was right. It must have been him that organised this.

'You will be welcome to join us at our lunch as soon as we have sorted out a few problems, madam,' said Simon smoothly. 'We have been talking to Harold Greencliff here, and we would like you to help us with a couple of points.'

To Baldwin it looked as though the blood immediately drained from her face.

'Well?' she asked composedly.

'In the first case. On the day that the old woman died, Agatha Kyteler, you went to see her. It was to arrange for a miscarriage, wasn't it?'

At his words, Greencliff covered his face with his hands, but the woman merely stared back silently, her face as rigid as a mask. After a moment she stiffly inclined her head in agreement, her lips pursed into a thin, bloodless line of rage.

'And while you were there, you left Harold minding your horse, didn't you?' Again there was a slow nod. 'While you were there, what happened?'

Shooting a look at Harold Greencliff, she seemed to steel herself. 'When I got there, the old woman was fine. I had seen her the previous Saturday to ask for the . . . medicine. She had said that it took time to collect the leaves and herbs, so she could not make it for some days, but it would be ready on the Tuesday. I went there, paid her, and took the draught. I did not wait, I drank it there, with her watching.'

'What then?'

'Then? I returned to my horse. Harold was there, and he gave me back my horse and I made my way home.'

Greencliff stirred, and his hands fell from his face. Staring at her bleakly, he said, 'No. That's not how it was. She told me she was going there to get a potion to make a child – *our* child – strong and healthy. She said she believed the rumours about old Agatha.'

'Harold!' she cried, suddenly scared.

'She thought Agatha was a witch, she said. She said the old woman could help her to have a strong baby. I didn't think she was right, but I wanted her to be happy, so I agreed. I held her horse for her while she went to the witch's house, and I waited until she came back. But when she was there, she looked sort of smug, and I knew something was wrong!

'Then she told me. She said she'd bought a draught and our baby would die. She'd always promised me we'd live

341

together, that we'd run away to her family in Gascony, where her husband wouldn't dare to come for us, and when she said she had gone there to drink a mixture that would kill our baby, I was horrified.'

'What did you do, Harold?' asked Simon, angrily cutting off the sudden attempt at interruption by the woman, who now sat with her magnificent eyes wide in her horror as she stared at Greencliff, shaking her head slowly from side to side.

'I tried to talk her out of the idea, tried to tell her we'd be all right, that we could get away and we'd be safe in Gascony, but she just laughed, and that was when she told me she'd already taken the potion. It was too late! She said that I was mad if I thought she was going to leave a wealthy husband to live the life of a pauper in another land. She rode off, and I was sort of struck dumb. Well, I had to do something, so I went to the inn and had a drink. I was mad, furious about the witch taking away my child. She'd killed him, sure as anything, because if she'd not given Angelina the mixture, she could have had our child.'

'Harold!' she murmured softly with a catch in her voice. He ignored her.

'Well, I hadn't been there for long when a friend arrived, frozen from the weather. He had not expected it to be so cold and had left his surcoat behind. When he saw what sort of a state I was in, he asked what was the matter, and I admitted to him what had happened, and he said that I should see the witch and make sure she kept her silence, otherwise she could make great trouble for me and for Angelina. I still hoped that she might change her mind, you see, and thought that if we could make sure that there was no gossip about us, she might decide to come back to me.

'We left straight away. It didn't take long to get to the old hag's place, and when we got there we went in . . .'

'Who went in first?' said Simon, frowning intently.

After a moment's consideration, he said, 'Me. I went inside while he saw to his horse, and the . . . She was on the floor, covered in blood. The dog, *this* dog, was on the floor by her head, whining. I think he had been hurt too. That was when I realised . . . Well, I thought . . .'

'You thought Mrs Trevellyn had killed old Kyteler to keep her mouth silenced permanently, didn't you?' The boy nodded dumbly. 'And you immediately thought that she must be suspected as the murderess?'

'Yes, I thought that if the body was found there, there would be bound to be an inquiry, and someone may have seen her going there and then what chance would she have? They would be bound to guess it was her, and I didn't want that. So I sent my friend away, and took the body to hide it. My friend, he was . . .' His voice trailed off uncertainly.

'You might as well tell us it all. Your friend will not be hurt for trying to protect you,' said Baldwin.

'I think he was sure that I must have killed the old woman. He thought I had done it while he was seeing to the horse. When he came in, he saw the body and stared at me, saying, "Why, Harold? There was no need to kill her!" He was very shocked. Anyway, he left me, shocked, and I took her body back to my house. It was too dark to do anything with her that night; the earth was solid, I would never have been able to bury her, so I was going to hide her the next morning. Then I went back to the inn as if nothing had happened. He was in Wefford, and I met him on the way, so we entered together. Next morning, when I was going to hide her

343

somewhere in the woods, old Cottey arrived and found her before I could, and that was when you were called.'

'I see,' said Simon, frowning as he concentrated. 'And what of the night when Alan Trevellyn died?'

'I had been trying to see Angelina ever since the day that old Kyteler had died, but she always refused. Then my friend managed to get a note to her, and he told me we could meet. He came with me through the snow and when we saw her, he left me to speak with her alone. I swear I didn't see Alan Trevellyn. Or kill him. I spoke with Angelina and tried to persuade her to come away with me, but she laughed at me. She told me she would never leave her husband while he was alive and told me to leave her alone.'

'Then what?'

'I went back home and tried to sleep. But no matter how much I tried, I couldn't. I just kept thinking of her and how my life would be. I couldn't face it. Knowing I would be always seeing her in the village, or out in the fields and the woods, it made me sick to think of it. So I decided I must leave. I decided to go to Gascony without her. At least there I could forget her and start a new life. I packed some things and went. I went . . . Well, you know the rest.'

Simon was nodding. Certainly it matched the facts that they had so far managed to piece together. Shooting a look at the woman, he said, 'Well?'

She started. For the last few minutes she had seemed to lose herself in her thoughts, staring into the fire roaring close by. 'Yes? Oh, I suppose it's true. It is how I remember it. But I didn't know it at the time. After I had been to see that old hag, when I heard she had been found dead, I was sure that it must have been Harold who killed her. Especially when I heard that she was found in his field. It was obvious. I was scared to see him after that. I thought he might try to kill me. That was why I insisted that he came without a weapon when he came to see me.'

'You insisted he came without a weapon?' Simon said.

Greencliff said, 'Yes. She took my dagger and gave it to my friend before we met. She refused to see me alone while I had my dagger with me.'

Simon leaned back in his seat, both hands on the table top, and stared wide-eyed at the youth. For a moment he was silent, but then he spoke with a voice slow and deliberate. 'When did you get it back? When did your friend give you your dagger back?'

'My ballock knife? When we left the Trevellyn house, I suppose. Oh, no. No, he must have set it down at my house. That's right, I found it on the floor in the house when I was packing. He must have put it there for me.'

'Tell me one last thing. This friend, it was Stephen de la Forte, wasn't it?'

The misery in his eyes was plain to see as the boy answered simply, 'Yes.'

After they had checked the story to make sure that they understood it, Baldwin told Tanner to hold both Greencliff and Mrs Trevellyn at Furnshill, and then led the way out. Simon and he quickly donned thick jackets and cloaks. The bailiff also grabbed a woollen scarf which he wrapped round his neck before tugging on his gloves. Then he went back to the hall to see his wife before leaving. Having given her a hug, he turned, and caught a glimpse of Baldwin.

He was standing by the doorway, and Mrs Trevellyn had crossed to his side, as if expecting to receive a similar farewell to that which Simon and his wife had exchanged. It felt as if his heart would stop when Simon saw the knight look at the woman without recognition, only to turn dismissively on his heel and make his way to the front door. Not from sympathy for the woman, but because he could see how much his friend was hurt at the story he had just heard. As if recognising the knight's despair, the thin figure of the black and brown dog followed at his heels.

Outside, Edgar was already mounted on his horse, and Hugh stood nearby, holding Baldwin's and Simon's. They swung up, took their reins, and made their way down the driveway towards the lane. The dog followed behind as, once on the road, they turned their faces to the south and set off to Wefford.

Whenever Simon glanced at his friend, Baldwin's face was set as solidly as the brass plate on a tomb. Although he maintained an expressionless demeanour, Simon could see the pain in his eyes. It was too clear, and it made him try to think of something to lighten his friend's mood. But what can soothe a wounded heart? In the end he gave up the struggle and stared ahead glumly, sadly aware of his inability to offer any comfort.

CHAPTER TWENTY-FIVE

They clattered up to the entrance of the house in the early afternoon, halting and dismounting before the front door. Soon hostlers appeared and took their horses while Baldwin tied the dog to a hook by the door. Then they entered. In the hall they found the lady of the house, sitting alone in front of her fire and looking up at them with fear in her eyes.

'Yes?' she said, her voice quavering.

Baldwin stepped forward, but Simon interrupted him quickly and, pushing in front, bowed quickly to the lady. 'Madam, we need to speak to your son. Is he here?'

She shot a glance at Baldwin and Edgar, her eyes wide and fearful, before they rested on the bailiff once more. 'You want to speak to Stephen again? But why? He told you all he knew the last time you were here, what more do you want of him?'

'I'm sorry, madam, but we need to ask him some questions. Is he here?'

'No . . . No, he's in Crediton. He left some time ago. He should be back tomorrow, though, so if you want to come back then . . .'

'No, I think we'll wait.'

'But why?'

Simon looked at her sympathetically. He was beginning to feel that all he could do today was try to offer support to those he was bound to upset. Trying to smile, he said as soothingly as he could, 'We have to ask him about the death of Agatha Kyteler and Alan Trevellyn. We think that . . .'

He paused at the sight of her pale, terrified face in which the eyes appeared to have grown to the size of plums, huge and startling against the pallor of her skin. 'Are you all right? Can we get you anything?'

Waving a hand in irritable dismissal of the offer, she held his gaze, and to his sudden distress, he saw a large tear roll down her dried and wrinkled cheek. It was as if he had upset his own mother, and he felt her pain like a band constricting his chest. Yet there was nothing he could do to make it easier for her. If her son was, as he believed, responsible for the two murders, she would live to see her only son die, and in a cruel and degrading manner.

He averted his gaze and settled to wait, but he had only just made himself comfortable in a small chair, while Baldwin and Edgar stood lounging against the screens, when Walter de la Forte came in, closely followed by the thin and perpetually anxious manservant.

It was apparent that he had not seen the knight and his man to his left as he entered, because he immediately strode to the bailiff and stood before him bristling with rage.

'What is this? I understand you're here to question my son again? What gives you the right to invade my house? You may be an officer, but you're not an officer *here*!'

'I am an official. I can . . .'

'Not in my house, you can't. I've a good mind to teach you not to molest a man in his own home. I could kill you now, and all my servants would swear that you attacked me and . . .'

At the sound of Baldwin clearing his throat from behind, he underwent a sudden transformation. His anger disappeared to be replaced by a kind of cunning sharpness before he risked a quick glance over his shoulder and found Baldwin and Edgar to be close behind him. He slowly turned back to Simon, who did not move or respond, but merely sat and stared up at him with an expression of faint disbelief. When it became apparent that the man was still wondering what he could say, Simon softly spoke. 'You just threatened an officer in the presence of two other men of high honour. You will sit and be silent. We shall deal with you later.'

At first it looked like he was going to attempt an attack on Simon. His eyes bulged with his emotion, and his hands clenched, but then the fire died. His shoulders dropping, he looked as though he recognised defeat. Turning away, he stumbled to a bench and sat, his face in his hands.

Looking up at Baldwin, Simon saw that his eyes were on the fire. However, Edgar was aware that the man could be a problem, and when the bailiff gave a quick nod, the servant walked round to take up a position behind the merchant.

On Simon's cloak there was a twig caught among the threads. Reaching down, he lifted the heavy cloth and studied it. Pulling at the stick, he murmured softly, 'It must have been hard, having to be suspicious of your own son. I don't suppose you really wanted your partner killed so that your son could take over his position. It sets a rather unpleasant precedent to have partnerships dissolved by death. I must admit, though, I don't understand why he wanted to kill old Agatha Kyteler.' He plucked the twig free and gazed at it ruminatively for a moment before tossing it into the fire.

The older man stared at him for what seemed a long time, then he turned to gaze at the fire, as if debating with himself whether to tell his story or not. After a minute or two, looking up, he said to his wife, 'You had better leave us.' She stared at him, and appeared to be about to say something, but then thought the better of it, rose, and swept out.

It was some more minutes before Walter de la Forte began to talk. 'It was so long ago, we never thought it could hurt us. You don't worry like that when you're young, do you? You think you're immune to any problems caused by your actions. You don't realise that they can return to haunt you in your later life. In our case, we thought the past was far behind us, but it was lying dormant, waiting until we should be so arrogant as to think ourselves safe. Then it pounced.'

The room was silent apart from the crackling of the logs on the fire, but even they looked subdued, as if the flames too were listening.

'When Alan and I were much younger, when we were beginning our business, we set up as traders from the money we made during the evacuation from Acre. There were no English knights to take over our ship, Alan and I did it ourselves. Our captain had died in the city. He was hit by shrapnel from a catapult's stone. We took charge of the ship. It was so easy!

'There were people thronging the docks, trying to escape, looking like ants swarming over all the land, streaming on to any old cog or carrack that would carry them. We were careful, we took on board only those who had money or gold. With the wealth in the city we could afford to be choosy. We had no need of furs, so if that was all the people had, they stayed. We took men and women and children. The children were best. They took little space and the mothers were often glad to see them sent away safely.

'There was one couple, a mother with her boy, who tried to persuade us to take them. She was a little older than us, a strong girl, but what a beauty! The boy was only a baby. Well, I was happy enough to take her for the jewels she carried, but Alan took a fancy to her. He was adamant. He wanted *her*, and that was to be her price for freedom. He always was a randy fool. I think it was because he had never managed to father a child. If it had been me, I would have taken her on board and then raped her, but he always was a fool about that sort of thing. He told her what the price of her passage would be and she refused. And with obvious loathing. So! He refused to take her or her child, no matter what she said. That was that!' He glanced up bleakly.

Sighing, he continued, now holding the bailiff's eyes as he spoke. 'Later, another woman came, one who was not the same in looks or in position. She had a young child, and she had money. We let her aboard. How were we to know that she had the son of the first? And we could not tell that the first was the woman of a powerful man in Gascony, the Captal de Beaumont, who had been in Acre to help defend the city.

'The boy was his son – his bastard, apparently. The woman was his nurse: Agatha Kyteler, curse her! When we let her off the ship at Cyprus, she managed to make her own way back to Gascony and delivered the boy to his father. The mother must have died. To our shame!' His head dropped into his hands, and although he did not weep, his emotion was all too clear.

Sighing, Baldwin tried to keep the contempt and disgust from his face as he watched the man. That any Christian man could have condemned a woman to the mercy of the Egyptians was horrific enough, but for so paltry a reason? It would have been kinder to have simply killed her. He sighed again as the man began talking again.

'And there the affair ended, as far as we were concerned. Alan and I began our new lives. We had made plenty of money in the escape from Acre, and we used it wisely. We bought new ships – heavy cogs for bringing wine over the channel – and spent years trading peacefully between Gascony and England. But then, of course, the troubles began to get worse in France, and our ships started to get attacked. We lost one ship sunk by pirates and another captured, with all the men aboard murdered. That only left us the one, and we needed finance to keep it going, which is why we had to go to the Genoese. Doing that we managed to survive until about ten years ago.'

His face was almost wondering now, as if in amazement at how far he and his partner had fallen after the high point of their lives. 'It was that bitch Kyteler, the old hag!' he declared, his head shaking slowly from side to side.

'I had only just built my house when she came to town. I don't know how she got here or how she found out where we were, but she did. She came here, to my house and introduced herself. Then she recalled the trip from Acre and told me whose son the boy was. I was horrified! I thought that at any time we should expect to have the Captal's men storming the house, but that was nonsense. When I told Alan, he said we should kill her, but I was against the idea. I thought we had enough dead on our hands already, so I said I would have no part in her murder.

'He went and tried to threaten her. He wanted her to leave the area, but I think she had decided to stay as a constant reminder of our action at Acre. A living token of our guilt. She threatened to tell the Captal if anything happened to her. That was why Alan built his house up and had the castellations added. He was scared of being attacked by the Captal's men.'

'So all she did was stay nearby? She only lived here, and that made Trevellyn go in fear of his life?'

'Yes! The Captal de Beaumont is a powerful man. If he wanted to attack us, we could hardly protect ourselves. Alan said we ought to have had her killed off years ago, it would have been easier, at least we'd have known where we stood. But it was too late after a while.

'Stephen got to hear about it somehow. He felt that she was a danger to us all. He wanted her gone, but what could we do? And then, when she was out of the way, he decided that our partnership was useless as well. He told me that Alan must be bought off. He said that Alan was a harmful partner, that he was destroying the business, that there would be nothing for Stephen to inherit if Alan remained. When I asked him what he meant, he told me to have Alan killed. At first all I could do was stare at him, and then I lashed out. That was where he got his bruise. It was after that I heard Alan had been killed.'

Just then they heard a horse approaching outside. The merchant looked up as if searching for sympathy, staring at Simon with a kind of desperate yearning, as if he was pleading for understanding.

He was surprised to hear the old woman's dog begin to snarl and then growl and bark savagely out by the front door. There was a sudden flutter in the screens, and then they heard the front door thrown open. Almost before Simon could comprehend what was happening, Baldwin had uttered a most uncharacteristic curse and hurled himself at the door, and Edgar had followed, leaving the bailiff and the merchant sitting in astonishment.

'Don't kill him, Bailiff. He's a good son,' said the man softly, and then Simon's senses recovered. Realising what was happening, he lurched to his feet and ran at full pelt.

CHAPTER TWENTY-SIX

Outside, the mother was standing and staring at the disappearing figure of her son, riding fast for the road. Baldwin stood fuming, waiting for Edgar to return with his horse. When he did, there was only his own and Baldwin's. Snatching the reins from him, Simon snarled, 'Get inside! Keep the father there until we get back!' And, somewhat to his surprise, Edgar obeyed.

Whipping their mounts, they launched themselves down the road at a gallop. They had their target some hundreds of yards away and all they need do was catch him. They could see him riding over the snow-covered grass to the right of the lane, then turning north as he hit the road. Whipping their horses, they kept their speed, although every now and again the knight glanced down at the snow rushing past their horses' hooves, wondering what would happen if they were to fall at this sort of pace. And it was likely that they would. While the snow was soft enough, he knew that a layer of ice could lie beneath its white covering, as slippery as oil on a metal breast-plate, and if they were to hit such a patch, they would be hurt.

And it was not long before he was proved correct. He felt his horse's hindquarters slip, and felt the great creature falter as if nervous, knowing that he was losing grip. It was only with care that he managed to stay in the saddle. When he heard the high whinny and gasp from his side, above the whistle of the wind in his ears, he knew that Simon had fallen, and turning and throwing an anxious glance behind, he saw the bailiff sitting in a drift and rubbing his head with a grimace of angry pain.

It was then that Baldwin felt the anger rising. Now this young fool had caused his friend to be hurt as well. With his jaw set and his eyes staring, he set spurs to his mount's flanks and raced on.

They had entered the cold shade of the woods now, and Baldwin felt that the dark trunks rising on either side and flashing past looked almost like disapproving spectators. He set his teeth at the thought. Why should they approve? This was a race to the death, after all. The boy would die, whether during his flight or later, and the knight must catch him or die in the attempt, now that there was only him left.

Then the trees seemed to pull back from the track as if in dismay, and Baldwin drew in his breath. They were coming into the village. The open space by the inn came towards them, then they had flashed past, leaving two surprised men trying to calm their horses at the entrance, startled by the speed of the two riders.

Leaving the village, Baldwin became aware that his mount was beginning to tire. He could feel the breathing becoming more laboured, the steps starting to lose their rhythmic pattern, and the head was straining as it stared forward. Biting his lip, the knight frowned ahead. Could the boy escape? No, he mustn't. He must be caught and made to pay for the murders.

The horse ahead was a blur against the white of the road, the youth a darker smudge on its back. All Baldwin could see was the snow whipped up by the hooves and the wind, flying upwards into a cloud like a trail of feathers in their wake. It was already becoming colder and the breath felt like it was freezing his lungs as he inhaled. It smoked as he breathed out, the cold damp mist being snatched away from his mouth by the wind as he rode. Every now and then he would catch a whiff of the dank breath of his horse as the grey exhalation was drawn past his nostrils, but he kept his eyes fixed now on the figure ahead: his prey.

He was aware of the light fading. The sun was gradually sinking behind the protective covering of clouds, and there was a pink and orange glow in the west, flecked with, purple and blue, which he could glimpse on his left. They were past the village, back in among trees, and then came a clearing. Here the youth sensed he had an advantage, and Baldwin saw his arm rise and fall in a steady rhythm as he beat his horse's flank. 'Fool!' the knight thought. 'All you'll do is lose his concentration if you keep hitting him. Leave him be.'

But it worked, and the boy reentered the woods at the far end of the clearing with a greater advantage. It was obvious that the knight would not be able to catch him. The youth was smaller in body, his horse faster, while the knight's mount was larger and slower. The contest was too unequal. He was about to rein in, when he saw a larger splash of snow, and then, when it settled, the horse and rider seemed to have disappeared. Uttering a quick prayer, Baldwin slowed to a canter, then a trot, and went forward hopefully to investigate.

'Get up! Get *up*! he heard as he approached, and then he saw the boy. Stephen was kneeling and struggling in desperation to make the horse rise, but the horse was lying dazedly, both forelimbs outstretched, and whinnying softly, clearly in great pain. When he was close, Baldwin saw that one leg was bent at an impossible angle from the forelock. It was broken.

'Shut up, Stephen,' he said as he dropped from his saddle, and the youth rose, to stand anxiously, eyes wandering from the knight to the woods. 'Don't even think it,' Baldwin continued evenly. 'If you try to run, I'll catch you. And if you were wondering about taking my horse, don't bother. He doesn't like other riders. He'd throw you within yards. Sit down over there, while I see to your horse.'

While the boy stumbled to the patch of ground Baldwin had indicated, the knight studied the horse. There was nothing he could do. The leg was broken, and it was easy to see why. Riding in among the trees, the horse had been unlucky enough to put his leg into a rabbit hole hidden by the snow. There was nothing else for it. Baldwin drew his dagger and cut the horse's throat with a single, quick slash that opened the artery. Leaping back, he could not avoid the fine spray and then thick gouts of blood that gushed. The knight was liberally spattered. It was soon over, and when the creature's shivering death throes were done, he cleaned his knife on the horse's flank before he stowed it away. Stephen de la Forte was still seated where he had been told, resting with his hands on the ground behind him, although now his panting had reduced. Baldwin kept an eye on him while he mounted, then cocked an eye back the way they had come. 'I think it's time we started back, don't you?' he said affably.

The youth slowly rose to his feet and glanced at the dead horse. Without moving, he said musingly, 'I suppose you know how wealthy my father is? He would pay well for my freedom. All you have to do is let me go now.'

'You have a long walk ahead of you, Stephen. Save your breath for that.'

It would have been foolish for the boy to try to escape. Similarly, he seemed to realise that it would be impossible to try to deny his guilt. He strode along amenably enough, hands clutching his cloak tightly around his body as they made their way back. Their mad race had taken less than a half-hour, but it took them nearly that long to get to the village with Stephen on foot, and Baldwin's better judgement might have persuaded him to stay and enjoy a drink, but he decided to continue. He wanted to see how Simon was after his fall.

It was almost another hour before they came to the track on the left that wound its way up to the house, and here for the first time the youth faltered.

'Do we have to go there? Can't you take me straight to the gaol? I don't want to see my parents like this.' There was a plaintive tone to his voice, the spoiled child who cannot have his own way.

Baldwin's sympathy was limited. 'Get a move on. At least you can get a warm drink inside you at the house.'

The last thing on the boy's mind was an attempt to break away and make his escape, but he was reluctant to arrive at his home, and the knight cursed the youth's slowness under his breath. Now he was nearly there, he wished to complete their journey as quickly as he could.

At the door they waited, and when it was pulled wide, it was Edgar who stood there to welcome them. Taking Stephen by the arm, he waited while his master dropped from his horse. When an hostler arrived and took the reins from him, they all passed inside.

'Simon! How are you?' Baldwin cried at the door, and crossed the floor to his friend, who sat swathed in cloak and blankets like a new-born child. The bailiff smiled, but his pleasure at seeing the knight could not hide the yellowish pallor of his features.

'I'm fine,' he admitted. 'But I landed on my head, and it jarred me.' He stopped and stared. 'My God, Baldwin! Are you all right? You're covered in blood, did he stab you?'

'I'm fine. I had to kill his horse: broken leg.'

'Thank God! I . . .' He stopped, his mouth open in apparent revelation, and Baldwin heard him mutter, 'Of course! That was why he was cold! Why didn't I realise before?'

Barging past the knight, Stephen stepped up to the fire and ignored the gaze of the others. His father was sitting with his mother on a bench by the hearth, his arm around her, and to Baldwin it looked as if they had both aged in his absence. She was sniffling and trying to hold back her weeping, while her husband sat stoically and expressionlessly, swallowing hard every few minutes as if trying to keep the tears at bay.

When the youth turned from the fire, Baldwin saw him glance at his parents for a moment. In that quick look, he saw only contempt and loathing, and he felt a cold chill at the sight of it. How long would it have been, he wondered, before this boy decided that his father was too weak or ineffectual to be his partner as well?

It was Walter de la Forte who broke the silence. 'Are you going to tell us why?'

'Why, father? Why I killed them? *You* know the reasons why. And I did it then because I had the opportunity, I thought, of getting away with their deaths. After all, they both deserved their ends.'

He walked over to a small chair and sat, staring at his father with apparent surprise, as if he expected that he at least should understand. 'She had been a threat for ages, and that was hardly right, especially now the business has been suffering. No, it was only right that she should die. She was a danger, and had been for many years.'

'But why Alan? He was our friend, your friend! Why kill *him*?'

'He was weak and a fool. He wanted us to keep on with the trading when it was clear we needed to change, to move into banking, beat the Genoese at their own game. That's where the money is going to be in the future. But he wouldn't see it. He couldn't. He was going to ruin our business, Father. I couldn't let him do that to my inheritance. I had to kill him.'

Simon interrupted. 'You knew what you did was going to put the whole blame on to Greencliff, didn't you? Did you want him to die for what you had done?'

'Harold?' The youth's face showed momentary confusion, near anger as he frowned, but then he seemed to realise that the bailiff was genuinely unaware of the truth and gave him an comprehending smile. 'Oh, no. You don't understand. I told Harold to go and escape. I knew he *could* be in danger otherwise. That was why I went to his house after the witch died, to make sure he had gone. I had to make sure he would be all right after I killed her. Then, when I had seen to Alan Trevellyn, I made sure he left for good. He was my friend; I was looking after him.'

CHAPTER TWENTY-SEVEN

It was late when they finally made it home, and both were ready to drop straight to sleep, but there was no opportunity for them to do so. Margaret, Tanner, Greencliff and Angelina Trevellyn were still in front of the fire, and their eyes rose to the door as the three men entered.

Margaret went to Simon as soon as she saw him, with a sigh of relief, hugging him with her eyes closed, 'I thought something must have gone wrong,' she whispered, and then, as she squeezed tighter in her joy, she felt him wince and heard his quick moan, and stood back. Now she could see his pain, and the paleness of his face. Even as she saw him try to smile, she turned an accusatory glare to Baldwin. 'What's happened to him?' she asked, and then gasped in horror as she saw the gore over his tunic. 'Baldwin! What has happened to *you*?'

The knight grinned. 'Very little, the same as your husband. But I fear we shall all three of us soon die of the cold if we do not get inside and sit before the fire.'

While Margaret bustled, calling for Hugh and helping Simon to a chair, Baldwin walked to his own chair by the fire and sat, pensively watching them. Hugh did not appear – he had fallen asleep in the kitchen by the fire – so Edgar went to fetch food and drink for them. It was only when he had left the room that Baldwin found his eyes being drawn to Angelina Trevellyn. Seeing her condescending smile as she watched the husband and wife, the knight nodded to himself as he turned his face to the fire once more. It confirmed his decision, reached with such difficulty on the ride homewards.

'Come on, then! What happened? And Simon, how did you guess it was him?'

The bailiff smiled at his wife. 'There were a number of things that made me start to think of Stephen de la Forte,' he began. 'I think the first thing was how so many people started saying how much of a friend he was to Harold, and how they were always together. It seemed as though they had no secrets from each other – Jennie Miller even said that Stephen knew who Harold's wealthy lover was.' At this, both Greencliff and Angelina Trevellyn stirred, but Simon ignored them.

'Then there was the fact that at both murders, although Harold was there or nearby, he was apparently alone. It did not occur to me at once for, in affairs of the heart, most men will leave their friends behind when they go to see their lover. But there was something odd about the prints back from the Trevellyn house on the afternoon we went to Harold's house after discovering Alan Trevellyn's body. It only came to me late. There were the prints of a man *and a horse*!'

He glanced at the farmer. 'You never owned a horse, did you? That's what Jennie Miller said too. What use would a shepherd and farmer have for a horse? And if you did have one, why walk the horse home? To avoid ice, maybe, but it would be rare for a man to walk unless his horse was lame, and this horse did not limp. No, I became certain that there was another man with you. You confirmed that yesterday.

'So what about the day of the death of Agatha Kyteler? Once again, you were seen while you stood with Angelina's horse, once again, you were alone there. Was it likely? Later, at the inn, you were seen with Stephen de la Forte again, but *he came in after you*. You did not enter together. If he was with you when you went to see your lover, when Alan Trevellyn died, surely it was possible that he was with you when Agatha died as well? In which case, where had he gone?'

Nodding, Baldwin leaned forward. 'Yes, I think that this is what happened. You two, Harold and Angelina, agreed to meet, but Stephen went with you. Harold, you waited with the horse while Angelina went to see the old woman. When she left, Stephen made some excuse . . .'

'He said that after seeing the old woman, Angelina would want my company, but he would probably be unwelcome,' said Harold dully. 'He rode off as if he was on his way home.'

'I see. So he went a short way, then tied his horse in the woods, and made his way to the old woman's cottage. When he saw Angelina leaving, he went inside and found her still at her table. He pulled out his knife and killed her.'

'I knew none of this!' the boy cried, and his face dropped into his hands.

'No, that much is obvious,' continued the knight. 'What happened was that Angelina told you what she had done, and you were shocked, horrified, by what she had done, when you had been looking forward to raising the child.'

'She said she wanted nothing more to do with me when I asked her to leave the village and come away with me.'

'Yes,' said the knight and threw her a glance. She appeared to be gazing at the youth with a small contemptuous sneer. 'I imagine she did. Anyway, feeling as you did, you went to the inn to get drunk. Half an hour later or so, Stephen arrived . . .'

Eagerly, the bailiff interrupted. 'And he was cold, you said! You said he had no surcoat!'

'Yes,' the boy nodded with surprise.

'Look at Baldwin's tunic, after killing Stephen's horse!' said Simon triumphantly. 'Stephen may have been able to clean his face at a stream in the woods, but he couldn't clean his clothes. That was another thing that stuck in my mind!'

'Thank you, Simon,' said Baldwin with an imperceptible frown of irritation at the break in his tale. He paused, trying to regain the threads, but Simon was too quick.

'So,' he said, 'Stephen appeared, heard what Angelina had said to you, and then started to speak about how the old woman would be sure to talk about such a wealthy woman going to see her, or something, yes?'

The boy nodded miserably. 'He said that Agatha never could keep her mouth shut. He said she had told everyone in the village about me and Sarah Cottey. I *had* to do something to keep her quiet.'

'Yes, that was when you were overheard talking about silencing the old witch!'

'Yes. And Stephen offered to come with me.'

'That's the interesting bit. I suppose he wanted someone to confirm that it was a shock to him to find her body there.'

'I don't know. He came up to the cottage, but when I opened the door, and found her there, her dog came out and started to attack him. He said we'd better go, and I held the dog back, for it would have taken him by the throat other-wise. When he had gone, though, I began to think, and . . .'

'You thought Angelina had done it,' said Baldwin flatly. 'So you chose to drag the old woman's body to your field, so you could bury it and hide the proof of the murder.'

Nodding again, the boy looked up with frank sadness. 'I went to the inn first, with Stephen. I left the body there at the house. I didn't even tell him what I was going to do, I thought it would be wrong to involve him. Then, when we left the inn I took her back with me, through the woods, and left her in the field. I was intending to bury her the next morning. But Cottey found her first.'

'Why did you run away?'

'I still loved – I still love – Angelina. But she made it clear that she did not love me. I was going away. I was going to leave and find my fortune elsewhere.'

'I see.'

Simon musingly poured himself some wine. 'Who suggested that you should go and see Angelina later? When Alan Trevellyn died?'

'Angelina did,' he said.

'I did not!' she declared hotly. '*You* asked to see me!'

'I assume, then,' interjected the knight suavely, 'that Stephen told you, Harold, that Angelina wanted to discuss things with you, and told you, Angelina, that Harold must talk to you?'

They both nodded, and she seemed to consider as she said, 'He threatened me. He said that Harold would tell all in the village about us if I did not agree to meet him one last time.'

'But you refused unless he came without a weapon?' asked Baldwin, leaning forward.

'That was Stephen's idea. He said that Harold was so depressed he could do anything. He said I should be very careful, and he offered to take Harold's knife if I agreed to see him. Stephen said he would stay nearby so that I should be safe.'

'So in that way he managed to get your knife, Harold. He used it to kill Alan Trevellyn. I don't know how.'

'He came to the house and asked for wine. Maybe he told my husband that he had seen me with a man up in the woods? The servants were all terrified by my husband's temper before he left to search for me. He was in a terrible rage.'

'It's quite likely. Yes, he knew your husband well, as the partner of his father, so if Stephen saw Alan, Alan would probably have believed his story. And he could have promised to lead him to you, as well. It would not have taken much to drop back behind, and cut his throat as he stood in the trees. Then he covered the body with snow to hide it a little, and went back to see you two.'

'Why wasn't he covered in blood this time?' asked Simon frowning.

'This murder was better planned. He knew that blood would cover the whole area after killing the old woman, so maybe he carried a fresh tunic with him, one that he only put on after leaving these two together. I don't know, but he's bright enough to manage that.'

'And then,' Simon finished, 'he joined you, Harold, after your meeting with Angelina, and went home with you. It was his tracks and yours that we saw. Your feet, his horse.'

'Yes, he came back. He stayed with me a while, I think, but I hardly said anything to him. Angelina had confirmed that she would not leave her husband to live with me, not even if I could get us away, to over the sea. I felt that I had nothing to live for in Wefford any more. After he had gone, I packed and left. The rest, I think, you know.'

In the silence that followed, Margaret found it difficult to keep her eyes from the miserable figure of the farmer. He sat huddled, deep in thought, but none of the thoughts seemed to give him any joy. The woman was different, she could see. Angelina Trevellyn sat with a measuring gaze in her green eyes, and they were fixed intently upon Baldwin, who appeared to be unaware of her presence. The story of love and misery had struck him with its despair.

'Oh, don't take her, Baldwin,' she found herself thinking with a shudder. To her surprise she found that the wish was so intense it struck her almost as a prayer. 'She's vicious, uncaring and grasping. Beware!'

As if he had somehow caught the drift of her thoughts, Harold Greencliff suddenly rose. Without a word, he swept from the room, his face downcast and his eyes avoiding meeting the gaze of any of the other people there. When she looked at her husband and the knight, Margaret saw the sympathy there, but the boy appeared not to have noticed as he slammed the door and stalked out into the open air.

After a moment, Baldwin stood and followed the boy.

Outside, the night was a grey curtain that hid the land around, and Greencliff was invisible in his dark tunic. But it

369

was easy to find him from the sound of tortured sobbing that came from the side of the house. Baldwin stood undecided for a moment, not sure whether to go and interrupt the boy in his misery or not. He made up his mind. Steeling himself he strode on.

The boy was leaning against the log pile, eyes thrown upward at the star-filled sky, heaving great breaths and sobbing them out again in his despair and misery. He did not turn as the knight came up beside him, but continued his solitary skyward stare.

'What will you do, Harold?' asked Baldwin softly after a few minutes.

'Do? What *can* I do? What is there for me here? I've lost my only friends: my best friend is a murderer who tried to put all of the blame on to me; my woman, the one woman I thought wanted me as her husband, has made up her mind I'm not good enough for her! Not good enough to sweep her stables! What is there for me? What can I do, where can I go to find peace?'

Remembering Sarah Cottey and her spirited defence of him, Baldwin considered. He said slowly, 'There are others who may be better friends or lovers, Harold.'

'There's no one. I have no one. No friends, no family, nothing.' The tone was definite, the finality as certain as the slam of a tomb closing. In the face of it, Baldwin felt unequal to any further battle for the boy's confidence. Turning, he stared away as he thought for a minute.

'Harold, if you need help, tell me. If you want to leave the area and go to Gascony like you said before, I'll release you from your villeinage. But remember, you can only run from things you leave behind, not from things inside you. If you go but take the woman and your friend with you in your heart, you'll never find peace. There must be another woman here that would be better for you, someone who can ease your life and . . .'

It was this that finally made the boy spin to face him. 'Why? So *you* can take my woman? She's told me that already, that you want her. It's obvious why – a wealthy merchant's widow and the wealthy knight – but don't try to tell me it's better for *me* when all you're trying to do is look after yourself. Don't try to tell me you're trying to help me when what you're doing is stealing my woman!'

Simon was sitting alone in the hall when the knight came back.

'How is he?'

Dropping into his chair, Baldwin gave him a grimace and puffed out his cheeks in a sigh. 'There's nothing *I* can say. He doesn't trust me. I think if he stays for a week he'll be here for ever, but if he goes far away I wouldn't be too surprised. You never know, it might be best for him. It certainly did me good when I went abroad.'

There was a slight noise, and the door from the screens opened to show Angelina Trevellyn. She walked in as slowly and gravely as a nun and sat opposite the knight, her face showing a sad and compassionate concern. 'How is he?' she asked softly, her voice low.

'I think,' Baldwin said, staring at her sceptically, 'that you should find out for yourself, madam.'

'What do you mean?'

'He was your lover.'

Simon wriggled in his seat. He had no desire to be here for this. He glanced at the door in mute appeal, but no one entered, and he dared not interrupt them himself. Cringing back, he tried to make himself as small as possible.

'That was before,' she said calmly.

Baldwin spoke drily. 'What, before you realised you were about to become a widow and could have your choice of the men – or should I say knights? – of the area, madam? Before you thought you could do better for yourself? Before you thought it would be pleasant to own a man with a title in preference to a mere merchant whom you had always feared and disliked?'

'That is hardly fair,' she said, giving a slightly nervous smile. Baldwin did not smile back.

'Isn't it? I think it probably is. When did you decide on me? Was that some time ago too? Or was it a snap decision, like choosing to take a local farmer as your lover? It must have been funny until you got pregnant. That was the one thing that surprised me. Why were you so upset about being pregnant? Why should a married woman be so fearful that she is prepared to go to a woman reputed to be a witch to force the child to miscarry before her husband can find out?'

'I thought it would be wrong to bring up a child as his own when it might not be,' she said with a hint of defiance.

'I doubt that, I doubt it a great deal. I think it was because you knew that he could not have children. Oh, yes,' he carried on as her face coloured, 'Walter de la Forte knew about that too. He told us. Tell me, though: when did you choose me? Was it when you saw my house here and realised how large my estates were? Or was it before, when you first saw me and thought I might be more enjoyable than a mere farmer?'

'I don't have to listen to this!' she said, standing and glaring at him angrily, the light reflecting from her eyes in green glints of cold fury.

To Simon, it seemed that the knight stared at her for a moment as if trying to remember something, perhaps how he had felt when he had first seen her and been so enamoured of the beautiful green-eyed Gascon lady. 'No,' he said softly, 'you can go whenever you want, can't you? Do whatever you want. You are wealthy now, and have money and lands. Well, go then. I wish you well.'

As his friend turned back to his fire, Simon thought he saw doubt in the woman's eyes, but then her rage took her over and she flounced from the room. Soon her voice could be heard outside, shrilly calling for her horse and servant, then shrieking when she felt that she was being thwarted.

'I think that you have probably just had a very lucky escape!' said Simon meditatively, but when he glanced over at him, the bailiff caught a fleeting glimpse of the deep sadness that passed over the knight's face.

The door opened and Margaret walked in, a tray with wine and minted water in her hands. 'Have you seen Angelina Trevellyn?' she asked in bewilderment. 'She's demanding her horse, and when I suggested she might be better to wait here the night and leave in the morning, I thought she was going to launch herself at me in her rage! What have you said to upset her? Baldwin, why what is it?'

But even as she set the tray down and leaned towards him with a compassionate frown on her face, even as he tried to smile, he found he could not. And only by blinking could he stop the tears that suddenly threatened.

CHAPTER TWENTY-EIGHT

When they had been back in their draughty castle for almost two months after the murders, Simon and Margaret received a letter from Baldwin. Of course, Margaret could not read or write, but Simon had been fortunate enough to have been schooled by the priests at Crediton when he was young, and he and the educated knight often exchanged letters when they had the opportunity.

'What does he have to say?' she asked, not bothering to rise as she once had done. Before, the novelty had made her look at the indecipherable characters over his shoulder, but now that he had been bailiff for a little over a year, she was well used to seeing missives arrive, and the event was not such as would make her leave her plate of food. Funny, she thought vaguely, that being pregnant can make one so hungry all the time.

'It confirms that young Stephen de la Forte is dead. Apparently he went to the gallows well enough, but he took his time dying and the executioner had to help. Anyway, it seems that Greencliff has announced in church that he is to wed Sarah Cottey. Baldwin thinks it's a good idea, even old Sam is happy with it. He'll be grateful for an extra hand, and Greencliff is a good strong lad.'

'Anything else?'

'His manor is ahead of itself already, and he's looking forward to a good harvest at last.' His face frowned suddenly, and he leaned forward.

'What is it?'

Glancing up, she saw a smile spread over his face. 'Angelina Trevellyn,' he said. 'She's decided to return to Gascony, apparently. And Baldwin has made some comments about her that I don't think I should relay to you! It's enough to say that he seems relieved to see her go. What he does say is that she was somehow embarrassed. It seems that some men took to heckling her in the street. Apparently, news of her affair with Greencliff got around the village, and spread further afield. Baldwin thinks it might have been Jennie Miller.'

'That's not very funny. It's not very chivalrous to treat a woman like that.'

'No, but it seems that the result was her choosing to leave, so it had a good outcome. It seems to have made quite a stir in the area. Anyway, he goes on to say that there's a widow over at Crediton that Peter Clifford is trying to get Baldwin interested in, who appears to be very suitable.'

'How suitable? Do stop grinning like that!'

'She is known to be generous with her alms and supports Peter's little hospital, so she seems quite sensible and kindly.'

'And?'

'And she's older than Baldwin, uglier than his mastiff, and he's begging us to invite him here for a holiday to escape her clutches as soon as possible!'

'Tell him I look forward to seeing him soon,' Margaret sighed. 'It'll be good to see him again. But tell him to come here in the summer. It's too cold in the winter! Oh, and ask him if he wants to bring this lady with him. After all, he might find things very boring here otherwise!'

Michael Jecks
Templar's Acre

The Holy Land, 1291.

A war has been raging across these lands for decades. The forces of the Crusaders have been pushed back again and again by the Muslims and now just one city remains in Crusader control. That one city stands between the past and the future. One city which must be defended at all costs. That city is Acre.

Into this battle where men will fight to the death to defend their city comes a young boy. Green and scared, he has never seen battle before. But he is on the run from a dark past and he has no choice but to stay. And to stay means to fight. That boy is Baldwin de Furnshill.

This is the story of the siege of Acre, and of the moment Baldwin first charged into battle.

This is just the beginning. The rest is history.

Hardback ISBN 978-0-85720-517-9
Ebook ISBN 978-0-85720-520-9